a Mickle, a Muckle, a Malt and the Moon

# The Eagle has landed
## *July 1969*

| | |
|---|---|
| **Houston** | That's affirmative. |
| **Eagle** | Houston, Tranquillity Base here. The Eagle has landed. |
| **Houston** | Roger, Tranquillity. We copy you on the ground. You've got a bunch of guys about to turn blue. We're breathing again. Thanks a lot. |
| **Tranquillity Base** | Thank you. |
| **Houston** | You're looking good here. |
| **Tranquillity Base** | A very smooth touchdown. |
| **Houston** | You are stay for T1. Over. |
| **Tranquillity Base** | Roger. Stay for T1. |
| **Houston** | Roger and we see you venting the ox. |
| **Tranquillity Base** | Roger. |
| **Columbia** | How do you read me? |
| **Houston** | He has landed Tranquillity Base. Eagle is at Tranquillity. I read you five by. Over. |
| **Columbia** | Yes. I heard the whole thing. |
| **Houston** | Well it's a good show. |
| **Columbia** | Fantastic. |
| **Tranquillity Base** | I'll second that. |
| **Apollo Control** | The next major stay/no-stay will be for the T2 event. That is at 21minutes 26 seconds after initiation of power descent. |
| **Columbia** | Up telemetry command reset to re-acquire on high gain. |
| **Houston** | That's affirmative. |
| **Houston** | Copy. Out. |
| **Apollo Control** | We have an unofficial time for the touchdown of 102 hours, 45 minutes, 42 seconds and we will update that. |
| **Houston** | Eagle. You loaded R2 wrong. We want 10254. |
| **Tranquillity Base** | Roger. Do you want the horizontal 55 15.2? |
| **Houston** | That's affirmative. |
| **Apollo Control** | We're now less than four minutes from our next stay/no-stay. It will be for one complete revolution of the command module. |
| **Houston** | You are stay for T2. Over. |
| **Houston** | That's affirmative. |

# a Mickle
# a Muckle
# a Malt *and*
# *the* Moon

*Bill Smith*

**Kennedy & Boyd**

Published by
Kennedy and Boyd
an imprint of
Zeticula
57 St Vincent Crescent
Glasgow
G3 8NQ

http://www.kennedyandboyd.co.uk
admin@kennedyandboyd.co.uk

For more information about The Arran, visit
http://www.arranwhisky.com

**ISBN 1-904999-06-9 Paperback**
ISBN 1-904999-07-7 Hardback

*To Janet, with love*

## *Thanks*

Many people have helped along the way, some less
consciously than others.
In particular I should like to thank, in no particular
order:

NASA, for showing the way;

John Rooney, man of letters and sadly missed

Janet de Vigne, for invaluable editorial assistance

Colin Robertson, photographer,
(www.iconphotography.co.uk), for his help and advice

Stuart Johnston, for contributing a lifetime of
experience in publishing

The twilight wine of Scotland, for its help and
encouragement.

# Prologue
## Christmas - 2007

The cable car was brightly coloured in crisp reds and greys. At this early hour, on the first trip of the day, the numbers travelling to the summit would be few. Somewhere at the end of the station a shutter was raised, and the smell of freshly brewed coffee drifted on the cold morning air. From down by the tall stand of trees came the sound of a radio and carols being gently sung. By the door of the waiting room a dog sat patiently, hoping to slip into the warm interior to lie hidden behind the big stove at the end of the room.

All around, the snow was hard packed following the latest blizzard a week earlier. For the last three days, the sky had remained cloudless and untroubled. Across the broad sweep of the valley, the tiny rooftops and winding streets of a scattering of villages could be clearly seen. Lower down the slopes, the Christmas tree in the town square was just visible, a beacon of twinkling colour in the deep early morning shadow.

At the boarding point, a handful of mothers with school children gathered at the edge of the platform, hoping to fill the window seats. Chattering noisily, clutching their new skis and brightly coloured knapsacks, the children clustered around in groups, eager for the doors to open.

Standing apart and waiting to board, the four men appeared to be strangers to each other; the two younger, fit and broad shouldered, carried rucksacks, while the two older men seemed strangely out of place with their windcheaters and makeshift headgear. Standing alone and separated by a few metres they were heavily wrapped against the sub-zero temperature, their collars turned up and their faces protected by warm woollen scarves.

As the bell announced departure, they boarded, until with a lurch they began the long climb towards the first platform on the way up to the summit. As the car cleared the confines of the station and the sun streamed into the cabin, the landscape unfolded before them. Behind, their view across the valley showed Chamonix shrouded in inky shadow. Above, and directly in front, the massive bulk of Mont Blanc towered over the surrounding valleys. Beneath, the densely packed trees on the lower slopes were soon left behind as the car climbed steadily up the valley.

Arriving at the station platform, the two younger men remained apart, casually observing the scene but watching the terraced levels and the only approach to the restaurant. The two older men made their way inside, eventually settling for a table in the corner away from the other diners. Soon they were engrossed in conversation. At the end of an hour, having breakfasted, they again boarded the cable car returning to Chamonix until, at the terminus, they left the carriage without a backward glance.

The next morning, Gregor McLeod, First Minister of The State of Scotland, collected his passport in the name of Eric Brown from the receptionist at the Excelsior hotel in Les Tines and drove the forty miles to Geneva Airport in a hired car. Lightly tanned and marginally fitter after a week of skiing and workouts in the hotel gymnasium, he boarded the Swiss Air flight to Edinburgh and fell almost instantly asleep.

# 1

## 2011 - Washington

Nathan Jackson, President of the United States of America, stood by the large windows in the Oval Office looking down on the rose garden that fronted the White House. Behind him, the door to the waiting room stood ajar, the voices of those attending his next scheduled meeting quietly heard, their manner reserved, holding back until the appointed hour then striding boldly in to take their places. Exchanging small talk and busying themselves, they moved as if arriving from some earlier tussle, clearly relieved to be entering the relatively sane surroundings of the Oval Office.

Turning and smiling, enjoying some brief exchange with Dale Johnson, his Secretary of State, he beamed a mature confidence in every direction, a president sure of his ground, at ease with the world and at ease with himself, increasingly aware that his first four years in office was shortly to end, and determined that in his closing months he would impart some legacy to the world, some gift to the American people; some worthy reminder of his three and a half years of near perfect peace in a stable world.

True, AIDS was still a problem and global warming refused to go away. The weather utterly refused to play ball and the recently published reports from the World Health Organisation, Friends of the Earth, and those persistent lefty bastards in Greenpeace made for grim reading if one was to take them seriously. Not that any president worth his salt could. With the economy flourishing as never before, with the distance between the third world and the developed countries widening by the minute, he could afford to ignore a few wild nights of storm and flooding, and those endless days of hot steamy rain that always seemed to fall so unreasonably on his golf outings, and now, so unseasonably at any time of year.

The slow, ongoing disappearance of the Maldives and now the losses being encountered in other island groups *was* a little worrying however. And then there was that recontouring of the flood plains in Bangladesh and the Nile basin that had so upset the cartographers at the Pentagon for a while. Oh, everybody *knew* that the sea levels were bound to rise. It had been predicted. No direct proof that the melting of the polar ice caps was responsible however. No sir! Of that, he *was* certain. The fact that half the major rivers in the world were running at reduced capacity, that water rationing would become inevitable within a few years in most civilised countries was, well, just the way things were. After all, there was only so much that one President, no matter how conscientious, could achieve in one short term in office.

Outside, on the lawn, the tall mature trees swung and lurched together in the wind, their branches ominously bare and strangely noisy. Their leaves, early browned and stained, deprived and rotting on the stem, rattled and rustled on this fine summer's morning, their shrinking roots failing to nourish cells already tainted with acid rain, their deterioration year on year so gradual that the loss of colour was hardly noticed. A squall of rain drifted over the area, clattering on the leaves; leaves that at an earlier time would have been broad and green, rich in colour, deep veined and full of life.

'An early autumn,' he told himself, 'a good time to reflect on our time in office.'

'Gentlemen, be seated.'

They seated themselves, his inner quorum of senior aides, good men all.

'Gentlemen, we can dispense with formality; please relax. Coffee is on the way. We have so much to do in the coming months, so much good work still to achieve.'

Murmurs of consent and general agreement flooded the room with shared bonhomie and endless good cheer. Outside the rain turned to a steady downpour. July was going to be just as disappointing as June.

'I believe it is time that we reflected on our substantial achievements and set about reminding the world and our own people of just how well we have been doing over these past few years. If we are to succeed in our bid for re-election we must start now.'

There was smiling and much nodding of heads.

'After all, we have a great deal to be proud of. The average American family is several points better off than when we came to office, our health service is now universally acclaimed and our schools and colleges are second to none.'

A half hearted round of applause greeted this last statement, slightly disconcerting all things considered, the applause faltering as soon as it had begun. Pressing on regardless, he stood and patrolled the carpet on his side of the worn desk, his mood rising again, his speech becoming more assured as he launched into his plans for a massive campaign to look back and record with satisfaction the achievements of his first term in the noble office of President of the United States of America.

'We could do a movie, full length!' his National Security Advisor Arnold B. Denham exclaimed.

'A week of country-wide carnival celebrations that will outshine Rio,' Levin, his Pentagon Chief of Staff roared. 'By God, we'll do it!'

Denham was on his feet again.

'Yes. I can see it; a full length movie that will record for all time the legacy that we hand on to future generations. Think about it! We can get that guy, what's his name, from out west, to do the whole thing? Yeah, the same one who did that beautiful job on Ronald Reagan. He's the guy for the job.'

With hands raised, waving in gratitude for the support being freely expressed, Nathan Jackson subsided into his chair, his protests lost in the sea of voices, each one throwing suggestion after suggestion at the meeting, each grander than the one before, each a certain winner destined to portray the years of glory to their best advantage.

'Hold on now, hold on now. We seem to be doing a whole lot of the same thing around here. Let's settle down and table a few of those ideas.

'Mr Secretary of State, Dale, let's have your views on the subject.'

At this, the room stilled noticeably, all eyes turning to the robust, stately figure of the man who had saved the nation time after time, routing the thief of Baghdad, driving terrorism from the free world, diplomatically settling historical differences and open warfare in a dozen locations from Northern Ireland to the Bekkah valley; the power behind the throne; the one man that not one of them would choose to cross, not in jest and certainly not in anger.

'Come now Dale, give us your views on the subject.'

'Well sir, you and I discussed this whole thing some time ago, as you know, and I am well aware of your feelings on the matter. Certainly we must mark your departure from the presidency and the long years of service you have given to this great nation of ours. I have no doubt that the American people will expect it, nay demand, that we must, in some suitable way, ensure that your time in office be set down in the record books as a time of peace and stability for the peoples of this great country of ours. Above all, I sincerely believe that we must establish some worthwhile event to act as a marker, a timeless milestone, for all the world to see, so that they will know, that we above all others, are undoubtedly the most successful and concerned nation on the face of this good earth ... '

As he continued, Nathan Jackson sat with head bowed, locking his hands purposefully in front of him, silent and serious. The others held their stances, heads held high, proudly aware of history in the making.

' ... and whilst I doubt if time is truly available for any long-term planning of major events, such as this film project, I have no doubt that we shall come up with something to be proud of, something that will stand for all time as a beacon of our faith, a symbol of our resolve and a monument to our achievements in this, our final hour in office.'

He paused for breath, and the gathering rose as a man, cheering him and their beaming president, sending the pigeons flying from the window sills and leaving the marines outside wondering ...

'Just what the hell kind of a party were they having anyway?'

As if suddenly reminded of something he must not forget, the head of the C.I.A. began to talk over the clamour of voices.

'There's just one little thing, Mr President.'

Joe Skinner was trying hard to be dutiful, trying to be heard over the euphoria of consent and concerned lest he dampen the mood of the meeting. He shifted slightly from foot to foot, raising himself slowly to his full height, awkward and tentative but building on the growing attention he was receiving.

'I have here a piece of intelligence that was dropped on to my desk earlier this morning. Frankly,' he paused, shaking his head, 'It scares the hell out of me.'

There! He had said it, wondering in the same instant if his choice of timing might not be ill judged. He pressed on.

'It's from one of our watchers in Europe, England actually. Details are still sketchy at the moment, but we *could* find ourselves in a touchy situation; one that will need very careful handling, and one that could have us facing up to a developing crisis in the coming weeks.'

He was fumbling for some document or other in his inner pocket, failing to find it, but continuing nevertheless.

'Whilst it's not the Cuban affair all over again, it's infinitely more delicate and could possibly pose a bigger threat than all the terrorist attacks put together.'

Somewhere in the room, a tiny pin thundered onto the floor.

'What in hell's name are you talking about?' asked a bewildered President, his eyes roving over the assembled faces, his mood deepening, his composure dwindling fast.

'Well sir, it's like this. Nothing is really a hundred percent clear at this early juncture you understand, and we have no reliable intelligence to corroborate our initial suspicions, as yet …'

At this, Nathan Jackson leaned forward to within an inch of Skinner's face, and with a grim smile tainted with displeasure said,

'Just damn well give it to us straight. Do we sit here planning the movie or is there something we should all damn well know about?' At this, he looked around the room seeking assurances.

'Well, sir, I would like a little more time to talk with my people, you understand, but as far as I am able to determine the salient facts of the matter…'

He paused again, distinctly nervous, spectacles steaming in front of his eyes, his bald head beginning to glow.

'For some time now we have been aware of something going on over in Scotland. They have, as you know, been developing a rocket system with a view to launching satellites into space. From what I am hearing, the technology is very advanced, and as far as we can ascertain, their rockets are propelled using some quite revolutionary fuel propulsion system that is light years ahead of its time. We now have every reason to believe that the work, currently being carried out on a remote island in the North Atlantic, could be being developed for offensive use.'

Nathan Jackson stood motionless, arms hanging by his side, his mouth open. The others were listening now.

'The feedback I am receiving seems to suggest that the extreme secrecy surrounding the work is an indication of its military importance. Moreover, the Scots are on good terms with the Russians, and we have evidence of collaboration between their respective space agencies that would seem to hint at something going on that requires investigation.'

At this, all heads turned towards their President, his expression denying them the assurances they so desperately sought. Minutes passed, or so it seemed. Dale Johnson looked hard at Joe Skinner.

'Why couldn't he have raised this at some earlier, altogether more appropriate time? Why NOW?' he was thinking.

Nathan Jackson was silent, tense and concerned, sombre and contemplative. He and the Secretary of State moved to the side and buried themselves in deep, urgent consultation for a few tense minutes. Jackson returned to the desk and turned to Skinner.

'Joseph, this is something we need to find out about. You say your intelligence reports are sketchy at the present time. This I can understand. I thank you, nevertheless, for bringing this matter to our immediate attention.'

He paused, stroking his chin.

'We want you to get your best people over there as quickly as is reasonably possible. I want to know more. They will report only to you. You will report only to me. Do you understand?'

'Yes Mr President, I sure as hell do.'

'We want chapter and verse on this one. This is serious. The English have always been our allies, our friends. But times can change. Check out the location. Find out what they are up to. Got it?'

'Yes Mr President. But, as far as I know, the English may not be involved. Since devolution and with the advent of full autonomy, the Scottish Parliament has taken complete charge of its own affairs as a sovereign nation, undertaking many new self-indulgent projects, some of which, when seen in the light of the world stage at large, have appeared to be of dubious merit, some bordering on the ...'

Showing a brief flash of anger, Nathan Jackson interrupted his flow,

'What you mean is that the Scots are an irresponsible bunch of bastards who can't be let out on their own. Why in God's name the Limeys didn't stick them on a reservation centuries ago I'll never know. And you, Franklin', he said, addressing the number two at the State Department, You should get on to your opposite number in the Foreign Office and see what you can find out. We have work to do. I need answers. Go to London as early as possible. Talk to them there. They may know something that we have missed. If anybody knows what is going on, they will for sure. It may be nothing at all. On the other hand...'

His eyes narrowing, watched by Dale Johnson, his mind racing with the possibilities, Nathan Jackson no longer needed a movie script to guarantee his re-election. He had a missile crisis! Maybe not on the same terrifying scale as the Cuban affair, but a crisis nevertheless; and what JFK could do, he, Nathan Jackson could sure as hell do better.

Trying to read his thoughts but still several paces behind him, Dale Johnson wondered just where this line of reasoning might be leading them. As the meeting broke up and the others left, the President crossed to the world map at the far end of the room, scanning first the Caribbean and then the South China seas as he endeavoured to locate the source of the threat.

'Over here, Mr President,' said his Secretary of State, just here, to the north of London. There!'

'Christ almighty, it's attached'. He turned, aghast, the truth dawning on him. 'We'd be declaring war on the British Isles if this threat materialises. There has to be some mistake. They're a party to the non-proliferation treaty and all that shit. There has to be some explanation. What time is it now in London?'

Dale Johnson checked his watch, answering immediately.

'It is early evening there at the moment, sir.' They walked slowly back to their seats, Jackson distracted, unsure of what the future held, but determined to match the threat, if indeed there was one.

'So far,' he said, 'we know diddley shit. It *could,* after all, be as they say, or a scientific research project. Needn't be offensive at all. But we need to know.'

Absentmindedly, his thoughts drifting from scenario to scenario, he crossed the room, lifting the decanter of fine Highland malt from the tray on the New England dresser, and pouring two modest drams.

'At the very least, Dale, we will go down fighting. Whatever the threat, we will meet it. Yes sir! This is a great nation, a leader in world matters and as your President I will not turn the cheek in the face of a challenge, no matter how great or how dreadful the consequences might be.'

He drank deeply, at which point Dale Johnson lifted his own glass, wondering all the while whether the constitution allowed for such an obvious act of treason, but more deeply concerned that, if hostilities did ensue, the supply of whisky, so essential to the running of a good senate, might some day soon be halted, bringing on a crisis of a different order, but one of equal concern to all good men of serious mind and good intentions.


Mark Brander, the White House Press Officer and spokesman on all things pertinent to the presidency, sat in a deep leather armchair nursing his drink. Not normally a hard drinker, his years in service in Washington had taught him to drift with the tide, run with hares and hunt with the proverbial hounds. Deep in thought, sitting opposite him, Nathan Jackson stared into the flames of the fire under the darkening portrait of Abraham Lincoln. Outside, the afternoon had faded, the night closing in earlier than usual, dark clouds obscuring the sky, a distinct touch of autumnal chill in the air.

'So you see, Mark, as I was saying, this intelligence, if it proves to have any substance to it at all, could be a God-sent opportunity for us to demonstrate this administration's undying dedication to the peace of the free world. If those bastards are planning anything, then we will expose it, challenging them to reveal their intentions; showing the world that we are still on the ball, forever vigilant, forever watchful.'

He paused to refresh his glass with ice. Mark Brander leaned forward.

'If we can assume that the information is correct, just for the moment, several questions spring to mind. Firstly, how can any country get so far down the line without our Embassies getting to know about it? Our satellite surveillance for Christ's sake! Secondly, just where *is* the funding coming from? Thirdly…'

At this Nathan Jackson interrupted him.

'I've been looking into it. They discovered natural gas at the turn of the century, tons of the stuff. They've been exporting it to a number of European countries ever since independence. On top of that, the recently discovered Ibrox field, with its massive reserves of top grade crude, has placed the Scots at the head of a short list of nations where every man, woman and child could become a millionaire in the next five years, even if they never lifted a finger to help themselves. The bastards are rolling in hard currency. None of your chicken-shit Euros for them. They print and mint their own, and it's doing just fine.'

At this, he paused again. 'So you see, if they chose to, they could fund their *own* star wars project, their *own* offensive or defensive systems or whatever else they chose to undertake. Rolling in the stuff as Levi would say; more money than sense. Anyway, now you are fully briefed, I intend to meet with you again, perhaps tomorrow, or just as soon as I have more information to hand. We must make this thing happen. I want to milk it until it drops.'

'I fully understand, Mr President. Opportunities like this are rare enough and one must endeavour to derive every ounce of spin from them.'

At this, they rose on cue, both swaying slightly, the Press

Officer moving towards the door.

'Goodnight again, and thank you, Mr President, as always it has been a privilege talking with you in so frank a manner. I'll hang fire until I hear from you.'

Standing alone by the fireside, mellow and again composed, Nathan Jackson was tempted to place a call to London. No! He would wait. Once armed with the latest reports he would enjoy a little chat with his British opposite number. Pay back time at last! Rattling his cage about his lost kingdom to the north would be a pleasure. Telling him of the emerging problem across his border would be certain to cure his constipation. Chuckling, he moved off in the direction of the living quarters of the great house, remembering that first official visit to London and the invitation to Chequers that never was.

'Ryder ! Eat yer heart out.'

# 2

Across the machair on North Uist, on the edge of the great swell of the Atlantic Ocean, the wind pulled and tugged at the tough beach grasses, their long roots binding the sand dunes, rarely giving ground to its wild roar or the surges of the great Spring tides. Below, the beaches ran the length of the island, wide and virginal, the white sand peppered by traces of brightly-coloured seaweed, far travelled flora from Caribbean shores, forever moving Eastwards as the Gulf stream stroked the shores of Scotland's sentinel islands. The Outer Hebrides, home to fable and fantasy, songs and stories and not much else.

In these June days, dawn came quickly, lighting the peaks of North and South Lee, Eaval, Roneval and Bhein Mohr to the South. Further to the West, the lower rise of Clettraval and the Valley of Glen Drolla caught the first glimmers of a rosy sun, the light moving quickly over the sea to arrive six hours later on the Eastern seaboard of North America, the first landfall in two and a half thousand miles.

On the slopes of Clettraval overlooking the tiny abandoned settlements of Balmartin and Tigharry, the road around the peninsula served the new complex. Above the road, the low outline of a vast array of buildings could be seen wrapping around the slopes, half buried into the rise and fall of the natural rock formations. The complex appeared to turn back on itself time and again, rising and falling with the contours, blending with the landscape, the tip of an iceberg of engineering buried far below the ground, aware of its intrusion into a delicate ecosystem and determined to hide itself beneath a covering of heather and gorse.

Below ground there was quiet disciplined activity, as scores of workers toiled at various tasks, surrounding the great natural underground chamber that housed the giant rocket, shiny silver and blue, glinting under the sea of overhead lighting tracks hanging high over the vastness of the cave. Gantries and frameworks of all descriptions snaked across the vast space. Giant cherry pickers, their reach fully extended, swayed gently as the operatives moved in the confined cradles, probing and occasionally disappearing into the many access panels remaining on the hull of the craft. On the giant platforms that ran along the four sides of the work area, dozens of white clad figures could be seen assembling and fitting, adding to the multitude of systems and components that made up the heart and soul of the great ship. In the transport hub, glass fronted lifts rose and fell, gliding smoothly to various levels, transporting people and materials in a constant cycle, feeding the needs of a massive workforce that worked, slept and ate in steady rotation, each serving the ends of a programme that had not faltered once in three years.

In the hotel area, staff slept while others retired after a long night shift. Quiet bells signalled the close of play as the station rested for the two hours between six and eight each morning when silence could descend, tools were laid aside and warm breakfasts were served to the outgoing and incoming shifts in clean spacious dining rooms. Here, soft music stilled the nerves and reminded the soul that the outside world, a world full of distant families and old friends, was only a short flight away once every four weeks.

Colourful carpeted spaces and sweet smelling out-of-season flowers. Reminders of Mother Nature in a man made environment. Elsewhere, the accent was on relaxation, the gymnasiums and saunas, the bars and Cineplex designed to woo the mind and body away from the stresses of a work ethic that demanded total commitment to the programme underway.

As senior administrator and project manager, Fiona McLeod was thoroughly at home in the environment. On target for completion in four months, she could look back on three years' hard work with satisfaction. Still only thirty, tall, slim and fair, an education at a red-brick university behind her, she carried her confidence into meeting rooms, dispensing judgements and advice with the skills and abilities of someone of more advanced years.

Rising early, she prepared for a day that would see a break in her normal routine. With a senior level delegation arriving from Edinburgh to review progress and to hear the monthly report first hand, she knew that her day would be fully occupied from the minute that the helicopters landed on the pads and the lift doors opened. There would then follow the inevitable barrage of questions and answers to be relayed in turn to the select committee meeting in Edinburgh, where Gregor McLeod would listen enthusiastically to the reports, sending his e-mailed congratulations to her, always polite, forever mindful of her responsibility to the project, and forever supportive in whatever demands she might make on him.

Gregor; the people's choice. Fifty-three next birthday after a lifetime serving his country in politics and industry, craggy faced and grey haired, lion maned, his broad forehead lined with the wear and tear of a hundred confrontations and more than a fair share of disappointments in left-wing politics, but with a reputation for integrity and courage that could not be matched by any man alive. Seizing his opportunity to serve his country at a time when independence was a remote dream on some fortune teller's horizon, he had started the Scottish Independence Party; a move he had never had cause to regret. With devolution behind them and their new found independence still a babe in arms, he could look forward with some confidence to years of stability and wealth for a country so long deprived of full sovereignty.

With the future wealth of the nation flowing beneath his feet and as leader of the party in power, his statesmanship and enthusiasm for Scotland's right to rise and prosper had fired the imagination of all parties for a series of projects destined to mark his country's emergence into the first decade of the new millennium, whilst ensuring that reserves were safeguarded and invested in the things that mattered most for generation after generation of Scots still to be born; born into a future that would see poverty, unemployment and social deprivation made things of the past, where job opportunity and work security were underwritten by a Government contracted to serving the electorate.

As the helicopters arrived and the noise of the rotors subsided, the doors opened and Gregor McLeod dropped to the concrete below, a spring in his step, the smell of the wild flowers rising through the smell of the exhaust, his face turning to the wide expanse of ocean where a continuous layer of ominous smog drifted slowly eastwards on the light morning air.

As if suddenly angered, his mood deepening, he moved quickly back on to the large lift area, as the helicopter pad slowly sank beneath the ground, the large overhead doors sliding and shutting out the sky. Transferring to the service lifts they descended quickly, then hurrying out, arms outstretched, seeing the look on his niece's face as he bear-hugged her, swinging her off her feet to the accompaniment of loud shrieks of laughter that turned every head in the cavern, letting them know, if they ever had any doubts, that the bear was on one of his irregular prowls and that party time was just around the corner.

Standing now, gazing up at the huge shape draped in protective covers, his serious composure returned to him, his smile fixed as his eyes roamed over the scene. With a clap of his hands they were off, Fiona leading the way towards the runabouts. Quite where the day would lead her was anyone's guess.


'So you see Gregor, mishaps apart, we are fairly sure to finish within a two week window of our projected date and I believe that with a bit of luck, despite the holidays coming up, we can hit the date for completion on the button.'

Gregor McLeod was impressed. Sitting, looking at the wall display, running his eyes over the great wall chart, the delays offset by overtime working, the milestones that indicated a target met, a snag uncovered, his years of advising industry had made him no stranger to the half truths hidden in progress reports.

'I can't help noticing that the key to your completing the next stage relies heavily on your receiving the electronic gyros from Jardine's. If they are delayed again, the whole workline, from mid-August until first week of September could very well see delays developing in a vital component of the inertial guidance systems.'

He paused. Her quick glance at the chart confirmed that his niece had missed that particular issue in her brief but general submission to the assembly.

'Yes. That *is* a possibility. But we do have a contingency supply that will be available to us by the end of the month. As you know we foresaw the possibility of delays in critical items and laid them off twice to separate independent contractors.'

He smiled. So that was where the rising costs were coming from.

'Fine. Fine. And if we choose to announce a date for departure before the winter sets in, can we do it? With any certainty?' He looked around at the faces, each one concerned in some way with the success of the project.

'What's your view on this, Murdo? Can we go for an autumn launch?'

Murdo Sinclair, scientist and mathematician, controller of the National Space Centre at Rosewell and a member of the inner quorum of Gregor's short list of confidants, smiled reassuringly, eased himself out of his chair and moved to the chart.

'We do have a launch window in October, that's true. However, as I see it, the problem lies here. The commissioning period is too short. The phased commissioning and the added complexities of these new systems coming on line are stretching the centre's controllers to the limit. For any launch date to be realistic, and to give ourselves a better than average chance of success, I need at least another month between handover and my people swarming all over the thing, fine tuning the responses and ensuring that the systems are working properly on the ship. Where are we now, end of June?', consulting his clipboard, 'If we were to run in parallel with the teams here, bringing over my key personnel for the last two months, it might just be possible. Where we would sleep is another issue.'

Seeing a possible window of opportunity Gregor lifted his hand:

'Let's see if this gives us a way forward. I believe it might. If the weather closes us down, we won't budge until spring next year. The costs are already alarming and opposition from the benches is never very far away. Now, who wants breakfast?'

As they made their way down to the leisure area, Gregor took his niece by the arm, taking her gently to one side.

'Fiona, there is, as you know, a great deal more riding on this project than I can tell you at present. I have plans afoot that make progress towards this launch date a damn near imperative. I want you to cancel all leave other than essential, medically recommended R & R. I want everyone at their posts night and day for the next two and a half months. Work three eight hour shifts if you have to. Murdo's lot can be fitted in, although I appreciate that accommodation is limited. If necessary we will board them out. But I want this done.'

Dropping his voice still further he spoke directly to her ear, secrecy essential, the urgency of his plea not lost on her, as she began to wonder just why the upcoming American elections had so suddenly been introduced into an equation already complicated with shifting political allegiances, lapses in project security and the ever-present, overriding need to keep the whole affair under wraps until just before launch day.


The Boeing 787 climbed steeply out of Washington's Dulles Airport, rising through the blanket of smog, the clouds thinning as the grey outside the first class cabin changed slowly to a snowy white haze and finally to a clear blue sky. Elmer Thomas Franklin, Under Secretary in the State Department no less, fifty, divorced and neglected by the opposite sex, prone to hard work and long workouts in his personal gymnasium, balding, lean of face and trim of figure, sat dwarfed by two large agents from the service, both of whom he had personally selected for their reputations in matters unspoken, for their long silences and above all, for their tact in delicate situations.

His final briefing had been precise, his President requiring answers and a direct line to his findings however irrelevant they might seem. He had noted that the situation was by now being referred to as "that missile crisis", a term he himself would not have employed, nor did he subscribe to the rising temperature surrounding the affair; an affair which was only three days in the making, and on a subject that had very little in the way of corroborating intelligence to justify raising it even to the level of a minor alert. To give it a priority rating at all was simply absurd.

At any rate, he would know soon enough. His meeting

scheduled with the British Prime Minister would surely reveal all. How often had he remarked on the quality of supplied covert material and the willingness of their British counterparts to share traffic intercepts from the most surprising of sources? He had no doubts at all that in the space of a short visit, his concerns, and those of his President would be put to rest. With his youngest daughter married to that chap from Oxford and his regular twice yearly visits to West End theatres, he had a definite soft spot for the British way of life, their mocking, humorous little ways, their self deprecating mannerisms, and above all, their longstanding relationship with their cousins across the pond.

'Champagne, sir?'

The stewardess, florid and fiftyish, flattering him with a busy smile, that extra second or two given out gratuitously, waiting for him to return to the present, unhurried and charming, determined never again to return to the rear cabin.

'No. Thank you. No. A glass of water perhaps; when you are free.'

'With ice, sir?' He had gone again, and she moved on.

'Franklin. There is a side to this investigation, this "fact finding" as you insist on calling it, that I would ask you to bear in mind. In the event that this thing could be seen as a potential threat to our great nation, no matter how small, I will deal with it as I have dealt with similar matters over the course of my time in office. I shall not hesitate to use force if needs be. In your discussions with the British Prime Minister, I want you to know that you have my full and considered authority to imply the use of force, in whatever circumstances you deem necessary, if you feel that the situation demands it. You will use the secure line at all times. Call me at any hour. I am at your disposal twenty four hours a day in this matter. I simply cannot believe that Ryder is unaware of this plot to undermine the peace of our world.'

He solemnly noted the escalation to the status of "plot".

'You will convey to him my best wishes of course and listen carefully to his tone. You will then relay anything you pick up directly to me. Do I make myself clear?'

And, with that, they shook hands. Leaving the inner office, he lingered in the ante room, unsure if he had read the unspoken signals from Dale Johnson for some last minute instructions. Then he felt his arm gripped, then they were moving to the side, out of earshot, conspirators in an instant, guilty with their fingers deep in the cookie jar. Dale Johnson was speaking softly into his ear, his tone mild but his concern at the situation causing his voice to tremble, leaning back now, his finger wagging ominously in the general direction of the Oval Office.

'Whatever happens over there, whatever it is that you find out, I want you to know one thing. There will be no fucking war over this issue! Let the rhetoric ring out, let the parties shout insults and rave at each other, but I repeat, THERE WILL BE NO SHOOTING WAR, not while that crazy bastard is sitting there with his finger hovering over the button.'

Heathrow Airport on a muggy, smoggy July morning, the airport filling at this early hour with holiday makers and business men. Safely through the VIP channel, they drove in convoy into London, the traffic building as they crossed the Hammersmith flyover, the discreet police escort ahead of them, turning along Knightsbridge, through Hyde Park Corner and finally to the door of the Connaught Hotel.

The small talk on the journey in had been predictable, the First Secretary anxious to please; his American opposite number similarly disposed towards the pleasantries expected, despite their many close encounters over the years.

'Oh, I am sure you will find the Connaught as warm and friendly as ever. Wonderful food. Good all round really. Their Sunday roast rib you really must try.'

Cutting across the small talk and regretting it instantly, Elmer Franklin enquired,

'And you say that John will only be able to meet with me tomorrow? Is that correct?'

'Yes. His schedule is rather tight at the moment. He was

wondering if perhaps you might choose to brief me, in general terms only I hasten to add, in order that we might prepare ourselves for any ...'

He paused, searching for the right word, the pause inviting interruption but expecting none. The sentence left hanging, untimely, the next question was out before he realised it.

'We could of course arrange to accompany you for shopping if that would be convenient. The afternoons are usually too busy with tourists, the early morning perhaps the more convenient time?' His eyebrows raised, another offer rebuffed.

Elmer Franklin was gazing out at the crowds, seemingly distracted. He was wondering just how long the Minister had allocated to their meeting. Perhaps dinner at the Ambassador's residence would present a better opportunity for exploring the complexities of a situation that the government must surely be cognisant of, but one that they had rigidly kept from sharing with their friends and allies.

'Shopping? No. I don't think so. Also my business with your Prime Minister is rather difficult, a matter of some urgency in many respects, and one that could affect both our countries in the near future. I regret therefore that the details of my mission must remain with me until we meet.'

At this juncture, the grey suit reached for the telephone and, speaking quietly, gave some terse, direct instructions to the other end. A pause ensued, until he nodded and replaced the receiver.

'The Prime Minister has asked me to enquire if lunch can be arranged at Number Ten; today at say, twelve thirty.'

'Thank you. That will be most convenient.'

As the doorman at the Connaught hurried forward, his experience told him that in the race for the handle on the door of the Jaguar he would come a poor second, as the man from the Special Branch shot out of the passenger seat in front, shielding the opening and moving (in line with his responsibility) all the way to the steps of the building, through the reception area and all the way to the "john" in the private apartment on the top floor.

They sat together at one end of the long table. In less than thirty seconds he was aware that he held the firm attention of the Prime Minister. Minutes later he had concluded his summary.

'Elmer, What you have just confided to me places my government in a very embarrassing situation. We are of course aware from our many sources that *something* has been going on ever since the Scots took their independence in two thousand and six. Exactly *what* is less clear. We have of course asked all the usual questions, made the usual overtures, tried our level best, in as friendly a manner as possible, to try to establish exactly what they are pursuing and why.

'Since independence, their treasury has been overflowing with reserves and we have had to stand by and watch as they have embarked on project after project, often, it seems to us on foolishly philanthropic ventures entirely devoid of return or foreseeable benefit long term. But I do have to commend many of them, if only as gestures of friendship and goodwill which have done them no harm worldwide, winning them many friends and creating influence with poorer nations.'

He paused as coffee was served. Alone again, he continued, choosing his words, at pains to defuse an awkward situation.

'Last month I called their Prime Minister, Gregor McLeod, an old friend of mine, a stalwart of the Labour Party going back many moons. He was affable as always, but curiously tight lipped about their projects, their future spending or their current undertakings. I told him that talk of rocketry was widespread and asked him frankly if we, or any other nation, neighbouring or otherwise, had any reason whatsoever to be concerned.'

At this, Elmer Franklin leaned forward.

'Did he give an indication of what was going on?'

'No. In fact he laughed. Roared, actually. Said he did not intend to invade us or any other nation in the immediate or distant future saying we had nothing they wanted so badly, insisting instead that in line with their current policy of investment for the future they were developing several projects, not just one, all with peaceful outcomes. I asked him to give me his assurance that he was not involved in developing armaments of any kind.'

He paused.

'We share, as you know a joint defensive strategy, and he readily gave me just such an assurance. "I can assure you that we are working hard towards a peaceful solution of some of the world's most troublesome problems and I have the full support of all parties in one or two ventures that will undoubtedly contribute towards that end. If Goliath himself came looking for trouble, I doubt very much if we could find a single slingshot between us". His very words as I recall them.'

They sat in silence.

'Tomorrow I have a meeting with George Donaldson, my Chief of Security here at Number Ten. Indications are that he has a more detailed folder for me to inspect. If there is anything you should know, I will of course inform you immediately. I am reassured that you do not consider the threat to have any substance to it. I was, incidentally, inclined to a similar view myself. However, these days, it pays in the long run to be careful at the outset.'

They arose, John Ryder wondering if it had all come out or if there was more behind this meeting than had at first appeared. Left alone, he placed several phone calls, waiting till each had responded, his mood uneasy as he wondered if Gregor had finally lost his bloody marbles for the last and final time.


Five o'clock and the Cabinet Room at Number Ten was filling on time. Despite the heat, the dark suits entered the room, uncertain of the reason for the hurriedly arranged meeting, but curious and by definition concerned, lest the screw-up was of their special making. For screw-up it had to be. Either known to a few, but not yet common knowledge, or one simply in the making, to be nipped in the bud before the indiscretion or whatever reached the level of scandal or worse.

The entry into the room of the head of the security services caused some feet to shuffle and some individual neck massaging, as each in turn adopted and developed his own particular body language that said, 'Please God, let it be *his* phone that was tapped and not mine.'

The Prime Minister hurried into the room moments later and joined them at the head of the table. Wasting no time, he came directly to the point.

'I met today with Elmer Franklin, who flew over this morning to brief me on some very strange goings on across our border to the north.' He smiled, as the mirth rumbled around the table, tension easing, their worries disappearing, the mood relaxing noticeably as he went on.

'It seems that the many rumours we have heard of late, of intensive rocket construction, have been picked up by our friends over there, and Mr Jackson, it would appear, believes that he will end his first term in office facing a missile crisis on a scale not far short of the one in the sixties.'

At this, the room erupted in laughter, any remaining concerns for their jobs, their security or their cabinet positions dispelled in an instant.

'Yes. I nearly laughed too. But we must not be ungenerous. We are well aware of the close ties between Scotland and the Russian states. We also know of their plans, most of them at least, for future co-operation on cultural and agricultural matters and for assistance with funding for several low key projects in the various independent republics. But what we have here today, is quite different. As I have said, I must reassure Mr. Jackson and his aides that we are not, and never have been party to the various,' he paused, 'adventures undertaken by our friends over the wall.'

He went on.

'Nevertheless, George here has something to impart that puts a slightly different complexion on the whole affair and I would like you to listen carefully to what he has to say. I am meeting with Franklin again tomorrow at noon, and I must reassure him that we have a handle on this business, and that we are not entirely ignorant of the affair that's bothering him.'

At this, George Donaldson slouched further in his chair, his chin resting on his collar, his tie almost hidden. As head of the department in charge of covert security he was known to some, but not to all. His manner however and the very fact that he was present raised the matter to a level of importance that obviously demanded a face to face instead of the restricted circular, stamped, "Top Secret: for your eyes only."

'Well,' he started, 'there isn't much to tell. Four and a half years ago we know that they swapped a contract to supply natural gas for a package of Russian equipment and know-how, with a view to investing in satellite launch technology and, as most of you are aware, it all seemed very harmless at the time. They never had a hope in hell of catching the Ariane programme, nor were they ever likely to develop the technical know-how to get the thing off the ground, let alone get a satellite into orbit. But, it now seems more than likely that they did. Or at the very least, they did in collaboration with the Russian team. Less than a month ago a rocket was launched that put just such a satellite into orbit. Still, nothing remarkable about that I hear you say. True enough.

'What is remarkable though, is that the rocket was less than a third the size of anything we know about, appeared to be not much bigger than the American Space shuttle itself, the fuel carrying capacity was clearly reduced, the burn at launch was noticeably different, and they climbed faster than normal, entering a very high orbit in a very short space of time. At no point did we note any separation of fuel capsules, nor do we have any record of them shedding anything before ...'

At this he paused, leaning forward, enunciating clearly, slowing his delivery until all eyes were on him,

' ... before re-entering the earth's atmosphere three days later and *landing*, we can only presume "shuttle fashion", in Kazakhstan.'

There was silence in the room. The impact of what they had just heard beginning to sink in, their minds now focused; not a smirk in sight.

'So as you might by now have guessed, they have developed, one must presume, in collaboration with their new buddies on the Steppes, a bird that can exit and enter, refuel and presumably be used more than once. There is talk of some revolutionary new fuel technology too. My people are fairly certain that they are on to something. I am also told that, without some enormous technological leap forward, what they have achieved would be nigh on impossible. So, believe it or not, the rumours of their success in the field must now be reviewed in the light of our most recent intelligence reports. One small thing, perhaps unimportant until we view it as a measure of the success and as an indicator of the quality of the fuel used, my man on the ground, who was less than five hundred metres from the launch pad, heard next to nothing One minute, the rocket was on the pad; the next, it had lifted and was gone.'

John Ryder glanced at his watch.

'Gentlemen, what we have heard today must be kept under the strictest of wraps. I am placing a further call to Gregor McLeod tonight and I shall be requesting a meeting with him. Before we go, we also have it on very good authority that they are planning a launch of their own to mark St. Andrew's Day, in less than six months' time.'

At this, a murmur of surprise was heard as John Ryder looking up, his face serious, giving nothing away, his expression belying the unspoken thoughts of them all; that their plutocratic neighbours in the north had undeniably come into their own; had used their skills and ingenuity to emerge yet again on the world stage as technical entrepreneurs and a force to be reckoned with.

Alan Redding, the Minister for Science & Technology, raised his hand off the table, his concern clearly apparent to those who knew him.

'Minister, if this is true and they have developed such a tool, it sounds as if they still have a long way to go before accelerating a man into orbit. The thing must have been unmanned for God's sake. Twice the rate of climb? I find it hard to believe. Really! And as for sprouting wings and landing as a shuttle; well, what can I say? The best brains on both sides of the Atlantic have pondered that one for decades. To get a satellite into space does not require a re-entry vehicle. A discarded staged rocket would suffice. Did our man on the ground actually see it land and taxi? I doubt it. Such a technology would be state of the art and I doubt if it exists. A vertical take off and a conventional landing? Really! it's ridiculous. I find it all too much to take on board.'

At this, George Donaldson, lifted one eyebrow frowning slightly. his gaze fixed on Alan Redding.

'Believe it or believe it not, I am of the opinion that we must conclude that they *have* been successful, since all of the evidence points to the facts as I have outlined them. And hear this, as far as we can ascertain from direct observation of the site, they re-launched the very same bird a day later without even bothering to stick it through the bloody carwash.'

# 3

Gregor McLeod sat in his office high above the Castle Esplanade looking down on to the city, a bustling metropolis stirring into life as it had done every day for centuries.

The panoramic view to the north was breathtaking. The estuary of the River Forth, the three great bridges connecting the lowlands to the Kingdom of Fife and the Highlands, where the rugged terrain of gorse- and heather-covered mountains could be seen on a clear day. And to the west on the very few truly clear days, the faint outlines of Ben More and Ben Lawers towered over the surrounding mountainsides.

Gregor McLeod was a happy man, his plans for his Party and his country running smoothly, coexisting in perfect harmony. In the few short years since independence, they had come a long way. Reaping the profits from the natural resources of the land, investing wisely in the things that were needed, seeing his people happy and industrious, were things that truly mattered to him. With his latest venture coming to fruition in a few short months, he had every reason to be happy. Everything was on schedule. Even allowing for minor setbacks, he was confident that the target dates agreed at the meeting could be met. A tall order perhaps, but worthwhile nevertheless. He had long since dismissed the nagging doubts that at an earlier time had dogged his nights. They would succeed. In this, he remained confident.

A light knock sounded on the door and his secretary entered.

'Mr Simpson has arrived, sir. Shall I show him in?'

Angus Simpson, features editor of the Scotsman, friend and colleague over many years, trusted and reliable, thrust out his hand as they greeted each other warmly.

'How was the trip? When did you arrive?'

'Oh, yesterday evening. Tiring as always, but productive.'

'You seem to spend a lot of time at that space centre, Gregor. Anything we should all know about? There are enough rumours running around the streets to fill a dozen dung carts. When are you going to let us in on the latest project?'

Gregor crossed to his desk. He was weary; too many late nights.

'Oh! soon enough; soon enough. When did I ever cheat you out of a good story? Just tell me that?' They laughed.

'But seriously, Gregor, the talk is that this satellite launch programme of yours is adrift, despite the fortune still being spent on it. That last payment to the Russian Space Agency was a king's ransom. The murmurs are rising and the voices of doom will not be stilled. The word on the street is that you've lost the plot. The socialists are after your hide and you are going to find in this next session of parliament that they will not be as easy to handle as before. Thus far, they have backed you against Labour all the way. But all that could change. You know as well as I do that it only takes one of these schemes to go wrong and they will be baying after you like a pack of hungry dogs.'

Gregor McLeod held up his hands in mild protest. It was true. He had kept them in the dark for too long. The Research and Development Fund allocated to the project had long since run dry, his never-ending appeals for fresh funding grudgingly but regularly conceded, his previous record of leadership and honest fair dealing winning the argument every time.

'Gus. If I never succeed in another thing in my remaining years of life, I would willingly surrender all of our previous good works and any future successes for just this one. If it works out, we will have accomplished something that will benefit all of us for years to come. It has come to mean a great deal to us, all of us on the team. I intend to go public shortly, broadcasting to the nation, when hopefully our plans will be made clear. I am also, as you so rightly predicted, in for a storm at Minister's Question Time on Thursday. It can't be avoided. As usual I'll refer them to the minutes of the Select Committee's last meeting. But, I know I must give them something more than just dates and financial projections.'

He paused, as if weighing up the situation.

'I asked you to come in today for more than just a chat. If I was to let you in on a little secret, I would need your firm handshake that not a word would get out until I am ready.' He glanced at

Angus, a shadow of indecision on his brow.

'You've known me man and boy, Gregor. My turn now. When have I ever let *you* down? Whatever goes on between us *is* between us. The number of times I wished it weren't so ...'

Gregor paused, thinking. In an hour he would go down to the debating chamber to face the opposition, but for now, moving to the window, his back to the other man, he stood considering for a moment longer, before returning to his seat.

'Now, not a word to anyone, nothing in print until I say so. And there are several ways you could prove to be very useful. In the coming weeks, days actually, I will need you to drop a few hints via your column or wherever. I need to build a climate of anticipation, create an interest that will bring everyone on board for what I have in mind. And then, God help us, we will have to batten down the hatches, man the ramparts and fight off the world's press. Hold on whilst I divert all incomings.'

'You see, it's like this ...'

At the end of an hour they were still there. Outside, the rain fell through the summer sunshine, dark clouds rolling over the Fife hills. High in the foothills of the Grampians, the plantations of Forestry Commission trees claimed the terrain, their tall trunks, closely packed, shutting out the sun in places. And here and there the inevitable traces of acid rain, the yellowing of the needles, the bare branches and the bark spalling to reveal the dead bones beneath.

Murdo Sinclair peered through the protective window of the bunker, looking out over the expanse of the runway towards the secluded area. Although some distance away, the monitors in front relayed action from a dozen camera sources, giving him a clear picture of the progress of the test under way. On the edge of the area, fire trucks and rescue tenders stood ready, prepared to move in immediately if the machine was to run out of control, side slipping and crashing on to the sand beds below. Around the target area, large nets, angled gently away from the ground, formed catchments on four sides; a safety measure that had, on several occasions, saved a very expensive piece of equipment from adding to the spiralling costs of an already over-budget programme.

Inch by inch, the craft slowed its descent. Hovering some twenty feet off the surface of the sand pit it tipped to one side, then corrected, righting itself, still hovering, stationary now, before beginning the balanced descent to the ground. Around the perimeter of the dish, dozens of tiny jets kept the machine level, the friction free gyros, their accuracy assured by the advanced software at the heart of the computer bank, countering the natural tendency for side slip and tilt, a process that reflected three years of design, sorely beset with failure after failure.

As the vehicle touched evenly on the bed of soft sand, a cheer went up from those standing by the tenders. In the bunker, slow grins replaced taut lines around the mouth as the team relaxed, congratulating each other on another near flawless exercise.

'I want to resume tests as soon as possible with the CM2 gas instead of compressed air. By tomorrow, we can have the vacuum chamber readied for at least two flights. One lift off, and, if we can manage it, another landing. This time, let Johnson have command of the first test. I want to carry out the second personally. We, all of us, must be fully conversant with the new revised control procedures in time for the final tests in September.'

He reached for the public address button.

'Well done, everybody. I am very happy with a good day's work.'

Releasing the catches on the fire doors, he moved away down the concrete corridor under the dome that housed Scotland's first Space Research Centre, the Rosewell Institute, home to physicists, mathematicians, astronomers, and scientists fully engaged in a variety of projects, from initially monitoring the endless sightings of UFOs over the Central Lowlands, to developing a programme that covered deep space photography, astronomy and signals monitoring of radio and infrared wavebands.

Returning to his office, he switched to a secure line and dialled. The voice of Gregor McLeod was as recognisable as his signature itself.

'Yes Murdo. Good news I hope.' He listened for a full three minutes. 'I am of course delighted. I never had a single doubt. Keep me informed after tomorrow's tests. Oh, by the way. I brought Gus Simpson up to date on our plans. Not the whole story, you understand, but enough to get him safely on our side. Take a look at Thursday's Scotsman for a preview of what is sure to follow.'

'Are we doing the right thing? Will he play along with us? We're too close to success for any risk that the House will overturn the decision to launch.'

'You leave the House to me. If we play our cards correctly they, as usual, will be in bed with the lights out before they realise what's happening to them. I'll be speaking to Fiona later so no need to mention anything to her. I'll let her know what's going on.'

At that he closed the line; his spirits rising. This was good news indeed. Slowly, ever so slowly, they were beginning to achieve their goals. The tests on the fuel had gone well, and now? With tests on the support vehicle proving positive they were now well on the way to the launch. With safety margins improved and work on the use of the new lightweight stabilising gases, progress had been swift. But could he do it? Was the risk too high? It was immaterial to his plan. He could still play his cards. It was irrelevant; either way; to land or not to land? That was the big question. To invite the Russians on board was yet another, but not on the first trip. No! Not on this one! To let them in on the progress made on the tests was something else he would have to consider very carefully. The recent success of the two orbital flights from Tashkent in Uzbekistan was progress indeed, encouraging and solid proof (if ever he needed it), that the new fuel technology was the key to future flights.

He must, he reminded himself, send a congratulatory note to Mikhail. They had done wonders in St. Petersburg. Astonishing progress, from the time of their first discussions, their first handshake, agreeing to share the secret of the fuel in exchange for Russian assistance. It had all been too easy; a future joint exploration combining Scottish funding and the long years of development expertise in orbital flight held by the Russians.

'Aye,' he thought. 'But not on this trip.'

This one was too important to share, too sensitive to bring them on board. This adventure required a deft touch, playing for keeps!

Gazing out at the traffic below, the early morning shoppers crowding the pavements of Princes Street, he realised that he had been sitting for over an hour lost in thought, something that he was aware was happening all too often these days, the burden of responsibility creating more questions than answers; answers that would have to be found, and found quickly if he wanted to save even his own tiny corner of the planet.


Elmer Franklin sat in the American Ambassador's office overlooking Grosvenor Square, manner alert, pencil poised, cuffs startlingly white against the deep rich mahogany of the desktop.

'Yes, Mr President. That is exactly the way he put it over to me. He was totally unconcerned. Yes! Yes, I said "unconcerned". Not in the least bit worried. No, he is aware of the project but it seems that he had sufficient reassurance in the past from the Scottish First Minister that …'

Long pause.

'No! Definitely not. I have made that clear. He is most definitely *un*concerned. He believes that the whole thing is positively ridiculous.'

Another pause.

'I see. I see. Well. I don't think so. I'm due to meet with him again tomorrow at noon. Yes, yes… "couldn't locate a single sling shot between them." His exact words.'

The receiver shifted to the other ear which was several degrees cooler.

'Well no, not exactly. He at no time indicated awareness of any active Russian collaboration. Tashkent? Where? In Uzbekistan? No. No such reference was made. I am certain. Yes. What? Two flights into orbit from Uzbekistan? When? Oh!'

The receiver shifted back as he wrote hastily on the pad in front of him.

'Yes. Yes. And re-entry was confirmed the day after. I see. I see. Yes. I'm almost certain that John Ryder has no information on these points you have just raised. He was on the contrary extremely frank. I said, frank. Frank who? No, I meant that he was being extremely honest. He agreed to call Gregor McLeod yesterday evening. So far, I have no information on that point, but he agreed to keep us in the frame if he learned anything that could be of use. Yes. I will. I will, certainly. Yes. Goodnight, Mr President.'

As he closed the line, Nathan Jackson turned to his aides, Johnson, Denham and his deputy, Joe Skinner of the CIA and the NASA Chief Administrator, Tom Sherman.

'What do you make of that? He claims they know diddley shit about any of it. Well we know one thing. The Scots *are* funding their space programme. Those payments to the Narodny Bank are astronomical, and regular. But what about those launches from Tashkent? It's obvious, they must be collaborating.'

Tom Sherman, as always was listening quietly. As the Chief Administrator at NASA, he had served several administrations in his time. Now close to retiring, his experience and wisdom had often been called upon in many a crisis.

'If they are funding the Russian space agency, with the know-how the Russians have gathered and with billions being poured into their coffers, we could be seeing a partnership in space that would rival our own great days in the sixties and seventies. It's a great pity, I always felt, that subsequent administrations saw fit to abandon our manned space missions during Nixon's term in office. We would have been around the solar system twenty times over by now, if those clowns in Congress had had their heads screwed on the right way. What a sad way to have to run an agency. Look what happened to our plans to soft-land on Mars, for God's sake. If you asked me to hit the Moon tomorrow, I doubt if I could find the expertise to hit my own back yard. This great country of ours has, frankly, slipped out of the era of manned exploration of space and, much as I regret having to say it, we're now in danger of becoming a second class nation in the race to dominate travel beyond the immediate airspace of our own planet.'

As he glanced up, the figure of Nathan Jackson brimming over with anger and frustration was not a pleasant sight.

'Godammit, Tom. If I've heard that piece once I have heard it a thousand times from your people. Please don't tell me what I already goddamn know. What I *do* need now is your advice on how this affects our national security. Do they have the capability to develop this to the level of a global threat? For Christ's sake, if they have the delivery system, all it needs is a warhead. So, are the Ruskies simply moving their I.B.M.s that bit closer? Fortunately, our Star Wars technology is firmly in place. Yes sirree. Thank God we had the foresight to bring that little number on line. No incoming rocket is gonna reach these shores.'

At this, he smacked his fist into his palm.

In the corner, Dale Johnson began to whistle softly, lifting his eyes skywards. Tom Sherman had begun to speak again, a note of resignation in his voice.

'I *am* worried, nevertheless. This reference to the sling shot. How did it go? - "not a single sling shot between them". Last time we heard those words used in any meaningful context was during *our* lunar expeditions as we accelerated away from earth's gravity and used the principal of the sling-shot to get our ship into orbit round the Moon.'

The room stilled.

'Good God!' said the President, 'don't tell me they have gotten together with the Russians to put a man on the Moon? Is that a possibility?'

Looking around the room, their faces gave no hint of any immediate answers. Judging by their startled looks, this was clearly news to all of them.

'Well? Is it possible? the President was asking.'

The stillness that followed was broken only by the quiet distracted whistling of the Secretary of State, who sat with legs crossed staring out of the window, his mind concerned with other things. Beside him, Jo Skinner turned slowly, his expression grave, his mood serious.

'I will say one thing. We had all better hope and pray that they are *not* heading for the Moon, and that's *all* I have to say.'

At this, Nathan Jackson leaned forward across the desk. He was curious. Something warned him intuitively that there was more to come.

'Come on then. State your piece. What exactly are you driving at?'

Jo Skinner was biting his lip, staring at the deep rich red, heavily patterned carpet. He avoided the President's piercing gaze, shifting uncomfortably in his chair. Tom Sherman looked around at them all, the senior figure among them, a look of quiet resignation on his face as he turned to Joe Skinner, who was sitting with head down, his face buried in his hands.

'Tell him Joe, since you were around at the time.' Then in a softer tone, reluctantly, 'He should be told.'

Sitting beside him, they all suddenly looked as though they might be getting ready to duet on the whistling caper with Dale Johnson.

'Told what, for Christ's sake?' The President, looking now from side to side, expecting ready made answers.

They were all now actively engaged in trying desperately to come last in the race to be first to answer, their body language expressing a mixture of hopelessness and inevitability as if suppressing some awful truth.

'Tell me what, for Jesus' sake!' Jackson was searching each of their faces in turn.

'It's about the Moon landings Sir.' Skinner was trying to explain quietly, but the words, when they came, were like distant sounding gongs in some far off valley.

'This is kinda hard for me to say, given that … well, it's true that I was around at the time as Tom has said, but only just. I mean…'

Nathan Jackson was on his feet, fearing some calamity, feeling the point of the sword suspended over his administration, desperate for clarification but fearing the worst.

'What are you trying to tell me?' The words chosen carefully, the slow delivery intended to settle the air of desperation that now seemed to be creeping into every corner of the room.

'Well, Sir, about the Moon landings. You see …'

At this point, Jackson exploded, his face turning purple, his blood pressure beginning to soar.

'What in hell's name is going on? Just give me the facts for Christ's sake.'

'Well Sir…about Apollo Eleven; about that first landing, you remember, that bit where Neil Armstrong gets down from the descent module, the famous line:

"One small step for man, one giant leap for mankind"?'

'Yes. Yes. So what? … We *did* land on the goddamned thing after all, didn't we? Everybody knows that! Every half-witted dog in the street knows that, for Christ's sake. Well, don't they?'

His mouth remained open, his confusion obvious. Tom Sherman had taken up the story, the pain on his face clearly seen.

'Mr President, there are one or two aspects of that story that we should perhaps be bringing to your attention. You see, at that time back in the sixties, things were just, well, just a little chaotic and …'

Across the room, the thin whistling suddenly died.

# 4

Across the great chamber, the members roared with laughter, the exchanges over the course of the afternoon enriched with humour and refined sarcasm. Criticism and argument, contentious issues debated with real fervour and genuine concern for the subjects under discussion. As usual, Gregor McLeod held the floor. Minister's Question Time was invariably the most entertaining show of the week, the public gallery crammed with reporters and members of the public enjoying the argument and the rhetoric exchanged between skilled politicians on all sides of the house.

The Liberal Member for Lennox was on his feet.

'Mr Speaker, the issue is not merely one of the overall cost of the project, but a question of whether or not the funds are being directed wisely and utilised properly. Whilst we are all of us in general agreement on the ultimate goal of the project, and if we are to believe the recently updated feasibility study report, it would appear that we are now very close to finishing. If we are to protect our investment at this stage of the proceedings, I can only propose that the request for additional funding be sanctioned, in the fervent hope that we will all see the promised returns beginning to materialise in the very near future.

'As you all know, I was, and I remain, a critic of this Government's spending on projects and overseas commitments to aid packages which in my opinion are of doubtful benefit to our nation in the long term. I have opposed spending on a number of these projects and whilst I am now reluctantly in favour of additional funding on the satellite programme, I wish to record my opposition to the high-handed manner in which the present First Minister drives his personal crusades through this House, selfishly taking the moral high ground in every debate, giving us the benefit of his, dare I say it, *dubious* rhetoric on everything from garbage collection to his dreams for flying the Saltire in outer space. It is high time that this Government was called to account for its philandering ways and high time that it told this nation the truth about its current programme for cutting the costs of getting satellites into orbit.'

The Speaker of the House called on the Chief Minister to reply. Gregor rose, and the room quietened.

'Mr Speaker, Honourable Members of this house. The moral high ground as I recall, is a very narrow ledge hovering somewhere above an abyss full of good intentions, half truths, unfulfilled promises and little else. No. We do not claim "the moral high ground". Instead ,we offer you the choice. The choice between remaining as we have been over the last five hundred years of our history, or of seeing ourselves as torch bearers for a better, happier, altogether more prosperous nation, culturally enriched and intellectually stimulated by the prospect of becoming a leader in world affairs.

'We have, as you all know, through the continuing good management of our resources, funded the talent and manpower in our centres of learning, reached for and sustained the quest for a better understanding of ourselves and our society at large, whilst we continue to maintain our position inside the Federation of European States.

'We have achieved a great deal of which we can all be proud. We have also created a growing list of successes in a very short space of time. We have influenced world opinion and we continue to do so by our example and our considerable philanthropy. Never at any time in this country's history have the government and the parties in opposition been so focused on these shared aims. You have supported us because you have believed in the things we were doing. We have been united in consensus, divided only by the call to prioritise the options open to us, on how we invest and dispense the great wealth at our disposal.

'Our term in office is not guaranteed. In a few short months the reins of power could very easily leave our hands. We wish the incoming party, whoever they might be, every success. We have shown the way forward. It would be churlish of me to suggest that our way is the only way. But I must agree with my honourable friend. From time to time we have been less than forthright in announcing our goals. You may agree or choose to disagree with our methodology but our successes are a matter of record. I recall fierce opposition to a number of our proposals. Opposition which, in any democratically elected parliament, is essential in moderating the excesses of ...'

At this, the laughter erupted again, drowning out the remainder of his sentence.

'But as you all know, my only wish was for us all to take pride in our nation, to see ourselves as qualified inheritors of a great tradition of free thinkers, a nation of inventors and philosophers, artists and poets who have sent their messages across the globe. We have, I believe, managed to sweep away the old shackles, the all too heavy reliance on a shabby tradition that appealed to choking sentimentality to sustain itself with cabers and shortbread, the kilt and the sporran and enough tartan weave to go around the world a thousand times over.

'No. We have tried to look to a future where we will replace these worn out images with a cultural identity built on solid achievement and by raising the voice of common sense in arguing our case on the world stage. As we sit in this great new Parliament building of ours, we can look back on things achieved, each in turn reflecting on our declared intention to ensure that the world we will hand on will be a better place for generations still to come. We do not condemn the past, nor do we commend the lack of achievement during the years in the wilderness. That view we carried of ourselves as a second class nation has changed forever. It is time to reflect on what we might yet achieve, what we might yet aspire to, using only the voice of reason, of moderation and genuine concern for others. I ask you to believe that I have held these things dear to my heart, not for myself, but for Scotland.'

Across the chamber, the cries rang out in response to the emotion in his appeal, the applause from the public gallery not the least among them.

'I now return to the question of investment in our Space Centres both here and on North Uist and our plans to deploy satellites in space for a fraction of the cost of our nearest competitors in the market place. I believe that we *can* achieve this. Some of you are no doubt aware that over the past two years, considerable investment has gone into the development of advanced fuels, without which we could not compete in any arena of space research. Many will no doubt have heard rumours of our recent successes in this field. Collaboration with our friends in Russia, and the agreement in place to share our gas reserves in exchange for their considerable expertise in re-entry technology have paid off handsomely.

'I can now reveal that in the past two months our new fuel has been used to launch and retrieve the prototype of our new space shuttle. I am assured that the tests were concluded without a hitch. The vehicle, developed conjointly in discussions with our own scientists, is capable of reaching a high orbit and has successfully re-entered the earth's atmosphere, landing on more than one occasion without sustaining damage of any kind.'

At this a murmur of approval was heard in the chamber. A lone round of applause raised heads for a moment before their attention returned once again to the speech.

'And now, my friends, I have a confession to make to you. A confession which will in all probability change the course of our lives forever.'

The members stirred in their chairs, their interest aroused still further. When Gregor McLeod confessed to anything it was rarely trivial. They waited.

'Until this moment, the results of our on-going work both at Rosewell and on North Uist have been a matter of conjecture for many of you. I myself confess to being surprised and delighted by results at both venues. Whilst it is true that aiming to put satellites into orbit *was* the original target of our effort...'

He heard the murmur rising again, the assembly beginning to sense the importance of the confession about to be revealed, beginning to feel the weight of the exposé that had been kept from them; something that they should have been party to; something that warranted debate and the approval of the House.

' ...I can now reveal...'

He held up his hand, waiting for the noise to subside.

'I can now reveal that we have made great strides in perfecting a vehicle that will not only orbit the earth, but which could, without modification of any kind, reach for the very stars.'

In the public gallery, Gus Simpson, watched the performance, marvelling at the ease with which his old friend held the gathering in his hands. At the announcement there was an immediate uproar, several Members on their feet in an instant, demanding the Speaker's attention. Tomorrow he would go into print, the copy already drafted, the full story and the first of a series of leaks about the government's plans for the journey of a lifetime about to dazzle a public already well used to unusual proclamations from a man they had come to love and respect. Gregor was talking again, his arms raised over his head, his composure unruffled.

'Mr Speaker, I ask for your indulgence for these few remaining moments.'

The great chamber stilled again, the final statement eagerly awaited.

'My friends, it is our intention, on the thirtieth day of November, St Andrew's Day, to launch a vehicle into space that will carry with it the hopes and aspirations of us all; a craft that will herald the arrival of Scotland into an era of space exploration, that will tell the world that the spirit of adventure and human endeavour is alive and well, and flourishing in this great nation of ours.

'Gentlemen, on that day we shall all see, with God's help, the first Scots embarking on a journey that will see them, four days and ten hours later, setting foot on the Moon itself.'

The stunned silence that followed his announcement was broken only seconds later when the Parliament rose as one man, the cheer heard across the length and breadth of Princes Street.

'You wily old bastard,' thought Gus Simpson. 'You've done it again.'


The news announcer returned to the main item of news, his voice faltering as the emotion he felt caught at his throat, causing him to cough lightly several times during the broadcast.

'First Minister Gregor McLeod today announced to a stunned parliament that plans are well advanced for a Scottish Moon landing at the end of November. Pressed for details, the First Minister declined to enter into debate on the subject. The Opposition benches have called for a full debate on the issue, claiming that they have been consistently lied to about the development of a space programme aiming to see a team of Scots on the Moon by the end of this year. The First Minister was however loudly cheered by his party and made an emotional appeal for the support of all parties, in what he described as "an opportunity without equal that would once and for all time place Scotland in the forefront of world affairs and in the long run be of great benefit to mankind". When pressed for details, he again declined to enter into debate on the many issues raised by his announcement. A round table discussion on the announcement will take place after this programme on a special edition of the Kirsty Monroe Show.'

'And now for the rest of the news.'

# 5

In the public bar of "The Bletherin' Skite", Rab Nicol was on the scrounge. It had been a bad day thus far. A very bad day, that is, for scroungers. This, his third pint of stout of the entire evening, was all but finished and prospects of an immediate refill were dwindling fast. The bar-tender, Charlie Smith, had his professional eye on him too. Rab Nicol was one nuisance he could live without. One more attempt to wheedle further beverage out of his better heeled customers, and he would retire him ungracefully on to the pavement of the High Street.

Rab too, was equally aware of the unspoken dialogue developing between them. As cautious as he was smart, he was acutely aware that time at the bar of this particular hostelry was fast running out. Not that this was the only pub in town! No sir. Rab knew them all. As a professional drunk, that was an essential part of the game. Knowing where to scrounge and which pubs to avoid was the way to stay alive.

The television set above the bar brightened into life, the volume adjusted to a low groan. With pictures only, the regulars could keep abreast of the day's happenings, without placing any undue stress on their ability to consume drink. But this was different. Something in the programme was beginning to claim their attention.

'But surely, if we *can* safely reach the Moon and return in one piece, surely this would be a magnificent achievement, given that it is now fifty-odd years since anyone set foot on our nearest neighbour in the solar system.'

Around the table' the pundits from several newspapers and a couple of commentators sat in heated discussion with a representative of each of the political parties.

'It was a waste o' money then, and it's a disgraceful waste o' money now! If Gregor McLeod wants tae bankrupt us he is goin' the right way about it! How much have we spent so far? Nearly three billion and that's no' counting' the development costs o' that fuel business. He never mentioned *that,* you'll no doubt have noticed.'

Kirsty Monroe was opening the debate, steering away from

the Honourable Member from Govan and searching for a less opinionated response.

'Tell me, Angus; do you believe that the people of Scotland are behind him in his efforts? Do you foresee him running into trouble in the House over this one?'

Drifting ever closer to the bar, watched closely by Charlie Smith, Rab Nicol was turning his good ear in his unshaven head towards the television set in an effort to pick up the thread of the programme. More a dedicated drinker than a dedicated viewer, he was intrigued by the numbers mentioned and the odd references to the Moon that were interspersed into the dialogue.

'Hey. You! Shuthefuckup a minute.'

'Hey. Fuck you!'

Heads turned to look at Rab then slowly back towards the set, the volume now raised by the barman, as they gathered around to listen.

'Naw. Naw. Listen. It's really interestin'. She says they're goin' tae the Moon. Honest! Listen, for Christ's sake'.

Gus Simpson was speaking.

'If Gregor says that they can do it, then we had better believe him. In all the years I have known him, he has never been known to promise anything he could not deliver. I believe that if we succeed, that it will place Scotland firmly at the hub of world scientific affairs. After all; the wonder of space travel has intrigued everyone, ever since that first Moon landing.'

At this point, the television studio debate gave way to stock footage of the descent by Neil Armstrong onto the surface of the Moon.

They leaned forward, silent now as they listened.

"One small step for man, one giant leap for mankind."

'That's it Jimmy. You gi'e it tae them; up the Celtic!'

Rab was beaming, his face alive, shouting across the bar, the other customers being swept along on a tide of uninhibited patriotism, not entirely sure why, but aware that somewhere along the way, Gregor McLeod, their champion, had done it again.

'Hey, you. Big mouth. You shut the fuck up aboot Celtic.

This has got nothin' tae dae wi' Celtic. Neil Armstrong's no' even a Catholic.'

'Who says he's no' a Catholic?' Rab was incensed.

'You two. Shut it. Now!' Charlie Smith was not about to allow sectarian blood letting on the premises. 'Aye. The pair o' ye'. Shut it.'

'Awfy sorry Jimmie if ah gave ye any offence,' the opportunity to ingratiate himself not one to be missed. 'S'no like me really. Just got carried away; us landin' on the Moon an' a' that. Ye ken how it is. Gets ye right here.'

'Nae offence taken, Jimmy. Here, have a drink. Let's forget aboot it. OK? Meet the wife.'

'Aye. Hullo. Nae problem, Jimmy. Ah don't really gi'e a damn if he was a Catholic or no'. It's a' the same thing tae me like.'

'Ah said shut it!'

Kirsty Monroe was off again.

'And as leader of the Scottish Socialist Party, what do you make of the announcement?' Kenny Paterson, leader of the S.S.P. launched into his party's position on the funding and the overall sacrifices demanded of a patient, suppressed populace controlled by bigots and capitalists intent on bankrupting Scotland in an attempt to erect monuments to their own vain glory.

'It's a situation that we have come to expect from the so called Scottish Independence Party. Whilst it's true that we have generally supported their efforts over their years in power, we dismiss this latest venture as outright electioneering in the face of rising social disorder, a noticeable fall in the standard of living for the poorer members of our community; and for the people of Scotland as a whole. We have always campaigned, and will continue to press, for investment in the things that help to build communities, where locals can integrate fully with asylum seekers and live side by side with those of different religious and ethnic backgrounds ...'

'Did ye hear that?

Rab was on his feet again, his pint nearly drained. It was time for further agitation.

'Did ye hear what he said? Live side by side wi' who? Different ethnic backgrounds? He's got some fuckin' nerve, ah'm tellin' ye. If it's no one bunch o' foreigners, it's another. They'll be importing Eskimos next. I don't want tae live next door tae some fuckin' igloo. D'you? Reindeer runnin' a' ower the gairden; keepin' polar bears fur pets.'

'Will you shut the fuck up about polar bears?'

All eyes were returning to the programme.

'And with that astonishing announcement today in the House, we end tonight's programme, so from me, Kirsty Monroe and the team, goodnight.'

Rab remained silent, nursing the last dregs of his pint. Sitting apart at the end of the bar, left on his own, it was time for action, time for his best effort to be called up. Biding his time until the conversation dipped, he spoke up, as if continuing a dialogue with some invisible entity next to him.

'Will ye listen or no'? Ah'm tellin ye, the Yanks never made it tae the Moon. It was all a set up. Oh, they *went* there right enough, whizzed around an' a' that, but they never *landed* on the Moon. That Apollo Eleven bit never happened. That bit was a set up! It was too dangerous. Aye. That's right. It wis too bloody dangerous. They couldnae control that lunar module thing. Wis fundamentally unstable. That bit about "one small step" and a' that; well that bit was done in a *fil-lum* studio in California. Ah saw a documentary about that one!'

He paused for effect, innocently checking out reactions around the bar. Every face in the room was watching him. He turned apologetically, a timid look on his face. A *thirsty* look.

'See you Jimmy. That's a very interestin' proposition you're coming oot wi'. Ye seem tae ken an awfy lot aboot the subject. Who says they never made it tae the Moon? Who? Just tell us who.'

At this, the empty glass began to speak volumes, the angled, questioning look on the story-teller's face, a page extracted from the unwritten treatise on the art of obtaining gratuitous refreshment.

Three hours later, alone again on the High Street, the pubs emptied and the pavements deserted, Rab Nicol wandered home, a great discovery made; one to dine out on forever and ever. All you had to do was start the argument. 'Did they or didn't they', and the rest was pure self indulgence and free Guinness for the rest of the night. All in all, he had a lot to thank Gregor McLeod for.


Midnight, and a full Moon. Elmer Franklin sat by the phone in his suite, waiting nervously for his call to the White House to be returned. Well into his third large whisky, he consulted the notes he had made to prompt his exchanges with his President. Daring to rise from his seat by the phone, he crossed nervously to the window, seeing the streets below dark and deserted.

Standing there, he knew that the news would be well received. There *was* no crisis. No need to bring out the big guns. Everything was neatly under control. Or was it? Surely if John Ryder was unconcerned, even happy about the development, why should the President be any less so? His earlier meeting with the British Prime Minister had been courteous but brief, the mission defused by the announcement made in the Scottish Parliament the previous day. The heat was off. Everyone could now sit back and watch the fun developing. In truth Franklin was also relieved. Keeping a cool head when everyone around was losing theirs was the trick. He was well satisfied with the turn of events. Sitting again, he reflected on his meeting with John Ryder.

'Well, Franklin, all I can tell you is that we were as flabbergasted as you undoubtedly were. We had no idea. The very idea of the Scots going to the Moon is preposterous. If we hadn't heard it for ourselves, none of us would have believed it. All I can say is that we do not seem to have an arms crisis on our hands. You can now reassure Mr Jackson that we are not facing a repeat of the Cuban affair and that we will be monitoring the whole business very closely from our side of the border. Indeed, I today received an official invitation to the launch ceremony. Many members of my Cabinet received similar. I believe they must have had a lot of assistance from the Russians. Six, or is it five years after independence, and already a world leader in scientific matters. It beggars belief. I hope that you will convey my best wishes to your President, who I am sure will be most relieved and delighted to know that our neighbours over the wall *can* be trusted to be responsible, if only up to a point, in matters of security and international protocol.'

'Yes, I agree. They *should* have consulted us; and your government. After all, what do they have to hide? This is hardly breaking new ground, is it? Your people led the way, showing the rest of us that the free world had the capacity, and the will, to reach beyond the confines of our tiny planet and reach for the first time ever for the stars. I remember, as a boy, those chilling moments as the Eagle swept in for that first historic touchdown. "The Eagle has landed". Prophetic words indeed. Your country led the way. And now...'

He paused, glancing out of the window of number eleven.

'Must rush. I'm meeting my cabinet for lunch. It has been a great pleasure renewing our acquaintance again.'

Franklin watched as the car outside sped off into the Westminster traffic. Leaving Downing Street, he had walked along enjoying the bright summer sunshine, seeing the placards boldly proclaiming the news.

## 'SCOTS HEAD
## FOR
## THE MOON'

Underneath someone had scrawled,
*The sooner the better.*

Franklin was not amused.


Franklin was in the arms of his mistress, the warmth of her body pressed to his face. Her hands roved over his muscular torso, titillating and soothing, her soft voice sending waves of passion coursing through him. They rolled together on the soft sheets, his lust rising, his mind blocking out everything except the driving need for her body, her softness and her radiant skin. He became aware of the cool sheets under his head, the sudden smell of stale whisky on her breath, realising it was himself, his mind struggling to throw off the dream, some other part of his subconscious self desperate to linger for precious moments longer. If only…

The phone rang several times more before reality finally clicked in. Grabbing the receiver, he rolled upright on the bed, fumbling for his spectacles, then bending to retrieve his notes.

'Yes, Elmer Franklin speaking. No. I will hang on.' Seconds passed, then minutes. He checked the line. It was still open. Then the sound of a transfer being made, a connection established. Tired and irritable, he waited as the minutes ticked by. And such a wonderful dream, gone like a drifting smoke. He was getting too old for public life; time soon to retire to the Bahamas and find some real love.

'What? Yes. I am here. Yes. Good evening, Mr President. I trust that you received the transcript of my report.'

Pause, as pleasantries were exchanged.

'Yes, of course I'm certain. No crisis at all as far as I can see. And John Ryder agrees with…'

'No. It's quite clear. Their so-called missile programme is in fact a space mission designed to take them to the Moon. Quite soon I understand.'

There was an extended pause while the other end conferred on another line. Was he picking up traces of anger, of regret, of dismay? Perhaps even a hint of fear, or was it…? Confused now, he listened.

'I really don't understand. I thought it was wonderful news. No. They have no military intentions whatsoever. Their plan, quite simply, is to land men on the Moon in the month of November. Yes. The news has been widely broadcast. People here simply can't believe it… The Scots are, literally, over the moon with joy. Widespread feelings of…'

Further heated exchanges were heard.

'No. Not at all. Well, as far as I can be certain, they *claim* to have the ability to make the journey. I hardly think that their First Minister would go on record, if there was even the slightest doubt they could carry the thing through to the end. Yes. In November.

'I see. It's possible I suppose; there are many factors that could delay them. Of course. Weather for one thing. Technical setbacks for another. From our own experience we know that mishaps can occur right up until the final countdown.

'I agree there *are* no certainties in life.

'Well, Sir. I really do believe that they intend to do it. Yes. To head for the Moon. No. That appears to be the situation. No preliminary test flights. That's right. Yes. Yes. They claim that their recent test flights over Uzbekistan have cleared the way for ... No. No. They are quite open about the Russian participation, even suggesting that...'

Elmer sat down again, listening intently, the conversation in Washington clearly being carried on in conference. After a moment or two it resumed.

'If I understand their intention clearly, it is to fly to the Moon on the thirtieth day of November, Saint Andrew's day, and return five days later, reminding the world of our own first historic trip in ...'

A further protracted pause ensued.

'No Sir. I believe they intend to make as much use as possible of the data that we published at that time and make for a landing at much the same spot in the Sea of Tranquillity. The media here is full of speculation about their ...

'Yes. I agree. I would suggest that we offer them every assistance. Oh, I see. Well now, that sheds an entirely different light on the matter. I had no idea that there was any problem at all.'

There was a long pause while the conversation went one way. Franklin stood hopping from foot to foot, suddenly stopping, his knees giving way, his frame seeming to crumple, his face showing distinct signs of bewilderment and not a little pain.

'But Mr President, Sir. They are a sovereign people, a member of NATO and until recently a good and stalwart ally of the United States. What you are suggesting is, frankly ...'

He stopped, the agitation from across the Atlantic clearly reflected on his face. He stood. Drawing himself up to his full height, anger beginning to harden the lines around his mouth, he suddenly saw his years of loyal service under a number of past presidents as hollow and unfulfilled, the integrity and dedication he had carried with him throughout his diplomatic career, suddenly snatched away, his hand shaking, his mind in a turmoil.

'Yes; if these are your wishes Mr President. I will do my best to further your instructions as you have directed. You will of course confirm everything to me …'

The line was cut. At this, Franklin collapsed onto the edge of the bed and wondered if his retirement would materialise a lot earlier than he had anticipated.

On the street six storeys below, the delivery truck dumped the first editions of the morning papers on the doorstep of the hotel. Stooping to pick them up, the hotel porter paused to read the banner headlines:

## SCOTS TO GO
## FOR MOON
## LANDING

'Fuckin' Jocks' he muttered, 'We should 'ave clobbered the bastards at Bannockburn, when we 'ad the chance.'

# 6

The two special agents, Paul Burke and Lenny Stern, leaned inconspicuously against the bar of the village inn, wearing assorted tartan trews and lumberjack shirts in dubious, tourist orientated colour combinations, setting them apart from visitors and locals alike. Behind the bar, Lachie MacDonald was explaining the coinage to them.

From the moment their helicopter had landed in a field outside the village, they had become the centre of attention. Now, feeling distinctly uncomfortable and increasingly aware that their attempt at integration had fallen on its face, they were listening to the quiet buzz of interest their presence had aroused and observing the covert grins on the faces of the locals across the tiny room. Rarely did the Covenanters' Inn offer such rich entertainment.

Through the doorway into the public bar, occasional faces peered out, then retreated, the dominoes silent on the table top, all interest in the game at a standstill, curiosity dominating the proceedings, the landlord all but ignoring the intruders, affable but determined to show no special favour toward his new customers.

'Ye'll no' be from around here, then?' he said, smiling, avoiding too much eye contact.

'Can I refresh yer glasses, or offer you something else?' Polishing the bar now, the silence deafening, every ear in the place hung on every nuance, on every syllable of each and every word.

Forced into replying, but grateful for the chance to strike up the conversation, Paul Burke nodded and swigged the remaining drops of warm ale.

'Give me two more of the same.' The American accent sent a buzz around the bar, guesses confirmed, arguments settled in a flash.

'Americans.'

'We don't see too many gentlemen, such as yourselves, around here at this time of year, but we do get the fishermen and the beaters in the season. Once we had two gentlemen staying from Edinburgh, and their two friends, all of them speaking Russian and drinking vodka like there was no tomorrow. A grand time we had then.' He set down their beers in front of them. 'Oh, we had such a party, that time. Drinking all night and singing, singing and drinking, like there was no tomorrow. Auchenlech had never seen the likes of it, not then and not since. Is the accommodation to your liking?' Polishing the bar top yet again, he noted the beers, untouched, the sudden exchanges between them at the mention of the two Russians.

'We only let rooms out in the summer, of course. Normally we close down the upstairs rooms in the winter time.'

He was settling into his routine. No direct questions. Simple interrogation techniques, practised over many years as a barman.

'The rooms are just fine. Say, do you serve dinner in the evenings?'

'At eight o'clock, but since it's only the two of you staying, we can arrange something for you at any time.'

Lenny Stern lifted his beer, the aroma strange, the warm flat texture not to his liking. So, this was Scotland? Flying up from London, he had noted the gradual changes in density of population, the dramatic topographical changes and the ever decreasing evidence of roads and townships the further north they had travelled. By-passing Glasgow, they had crossed the country under cloud cover seeing the terrain below them gradually becoming rugged and inhospitable, villages linked by minor roads, the area dotted with endless lochs and crossed by streams and rivers. Crossing the Minch, they had made for landfall on the island of North Uist.

'Yeah. We want to do some fishing while we are here; maybe a bit of hunting as well. Say, is there anyone who could take us out, show us around, maybe find us some good shooting?'

At this he turned for the first time looking around the bar at the tiny windows, the darkened beams and the worn fittings, the old fireplace where, despite the warm weather, a wood fire burned briskly in the grate. Above the bar, the glass-fronted salmon and the mangy stoat, dead and dull, stared down on an oak floor, blackened with the slops of generations of drinkers.

'Oh, I daresay old Duncan McAskill would be happy for a day's work. He's the best around here. I can tell you, he can find the game better than any man I know. Never been known to fail!'

'Oh,' said Paul Burke, 'There's one other thing. An old friend of ours in Washington said to say hello to an old friend of his from hereabouts. You wouldn't happen to know him by any chance?' ( At this, he looked straight at Lachie.)

'So this is it. This is what they have come for. To see Hamish,' he was thinking. 'And who might that be?' he enquired casually.

'His name is Hamish McLeod.'

At the mention of the name the bar stilled.

'Och, yes. Hamish. We ken him fine. He'll be a friend of a friend no doubt, so to speak?'

'In a way, yes.'

Aware of the stillness brought on by the mere mention of the name, wishing he could see around the corner of the bar into the other areas, uncomfortable with the fact that they had not yet checked out the layout. The only door into the place secured, but unsure of the existence of any secondary exit, Paul was uneasy, his training and instinct disturbed, the strangeness of the surroundings beginning to get to him.

'Well if it's Hamish McLeod you are after seeking, you need look no further.'

The speaker had entered the room quietly behind them. Dressed in worn jeans and an old pullover, a faded shirt and with a mop of white hair, he stretched out his arm in greeting, the book under his arm, the cracked lens on his spectacles and his quiet air of confidence placing him apart from the others in the room. He signalled quietly to Lachie.

'Bring three of The Arran if you please, and a drop of your finest tap water.' He led them towards a table in the corner carrying the glasses of whisky. 'Gentlemen; a touch of Highland hospitality before we get down to the serious business of finding out who we all are and which of my many pen pals is sending me greetings from Washington of all places. I was in New York once. Now there's a lovely city. Denver too, visiting an old aunt. And, I once got an invitation from a University in Massachusetts, no less, to go and talk to them about matters scientific, although why they asked *me* I never did find out. In the end I didn't go and I felt none the worse for missing it! But, Washington; never!' He laughed quietly. 'Now there's a curious thing,' he added wistfully.

At this, he sat down facing the other two, their huge frames blocking out the light from the window, their long shadows falling across the room. The taped sound of the pibroch began to fill the room, as Lachie discreetly covered their conversation with the sound of the pipes, killing off the chance of further eavesdropping by the patrons of the bar. Lifting his glass, Hamish toasted the two courteously, placing it back on the table empty. Half turning towards the bar, the merest of signals given, three more glasses of Scotland's finest appeared on the table.

'To your health again, gentlemen. And now, tell me. Exactly what kind of fish are you looking to catch? And what, if I might be so bold as to enquire, is the kind of game you are after? For deep sea fishing rods, such as you have there, will rarely land a salmon. And as for the deer, I doubt that the magnum you'll be carrying will be of little use unless you are very, very close to the beast. And I'm also thinking that, dressed as you are, you would be lucky indeed to get within twenty miles of the creatures who can see better than you or I at far greater distances.'

He began to chuckle quietly to himself, his laughter suppressed.

'No. To get within shooting distance of the big stag, you need stealth and a fair degree of cunning. You have to stalk your prey with great care. Cheers! Sometimes for the whole day. No sooner do you have it in your sights, but it moves on; a forever shifting target. I've seen grown men, after hours of crawling in the heather, wet through and determined, throw it all away with one shout of frustration that would send the entire herd running like the wind into the next century.'

At this, he paused.

'Now gentlemen, before we have another wee dram, is it the friction free gyroscopes or the new fuel that you are interested in?'

The night had come to Auchenlech and around the tiny hamlet the dark hills blended into one with the darkness beyond. Here and there, the lamps in a half a dozen cottages were the only signs of life. Across the single track road that ran the length of the village, the cobbled yard outside the Covenanters' Inn was warmed by the light from two small windows set low in the wall, screened from the road by a collection of dense fir trees that now swayed as the wind moaned and whistled through the branches. Outside the pub, the lonely telephone box stood guard over the disused horse trough.

From inside the bar, the sound of fiddles and singing was heard, joyous, hearty sounds, accompanied by the ringing of the till forever joining in every chorus, fitting in with every change of key, hardly a discord, and never a note of complaint.

And in all this *burrach*, running through this din of pipes and fiddles, drums and voices, a great sense of well-being flooding the rooms, the place packed out as never before. The two gentlemen in the corner, still seated beside Hamish McLeod, chorused louder than anyone else, their arms around the village filly and their table a mess of used glassware and spilled whisky. Somewhere in the next room, a lone piper struck up a lament, tuneful but sad, the melody drifting through into the other room, the bar quietening as the tune was caught, the magic settling over them, as moments long forgotten were distantly remembered.

The two Yanks were respectfully silent too. After five hours of Olympic-style boozing they were in solicitous mood, the object of their travels now a lifelong bosom friend that they swore they would never forget. Lachie stood behind the bar taking in the scene, seeing the old fox at work once again, his charm and intelligence easily digested, even by total strangers.

'I'll tell ye both something; ye'll never get an evening like this back in Washington. Why, there's more talent in here tonight than ye'd find at the whole of the Edinburgh Festival, I dare say. Old Matt here has never had a fiddle lesson in his whole life, but I would have him play at my funeral first, before all the world acclaimed orchestras you might name. You can never beat a lone fiddle, or a single piper, for reducing grown men to floods of tears.'

They all nodded wisely, Lenny Stern trying desperately to remain upright and awake. He could no longer feel his feet where the fiddler's dog had been camping on them for the last two hours. His buddy, Paul Burke, was calling for more Scotch.

'Lachlan, my fine friend, Lachlan, we are dry again! Fill them up, laddie,' his attempts at mimicking a West Highland accent sadly awry.

'So tell me, Lenny, from where did ye get the fancy notion that I was the one to talk to? Who said "talk to old Hamish" ? Not someone from around these parts, I fancy?

Hamish was smiling in a friendly, mildly inquisitive way, his glass of whisky held up to the light as he savoured the taste. Lenny was having some difficulty focusing, his brain still active but his defences all but gone. He leaned forward across the narrow table until they were almost head to head, deep concentration etched on his face, as he struggled to come to terms with remembering the reasons for their visit, and not in any way sure that he cared.

'Frankly, Hamish, I don't think it matters a bit. Do you? The word is out. You boys are all off to the Moon come Thursday. And not a shot fired across your bows! Not a single goddamn missile in sight. Our noble President will not be very happy, you can be sure of that. From what I hear, he was hoping to go out with a bang. Make a big splash so to speak.'

He grinned inanely, throwing his arms wide, rocking backwards, his whisky decanting over the fiddler who never missed a beat.

'So that was the story,' thought Hamish. 'He imagined that there might just be some capital in riding out a missile crisis in the dying weeks of his first term in office. Well, Mr Jackson, I am sorry to have to disappoint you, but if you hang on for just a couple of months or so, I think we will be giving you plenty to think about; something to make your petty missile crisis look like a walk on the hills. No. Just you rest easy. We have many a long mile to travel yet.'

Making his excuses, he moved towards the door, standing in the fresh air, a light rain beginning to fall, the Moon bright and full.

He crossed to the run-down telephone box and dialled a number. He waited.

'Hello Gregor, how are ye. Yes, I know. It *is* late. But I've been out and about doing a bit of bird-hunting. I've got a couple of rare ones bagged at this very moment. Oh you *had* heard. Yes. Yes. They arrived in one piece. It would seem that they have a great interest in our project, wanting to know this and that, and then this and that all over again. Never heard any pair talk like them.'

The conversation switched for a moment or two.

'It would seem that our Mr Jackson had some vision of his own, seeing himself as saviour of the world by stirring up talk of a *missile* crisis of all things, seeing Scotland as some kind of *terrorist state* intent on taking over his kingdom. Now fancy that.'

He stood grinning, listening to the roars of laughter booming down from the other end of the line.

'And now it seems he is very put out. Very upset indeed; seems that we have ruined his little party. Yes I agree. It is a shame. So, as we have agreed, I will take our new friends up to the plant tomorrow to show them the production process. Yes I know, very, very cautiously. Have no fear. By the time that I'm finished with them, they'll know even less than they knew when they started out. So I'll say goodnight, Gregor. This is a proud time for all of us. Your delivery to the chamber on Monday was pure theatre. You never missed a beat. Why did I have to be the one in the family with all the brains *and* the good looks as well?'

More laughter as they bid each other goodnight. Somewhere overhead, the sounds of straining, bumping and lifting were heard coming down the narrow staircase and through the ceiling, as the sleeping forms of the two agents were laid out, arms folded across their breasts, as the regulars of the Covenanters conducted a mock ceremony over their limp bodies. To the discordant strains of the "Stars And Stripes Forever", the small band of press-ganged porters and itinerant musicians stood with bowed heads, their fists clenched firmly against their bosoms, as they saluted the bravery of two drinking comrades, recently fallen in the solemn line of duty.

# 7

Gregor entered his office. Seven thirty on a warm summer's morning, the cirrus clouds high and light, the promise of fine weather confirmed. His coffee pot was filling, the rich smell pervading the room, his Scotsman folded and pristine on his desk, his mail neatly stacked in order of priority. Sitting, he opened the newspaper, the featured article by Angus Simpson tucked into the middle pages dominated by photographs of the earlier American landings. He started to read.

### FIRST MINISTER TELLS OF PLANS FOR MOON LANDING
### *Only Months Away From a November Launch*

Yesterday began as a perfectly normal day for most of us and ended with few of us getting much rest. Whilst it is true that we are all, by now, becoming used to the driving leadership of Gregor McLeod, his Merrie Men on the Castle Rock and their many commendable and often far reaching proclamations of one sort or another, it would appear that yesterday's announcement of the Government's plans for a landing on the Moon may just have eclipsed every previous achievement or any future event that is likely to be dropped on us in the short time remaining to this present administration.

This writer sat, as with so many others in the public gallery, and listened in awe as Gregor McLeod spelled out his plans for Scotland's future, its hopes and expectations for future generations, ending with the announcement that has today shocked the world.

'On the thirtieth of November, this year, the Space Shuttle *Caliban* will blast off from the specially prepared landing site on North Uist and head into orbit, before thrusting off towards the Moon that will see it undertake a 231,000 mile journey and back again. In reply to the many questions thrown at him following this historic announcement, he insisted that their original programme for using the technology to place satellites into orbit was still their objective and remained the main thrust and payback of the project. The possibility of pushing the technology further, once the realisation that a Moon shot was within their grasp at little additional cost, was one that they had seen fit to endorse, and for which he offered no apology. He did however plead for an understanding of the introduction of strict security measures imposed during the final year of the project, and he begged their forgiveness for undertaking an adventure which, he claimed, "would ultimately ensure that our children and their childrens' children could look forward to a brighter, sunnier and altogether healthier future."

'It is clear that we have been fortunate as a Nation to have had the dedicated services of Gregor McLeod over these past years, if only for the delights and the surprises that he is wont to spring upon an unsuspecting electorate. When one recalls the long string of accomplishments to the credit of this administration in the space of a few short years, one can only wonder where we would be now, had he not risen from the ranks of academia to lead us into this current period of new found wealth and freedom.

'There are nations around the world today who give grateful thanks to his leadership; institutions, many of them nameless, researchers both public and private who all, in their own way, owe a debt of gratitude to this man who has swept aside the petty bureaucracy that might have blocked fulfilment of their dreams, fuelling their ambitions and making it possible for their work and programmes to reach full maturity.

'If, and when, we ever do set foot on our nearest neighbour in the solar system we should remember that we do it, not for ourselves, but for the many who went before us; for those who surrendered their lives and freedom over the centuries, so that every man, woman and child would some day inherit the God given right to live their lives as free men in a free society.

'I would like to think, that as we step down on to the Moon's surface, that we do so without declaration of any kind, with simplicity and reverence, conducting ourselves with dignified reserve like guests at some honoured gathering, respecting the eternity of total silence that has always existed on the Moon, aware that we are intruders into some gigantic apparatus that, for all time to come, will remain God's best kept secret.'

Gregor laid the newspaper down, his eyes wandering to the windows, a serious look on his face.

'Amen to all of that,' he said quietly, before turning to the business of the day.

Rab Nicol sat in the corner of the pub, holding court, his ever growing host of followers and disciples spilling over onto the floor, as they waited with bated, beery, breath for his next pronouncement. The table in front of him bore the evidence of a hard day's drinking, the ashtrays overflowing, the empty glasses feeding the washing up area with a steady flow of work.

Up at the bar, Charlie Smith was keeping a wary eye on the proceedings, unsure of the sudden reversal in the fortunes of one Rab Nicol, unemployed vagrant and serial sponger. For the last four nights, the 'Bletherin Skite' had been filled to capacity, with punters and tourists hanging on his every word, his powers of invention never subsiding, his ability to wheedle drink from the earnest, gullible throng sitting at his feet enhanced by his apparent insight into matters scientific, philosophical and spiritual.

After four successful forays into this new field of endeavour, Rab was quickly becoming adept at manipulating his audience, always ready with a witty rejoinder, a mote of praise for a well considered question and as ever, a willing recipient of unsolicited bevvy, for which he always remembered to express undying gratitude.

'In short,' said Charlie the bartender, 'the bastard is on the make!'

'That is a scandalous lie!' retorted Rab, 'I am merely exercising my rights as an individual to express ma opinion on certain matters, and if the good people of this scabby hostelry wish to partake of ma knowledge and discourse with me, who am I to refuse to allow them to share with me this historic moment in our nation's history?'

'Get tae fuck, Rab. Ye never did a day's studyin' in yer life. Yer heid's in a tinny; ya big lump that ye are!'

And so saying, he strode off to collect glasses and sweep up for the umpteenth time between the legs of the faithful, their heads turning, their fervour rising, as they awaited the return of their mentor from the cludgie.

'Far be it from me to point out anything to this present administration. It is not for one of my social rank tae offer advice o' any sort tae the high heid yins up at the Rock. Now is it? If they've decided tae go tae the Moon who am I tae question it?'

At this, his face adopted the look of the retard, the simple look of one cheated by life of the opportunity to develop to his full potential.

'Rab, tell us, what's yer view on the possibility that we'll get there and find nothin'?'

A hush fell over the small room.

'I have made my voice clear on this issue. As I understand the situation from my *many renowned sources*, the possibility might just exist that the Yanks never made it tae the Moon. If they did...'

He paused for effect, his eyes narrowing,

'If they did, why huv they no' responded tae the many and varied criticisms that have been flung at them by me, and by others like me, from aroond the world on this very subject? Eh? Just tell me that, if ye wull?

'There have been observations made, that clearly show that the Moon landing was a fake, a stitch up.'

At this he paused to take a long thirst slaking draft of Guinness, wiping his hairy hand across his mouth, watched adoringly by the young ladies in the front row.

'In ma honest opinion, they couldnae dae it, simple as that. No' fur the want o' tryin', mark you,' his finger wagging, his face angelic.

'It was jist too dangerous ye see. The Eagle, the descent module was inherently unstaple.'

'Ye mean, "unstable", Rab?'

'Yes; that *is* what I said.'

A murmur of concern filled the room. If true, and they had no reason to doubt, this put an entirely different complexion on the current plans for a November launch. Across the other side of the room, steadily polishing his bar top, Charlie Smith glowered and fumed, listening to every word, his growing distaste for the rising star showing, as each item of imperfect knowledge was shared with all who would listen.

'Fur it wis in the desert, ye see, they were tryin' and tryin' tae stabilise this thing and it wis too difficult. Ye see, yon Neil Armstrong bloody nearly lost his life tryin' tae get it on the ground. It's a fact; the thing nearly couped. So ye see when they got tae the Moon, on the Tuesday night ah think it wis...'

At this, Charlie Smith, his ears burning with embarrassment, broke his golden rule and poured himself a large whisky to ease the pain.

'...they made the decision at NASA control, tae abort the landing. Now then, until this moment, I can tell youse, I have never telt a livin' soul this story. I wis sworn tae secrecy by those in control.'

At this he hung his head as if suffering the humiliation of having taken distasteful orders from those whom he had held in contempt, those who had held him in their power. A pawn in the game of life. Another murmur of sympathy rolled across the bar. He shook his head, as if trying to throw off a past that he could not lose.

'So, as I huv said, they hud tae come tae a decision, one way or the other, on whether or no' tae go fur the landin' or no', and efter hours o' wrangling and fightin' wi' NASA control, they were telt tae stuff it, and the order went oot, "jist youse yins stay up there fur a while longer until we tell yees tae come hame".

'So, although they whizzed around and around fur ages and ages, they did not land on the surface of the Moon. Ah'm tellin' yees all. Believe it, or believe it not!'

His emphasis sent Charlie's arm on a return journey towards the whisky dispenser in another vain attempt to quieten the shame. All heads were turned to the corner, their eyes riveted on their prophet. Behind them, the television set above the bar droned on, all of the programmes at some time or another over the course of the evening, dedicated to the news story of the week.

The outside broadcast showed a hillside and an unremarkable collection of roofs, the commentator standing, his voice barely heard, his arm waving around, indicating the extent of the giant chamber that housed the *Caliban*. The cameras mounted within the huge cavern sent out a picture of the vast array of supply platforms that surrounded the giant ship, the craft brightly lit, its metal skin reflecting a thousand lights. The shuttle stood proudly, decked out in the national colours, a massive blue Saltire painted along one side. At that moment, Rab, leaning forward to take charge of further supplies of drink, became aware of the programme. It suddenly dawned on him what he was seeing.

'And there we have it, ladies and gentlemen. The *Caliban* herself in all her glory.'

All heads turned, many moving immediately closer to the bar to listen. Soon the area was thronged with people. The sound was turned up as they listened. The commentator was in discussion with Murdo Sinclair.

'Yes, that is quite correct. There will be three astronauts on board. Each one of them will be capable of either piloting the main shuttle or of descending to the surface in the *Moonraker*, as we have named the descent vehicle. Altogether we have a team of ten men and women, who have been in training for this moment for the last two years. As you can see they will be very well accommodated in these spacious cabins serviced by the latest in space technology.'

The interviewer interrupted, 'All mod cons, in fact.' They laughed together.

'So, there we have it. On the thirtieth of November, a truly wonderful day to look forward to, three very brave young Scots will lift off from the launch pad here in North Uist, returning a week later to the undoubted acclaim of a grateful nation. When it happens, we at Scotland Television, will be here to bring you the news, and to give you a minute-by-minute account of the flight.'

The captions rolled over a stock shot of the Parliament building towering over the castle rock.


In his eyrie on the twenty third floor, Gregor watched the captions roll, well satisfied with the way things were going. Gus Simpson lifted his glass and toasted the screen.

'They did well. Good coverage. Not a single word spoken that could be considered contentious in any way. I believe they are firmly behind you in this one. That first view of the *Caliban* was breathtakingly beautiful.'

'Yes. I agree.' said Gregor. 'The nation *is* ready to take this on board. I did have however, a very heated discussion this morning with Kenny Paterson. He raised objection after objection, some of which I find myself in agreement with. He demanded that I explain the real reasons for this "unjustifiable expenditure on a vain monument to a party without principles", I think he said. I asked him to give me some time, to trust me in fact and I think he will wait. He knows that there is more to this than I have announced. He feels it, but he doesn't yet know exactly why. He is a real hot head, that one. But honest to a fault. One day he'll be a great asset to this country, if he stays the course.'

They laughed kindly. Down on Princes Street the summer

crowds were thronging the pavements, window shopping and enjoying the fine weather.

"They tell me flights into the airport are packed. Not a single seat available anywhere. I have had the Director of the Festival Committee up to see me yesterday, complaining that there will not be enough beds available for visitors in August, due to the influx of press and media turning up to cover the conferences. I could give her no reassurance, but it's something we should have considered. We will have to broadcast an appeal for anyone with spare accommodation to make it available. I only hope the sewers can cope with it all.'

It was late. Back at the "Bletherin' Skite" Rab was thinking, many sheets to the wind, trying to figure out a way to further his career as a pundit on all things pertaining to the American Moon-shots. This latest announcement was surely a God-sent opportunity to set himself up as an authority on the greatest failure of the twentieth century.

'And when we get there' he was thinking to himself. 'Just what will we find? I can bloody tell yees all. Nothin'. Bugger all. They never made it doon tae the surface. No sir! They couldna make it happen. And when we get there and find nothin'. What then? The world will know the truth! An' ye canny fuck aboot wi' the truth. Now then, boy!'

'Hey! You. Shut the fuck up!'

Unaware that he had been thinking aloud, he glanced around him. Heads were returning to their drinks. At nearly midnight the tourists and punters safely home in bed, the "Skite" had returned temporarily to its regulars. Nursing his pint, his mind scanning the possibilities for extending his recent run of good fortune, he considered his prospects.

'Ah could've been an astronaut so ah could. S'no as if ah couldna dae it. Wid have been a bloody doddle really. Ah'm as fit as the next man, so ah am.'

'Hey you, Rab.' Charlie Smith was addressing him from the safe end of the bar; the end furthest away from Rab Nicol.

'Me?'

'Aye, you. Shut the fuck up.'

Ignoring the provocation, sipping his beer, unwilling to let the subject drop, he considered again his change of fortune. He was on to a good thing. He might even consider selling tickets. Hold séances or something. Everything was possible.

'Ah could rent a hall,' he was thinking, 'find an agent.'

Wandering and weaving his way homewards, Rab Nicol discovered that he had a goal in life. A horizon was opening up in front of him that offered the prospects of recognition for his undoubted talents. As a spinner of yarns, his long founded ability to charm the gullible and wheedle drink out of the most stubborn of bartenders had, up until now, been honed and polished to a keen edge; an edge that would now cut swathes through the thickets of social alienation and deprivation, that had always marked him out as "professional layabout" or "work-shy bigot" to the counter staff at Job Centres across the City.

Stopping to raise his beer-flushed face to the Moon, Rab swore a solemn oath. To raise himself out of his meaningless self-imposed, day to day, hand to mouth existence and to portray himself as a seeker of the truth. Alone, he would take on the might of America, exposing her shabby lies for the world to see! Let wicked administrations tremble, let false governments tumble and fall, let corrupt authority and unfair justice wither and die! Rab Nicol had his beady eye on all of them.


The next day, a press conference took place in the auditorium of the new Parliament building. Projecting out from between the frames of the supporting structure, overhanging the rock face, the glazed floor around the perimeter available to the few who dared to walk on air, the room was a magnificent tribute to its designer. Far below, the ribbon of rail track snaked though the gardens that separated the high level of Princes Street from the Rock and the Old Town of Edinburgh.

Entering the room, Gregor McLeod received a round of

applause, an unusual, but not entirely unexpected occurrence, given the importance of his recent announcement. At his side stood his niece Fiona and Murdo Sinclair, the Director of the Rosewell Institute.

Gregor moved to the podium, raising his hands, receiving instant attention. The room was crammed with reporters, newsmen and media hacks from a number of countries, some arriving as he spoke, others still on the way.

'Ladies and gentlemen, I thank you for arriving on time this fine morning. I intend to make a short statement, copies of which will be made available to you with an information pack containing photographic material providing an insight into the work being carried out on at North Uist. I regret that access to that establishment on the island is restricted. Even if that were not so, we would be unhappy to see the place sink beneath the waves with the weight of numbers I see present here today.'

A ripple of easy laughter filled the room, simultaneous translations coming in seconds later and providing an echo of laughter from the foreign reporters.

'Let me begin by reassuring all of you that there is nothing sinister or threatening about our announcement. We are a sovereign nation and we will decide our priorities as we see fit. As many of you will know, for many centuries we failed to bring home our own harvests or ring our own tills. Much of that has now changed for the better. We are in the process of building a nation of which we can all be proud. With income tax almost abolished, our health service and educational institutions second to none, we can, I believe, feel some degree of satisfaction at how far we have travelled in a few short years since independence.

'This latest venture of ours is no more, or no less, than an extension of our ambitious plans to further our knowledge of our environment, to better understand the nature of the planet we inhabit, and to continue to invest in and research those subjects which touch on our lives. They require our deep understanding and continuing good management, if we are to secure the well being of planet earth for future generations.

'Some of you who have travelled from afar and who have visited us on numerous occasions, will no doubt have watched our progress in these matters, noting that we have not retired into our tartan covered shell, but instead have made our voice heard in the European Parliament on a number of global issues which must concern us all. We believe that we have contributed wisely to these debates, casting away cant and prejudice, offering instead the steadying hand of reasoned argument and common sense.

'Here at home in Scotland we have, through our continuing review of standards in daily life, bettered the lot for the majority of our people, showing the way ahead by example, throwing behind us the tatters of a tartan tradition that constrained and diminished us, at the same time leaving us with our heads stuck firmly up our kilts, with no worthwhile future staring back at us.'

A burst of laughter greeted this remark, the less agile of the translators failing to get the meaning across, the faces of the Oriental and Arab delegates registering serious confusion.

'This great building we sit in today and the many changes for the better that you will see around the city, epitomise our new approach to how we now see ourselves. In raising the new on the very foundations of the old, we have proclaimed our right to remake ourselves, whilst recognising and acknowledging our past history, dispensing with cultural dead wood and trimmings of pantomime, retaining only that which we perceive as being relevant and true to our new image as forward looking Europeans.

'We see no conflict between integrating the new with that which has gone before. Nor do we condone preservation as the sole mainstay of our traditions in art, architecture or learning. Treasured artefacts from the past have their valued place in our developing present. We do not seek to devalue them but instead we welcome them as historical milestones in the process of ongoing cultural development. We do not decry the past. Instead we see it as a starting point for a better more promising future; a future where we can all learn to live one with the other, upholding our truly great tradition of defending freedom for all at any price, and confronting injustice, prejudice and want, wherever we encounter it.'

A round of applause terminated his speech as he turned to Murdo, indicating that he should take over.

'Thank you. Thank you all on behalf of our First Minister. Let me begin by giving you some background information on our work both at Rosewell and at North Uist. From small beginnings, we have structured a research institute that I believe is second to none at this time. With a staff approaching three hundred, we have interests in everything from mathematical conundrums to the meaning of life itself. When Gregor walked in one day and enquired how we all felt about going to the Moon, it was just another example of how familiar we have all become with his frequently outrageous suggestions as to where, and on what, we should be spending his very generous grants. We have to say that these have enabled us to study and learn a great deal about a number of deeply troubling questions which have concerned scientists and astronomers alike for generations past.

'We do not expect or anticipate that our Moon landing will add in any significant way to the store of information already derived from previous trips made by the Americans, but we *are* hoping that the fuel we are using, which at the moment is high on our list of "don't tells", will prove to be revolutionary. It delivers a totally disproportionate thrust to volume of product burned. Moreover it is almost entirely environmentally safe, achieving less than two percent of current standards on solid emissions.'

At this statement the room filled with agitated discussion, heads turning. The buzz in the air abruptly suspended as he continued to speak.

'It is, in every sense, a major breakthrough in chemical engineering which we hope will, in the very near future, be adapted for use in domestic cars and public transport. Moreover, the product, and this I *can* tell you, the product derives, in part, from oil, a raw material for which we predict a very rosy future and one where we do not foresee any immediate or future shortfalls.'

Again, there was laughter, the extent of Scotland's massive reserves in fossil fuel already well known and widely publicised.

'So, if you have learned nothing else today, you will appreciate that we, at Rosewell, have *not* been standing around with our heads up our kilts!'

Roars of laughter, Gregor amused and applauding loudly, leaning forward, his remarks to Murdo almost lost in the din.

'Gregor has reminded me of one more thing before we take questions. Our intention is to make this knowledge available to all. Clearly there will be concerns on security and how, and to whom, we should dispense this information. Our view is that anything which assists in cleaning up the planet must not be held back in any way. We are therefore convening a conference of world leaders in the coming months to advise them of our findings and our concerns for controlling the production, under licence, of this new fuel. But we feel that the importance of this issue warrants us making it readily available at the earliest possible time.

'We will now take questions. Please be patient. We will get to you all in due course. For those of you who have submitted written queries these are currently being responded to and may be available for collection by early this evening.'

'Now, who is first?'


As the press conference started Rab Nicol was embracing his first pint of the day. A serious business, especially since it was now nearly noon and, owing to unforeseen circumstances, he had already lost half an hour out of his busy drinking schedule. He had had to walk the mile and a half to the pub, determined to suffer the indignity of exercise in order to preserve his meagre funds.

'Are ye no' goin' tae put the telly on then, Charlie?'

The question was innocuous but coming from Rab it sounded like a summons to be obeyed. Reluctantly, the bartender switched it into life for his sole customer.

Rab was entranced, watching the press conference unfold. He listened intently to the questions and answers, many of them complex but within the limits of his understanding. Nevertheless, he stared in awe as Gregor and Murdo Sinclair parried and discussed the many issues raised by the men of the free press.

'Can you clarify for us exactly how you resolved the problem of vertical take off and horizontal landing? Does the vehicle have any additional booster rockets at launch or are you saying that the fuel it carries is sufficient for lift off, the flight to the Moon and the return journey?'

Gregor sat down handing the question to Murdo. He in turn motioned Fiona forward to reply.

'The answer, in a nutshell, is yes. The fuel is enormously powerful, developing ninety percent of its maximum thrust immediately after initial ignition. It is under full throttle control at this point, and we can increase or suppress the thrust to avoid the G-forces usually experienced during initial acceleration. Because of the displacement of the fuel around the jacket of the *Caliban* and our system of primary and secondary thrusters we can stabilise lift off, slowing the progress of the vehicle right down to almost a hover.

'Of course, this tends to eat up the available reserves of fuel, so in tests we have tended to adopt the more conventional technique of accelerating the ship to a comfortable level, since fuel saving is not our primary concern at any point of the journey. We do not require booster rockets of any kind. We land the ship on the newly constructed runway, and then prepare it for its next operational flight, as we can now demonstrate.'

She pressed a few buttons in front of her and the auditorium slowly darkened. The giant screen appeared as if by magic, silent covers sliding away to reveal an IMAX spanning the full height and width of the chamber.

'Jesus, dae ye see that? Is that no' impressive?' Rab was entranced, his Guinness barely touched. An image appeared over the opening captions, descending through the clouds. All eyes watching as the cameras struggled to monitor its approach, the blue Saltire on the side of the craft becoming ever more evident as it appeared to glide in for a perfect landing.

'You will all note that unlike the American Space Shuttle our bird has wings.'

'Aye ye're right there, darlin'. You just tell 'em!'

A murmur of appreciation was heard, all eyes firmly fixed on the IMAX screen. She continued.

'The wings presented us with the biggest problem. As you can imagine they must only be deployed gradually after entering the atmosphere. They are controlled automatically, deploying initially to act as stabilisers and eventually for lift, as we use the engines to control our descent. The covering used in the manufacture of the wings is also quite new.'

'See that. See that. The thing's got wings as well. Fuckin' amazin'. So it is.'

As if in reply to Rab's finger pointing, Fiona went on.

'The complexity of the design will not have escaped many of you. We believe that we have broken new ground in avionics with this new technology. The rotation of the wings moving out and opening as we see here on the following diagrams, gives you some idea of just how difficult it has been to resolve the many issues that we had to face in dealing with the whole notion of a re-entry vehicle of this type. We believe we have succeeded.'

There were spontaneous and simultaneous rounds of applause from Rab and the delegates.

'Aye. Well done lassie. Ye deserve a medal, so ye do. Ye've got what it takes. That's for sure.'

Charlie Smith strolled slowly down the bar apparently to get a better look. Avoiding eye contact, he spoke over his shoulder, his evident distaste for his only customer thinly disguised.

'Should ye no' be up there telling them Rab? Seems tae me ye're wastin' yer time sittin' here. I'm quite sure they would like tae hear frae you, you being such an expert and a' that. I'm surprised ye have no' been invited tae address them. Maybe they dinna ken ye're back in town. "Tell me, Mr Nicol. Are you of the opinion that this thing will work or no? Excuse me asking, Mr Nicol, but I'm sure you'll ken the answer tae this one." '

Rab's anger was darkening, his temper rising, a snarl developing on his round face.

'See you boy, ya piece o' shit. Don't you try to take the mickey out of me. Ah'll huv you know that I have begun tae take a scholarly interest in this subject, as it so happens, and what's more, before I take *ma* business elsewhere, please note that it's nane o' your damn business. So, bugger off.'

# 8

Lunchtime, and the restaurant was quiet. Away from the hubbub of the main thoroughfares, the side streets of downtown Washington were a world away from the high life and intrigue of the diplomatic and political rat race that dominated the social life of the city.

Sitting in the corner under the stucco arched roof, surrounded by the rough plaster and fading scenes of the canals of Venice and the pines of Rome, Tom Sherman and his deputy Sam Cavanagh were deep in discussion. Around them, the other diners were intent on disposing of their meals and returning to their air-conditioned offices, the heat of the day stifling ambition, leaving the workforce listless and longing for cool breezes from the shore after sunset.

'Are we secure here? I don't remember the place.'

'Yes. I know it well. We're OK. So what do you think? How are things up at the palace?'

'I don't know what to believe exactly. He changes daily. Ever since Franklin sent him that report from London he has been like a bear with a sore head. Mark Brander told me yesterday that he practically threw Levi out of the office on Tuesday. He has been calling around too. Calls placed on his direct line, asking people in the department to check out this and that. Everybody is wondering what the hell is going on.'

Sam Cavanagh, long time executive director at the Cape Kennedy Space Centre listened patiently. The two men were lifelong friends, having shared the same dreams at various stages of their coinciding careers. Having watched the slow decline of activity at the Cape, budgets reducing year on year, he saw no future for himself as senior administrator of an enterprise that had no brief to do much more than monitor the few space probes either on their way to, or past their targets and heading into oblivion. He looked up.

'I hope you all know what you're doing. If he discovers what you are up to, it will destroy him. Getting him to revitalise the space programme is one thing. Telling him we all screwed up at the time is quite another.'

'Leave that to me. If he thinks that this latest Moon shot by Scotland has a chance of succeeding, I think we can expect an announcement soon after that America sees a future for further exploration of our solar system, even if it's only to rewrite history. As it stands at the moment, he doesn't know what to think. Joe spun him the bare facts. I thought he was going to faint. Whether he believed him or not, I can't say. But these calls he is placing are worrying. Joe says he has them covered. I presume that means that he's getting everything.'

'Christ almighty, tapping the White House lines is nothing short of treason. I don't think I want to hear this. If this should leak out in any shape or form, Watergate will be reclassified as a slight hiccup!'

'Yes. I hope to God we know where this is leading us. If the worst should happen and we have to tell him the truth, I will do my best to keep you out of it.'

'How long does Solly think it would take us to mobilise again if we get the go ahead?'

'He's never sure of anything, but he's looking into it; a few months, maybe. We have had everything in place as you know, for the past year. Winding it all up is the only challenge. It might need a bit of time. Who knows? When are the Jocks due to go? November? Well, it should be possible.'

Outside the truck, turned the corner and began to hose down the sticky tarmac. As it came level with the restaurant it stopped, the engine running. In the back, the two F.B.I. agents monitoring the conversation looked at each other in surprise. As they rewound the tape and listened again to the unintentional interception, they shook their heads, shrugged and filed it for future appraisal. The truck moved slowly forward, the jets of cooling water evaporating even as they settled on the hot shoulder of the road.


On the sixth floor of the Rock, Rod Cameron, the Minister for Education, was speaking softly into his telephone. Fit, forty with rugged good looks and a bad back from his days on the international rugby field, he was in his prime. Married with two children, a mistress and an overdraft, his life was a tangle of deceit and half truths that had stayed with him most of his adult life. With current responsibilities looming larger by the day, his portfolio extending by the hour, he was a busy, and irresponsible, philanderer.

'Yes. I know. It is difficult. I simply couldn't get away. By the time I got home and we got the kids to bed it had gone nine. I knew I would be late and the thought of you sitting…'

'Yes. I have said I'm sorry. I'll make it up to you this weekend. No. I have told her I am expected over in Glasgow. No. I don't have that problem. Anyway, we'll see how it turns out. Yes, of course I miss you. You know that. Yes! I love you. Who wouldn't?'

The conversation continued for some minutes, his secretary entering the room and placing some files on his desk. Signalling their importance, she left. With the door closed, he continued.

'No, it was Sarah. She came into the office. No, she suspects nothing. Don't be silly. Nobody knows anything.'

His other telephone rang.

'I must go. Things to get done. Call you at five thirty. Bye.'

At the other end of the line, Sally McIntosh felt the dismissal in his voice all too keenly. It seemed as if she spent her life waiting for the call, waiting for the pick up, waiting for the door bell to ring; always waiting. She replaced the receiver slowly. Blonde and beautiful, twenty-nine and vivacious, she knew in her heart that the affair was doomed. Four months was a long time, however, ever since she had applied for the job as Advisor on International Law to the new government. With a brilliant university career behind her, her own car and apartment in town, she had everything a young lady could wish for, everything except peace of mind.

Since being swept off her feet by Rod Cameron in the first two weeks in her new post, she had been rocketed into a life of high living, sweet loving nights and lost weekends stolen from his family. She regretted many things. It could never lead to anything more than this. It was hopeless. She had contemplated changing jobs, going away, finding a single unstressed lover to fill her nights and complete her days. All in all it was too much of a strain, keeping up pretences she could not sustain. She worried that their chance encounters and exposure to each other in business meetings were sending clear messages to everyone that they were an item. She dialled.

'Hi, Mary. Me! No, I needed to talk to someone. The rotter never turned up. Waited until ten, then…

'No. I have to stay in tonight. I might see him for an hour after work but that's all. I have some things to get done in the flat.

'Oh, I know. I wish I could. We'll try to set a couple of dates up for the end of the month if you can manage to leave yourself free. By the way, I saw that movie the other night. Great. You were right. Yes. Isn't it. Look, if you're busy we can talk later tonight. OK? Talk to you then. All right, that's a better idea; we'll do it Thursday. I don't mind. Eight at "Fishers". Great. See you then. Bye. Call you tonight. Bye.'

As she took the lift down to the staff canteen she caught sight of him entering the executive dining area. Their eyes met across the busy room. He was smiling, she quickly looked elsewhere, her heart beginning to race.

'Why does he do this to me?' she thought.

'What'll it be, Miss?

'Oh! The salad and the yoghurt, thank you.'

'If only I could order up my future with such certainty,' she was thinking, 'life would be a lot easier all round.'


Ten thirty and the "Skite" was packed to the doors. Outside, the crowd of six or seven crowding around the doorway, strained to see into the pub, wondering what the action was and if they were missing out on something of interest. Seated in his usual place on the bench at the rear of the premises, Rab sat looking positively Messianic. He had shaved and was wearing a T-shirt with the graphic across the front, "I love U.C.L.A." an item that had come his way from Susan, his fat American student admirer seated in the front row of the adoring audience.

With his shaven face and the faintly discernable scent of rosewater, he resembled nothing short of an ageing student with a serious drink problem. At this point in the evening, he was already well into his second major performance, the previous one having been a huge success! He was improving with every fabrication, his confidence building with every lie swallowed, his wit sharpened to a point, deadly and direct, Rab Nicol was coming into his own. Yes sir.

Up at the bar, Charlie Smith was busy; busy and amazed.

'How in hell's name does he manage tae keep foolin' them night after night?' he thought. The till, however, continued to ring throughout the performances and, reluctantly, the bar staff were beginning to send over the odd pint or two, in return for the continuous entertainment that was cramming the pub nightly.

'So you see, if the expert who *made* the cameras says it wis a fix, then I think we are bound tae accept his word. Whit he said wis that ye canny take decent pictures looking intae a wee reflex camera, wi yer heid cocked up in the air at an angle, and yer chin getting' in the way o' bein' able tae look doon tae get a decent shot. Of course…'

At this, his expression became conspiratorial and coy,

'Of course, unless ye *knew* that no matter where ye pointed the camera ye were always goin' tae take a good picture.' He paused, cocking one eye, the other winking ominously, a sneer developing on his face.

'Dae ye mean tae say Rab, the photies were faked as well?'

He slapped his hand on his thigh.

'Of course they were faked. They were done before they even took aff. Can you imagine trying tae look through that big black visor, which is six inches in front o' yer face, havin' tae look doon, at a wee viewfinder that yer tryin' tae operate wearing a pair o' bloody steel-lined, anti-radiation, size twenty-two gloves the size o' bloody mattresses?'

He paused, looking at them scathingly.

'It never happened, believe me boy! It never happened!'

'That's amazin', Rab. Whit ye've just said. It's amazin'. Really. When ye think aboot it, it wid have been difficult as you say. Ah can hardly find the button on ma camera wi' ma bare hands.'

'Not only that, but every last picture wis a winner. Every last one o' them in perfect focus! Now then, boy.'

He gave them an old fashioned look that said, 'believe it if ye will.' The room nodded in agreement. Charlie Smith was thinking…

'The wee bastard could be right. Wee camera, huge gloves. Makes ye think, right enough.'

'Tell us Rab. What aboot UFO's. De ye think they exist?'

The pub stilled as Rab screwed up his face, pondering the nicotine stained ceiling.

'As you know, these things are not new. They have been talked aboot fur centuries. I am told, and here I must say I am only quotin' frae a book, that the ancient Egyptians themselves had a wee drawing in the corner o' wan o' their tombs, showin' a flying' saucer landin' on tap o' wan o' their pyramids.'

His glass seemed to raise itself to his mouth unaided, a smooth transition of the arm, punctuated only by minor tremors in the region of the hand, as he paused to take stock.

'And…' he said slowly, 'the Egyptians kent a thing or two.'

'Rab, whit aboot the number o' times people huv seen UFO's aroond Bonnybrig and the Central Lowlands. Does that no surprise ye?'

'Nothin' surprises me, boy. I believe that in ancient times, lang before even people ran aroond on this earth, that aliens came to these fair shores.'

He paused for effect, fat Susan visibly shivering despite the heat in the room.

'I believe that they have continued tae visit us up tae the present time and I huv ma own solution fur that issue as well.' He smacked his lips, his hand nestling comfortably around the fresh pint that had quietly appeared under his nose.

'I think that we should all go down to that big scientific Institute at Rosewell and demand that the bloody director, that Murdo Sinclair, paints a big sign on his roof, sayin',

' "Can youse no read? This is Rosewell, no' Roswell. If ye're lookin' fur yer wee green pals, they're no here. So, bugger aff!"

'And if we did *that*, ah'm sure we'd never hear another beep oot o' any o' them ever again. Ah'm tellin' ye, boy.'

They sat round the wooden table in the tiny cottage overlooking the Atlantic ocean, a squall developing far out at sea, the winds light, the sunlight streaming in through the small recessed windows set into thick stone walls.

'I rarely drink coffee myself, you understand. I am more of a tea drinker; but only when I'm not at the whisky.' They laughed, the two agents wincing at the very mention of the word.

'Well now, seeing as how you would like something to stick in that report you're always taking about, I thought we might just take a run over to the base at Clettraval and I will show you around. Normally, it is strictly off limits to everyone except the base personnel, but I made a few phone calls last evening and permission has been granted. You have the word of the First Minister himself no less!'

At this, they both sat up, the hangovers which had threatened to hospitalise them beginning to fade, the paracetamol and caffeine killing the fatigue and lifting the soul.

'You see, he is my brother.'

He was busying himself around the tiny kitchen, preparing lunch for the three of them, the two Yanks meanwhile exchanging telling glances and waiting for him to call the shots.

'As I told you, the production unit that develops the fuel for the propulsion system is under my direct control, so we don't have to take the permission of anyone too far away.'

Hamish laughed quietly.

'I have been directing the operation as senior research chemist up here and in Edinburgh for more years than I care to remember.' He continued to chat to them in his soft mid-Highland accent, each vowel set in gold, each syllable a chord of ancient music.

'But before we saunter down the hill, let me show you something that I do now and again to amuse the children.'

He moved to the outside yard and disappeared into the

lean-to shed adjoining the cottage. After a moment he reappeared holding a crude aluminium tube capped and pointed at one end, fins protruding from the sides, the whole affair no longer than a rolled newspaper.

'The children love to see these things.' He held it out to them.

'You see, we place a small amount of fuel in here, not too much of course, then I ignite it remotely with this. Then just watch it go.' He gave a deep chuckle. 'Give me a minute or two to set it up.'

He disappeared back into the shed, unscrewed the base, connected some wiring to a standard battery and made some minor adjustments to the fuel cell. He emerged smiling.

'Oh it doesn't take much I assure you.' He walked to the end of the patch where the wall ran into some flattened earth and centred the rocket. I have a young lad in the village making them up for me. I lose so many. They drop in the sea you see. Sometimes on a Sunday we will do this over and over again. The children listen for it falling then run to pick it up. Whoever finds it gets to push the button next time around. But sometimes the winds carry them away and we never find them.'

The two agents exchanged further glances. The sea was at least two hundred yards away at its nearest point.

'Now, let's retire a pace or two and you'll see. Watch carefully. He pressed the control and a second later the rocket shot skywards at an ever increasing speed until they lost sight of it in the cloud cover.

'Gee whiz,' that was amazing.' Paul Burke, his hand raised, shielding his eyes, until realising that it had gone.

And now gentlemen if you please, we can take the path down to the road and I will drive you up to the base.'

They set off down the path, the smell of heather and mountain thyme filling the air.

'That was an impressive demonstration, Mr McLeod. And just how much fuel was in that thing?'

'Oh, I can't quite say with any certainty, but less than the full eye dropper thingy. Maybe three or four droplets.' Behind them a sharp clatter rang out on the path.

'Aye, that'll be it back down. We'll maybe get lucky and pick it up on the way back. And now gentlemen, we'll pop over to the base, then come back here in time for a quiet lunch and maybe a glass or two?'

He opened the door of the car. Glancing at his watch and trying desperately to calculate how long they had been on the path, Paul Burke reckoned that the thing had been aloft for at least thirty seconds. Given that it must have weighed just less than two hundred and fifty grams in weight, assuming a rate of climb of... As he began to calculate, the truth began to dawn on him. Whatever fucking which way you looked at it, the thing must have reached an altitude of close to two thousand feet before running out of fuel.

Sitting silently beside him, Lenny Stern was trying to work out which one of them had the best chance of getting hold of a free sample to carry home and wondering at the same time, if the old guy might just be carrying more of the stuff around on his person.

# 9

Nathan Jackson spoke first. The others listened and waited their turn. Whatever was troubling him had been around now for days, each and every one of them from the lowest volunteer worker to the Secretary of State himself feeling the sharp end of his tongue on more than one occasion. Not that they hung around to find out. Since the debriefing of his envoy to London, and with the stuff he was receiving back from Scotland, the President was a less than happy camper.

'I have called you all here today to try, one last time, to establish the truth about our Moon landing programme in the sixties and seventies. Forgive me if I appear to be the only dude not in the picture, but my understanding of the situation up until very recently has been as follows: The United States of America landed men on the surface of the Moon for the first time ever in July, 1969. We then successfully followed this up with further missions all of which, including one near disaster, were concluded successfully with no loss of life. But I am now led to believe that along with the entire population of the world at large, that I might have been mistaken. Am I correct in assuming that this is the case?'

There was much slow nodding of heads and not a few quiet murmurs of assent. Watching them all intently, he noted the dissenters for future questioning.

'So, from what I have learned since our last talk together and because of *certain reservations* that some of you have expressed about the Scottish launch later this year, I am slowly reaching the conclusion that there are aspects of our space programme dating from the 1970s which were not made public, for reasons which I now understand were closely guarded secrets then. Joe Skinner here has reported to me that their investigations at the time, as far as the records can show, revealed that Apollo Eleven was aborted for technical reasons and that it took many months of patient investigation to uncover the story you're telling me now, that what we all saw, or thought we all saw, was in fact a fabrication.'

He paused, his voice unsteady, his expression one of grim

resignation.

'All right, I say to myself. So the pictures that were actually shown as being beamed back from the Moon were actually being transmitted from across the country in California. OK. I buy the reason. I *even* buy into the need for preparing a back up at that time, given the high profile of the project, but I do not buy into the conspiracy that has kept every President since that time standing around like an ostrich with its head up its ass, waiting for a big yellow taxi to drop by.'

His anger rising, concern beginning to show through the thin veneer of restraint, he began patrolling the carpet again.

'You are telling me that our people out there have been persistently lied to about a period in their history they all refer to when acknowledging the greatness of our many accomplishments, lied to about men whom they have held in the highest regard as heroes of our times, and lied to about our government's inability to come clean, to tell the truth and to admit to our shortcomings in the face of world opinion. Gentlemen, if this indeed is the text of the matter, then I am astonished, bewildered and saddened by it all.'

'Mr President.'

Tom Sherman was speaking softly.

'Joe here has given you a version of the situation as it played out last time we met. Frankly, it is something that the four of us wish had never happened. You see, following the success of the earlier orbiting missions, we were faced with the next mission in line. Apollo Eleven was scheduled to make the first landing on the surface. We simply weren't ready for that one. But, we went along with it, blasted off and settled into orbit around the Moon. Then the big moment arrived. You see, as I have already explained to you, we had a limited time frame in which to make one crucial decision; whether to go for an attempt at the landing or to abort. It was touch and go. The "Eagle" was inherently unstable and in our hearts we all knew that it was a risky manoeuvre. We had had failure after failure. Jesus! When asked by your predecessor how things were going, that dickhead director of ours gave him glowing reassurances that everything was fine; just fine.'

He was in his own world now, remembering, thinking back to an earlier time of instability, of nuclear annihilation and the threat of Communist domination of the free world. Across the room Dale Johnson was watching him with a look of disbelief on his face.

'I don't have to spell out to you the repercussions of staring failure in the face. The cold war, the Cuban crisis; my God, it was a bad time. We had to succeed at any price. The possibility of not fulfilling our pledge to land men on the Moon was just too awful to contemplate. The Russians, for Christ's sake; they would have had a field day. Can you imagine?'

Tom Sherman dropped his head into his hands, rubbing his face before continuing.

'Anyway, nobody knew if the thing would perform in an airless environment or not. For Christ's sake, we could have lost a couple of good men up there. Up until that moment we really thought we had all the angles covered. Even the fall back situation with the back up movie we had put together in case of poor reception was convincing. Everybody said so. We didn't expect the rest of the world to nit pick over every goddamned frame, year after year as they have done.'

His expression was anguished, his voice dropping as he attempted to convey the guilt he had carried for all those years of cover up and silence.

'So you want me to tell it just as it happened. Well! For one thing, I can tell you that we *did* reach the Moon, settled into orbit, everything on course for the descent. Then, as planned, we sent down the unmanned kite to test responses and the damned thing just dropped like a stone, all controls from the ship failing to make an impression or reverse the plunge onto the surface. At that point, we all knew for sure that our assumptions and calculations for the projected landing were seriously compromised to say the very least. We all had to quickly get our heads around the problem, and make a decision one way or the other. It was a bad time as I recall it. Nobody wanted to make the decision either way. There were just the four of us in the picture. Christ! Even if we had taken a vote we could have been tied.

'Eventually, we decided, with only seconds to spare, to abort the landing. It was at that point, that it happened. As we sent the signal to the ship to stand down, the emergency back up programme began to roll automatically, broadcasting the descent that never was, the landing and the whole miserable shebang. Before we realised what had happened, the room was cheering, the world was electrified and we alone knew the truth. We were truly stunned.

'Slowly, it dawned on us what we had done. The crew kept asking us for clearance to return. We kept them up there until it was time for them to come home and that's the goddamn truth. We swore the crew and everyone else to total secrecy and that's the way it has been ever since.'

There was complete silence in the room as he finished speaking. Nathan Jackson sat down slowly, his face betraying nothing, his crumpled body language saying it all. Minutes later, he spoke, his voice faltering and unsure.

'So, now we know. And it is we alone who know. This stays right here with us. Do I make myself clear?' They all nodded glumly, until Tom Sherman began to speak.

'Mr. President. We have been discussing the problem we all know is now pressing with the news of this Scottish launch in November. If they succeed where we failed and then discover that there never was any substance to our claims of having been first on the Moon, we will be facing the biggest diplomatic catastrophe in our history. We could never expect any other nation to underwrite the biggest lie of the twentieth century. *At least* I don't think so.' He was wringing his hands, beginning to sweat profusely.

'For years now we have dreaded this moment, waiting for that announcement from Russia or China that they were planning a trip to the Moon. The hope *was* that it would never happen and, until now, it never has.'

Nathan Jackson was sitting with a stunned looked on his face.

'Did I hear you say that there was *no* substance to our claims of being first to land on the Moon? What about the later expeditions? Are you saying that we *never* landed at *any* time?' An even deeper silence settled on the room at this point. Nathan Jackson, disbelief imprinted on his face, looked from one to the other, sensing the unspoken epitaph, the final line, the last word still unsaid. It was Tom Sherman again.

'Well, actually, Mr President there are several aspects related to the later flights that we should perhaps be focusing your attention on at this time. You see…'

Nathan Jackson slowly turned to him, by now familiar with the opening gambit, the rambling introduction being offered whenever the news was so bad that it needed the softening touch that only the wisdom and experience of Tom Sherman could impart.

'Please don't tell me that we *never ever* landed on the surface!' He was distraught now, searching their faces for confirmation or denial.

'Will somebody please tell me?' The deep silence and heads bowed in resignation told him the whole story. Tom Sherman lifted his head.

'Mr President. We never returned to the Moon after Apollo Eleven and that's a fact. There wasn't any point. It was a lot cheaper to do it in the studios.'

Dale Johnson jumped to his feet completely exasperated.

'Not once? Not one fucking time? I can't believe this. The billions spent just to look at the other side of the Moon.'

A long pause ensued, nobody rushing to make the first move. Sam Cavanagh rose, speaking more to the assembly than to anyone in particular said,

'We seem … we seem to have two choices. Firstly, could we not declare that part of the Moon off limits to other countries? Declare it to be somehow or other, sacred turf … Declare it to be a wholly inaugurated piece of America, or …'

He paused, unsure of whether or not to continue.

'Or …

Jackson leaned forward, eager to hear the second option, ready to grasp at any straw no matter how insubstantial.

'Well sir, I suppose we *could* get there before they do and plant the …' He was straining to find the right word.

'The evidence!'

There was a stunned silence until he continued, unaware of the impact his speech was having on those around him.

'We could explain the absence of the hardware on the Moon by saying that the equipment and runabouts were dismantled and brought back after each subsequent trip to be set up in some future space museum here in Washington. Then we could get the stuff we need out of the stores up at Area 51, knock up a copy of the original descent vehicle and carry it with us, installing it where we said it landed, setting it up as a monument for future travellers to marvel at. By the time we have stirred up the site a bit no one will ever know that we faked the original images.

'We then stick the flag in the dirt, drop a few golf balls around the place. We would have to make sure we used the same boots.'

He paused as a thought struck him. 'The only problem would be ...'

'Yes. What? Go on man. Speak up. What?'

'Well, Mr President Sir, whilst I have no doubt that we could achieve it technically this time, I doubt if we could mobilise fast enough to get into the race. We simply don't have that kind of budget. The essential components are still, thank the Lord, as of this moment in time, in mothballs. Regrettably, we decided to destroy the original lunar lander for obvious reasons as I am sure you will all understand.' He paused, unsure how his ideas were being received.

'We would also need to unpack, test and re-invent the entire control apparatus, set up the communications, install security systems, and a million other things ... '

He looked around, suddenly realising that he might have overstepped the mark, but recognising at the same time that he had their undivided attention. His voice dropping, the passion ebbing, he continued:

'... and even if we did assemble a competent team and get the show on the road again, what excuse could we possibly give for returning to the Moon at this time?' Tom Sherman was watching Nathan Jackson's reaction intently.

It was at this point that the President began to see his problems disappearing, like new snow melting on some warm sidewalk. His horizon brightened as he saw the way clear to cleaning up the mess. He would cap his term in office with an announcement to the world; America would be there to play host to the Scottish travellers upon their arrival on the Moon; the first international handshake on another planet. If he couldn't have his missile crisis, he could at least go down as the President who re-invented space travel. As the idea grew in his mind, and as the realisation dawned that he had no serious alternative option open to him, he knew that, if America was to retain any credibility on the world stage, this was *one* race that they would *have* to win.

'Gentlemen,' he said. 'I propose to invoke my presidential power to instruct you all, as of this moment, to begin mobilising for a return trip to the Moon, to ensure that the reputation of this great country is not tainted by the failure of a previous administration to fulfil its promises to the American people. You shall have the required funding made available to you, but on one point I must be clear. We must not fail.'


'Frank? Sam here. You heard? Yeah. Great news. He bought into it hook, line and sinker. Yeah. Presidential decree. The whole shebang.'

'Yeah. Tom was there too.'

'What? No. No sign of any comeback. It seems perfectly clear to me. He sees a way now to cap off his presidency, while at the same time he thinks he has found a way to cover up the biggest fuck-up in our country's history. No. He believed every last bit of it. Stop worrying for Christ's sake.'

'I'm not sure about that. Could be. But does it matter? They won't say a word out of line, even if they do suspect the truth. We got what we wanted and they all know it. He's talking billions. We'll still be in business ten years from now. Yeah. That's right. We start immediately. What? Stop worrying, I said. He'll be out of office and gone before any of this ever leaks out. Now here's what I want you to do ...'

Down on the street, the truck from the municipality sat with its lights out at the kerbside.

The evening of the day following the press conference, the delegates were enjoying the sights, dining out, filling up with local brews and touring around the Old Town visiting pubs and show venues. At eight o'clock in the evening, business was picking up, even for a Tuesday night. As Rab strolled down the High Street heading for the "Skite" he was greeted with waves and smiles from passers-by, who had already drifted out of reach before the idea of tapping them for a sub occurred to him.

He was becoming known around the town. Not that he was penniless for he was now employed. Admittedly, not full time. Rewarded might be a better description, although twenty quid a night to talk to total strangers was better than a poke in the eye with a sharp stick! All things considered, his life was changing for the better. And ... that wee doll Susan had her eye on him.

Rab pushed through the crowd, the room packed out, solid wall to wall punters. A hush settled as he entered, the buzz picking up again as he ordered his drink. Looking through the mirror, he noted that his seat against the wall was apparently reserved.

'Well, well, whit wis this.' Things were beginning tae look up. His pint sat in front of him.

'There's nae charge for you tonight Rab. It's on the house! OK?'

'Aye.'

'Things were *certainly* looking up,' he thought, crossing to the seat against the wall, apologies all around,

'Oh sorry hen, didnae see yer big feet there. Ye a' right then? Sorry. Ma fault entirely. Oh! Sorry Jimmy, nae offence, ah hope. Difficult tae squeeze past ye! Is this seat taken? Naw? Oh good.'

'Hey, Rab. Ye're a bit late. Ah thought the show wis due tae start at eight. Ye couldna get away wi' turnin' up late at the London Palladium.'

'Hey, Rab, did ye no read that bit aboot them pickin' somebody fur the trip tae the Moon. Seems as though they're goin' tae set a question oan the Kirsty Monroe show one night next month. First wan tae answer correctly goes tae the Moon. Dae ye no' fancy yersel' as an astronaut?'

'Is thatafact? Whit time is it usually on pal? Whit wull they think o' next?'

'Hey Rab, Ah wis askin' ma pal aboot the camera thing, and he agrees wi' ye. Says ye need tae be right on tap o' a Hassleblad tae see the picture. He's a photographer. Says he wants tae take your picture an' a' that.'

The crowd was hanging on his every gesture. Clearly he was the centre of attraction. Susan sat in her usual place, her big blue eyes never roaming far from his face. He had even shaved again. Twice in two days. He might find himself going to bed the same day that he got up!

'Hey, big yin. What's the story behind the film studio ye were talkin' aboot. The one that faked a' the fillums?'

Rab put down his pint slowly, pausing until he saw that he had the attention of the crowd.

'I am not sure o' the name of the studio that wis involved, tae let ye understand, but it wis one o' they specialised ones that dae a' the special effects an' things. Jurassic Park an' that kind o' thing. Ye see, whit they did wis, they built this big studio and created a lunar landscape. Now I ask ye. How does anybody know whit a lunar landscape looks like if we've no' been there? See whit ah mean? But that wis precisely the reason they could get away wi' it. Because naebody could contradict them! But they made one or two mistakes, did they no'?'

He paused waiting for his words to register, for the faithful to draw even closer.

'When, fur instance they stuck the wee American flag into the sand, they forgot one wee thing. They made the flag as if it wis waving aboot. Skittering about as if it wis oan the bloody high seas in a force ten gale.'

He paused...

'But there's nae air on the Moon, nae wind tae move anything. So ah'm askin' yees all, does it make ony sense?'

'See that, that's very thought-provokin' stuff yer handin' oot. Huv ye got any mair where that came from?'

'Aye. There's plenty mair where that came from.' Rab was getting into his stride, the faithful encouraging him, his disciples ever supportive of his teachings.

'See when ye're on the Moon. Where's the sun? Is it up there, or is it doon here? Ye see ye don't know. Well I'll tell ye boy. The time that they landed oan the Moon ye can clearly see on the film they're *supposed* tae huv sent back, it's stuck up there at eleven o'clock...'

his arm outstretched,

'... when it should have been doon here at seven o'clock; as far as I can judge usin' the astronomical data currently available tae me.'

This last delivered with the modesty demanded of someone with a serious command of his subject. There was buzz of chatter at this new information.

'The man's a genius,' somebody whispered.

'A walkin' encyclo....whitever!' said another.

'Rab, are ye sayin' that wi a' their great thinkers an' scientists an' everything, that they couldna' get a simple thing like that right?'

'That is *precisely* whit I am saying to you boy. I think they had tae come up wi' the fillums in a hurry like, an' they got it wrang, Simple as that.'

A couple of pressmen from the conference entered the bar, curious about the crowd and the hush as they entered. Standing there, listening to Rab Nicol in full flight, they were obviously greatly amused by his pronouncements.

'Tell me something,' one of them shouted, 'If you're so certain that the Yanks never made it, how do you account for the endless data retrieved, their almost continuous commentary sent back, a commentary that was monitored by the entire world? I mean, in themselves, these were surely proof enough, if proof were ever needed, that they were on the Moon. What about the Moon rocks they brought back? What about the televised pictures, everything...'

He tailed off, shrugging indifferently, unconcerned as to whether he received a reply or not, convinced in his own mind that he knew the facts, the undisputed facts. Rab stood up and took a large swig from his latest draught of the evening session before considering the question.

'I will tell you this, sir. Whether or no' they landed on the Moon and did a' the things that they said they did, there remains sufficient doubt in ma mind, and in the minds o' other learned and well informed people after havin' reviewed the facts, tae cast doubt on the assumptions that you huv jist made.'

He sat down. It was his longest speech in a very short academic career.

'Because, ah'll tell yees why. Some o' ye might know, and ithers no', that goin' tae the Moon is no' a simple thing. Ye huv tae get dressed up fur the part. Oh, ah know that they had their boiler suits and divin' helmets an' a' the gear, but it wisnae enough! Ye see, once ye leave the protection o' the earth's atmosphere, ye get bombarded wi' radiation an' stuff like that. Oh, I hear ye say, "but they were inside the spaceship," an' ye'd be right of course. But it has been said by those who know,'

At this, he paused, his eyes roving over the ceiling as if unable to remember the exact source of his information ...

' ... that anyone passin' through the Van Allan belt, which as we a' know is highly radioactive, wid need a ton o' lead around him, if he wis tae huv even a wee chance o' surviving the trip. Now I doubt very much if the Yanks lined their wee ship wi' lead, but I don't think so!! Dae you?'

'So ye see Sir, we're no' as daft as we seem. We've looked intae this thing and WE ARE NOT CONVINCED. If they, on the ither hand...'

Smiling now,

'If they huv discovered some wonderful new way tae get 'round  the radiation problem, then that would be another matter a'the'gither.'

The reporter moved forward to interject,

'I am quite sure that they did. My God, man. They spent years on research and development before they even contemplated heading for the Moon. I must say. Really ...'

'Is that so. Well. Can you tell me this then? If they are so damned sure that their wee boiler-suits are up tae the job, then why don't they all toddle aff doon tae Three Mile Island and get stuck intae the problem they huv there? Tell me that boy. If ever a place needed a good clean up, it's Three Mile Island! Ever since the melt-down, the place has been aff limits, even tae the burds. There's bugger all skippin' aroond wi' the joys o' life on Three Mile Island.'

He looked around, basking in the silent appreciative adoration beaming back at him from his ever increasing following.

'So ye see, if they had the technology, dae ye no' think that they wid tend tae clean up their own back green first? Seems tae me, that that's one wee problem that they've still tae solve.'

'Aye. Fair enough Rab. It makes sense, whit ye're sayin'. If they had the suits and the gear, they'd surely use them.'

'Exactly, boy!'

A murmur of general agreement filled the room. The reporter shrugged and gave up. As he left the pub, he paused to chat with Charlie Smith.

'See that one. With him sitting there, yer pub's well named. He's a blethering shite.'

'Aye. Yer right. The pub's full o' them. Thank God!'


The two agents looked and listened as Hamish McLeod showed them around the extensive plant, carefully noting the layout and filing away items of interest for later use. Although untrained in such matters, they carefully noted the level of general activity, the arrays of laboratories and the endless pipe and services runs that covered the walls and ceilings. Listening now to one of the senior chemists, they nodded wisely as he explained the processes that ended with the product that had been so convincingly demonstrated earlier that morning. Hamish led them towards the exit.

'Now that you have seen the plant, I think it would be unkind of us not to take you over to the main assembly area where the *Caliban* is currently undergoing tests. Under normal circumstances, you will understand, the entire area is strictly off limits to most people. We are slightly behind our schedule at the moment, but we're getting there.'

He smiled, leading them towards the bright summer sunshine, down the long corridors, through the pairs of heavy blast doors and out into the parking area. As they drove off through the security fencing and along the deserted road that led to Clettraval, Lenny Stern was taking careful note of the security arrangements.

'So, tell us, Mr McLeod. How long has the fuel been around in its present state. Was it developed solely for your space programme, or did you have some previous agenda in mind when you started out?'

'Och! Ye know. We have been fiddling with this thing since independence in one way or another. We were given a huge grant to try to discover some way of reducing emissions on standard motor cars and the likes, and we just sort of carried on - until one day, we surprised ourselves with the results that I showed you this morning. It was, I suppose, what you might call a breakthrough. As the First Minister has announced, we will be making the formula available in due time, which should go a long way towards reducing acid rain across the developed world.

'The problem at the moment is the cost. We are working on that one too! Anything that derives in part from oil is bound to be expensive, and, if it costs more to produce that ordinary petrol, who will use it in God's name? But we are hopeful. We have several possibilities open to us.'

Paul Burke stared out at the ocean, still overwhelmed by the scale of the undertaking they had just witnessed and anxious now to see the *Caliban* being prepared for its long voyage. They pulled up at the first barrier and Hamish was waved through. Soon they were entering the panoramic lifts and descending slowly to the deck below. At their first sighting of the vast cavern they were immediately awe struck.

'Was this cut from solid rock?' asked Paul Burke.

'No. No. Not at all. It was a natural cavern, formed in pre-history. All we did was use what nature had already provided. Of course we have added a large complex of accommodation and workshops and the like. You'll see soon enough.'

Fiona McLeod was waiting as her father stepped from the lift.

'Gentlemen, my daughter Fiona. Fiona, this is Mr Burke and Mr Stern, both from the United States of America no less. They came over for the hunting and fishing, so they say.'

This, with a distinct twinkle in his eye.

'For spies,' she was thinking, 'They are remarkably presentable. Even good looking.'

Paul Burke stood and stared. The fair good looks, the long flaxen hair, and the green eyes staring frankly back at him, leaving him with feelings of inferiority that were most unwelcome.

'Well, there she is, gentlemen. And you have my personal assurance that she is designed to carry crew and not warheads.' At this, he peered over his spectacles to gauge their reaction to the truth!

'No. In a few short months she will be heading for the Moon. I believe you will be able to reassure Mr Franklin, and your President, that we will not be declaring war on you just yet.'

At the mention of Franklin's name, they both reacted. Then they were all laughing, Fiona busy answering questions, Hamish pointing out the various components of the ship. After an hour, having toured the facility, they were ready to leave.

'Well, we planned to travel back to London tomorrow. We're lodging at the Covenanters' Inn down in Auchenlech tonight. Our business is concluded here. Our job was to see what was going on, and frankly you have all made it very easy. Why don't you and Hamish come down tonight and we can have supper together? It's on the government this time.'

She smiled.

'Talk to my father. He may be flying back to Edinburgh tonight. Let's see. If not, I will accept.' She crossed to her father's side and spoke to him briefly.

'Well gentlemen, your offer of dinner, and no doubt a few drams along the way, is accepted with pleasure. And you're leaving tomorrow? And not a fishing line cast. Not a cartridge fired! And here I was believing that you were only interested in the hunting and the fishing. My, my. It's a queer old world gone wrong, if I'm not mistaken.'

They smiled wryly, as the sound of the Atlantic breakers reduced the need for some sort of reply. Driving back along the short road to Auchenlech, Paul Burke was totally unconcerned with the state of the world, the prospect of global incineration or any of the many horrors he might be expected to react to. Instead he was thinking only of the beauty of the gigantic *Caliban* standing in the middle of the vast cavern, and of the equally staggering beauty of the tiny Fiona when she had held his hand for that split second longer than necessary as they had uttered their casual goodbyes.

As the lunchtime session in the bar was drawing to a close at the Covenanters' Inn, Lachie MacDonald was regaling the regulars with his version of the "Night of the Two Yanks"; a night that would be etched forever into the memories of those present and assimilated into the folk culture of the island for generations to come; the story becoming richer by the telling; the telling becoming richer by the dram.

'Then they asked him about the rockets, and the fuel. Well he played them like the old poacher that he is, giving them this and that, and then confusing them with his technical talk and the like. Och. Ye know fine how he is with the drink in him. Well, I says to myself. Do they know who they are dealing with? He'll drink them both twice over and under the very table, I said to myself.'

They all roared with laughter.

'And he did! They could hardly speak, one of them falling off his stool and the other spending hours and hours trying to lift him up.'

They laughed again, tears beginning to course down the cheeks of the old fiddler.

'I never drank so much liquor, or laughed so much in my whole life,' he said.

'Yes,' said Lachie, 'the damned till was red hot at one point;

and the pair of them, signing for everything. When they see their bill tomorrow, I have a feeling they will be back down to the bar again to drown their sorrows. Nearly three hundred pounds was the price of a damned sore head.'

'Tell us, Lachie. What, if anything, did he tell them? Did he let on about the *Caliban* at all? Did he tell them anything worthwhile? Did he let on about the fuel?'

'Ah. Well now. Ye see…'

They all leaned forward, anticipating some finely tuned tale, the ability of Lachie MacDonald to weave just enough truth into a good story already a legend on the island.

'Well,' he said, turning to fill his glass, sniffing The Arran, 'It was like this.'

And as he wove the tale of the drunken antics of the two spies, of their singing and dancing and general carousing, interspersed with the serious lucid moments when the need to find the answers to their questions struggled in vain against the onslaught of the whisky, making them more receptive to the fanciful wanderings of one Hamish McLeod, the listeners sat, many with tears running down their cheeks at the very thought of the two agents, the memories still fresh in their minds, as they roared their approval of the art of the storyteller.

'And, says he of the tartan trews, "Tell me, Hamish, about the fuel." And Hamish looked at him and with a serious face he told him, 'It's a sad tale, laddie, and not one that folks from hereabouts are proud of. Ye see, over here on the islands, we have a centuries old tradition in the making of illicit booze. Call it what ye will. Whisky, the water of life, it dances under many names. Well, there was this fellow, not from these parts I should add, more interested he was in making money from his operations, you will understand, than in the gentle art of perfecting the God-given instructions on the making of fine malt whisky. And, believe you me, everyone knew what he was up to. Now, mind you, none of the locals would touch a drop of his concoctions; not if it had been the last drop on earth!

'And then slowly, ever so slowly, the stories begin to filter back to us. Since he canna sell it on the island, he's after heading for the mainland to see if he can improve on his "market projections" and the like over there. And sure enough, he sells and sells, returning every so often to make another batch or two.'

Around him, the faces were full of grinning anticipation.

'Until one day, he begins to experiment like. Adding a touch of this and a touch of that; looking to give the mixture an "extra little kick". An "extra kick" I ask you. Did the great malts ever require an "extra kick"?

'Well it seems that he was arrested shortly afterwards in Elgin of all ungodly places, selling his mixture to "ravers" at a hop, and the police confiscated the lot.' He paused to wipe the bar, everyone hanging on his words.

'And that might well have been the end of a sad story, had it not been for one small thing.'

The crowd was giggling now, knowing the ending, waiting for the climax of the story as it slowly unfolded, the laughter gathering strength as he steered them quietly to the end of his tale.

'Ye see, the trouble was, that the sergeant who arrested him, carted him and the leftovers back to the station, where he and his constable had a rare old time polishing off bottle after bottle. Well that would have been reason enough for concern as you might well imagine, but when the telephone rang at some ungodly hour the next morning and the sergeant heard the trembling voice of his constable at the other end of the line, he was very surprised.

'What on earth is the matter with ye?' says he.

'Well,' says the constable, 'I don't rightly know. It's funny like. One minute I was sitting on the old thunderbox this morning and the next thing I know, I am telephoning you from somewhere in Japan.'

# 10

The early morning mists hung over the Sound of Kerrera, the dim outline of the Isle of Mull faintly seen across the open water. Outside the hotel at this early hour, the town of Oban remained quiet, the harbour silent, the gulls still asleep. Moving slowly over the water, an early riser, a lone swan, appeared between the fishing boats and the pleasure craft, its wake the only disturbance on the dark, glassy surface. A crack of dawn light crept over the buildings, sending shafts of pale sunlight dancing over the waters, lighting Kerrera and the tips of the mountains on Mull and Morvern.

Sunday morning and Sally McIntosh looked over at the still sleeping form of Rod Cameron, sprawled over the disordered bed, his huge frame dwarfing the room. The half empty champagne bottle sat on the table, the drinks unfinished, the discarded clothes, the empty shoes and the bed cover thrown carelessly over the settee, brief reminders of their haste after entering the room at midnight, their need to be away from the other guests, away from the public gaze, to be safe behind locked doors and left to themselves. Responsibilities forgotten, living only for the moments that were becoming fewer and fewer as exposure threatened their affair, the deceit and the invention were taking over her life, leaving her unhappy at her betrayal of self.

At seven o'clock she showered and dressed, and, carrying her shoes, she carefully closed the door of the room and made her way downstairs. An early breakfast was called for; coffee essential, followed by a walk around the harbour to chase away the hangover.

Sitting by the window in the tiny dining room, looking out over the calm water, she reflected on her life and her present circumstances. His conversation with his wife as they had sat at dinner, his assurances, his lying, his calm assertions of undying love and fidelity had all upset her; imagining herself at the receiving end of the telephone, feeling the uncertainty that his wife must be feeling, the worm of suspicion constantly suppressed, in the hope that his work *was* the reason, the *only* reason for the extended separations that dogged their time together.

Feeling suddenly overcome with guilt, suddenly responsible

for the unhappiness that she was causing, aware that in all her life she had always been considerate of others to a fault, never willingly hurting or criticising, she realised that she was now an accomplished liar and conspirator in a game of love and deceit that could only end badly.

All too often these recurring feelings of guilt would call her from her sleep, leaving her anxious and restless in the early hours of the morning, thinking of him with his wife. Knowing that he carried none of his share of the guilt, only too aware that he had no remorse after each of their stolen nights, and certain that in the end they would be discovered, exposed and shamed, she dreaded the truth of their affair being splashed over the tabloids for her friends and family to see.

Moving out into the bright fresh morning, the gulls now noisy, their scavenging taking them to the steps of the hotel itself, she crossed the road and began to stroll along the seafront, watching the departing ferry. As she observed the bustle of early morning activity on the boats, she wished for an earlier time when she had been free from doubt, free from the burden of the lies and the longing, free to choose and above all free to plan her life in an orderly fashion, without ever having to react to the telephone summons, the furtive signals and the stolen guarded conversations always designed to sound so casual.

Back in the bedroom, the curtains still drawn, the room quite dark, Rod Cameron awoke to the sound of his mobile phone ringing on the side table. He opened the line.

'Yes, Angela. No, I've been up for an hour. Yes. Still in Glasgow; just had breakfast. Yes. Papers to get ready before ... No. I should be out of the meeting by three, possibly four at the latest. I promise. No. I will. I promise. Yes. I do. I will drive straight there. Yes, dinner tonight? With them? Oh yes. Fine. No problem. No. I am sure. I will be home by five or six at the latest. Yes. I'll call you when I'm through. Yes. Bye. Bye for now.' He closed the phone, buried his head back into the cold pillow and was almost instantly asleep, totally unaware, if he ever cared, that he was alone in the room.

Down on the slipway, feeding bread to the swans, Sally

McIntosh was feeling much better. Her decision made, she would get on with her life, bury herself in her work and make some new friends. Above her, leaning over the railings above the harbour, the hack from the local newspaper was wondering if any of the "national dailies" would be interested in photographs of the Minister for Education for Scotland furtively holding hands the previous evening with the blonde bimbo in the yellow dress talking to the swans barely fifteen feet below him. Raising his camera once again, he snapped off a couple more just to be sure.

In Edinburgh that evening, Gregor McLeod awaited his guests for dinner. The table was spread and the food prepared, a task he enjoyed when not pressured by work. He measured out a dram of whisky, turned the lights down and set some music to play quietly on the sound system.

'Mrs Jeffries, if I could ask you just to hang on long enough to see them all inside, it would be a great help. You've done wonders with the table. My thanks are due.'

She brushed aside his praises, pleased that finally he was appearing to relax more, taking time off to entertain, to watch television and socialise away from the demands of his job. Having served him ever since the passing of his wife ten years earlier, she maintained a wary eye on his well being, always ensuring that he was well provisioned and fed, proud to serve the man who was responsible for much of the change to the country since independence.

'If you want, I'll stay to serve and clear away too. You can't do it all and look after your guests at the same time.'

'No. No need. Fiona will be here and Gus Simpson's wife Jenny will no doubt lend a hand. In any case Murdo Sinclair is always willing to help out. If nobody else volunteers, he will for sure! And, brother Hamish is not bad in the kitchen.'

Half an hour later, with the guests assembled, Gregor led the way into the dining room.

'Well now. We don't sit on ceremony in this house! Jenny, you sit over here beside me, and your husband can have the company of

Fiona, my niece. Gus, you don't mind? Hamish, if you please. And Murdo, try sitting yourself down between the flowers. There we are. And I will be back in a moment. Hamish, perhaps you will look after the wine?'

'Consider it done.'

The mood settling, the ambiance conducive and the conversation weaving around on a variety of subjects, not least the coming Moon shot, Gregor served a superb meal, the laughter and the stories flying across the table enlivened by Hamish's account of the Burke and Stern gang's intrusion into North Uist.

'They dropped from the skies and they never knew what had hit them; whisky after whisky until three in the morning, and such singing. At one point they both had distinct Highland accents. I have to say, as undercover agents they would have done much better as town criers.'

They all laughed, Gregor wanting to know more.

'I've no doubt that their tour of the installations opened their eyes a fraction or two? Helped to blow away some of the cobwebs even? Stepping out from a drunken ceilidh in the Covenanters' into a world of high tech engineering half a mile up the road, on a near deserted island in the middle of nowhere, must have been quite a shock to the system, I dare say.'

Hamish continued his reminiscing.

'They were taken aback. The scale of the undertaking impressed them of course. But it's the fuel they are interested in. The formula. Once I found out how the ground was lying I was very careful to steer them in every possible direction, some of them slightly misleading, but informative enough to convince them that we had made big advances and were very, very serious, about going to the Moon. The plant was impressive of course, but until the moment that the lift descended into the cavern, I'm sure they thought that they had landed in Hicksville. We soon changed their opinion on that score.

'By now, the news will have been relayed back to Washington. They will have reported in detail on the project. After all, we showed them everything. As far as they, or anyone else is concerned, we are a small enthusiastic bunch of well-heeled amateurs indulging ourselves in a very expensive hobby. They must be wondering when we are going to ask for their help.'

Fiona was listening quietly, her evening at the Covenanters' Inn still fresh in her mind, the good looks and the gentle manners of Paul Burke winning her attention throughout the course of the dinner. Before leaving for London the following day he had called her to say "thank you" and to wish her well in completing the project.

'If you are ever over in Washington, look me up; here, take my private number. You never know; maybe some day.'

'Why is it,' she was thinking, 'that you always meet the really nice one on the last day of the holiday?'

Gregor was talking.

'So, they are still not convinced that our craft will take off, head for the Moon and be able carry enough fuel to orbit and return to earth? Well, well. But I suppose it is a mouthful to swallow. Worried about the Russian participation, were they? I hope you reassured them in that direction. I spoke to Mikhail in St Petersburg the other evening ...'

'How is he?'

'Och! They were fine, just a mite disappointed not to have been included in our plans. I told them we would collaborate on future missions and assist in putting a Russian on the Moon by the end of next year.'

'What did he say to that?

'He was delighted. I also asked him to give us a clear field in the coming months promising to bring him up to date on our plans as soon as I felt it was practical to do so. You know, we have such a good understanding with those people, it's hard to believe the cold war ever existed. I trust Mikhail implicitly. If only we had more like him around the world. If only.'

Fiona had entered from the kitchen, a tray of coffees in her hands.

'I suppose you men will have other business to talk over. Jenny and I will make ourselves scarce for a while. The kitchen needs three

Mrs Jeffries to bring it back to a state of order. Now, easy on the whisky, all of you.'

Throwing her arms around Hamish's neck; 'And that means you, *and* your big brother over there.'

The four men drifted into the sitting room. On the coffee table a selection of brandies and whiskies was laid out as they eased themselves into well-worn leather chairs that had seen better days. Gregor turned to Murdo.

'Now, tell me Murdo. It seems that your forecasts for getting the systems up and running were right on target? Fiona tells me that we will hit the date that we set, with plenty of time to spare?'

'That is correct. We have done quite well really. No hitches so far, but you never know…The *Moonraker* is behaving very well. The relay systems are functioning perfectly and morale at both centres is, frankly, very high. As you know a large number of our operators from Rosewell are over there at the moment, sleeping on the floors of the corridors.'

Gregor nodded sympathetically.

'I never had a doubt that it would all come right in the end. And Hamish tells me we have enough reserves of fuel to get there and back every week of the year for the next decade.' They laughed at the notion, the preparations for the first trip having all but killed them with the effort.

'But it's only the first trip we have to worry about I can assure you.' Gregor paused as if recalling something, 'It seems from Hamish's encounter with the two Yanks that Nathan Jackson thought that he might just have a missile crisis on his hands.'

'I don't believe it,' said Murdo. Gregor was chuckling, shaking his head, as he poured stiff measures into four glasses.

'What a story that might have been.' said Gus Simpson. 'He presumably believed the rumours of rocketry for military purposes. We even had serious enquiries from the "Nationals" down south about that possibility. When you come to think of it, from an American perspective, it would make little sense. As far as they are concerned we hardly figure on their scale of strategic thinking, rating as we do, as no less, and certainly no more of a threat than say,

Sicily, Iceland or even one of the Baltic States. Try explaining to a mid-western American the basic geography of Europe, and he would have a major problem identifying the borders of Germany, France or any of the other players. Take away the references to the towns and cities, and half the European Parliament would be in much the same pickle.'

Gregor smiled and nodded in agreement, now relaxed, enjoying the conversation between close friends. Gus continued.

'I may have told you this one already, but it does illustrate the insularity of the majority of Americans when it comes to knowing their world geography, not to mention their awareness of the geography of their own country. Back when I was covering the '82 Israeli invasion of the Lebanon, there was a story on the go around the Commodore Hotel about the two American Senators who had flown over to offer support to Chairman Arafat in his bunker. They promised undying support for a worthy cause. The Palestinians were under serious threat of annihilation at that time; the Israeli armour was only a mile away at Khalde and closing. The American envoy, George Habib, was desperately negotiating the latest cease-fire, while Reagan, if you remember, was in head to head heated discussions with the Israeli Prime Minister. It was a chaotic situation. Water and electricity had been cut off, food was scarce and the living conditions inside Beirut were appalling *Anyway*, one of the Senators declares at the end of the meeting, that he will ensure that the question of the Palestinian claim over rightful ownership of the West Bank of the river Jordan will be pressed home in the Senate. They will then push it through the U.N. Well! At that point, Arafat gives them an old fashioned look and turning to the map on the wall of the bunker, asks each of them in turn, to show him exactly which West Bank they had in mind.'

The other three roared with laughter, anticipating the responses.

'... and do you know, neither of them could find the river Jordan, let alone the West Bank.'

'Obviously, not baptised,' said Murdo quietly.

'A pity nevertheless that they failed to ensure they were

properly briefed,' said Hamish. Gus continued.

'Oh, the idea was fine. The trouble with enthusiasm is that it tends to make for carelessness and haste. Had they been up on their subject, it might have helped the peace effort with a show of informed solidarity, if only for that day. The Americans were getting a really bad press at that time. Not long after, hundreds of their young marines were blown to pieces at the airport. They never fully appreciated the position they were in. The situation at the time needed a firm hand. As their landing craft hit the beaches they were handing out chewing gum to school kids with limpet mines in their schoolbags. And, don't forget, the schools had been closed for months due to the war.'

Gregor lifted the decanter.

'Seconds, anyone?' He poured another round.

'Any minute now and we will be back on to the subject of politics and I am off duty until tomorrow. With the elections due at the end of the year, I find myself being pulled into meeting after meeting. All I really want to do is keep my mind focused on the game in hand. This is the first truly free weekend I have had in many months. Not that I regret a minute of it. I wouldn't change it for the world.'

Hamish was peering through his crystal ball, the amber of the whisky rolling in his glass and colouring his world.

'Gregor, at this juncture of the evening and just as the ladies rejoin us, I feel a toast coming over me.' He paused, as they all awaited his next statement.

'Looking back over the past years, we have come a long way as a nation. Things we only dreamed and talked about as students, are now being taken for granted, with our lives much improved and changed for the better. Although I elected to stay out of politics, you have always enjoyed my support in everything that your Party has undertaken. With a popular mandate from the people, with the power of the banks and big business firmly under control, with the economy on a sound footing and with good whisky retailing at an exorbitant five pounds a bottle...'

They all laughed.

'...I do seriously believe that there is little doubt that you will be re-elected for a further term. How could it be otherwise? You have not failed to deliver. The power of the other parties diminishes on a daily basis. If Christ himself was to walk down Princes Street performing miracles, he would convert fewer numbers than you yourself have done in the past few years.

'Oh, the Tories will moan, the Socialists may complain, Labour will fume that the future status of democracy itself is being challenged, but in truth, they are all united behind you. And I mean you. It is *you* they truly support, and it is *you* they will carry forward into the next government. We all know it. Oh, you smile, you shake your head, but you know it too. And now, this latest business cannot but help to place us on the world stage, as serious contenders in the campaign to clean up our planet and right the wrongs of past decades of exploitation and greed. Gregor, in supporting you, they in turn are expressing their faith in the new, revitalised Scotland.

'So, I give you the only toast worth a damn after a wonderful dinner. To Scotland, and the man who will lead her into another term of government. May they both survive and prosper.'

# 11

## Letters to the Scotsman

*Westminster, 26th July. '11*

Sir,

Recent correspondence from your readers on the subject of this week's announcement by Scotland's First Minister of this country's proposed trip to the Moon vary widely in their denunciations or support for the project, many of them accurately forecasting the precise date of our descent into hell for our sins or otherwise rejoicing in the almost spiritual release that so many of your less gifted readers seem to have experienced over these past days in coming to terms with Scotland's latest adventure.

Indeed, reading between the lines of the letters published thus far, one might be forgiven for anticipating a return on the one hand, to the re-introduction of the hair shirt (Tories only, if you please), and the Iron Maiden, (Scottish Socialists please queue here,) whilst on the other hand the suggestion by the Church of Scotland calling for mass pilgrimages to Arthur's Seat to sing loud praises to the Deity for his continued blessings (Liberals with hiking boots only) must surely give to those of us of more cautious disposition some hope for an early return to mature, rational journalism in the shape of an editor with the courage to bin all such feeble minded contributions to future issues.

I remain,
Dennis Turnbull M.P.

*"Dunrovin"*
*Moray Place.*
*27th July, 2011*

Sir,

Somewhere along the way we seem to have lost sight of the essential message being carefully screened by this present administration - what is deemed to be right for them is, by definition, right for the country as a whole. The high handed attitude of Gregor McLeod in redirecting funding away from areas where real benefit to the nation can be demonstrated, e.g. repairing the damage done to our schools and hospitals by PPP, etc. is typical of his single minded approach to deciding what is best for us all. Does he recognise these outstanding issues as items that require immediate government intervention? No. Instead he sees fit to lavish the undoubted *wealth of this foundling nation on an obsolete adventure, which forty years ago was shown to have served no worthwhile purpose other than that of political one-up-manship, at a time when the world was poised on the threshold of nuclear disaster, not to mention global poverty.*

*Sadly, the voices raised against the folly of sending men to a barren planet were not strong enough to deter outrageous overspending in the U.S.A., at a time when her under privileged minorities were living in squalor, facing hardship and hunger, with no opportunity for redress or reprieve.*

*Is it not time for this man to be brought to book for his excesses? Should he not be made to account for his gallivanting ways, his squandering of this nation's resources? Is it not high time that he told us the truth that lies behind his political manoeuvring, his sinister manipulation of the so called "free press" and stood up to be counted out in the forthcoming elections?*

*K. Paterson*
*Scottish Socialist Party*


*The Manse, Gogarburn*
*27ᵗʰ July. 2011*


*Sir,*
*Your contributor's comments, (Letters Page, T.Wodehouse, 24ᵗʰ inst.) that God may only be found in outer space since he has clearly forsaken earth, raises several fundamental theological issues that I beg leave to address.*

*In the first place, the notion of God as a being, an entity with form and boundaries, is as far removed from the modern concept of deity as can possibly be imagined. God is everywhere and within us all.*

*He knows no spatial limitation, no time constraints, being timeless and ever lasting He is ever present and ever watchful. As we endeavour to reach for the stars, we can be certain that we do not leave him behind.*

*His goodness and love are essential items of personal baggage on each and every journey that we make throughout our lives.*

*I remain etc.*
*Rev. J. Milligan*

*Tinkerbell Lodge, Aberfeldy.*
*29th July 2011*

Sir,

It would be perverse of me to suggest that I have come to detect a vulgar note of derision creeping into the various items of correspondence flooding your Letters page on a daily basis. The general bias seems to point in the direction of finding fault with everything accomplished by our present administration.

As one with no great love for Parties of any persuasion, I take issue with the countless occasions when pernicious and often actionable matters are dealt with in your columns without reference to their accuracy, philosophical inclination or political correctness.

The very recent, (Letters Page, 27th July) argument put forward by Mr Paterson M.S.P. that only those projects deemed by him to be of benefit to the community as a whole should be considered as worthwhile and seen to be praise worthy, is a shocking indictment of the state of cultural and historical awareness of so many of our young men and women in public service today.

I would remind all of them that the great constructions undertaken in the past, the Pyramids at Giza, the Hanging Gardens of Babylon, The Lighthouse at Alexandria, The Colossus of Rhodes, The Great Wall of China and our own Holyrood Project were all, in their time, monumental undertakings seen as great adventures set in stone for future generations to marvel at.

Joseph Numbthumb, Director,
The Precast Stone Co.


Sir,

On behalf of us all here we wish to dispute the assertions that have been put forward that Scotland will be the second country to land on the Moon. We, "The Friends of Robert Nicol", state our case here and now that the Yanks did not land on the Moon. After careful consideration of the available facts we are forced into the conclusion that they never made it!

If anyone wants to debate the matter we are ready to listen. As it stands now, Scotland will be first on the Moon.

Yours sincerely,
Susan Cramer.- Graduate — UCLA
Sec. "The Friends of Rab Nicol"

Sir,

Recent criticism of our work at Rosewell has highlighted for the directors the need for some recognition that the scientific nature of our work needs to be explained in general terms to a public, who, for the most part, have very little idea of what we do, and why we exist at all.

First of all, I should explain that we are a Public Institution answering to a Select Committee, to whom we report on a quarterly basis. We are funded directly from the Treasury by grants that are approved on the Rock and audited independently in the City. All in all, our expenditure is closely monitored and controlled at every stage, and future funding is entirely dependent on our ability to show justified need and measured results.

Any suggestion that we are loose cannons running around without supervision, (Letters Page, 23<sup>rd</sup> July) is entirely unjustified.We exist to serve our nation, drawing on the best available manpower from our universities in our quest for answers to some of the more pressing of the world's problems. In many cases, these problems are long term, and results are inevitably slow in the making.This should not be made an excuse for criticising an institution that has won the acclaim and respect of similar "think tanks" worldwide, nor should our status give us unconstitutional protection against our critics, who see the costs rising year on year.

Many of you will know that a great deal of our work over the past ten months has been dedicated to developing, testing and commissioning systems for guidance of the vehicle which on November 30<sup>th</sup> will leave North Uist and set course for the Moon. On that day, the dedicated work of three hundred women and men will reach maturity. It is our fervent hope that the effort and talent expended will result in the safe return of our astronauts to Earth.

No one should doubt that this is, and has always been, our first priority over the past year. If, in the course of getting there, some of you have been left in the dark, I am sure that you will realise that in the very nature of the work there is always a need for a degree of secrecy. We need to protect our interests in a competitive market, where industrial secrets are traded for high premiums between countries that, as yet, we have failed to win over to our very open-handed way of thinking.

I remain,
Murdo Sinclair  - Director
The Rosewell Institute

*Dove Farm, by Biggar.*
*29th July, 2011*

Sir,

As a journalist, I deplore recent correspondence on the subject of the 1969 Moon landing. Conspiracy theories are forever popping up, whether it be the Kennedy assassination, crop circles, alien intervention or world cartels controlling coffee bean prices.

It is truly sad to see a great newspaper, such as The Scotsman, reduced to printing trivia that would not warrant five lines in the Tiny Tots corner of most other major publications. However, since we are discussing the issue of Moon landings, I will be interested to see details at some stage of just how we intend to fly from Moon orbit to reach the Moon's surface. Will Superman be there to guide us? Will Spiderwoman be on hand to slow our descent?

So far we have been told little or shown anything other than a few distant shots on Monday evening of the intended launch vehicle, nor have any of us been graced with even the narrowest of technical explanations of how we are to get there. Whilst we are well used to this Government keeping its news to itself, (try sitting in on a government briefing, if you will), it is truly disheartening for those of us trying to extract the tiniest bit of technical information from any government department on anything to do with this mission.

I take this opportunity through the columns of your newspaper to appeal to the ministers concerned, to realise that an open discussion on these matters is infinitely preferable to the conspiracy of silence that exists at present.

John Stollar – Science Correspondent
The Independent


*St. John's Wood.*
*England*
*29th July 2011*

Sir,


The creeping assertions that the Americans did not in fact land on the surface of the Moon are indicative of a much wider malaise prevalent today in our society. When a great nation such as the United States of America puts its money where its generous mouth is, spending billions and trillions on advancing our knowledge of the universe, sending back exotic photographic evidence that life here on earth is infinitely preferable to that on any of our nearest neighbours, we should give thanks to that great country, that we are the privileged few to whom this immense volume of data is freely available; knowledge which in time, will no doubt alert us to the distinct possibility that we are, all of us, little more than God's accident in an ever expanding cosmos.

I call on all of you, believers and doubters alike, to get down on your knees to give thanks that we have survived two great wars, a dark age of nuclear uncertainty during the 'fifties, 'sixties and 'seventies, the years of Maggie Thatcher in the 'seventies and 'eighties and the demise of old Labour in the 'nineties only to have to face yet another sanity threatening onslaught in the form of conspiracy theories that seem to target only the good, the virtuous and the great; theories which can only in the end be countered by the truth, the light and the general pursuit of knowledge. I trust that when we do eventually set foot on the surface of the Moon, we will find sufficient evidence remaining there to silence the voices of those doubting Thomases who would have us believe that the claims of NASA in the late sixties were little more than ethereal Moonshine.

Erwin Kapolski — Chairman of the Anglo-American Society


Unpublished letter to the Scotsman

*Whisky-a-go-go, L.A.*
*29th July. 2011*

Sir,

As a fervent bystander but nevertheless an equally fervent supporter of all things Scottish, I deplore the unbelievable shite that has decorated your letters page over the past few weeks ever since the announcement was made "that we are all goin' tae the moooooon".

To all of you people back home I say,

'Be proud. Hold yer heads high and realise, just this once, that you have made it. It's great. See it for what it is. A triumphant conclusion to centuries of enterprising, Scottish, pioneering engineering, most of it washed down the pan in recent decades by years of under-investment, mismanagement and Tory rule.'

So. Get off yer bloody knees and let me hear it ring out. Let me hear you say it! We are the people!... and don't you forget it.'

Andrew McPherson

# 12

"The Bletherin' Skite" was filled to capacity, the crowd spilling over into the lounge bar, the lucky few able to see over the crowd to where an adoring audience of students, lefties, intellectuals, divorcees, poets, artists and washed up Tories lay sprawled at the feet of Rab Nicol. Sitting there, his face beaming and alcohol tinged, he was as smiling and shiny as a Toby jug in a dishwasher.

Fat Susan sat beside him dressed in virginal white, her face painted like Hiawatha at his wedding feast. The Pharaoh and his moll. At her feet sat the velvet collecting bag that had already been round the room twice in as many hours.

Rab sat too, his new found wealth reflected in the second hand jacket he was wearing, the check pattern faintly seen shining through the years of neglect. Elsewhere, the creases, the dirt and the burn marks, all radiated a sense of carefree, artistic recklessness that reinforced the image he carried with him; the ageing boy scout with a serious booze problem. And as usual, the drink was flowing around them.

'Hey. Susan. Huv some o' this, hen.'

The pint tipped to sharing point, her glass generously filled from the master's keg, gratuitous Guinness all over the floor.

'There's plenty more when we're *ready fur it.*' This with a sly wink returned by Susan with a coy sideways smile.

'Hey, Rab. Aye. It's me again. Jamie. Aye. How are ye? OK? Great tae see ye. Everything OK? See you, Rab. That bit aboot the shadows. Could ye just explain it *wan mair time* for Josie here. Ye see, she wisnae here when ye telt us the last time.'

Rab considered the request, waving his hand graciously in dismissal of any objection to a repetition of his earlier ramblings.

'Nae problem, son. Nae problem at a'. As a matter o' fact, sunshine, ah wis jist aboot tae get stuck back intae the plot when ye rang.'

Smiles all round, everybody hunkering down, the master about to speak. The audience settled, the buzz of conversation falling away as the Tartan Messiah raised his hand slowly until satisfied with the mood of the crowd, his hand falling slowly back again to rest on the shoulders of a bashful Susan.

'Ye see, on the fillum they made, or *were supposed tae huv made*, there's wan shot o' the lunar lander and ye can see one o' the legs o' the thing stickin' intae the dust. Now, in itself the photie is *no'* that remarkable. Just a wee bit o' alloy stickin' intae the dust, *so tae speak.*'

He paussed looking around at the faces, biding his time until the moment was right.

'An' on the ground, there's a wee shadow of course. But where was *the sun*, I asks you? Wis it up there or wis it ower here? An' the answer is…'

He paused again.

'…the answer is… it was in *both* places. Now. I hear ye say. How can that be? An' ye'd be right. Fur looking carefully at the photie fur just a minute or two longer wi' the trained eye o' an investigative mind, somebody, in the know, might jist say,

"what dae we huv here"?

'FOR JUST WHAT DO WE SEE?'

There was silence in the room. The dominoes quiet, the fruit machine patiently awaiting the arrival of autumn.

'Well, if it's no gonna upset yees all, Ah'll tell ye. It's simple. We see *two* shadows. Now, unless I am very much mistaken, unless I qualify for the job o' village eejit, I know of only *one* sun in our immediate solar system. So?'

Pause again, a further glance to the side.

'So, how is it we can huv *two* shadows?'

He looked around the room, his face carrying the look of a simple man, baffled by a simple question.

'Two shadows. How? How on earth can ye huv *two* shadows frae one sun?' He paused, looking slowly around at the upturned faces, all waiting spellbound for the lesson to resume.

'Now notice that I said…"how on *earth* can ye huv two shadows"… I did not say …"how on the *Moon* can ye huv two shadows", fur it is my contention that whit we are seeing was a set up. A set up wi' studio lighting and because, as I huv often said, they were in a hurry, they never checked the lightin' on some o' the shots. An' it's no jist one photie that's wrang, there's more!'

This last delivered at pace, his hands crashing down on his thighs to deliver home the message that could not be denied. The truth must out! A ripple of discussion filled the room, then quietened to a hush as the hand was again raised, his signal swift and light, thick with innuendo.

'Now I huv heard it disputed, that there is a simple explanation for this. A *simple* explanation. *Ah'll bet there is.* But no sae bloody simple, boy! Ye see, some big shot scientific guy comes oot o' the widwork wi the explanation that whit we are seein' is caused simply by a *reflection,* no less, frae *aff the side* o' the lander.'

He looked around him, over his shoulder at the bare wall, then at the ceiling above, as if expecting an answer to his confusion to be delivered into his lap. With a bewildered look, a slow shaking of the head, his expression turning to one of anger, a sneer beginning to surface, he began again.

'A *reflection*? Tell me how. From what? Both light sources are coming frae *behind* the lander, an' we're telt there's nothin' else on the Moon fur Christ's sake. Nothin' that could possibly *cause* a reflection. For it tae *cause* any kind o' reflection, the light wid huv had tae be in *front* shinin' *on* tae the thing! But how could that be possible, I ask maself? How?'

Again he searched their anxious faces for a hint of assistance, a morsel of hope, finding none.

'Because it never happened. That's why. Just another bit o' proof, if ever we needed it, that the Yanks never made it tae the Moon.'

At this, the applause and the cheering lifted the roof, the crowd on their feet, showing their appreciation of the performance in their every action. Behind the bar Charlie Smith paused on the way to the safe to deposit the bar takings at half time.

'He's right. The bastard is always right. How the fuck does he dae it?'

Back at the bar the staff were frantically pulling pints, dishing up whisky and rattling the overworked till.

'An' one fur Rab. Guinness. Aye. A pint. No. Make it two pints, one fur the lassie as well. Didn't ah tell ye, he's brilliant. Is he no'? Knows his stuff a' right. Last night he was amazin'. Fuckin' amazin'. Wis telling us aboot the Van Allan Belt. It's full o' radiation. He says it wid roast an elephant in a split second, an' if ye even got close tae it you'd be deid! The man's a wonder. Kens his stuff a' right.'

Rab sat at ease with himself contemplating his rise to fame and fortune. The bag was on the move again, the clinking of the loose change announcing untold happiness in its wake. With the Festival Fringe due to start in a month's time, he would have to start looking for a more salubrious venue to carry on his crusading, somewhere to hang his hat for the three weeks of rich Festival pickings.


Minister's Question Time, and the chamber was packed, the public gallery spilling over with eager members of the public with nothing better to do on a Friday morning. In the press boxes below, the men and the women from the media were similarly represented, attendance running at an all time high since the announcement of a date for the Moon launch.

Already an hour into the debate, the Right Honourable Member for Edinburgh Central had the floor.

'...and where if any, are the marketing studies, the profit and loss projections for future marketing of these marvellous spin-offs that we are told have been developed in parallel with the main programme? Where are we to look for immediate, or even long term returns from the enormous sums that have been expended on this costly affair? Where will we discover this elusive, unseen, unspecified benefit that the First Minister so tantalisingly waves in front of our noses, every time someone in this house dares to raise an objection or put the question "why"?

'Why indeed? Returning to the point raised earlier by my Honourable Red friend Mr Paterson, it would seem that even if we do succeed in perfecting the manufacturing processes for the fuel and its by-products, will we, at that point, be given any assurances that continuing investment will result, in the long run, in the emergence of a viable fuel that will reduce harmful emissions and still be *adaptable* for use in commercial airliners and family cars? Furthermore, is it not the case that work has been on-going for the past year to refine the production method sufficiently to bring the resale price of the product *below* that of the current retail price of the high street pumps? As I understand the present state of affairs, the cost of a litre of the stuff is nearly twenty per cent more than that of standard petrol. I would ask the First Minister to clarify, if he can, the points I have raised.'

Gregor McLeod rose to his feet. As usual, he carried no notes, his command of the subject never in question following his many discussions with Hamish on the very issues raised.

'Since my Honourable friend is clearly intent on widening the debate, I will accommodate him by widening it still further. On the many issues tabled, I can promise him no quick answers. Many of the objections raised here today will either survive to maturity, or fall by the wayside as we resolve the minor difficulties we are at present addressing in refining the product for commercial resale. But, when we *do* succeed, I am certain that we will have the support of all sides of the house. We will have taken a giant leap forward in our quest for a cleaner alternative to fossil fuels. If, one day we can get into our cars and drive off, knowing that we are not polluting the air we breathe, we will have achieved something truly worthwhile in every sense of the word.'

A brief round of applause greeted his opening remarks, the members settling down to enjoy the debate.

'If we can go one step further and persuade other countries to manufacture and market the product under licence, then we will have made considerable progress towards alleviating the terrible global damage being caused by acid rain. This will have been no small achievement. Let no one doubt that our efforts, so very close to achieving their ends, will be seen, one day, to have been the turning point in our fight to clean up the planet.

'And I do not need to remind any of you of the perils of doing nothing. The United States of America continues to defy the pleading of the majority of the world's leaders, who seek to persuade her to sign up to the spirit of the Kyoto agreement; to recognise for the sake of generations yet unborn that we can no longer live for today and ignore the damage that is being done now. As we sit here, day by day, countless tons of pollutants drift over the oceans of the world, turning our Garden of Eden into a dangerous hell on earth. We must continue the struggle to reduce emissions. There are others who continue to undo the best efforts of the more responsible nations of the world by ignoring the mountain of clear and incontrovertible scientific evidence that we are slowly but surely poisoning our planet.'

In the press gallery, the note taking and live transmissions continued.

'We now know that within a short space of time the great forests of the world will have shrunk to a dangerous level, they will, in all probability, eventually disappear because of over development and the effects of acid rain. You need no reminding that without the forests, we have, as a species, no long term future. We have, all of us, the responsibility to ensure that we do everything within our power as governments and as individuals to reverse the trend, and to impress on all countries, as forcefully as we can, the need for all to climb on board as quickly as possible, to save what we can from a rapidly deteriorating situation. In licensing the formula for the development of the fuel to other nations, we will of course insist that they make every effort to cut back their dependence on fossil fuels.

'Of course there are still many substantial hurdles to be overcome, still many difficulties to be resolved. But every step forward that we take is a step in the right direction, putting commercial values to the rear in our thinking, promoting instead the ideal of cleaner fuel for all by the year two thousand and twenty.'

He paused.

'Will it be profitable in the long term? I believe the answer is "yes". If only because we have no alternative solution at present, short of surrendering our right to own personal transportation vehicles. But that commercial consideration is not the only deciding factor that we must face. The automobile industry must also come on board. And heavy industry; and quickly too, if we are to halt the damage. We must undertake to convert all vehicles of a certain age and subsidise owners who qualify for assistance. All public transport will need to be upgraded, or scrapped and replaced, under the terms of legislation that we will shortly place before the House.'

At this statement, several members were instantly on their feet trying to attract the attention of the Speaker.

'I now return to the point of the debate. You have asked me if development work surrounding our space projects will have an impact in due course, in going some way towards reducing the considerable sums that have already been invested in the programme. The answer I believe is an emphatic "Yes". All the predictions for this year and up until the end of our present term in office indicate that we will be in a position to hand over to the incoming administration a set of books that are firmly in the black.

'But are we going to measure the success or failure of our tenure in government in this way? Are we to return to the days of leadership by accountancy? Are we really accountable in the long run to a set of figures to be weighed against a period of undeniable progress and improvement in the standard of living for every man, woman and child in our land, at a time in our history when our global environment is so seriously threatened by the lack of good will on the part of those uncaring individuals who have failed to unite with those of us who believe in the cause of our ultimate survival?'

He paused, the chamber silent, no voice raised in opposition. His manner resigned, his voice even and softly pitched his composure evident as he weighed his own words. Nodding, his expression serious, sensing the unity of the house on a subject above party politics, he continued,

'Mr Speaker, Honourable Members of the House, I believe that the coming three or four months will see us in a position to substantially influence and alter the stand being taken by those states who have so far failed to respond to the pleas of the United Nations to reduce their emissions of greenhouse gases, to halt the destruction that now threatens our existence by the selfish pursuit of financial gain and material exploitation. By promising to share the formula for the fuel; by encouraging its development and by subsidising its use, I believe that we will advance our argument for environmental protection to those nations who at the present time would find the cost of adopting it too great a burden to support on their struggling economies. At the same time we intend to step up pressure on the United States to recognise their position as leading industrial culprit in the failure to clean up our planet, asking them to recognise the scale of the problem, and the urgency with which we all now must view this developing crisis.'

He sat down to sustained applause.

Up in the press gallery, Gus Simpson was listening and thinking... 'Something he said at dinner the other night. Now what was it? His reference to America. How did he put it? As passively destructive as Genghis Khan was actively ...'

In an instant, Gus Simpson thought he could see where his old friend was heading. Still not sure of the way ahead, he was none the less convinced that he could perceive the thread of an idea developing. An idea that had been carefully constructed and artfully concealed. *Was* it possible? With Gregor McLeod *anything* was possible. But *this*? Surely not!'

Determined to find out and concerned about confronting his old friend with a premature exposition of his plans, he decided to wait. In waiting and listening, he was certain that he would eventually be brought into the picture. One thing, however, was certain. The waiting was going to kill him.

# 13

Carefully omitting any mention of "the night of the two Yanks", Paul Burke completed the report on his five days out of station, his mind constantly returning to a wind swept landscape, a cosy inn with a friendly bar and the persistently recurring image of two of the greenest eyes he had ever seen. A curious dissatisfaction haunted him as he returned to business, a tendency to day-dream staying with him through the first week back at his desk, a feeling of loneliness developing each evening as he ate alone, sitting, sometimes staring at the television set, seeing little and paying only scant attention to the run of the programme.

'I must be going down with something,' he thought. 'Some rare Scottish disease unknown to medical science, some exotic reaction to the midge bites' that still showed on his wrists and ears.

Pulling on his jacket, he left the apartment, exiting the building into a sticky hot July evening, now dark, the streets quietening now as traffic slowed to a trickle. Passing a bar on the corner, he turned and entered on impulse, a thing he had never done in three years of living on the avenue, walking into a world of soft lights and cool air conditioning, soft music and a scattering of customers.

The bartender eyed him without curiosity, waiting as he slipped into a seat at the bar. On the wall the clock showed that it was after eleven, a fact that surprised him. He had little recall of the hours since six when he had arrived home. Aware that he was hungry he called the barman across.

'Give me a draught Bud please. Say, is there any chance of having a burger? I clean forgot to eat today.'

The bartender indicated a menu on the bar and he ordered a steak. Pouring the beer, his eye roved over the shelves. Ahead of him the label on the bottle of whisky caught his eye. The familiar image of the distillery and a quiet stream set against a backdrop of lochs and mountains, receding into a pale blue sky. The bartender was polishing the bar top in front of him, handing over the cutlery, the condiment tray and a pile of napkins.

'Hey. Could I trouble you for a drop of whisky? Yeah. That's the one. Mind if I look at the bottle?'

'Help yourself.' And he strolled off. From the kitchen the smell of steak on the grill stole into the room, sharpening his hunger.

'Say. If you don't mind… I'll have another shot. Just arrived back from Scotland. Drank a few of these in a hurry one night; too many if the truth be told.'

He smiled, the bartender shrugging indifferently, pouring a second measure of whisky into the glass before replacing the bottle on the shelf and retreating into the kitchen. Lifting it to the light, then sniffing the glass, then lifting it once more to catch the light, his mind flooding with memories of his nights at the Covenanters' Inn, he sipped slowly, the minutes passing.

The bartender was standing in front of him, a curious look on his face. The plate of steak and fries ready to lay in front of him.

'Anything wrong with the glass, buddy?' He laid the meal down.

Startled, Paul Burke came out of his dream.

'No. Nothing at all. It's perfectly OK. No problem. I assure you.'

He started to eat, the taste of the whisky cutting across the mouth watering experience of the steak, so strongly reminiscent of his time in Scotland; that soft wave of dissatisfaction beginning to sweep over him again, reaching for the glass, sniffing the golden liquor, sipping again and drifting once more into his own sweet Celtic twilight; his beer undrunk, the memory he was savouring too rich to let go. He looked over at the bottle, staring at the label, a window in time and space, opening up a response in him that was novel and sweet tasting, illusive and nameless.

Half an hour later, returning home at twelve thirty, he checked the time and lifted the receiver. The phone rang twice, and her voice came down the line.

'Hi. Sorry to call so early. It's Paul Burke. Yeah. I'm back in harness. Been back a full week. Felt like giving you that call I promised you.'

The conversation swung to her end. At the end of half an hour they closed the line. Feeling happier than he could ever remember, for reasons he failed to fully understand, aware only of a lifting of his spirits at hearing the sound of her voice, he cracked open the bottle he had carried back from Scotland and poured himself a generous measure of liquid gold to nurse the bittersweet heartache that refused to go away.

Lunchtime, in the rear of "The Bletherin' Skite" and Rab sat between Charlie Smith and the man with the briefcase.

'Well ah'm no sayin' ah'm no interested. Ah am interested. Really. It's an offer ah should'na refuse. Whit ye're sayin' is, if ah work here every night for the three weeks o' the Festival ye'll pay me a hundred and fifty a week plus ma bevvy. It's a good offer, ah suppose.'

Rab's mind was working overtime.

'Work. What work? If this is work gi'e me mair o' it! A hundred and fifty quid a week. Whit? A fortune tae a hungry man.'

The man from the brewery was off again, talking in terms of contracts and bonuses. Charlie tapped Rab on the arm, pulling him back from the day dream, the door of the Rolls Royce held open, the chauffeur sitting primly in the driving seat, his moll Susan decorating the inside.

'Whit. Oh aye. Ah'll certainly gi'e ye an answer as soon as ah huv discussed the matter wi' ma business manager and partner. Two shows a night and three on a Saturday? Ah suppose it's a'right. Ah mean. Ah've nae real objections like. It's a' the same tae me.'

Laughing now, seeing the prospect of raising the offer, squeezing another fiver or so out of the deal. The man from the brewery was off again.

'Charlie tells me you certainly know how to pull them in; please the punters. That sort of thing. Good business. What sort of an act do you have. Sing? Play the guitar?'

'Naw. Naw. S'no an act. Nothin' like that. Just talkin'. Aboot nothin'. Load o' rubbish really. Come wan night. Ah'll gi'e ye a wee mention like. Ye could bring the wife.'

Charlie was pushing for the deal.

'Best tae agree something now Rab. Might no' get another chance. Ah'll need a couple o' days tae organise the lights an' the microphone. S'no a problem, just takes time. An' two stools? Why two?'

'I shall require one stool,' says Rab pointedly, 'for ma prompt notes an' ma glass o' stout. The ither stool is fur me tae stick ma backside on.'

'So Rab. You will let Charlie know if it's on or not. I hope that we can bring in the same business, or better, over the Festival?'

'Aye. OK. Ah'll let ye know. Thanks a lot. Be seein' ya.'

Rab was solicitous in his farewells. Charlie Smith had drawn two pints and with the doors shut to the street he and Rab sat at the bar. Behind them the telephone rang unexpectedly. The voice at the other end was asking for Mr Robert Armstrong Nicol.

'Mr who?' said Charlie. 'Robert who? Never heard o' him. He's no a customer is he?'

Rab was on his feet reaching for the phone.

'Hey. Haud oan. That's fur me. Robert Nicol. Here. Hand it over.'

The receiver changed hands, Rab's voice becoming sweet and angelic in an instant.

'Yes? Who is speaking? Mr. who? Ma name's Rab Nicol. Aye that's right hen. Ah'm the one. That's me fur sure. Aye. The wan an' only.'

Laughing now.

'Nae problem doll. Honest. Nae offence taken. Never use ma middle name. Jist Rab. Aye Rab. It's short fur Robert. Naebody ca's me that. No. So, whit can ah dae fur ye hen? Has somebody died or somethin'? Has somebody left me a fortune maybe?'

The voice at the other end continued for some time, with Rab's face expressing disbelief at one moment, satisfaction at another, bewilderment at all times.

'Ye want me tae what? When? Wednesday night. Never heard o' him. A chat show. Whit, Ye mean like Kirsty Monroe, that kind o' thing. Aye nae problem. Ah wid be delighted. Aye. Nae problem hen. Jist you dae that. Ah'll be here.'

With that, the line closed, leaving a mystified Charlie Smith, waiting for some explanation.

'Well?' said Charlie expectantly. 'Whit the fuck wis that a' aboot?'

Rab was pensive, sipping his Guinness. A television interview. An invitation to join a national chat show. First class train ticket tae Glesga' an a'! Well, well. Things *were* lookin' up.

'That wis ma *local* agent' he said suavely, stroking the day's growth on his face.

'Want's tae know if ah can dae a chat show tomorrow night. Huv tae go through tae the Television Centre; down at Pacific Quay. No sure ah should huv accepted. Ah'm really verra busy at this time. She says she'll send the contract an' the ticket tae the pub, here, tonight. Special *courier delivery* no less!'

'Christ!' said Charlie, in wonder, his eyes widening.

'Ye're a fuckin' star already.'

'And,' said Rab disdainfully, 'you can inform Mr what's his bloody name frae the brewery that it'll be four hundred a week…jist tae turn up.'

And with a toss of his chipped head, leaving the remainder of his pint unfinished like the toff that he was, he strolled confidently out into the bright July sunshine to prepare himself mentally for the task ahead.


The news announcer was winding up the broadcast, preparing to recap on the main items of news.

'And now to remind you of the main items of this evening's news…' The scene changed to a panoramic view of the Rock, the camera zooming in to fill the screen with the outside elevation of the castle ramparts panning down to the great council chamber before steadying.

'… where the Council of Ministers was in session. A statement will be issued tomorrow. Elsewhere, preparations it seems are well underway for the November launch of the spaceship *Caliban*. Today, for the first time, news cameras were allowed in to tour the facility at

North Uist and our reporter Steven Harris was there to bring us up to date on the progress of the launch.'

The reporter was in conversation with Fiona McLeod. Behind them, the area in front of the ship was a hive of determined activity.

'Fiona, apart from everything else we have said, I am told that you are still on target for the launch date, and that with luck, we shall see it all happening here on the thirtieth as promised. Is that correct?'

'Well, as you can see, we are certainly very busy. It is however fair to say that the date looks more realistic now than it did a month ago, but I am confident that it will all go according to plan for the November launch. We anticipated no delays, no snags that we have not foreseen. We are blessed with a magnificent workforce who have put their hearts and souls into this project, delivering on target and making life, for me at any rate, a lot easier than it might have been over these last twelve months.'

The announcer was off again.

'And the new runway? Will it be completed on time? Do you believe that test flights will take place as stated in early September?'

The cameras outside took in the view of the long construction site running off into the distance, crossing beaches and headlands for several miles, its terminus lost in the low hanging mist.

'We'll be ready before that. The data from the Uzbekistan flights has already been downloaded, and we are confident that we will be fully prepared for the start of the final commissioning period by the end of August.'

The camera moved around the tall cavern, the interview running to a close.

'... so with thanks to Fiona McLeod and everyone working on the project we return you to the studios in Glasgow.'

Back in the studio the announcer was being handed a piece of paper.

'And, before we close, we have some breaking news just in. Later today, the American President will go to Congress to ask them to endorse his plans for reinstating the American manned space programme with an early return to the Moon by the end of this year. The news has been welcomed here in Scotland, with the First Minister Gregor McLeod expressing some surprise that America should be returning to a programme of space exploration now. He nevertheless applauded the decision to initiate a return to the Moon, jokingly suggesting that his ten dollar bill was on *Caliban* getting into orbit around the Moon ahead of NASA. He refused to be drawn, however, on why the Americans had seen fit to announce a resumption of the manned Moon missions of the seventies at this time.

'And with that late item of news, we conclude our programme for this evening. We are of course back with you for the late news at ten o'clock, but until then, from all of us here in the newsroom, we say

"have a pleasant evening".'

# 14

Sally McIntosh heard the telephone ringing as she stepped out of the shower. Wrapping herself in a towel, she lifted the receiver in the hallway, hearing the voice of Rod Cameron telling her not to hang up.

'Please. Just give me a minute to explain. I can't talk for long but I had to talk to you, to explain.'

'Look,' she said, 'I don't think that an explanation is called for, do you? After all, I have told you I will no longer go on as we were. I see no point in it. That last weekend convinced me ...'

He stopped her.

'At least meet me for a drink. I could be there by ten or just after. Say you will. Hear me out. For Christ's sake, that's not too much to ask, is it?'

She heard herself reply, one part of her persuaded to accept, dividing her earlier uncommitted self and her new found self esteem.

'No. I've told you it's better this way. Let it end. We can still be friends. I don't dislike you. If anything I dislike myself for having carried on the way we did. It was wrong and I am aware of that at least. It won't happen again.'

'Don't hang up. See me for lunch tomorrow. I'm free before one until three. Say you'll come. I'll book for two. Usual place.'

Again she wavered, a part of her longing to go.

'No. Please don't go on. I have to go. I am just out of the shower. Look...I need to go.'

She replaced the receiver, then left it off the hook. Turning back, she replaced it again. On the hallstand, the film she had taken in Oban stood ready to go for developing. Picking it up, she went through to the kitchen and binned it. Another furtive piece of evidence of their relationship out of her life. Hardly a photograph of him, almost all of them of her. Never together.

As she dressed, she tried hard to dismiss the nagging doubts that she felt. If only he did feel for her and had been single. If only. No. It was over. No more hiding. It was over. As eight thirty approached, she left the apartment and made her way across the city, down the Mound and across Princes Street, the sun sinking behind the spires at the West End, the light still strong, the evening warm, the long shadows beginning to creep up the sides of the buildings as she walked towards Fishers in Thistle Street. The restaurant was full, her friend Mary seated at a table close to the bar, the bottle of wine already dented and the bread basket empty.

'I'm starving. You're late. Don't tell me, he rang again?' She nodded.

'Half an hour ago. It was terrible. He wanted me to meet him here for dinner tonight or lunch tomorrow.'

'So ... ?'

'I told him it was over. Finally over - for me if not for him. I just can't take it any more. I'm beginning to hate myself. Thinking like a spy. Constantly reminding myself to guard my tongue, unable to react. Every minute thinking I'm being watched. It all comes from the last few months of hiding in corners, watching out for the cameras. It's a nightmare. Now I've made my decision, I feel much better. Hurting, but relieved that it's over.'

'He's still very handsome. Say what you like. A guy like that won't change. His wife almost certainly knows the score, even if she doesn't acknowledge it.'

'Let's forget about it. I want to hear your news. How is Alex? No ring yet, I see. You'll be fifty and pregnant for the tenth time before the idea of marriage occurs to him.' They laughed, the waiter approaching to take their orders.

'Good evening! Don't tell me ladies. One Caesar salad and one deep fried goat's cheese, followed by "frito misto di mare" for two. Oh! I nearly forgot. One side salad of tomato and basil and garlic bread. Coming up!'

As they settled, now relaxed, the problems faded and softened as the frascati reached the spot. The restaurant continued to turn over covers, a steady stream of customers coming and going, as across the narrow street Rod Cameron stepped from the taxi, his arm around Sarah, his secretary.

'Oh. I guarantee this place. Never had a bad meal here. You'll see. The fish soup is excellent. Let's hope they kept our table. Matter of fact I've booked for two for tomorrow lunchtime. Some business to attend to. Good place to have a chat.'

Mary looked up, saw them approaching across the narrow space and on to the stairs and hoped that the potted palm would be wide enough to screen the broad figure of the Minister for Education as he climbed unhurriedly into the room at the back, his hand resting lightly on the beautiful backside of the elegant Sarah as he steered her to a secluded corner in the rear. Across the room, the quick glance of the head waiter was rewarded as he realised that the Minister's entrance had gone unnoticed by Sally, all his customers happy and contented; for the moment.

Gus Simpson was already at the bar in The Doric. As Gregor strode in, all heads turned, his tall broad frame, the all-too-familiar jacket and striking hair instantly recognisable features of the best loved man in Scotland. Eyes quickly dropped, as conversations were resumed, his privacy respected, no pointing fingers or uninvited intrusions ever likely to surface to disturb his rare appearances in pubs and restaurants across the city. On occasion, he would be seen swinging down Princes Street or heading up the Mound, his characteristic stride recognisable at a hundred paces, head high, returning the smiles and waves from well wishers as he headed back to his office on the Rock.

Refusing to own a car, he was seldom seen in public, his all too frequent appearances on television more than compensating for the lack of face-to-face encounters on the streets and alleyways of Edinburgh. On occasions, his presence would be welcomed in the Rose Street pubs and watering holes, where informed debate and intelligent discussion continued a long tradition of often heated argument on every subject from the politics of the day to arts and literature.

On these occasions, he became just another pundit, his views expressed as an individual, leaving aside party matters, the fellowship of like minds more important than dissension and controversy in any conversation. Not that he was slow to respond if he felt the need. In his earlier days at university his debating skills had been honed to a fine edge, his ability to see through the rhetoric used to defuse an argument and still many an opponent. In his company, even his closest friends took great care to be informed and well versed, leaving loose talk and speculation to others, in favour of accurate and considered reporting

At an earlier time, his regular "flytings" through the letters pages of the national dailies were a frequent source of ready wit and thought provoking entertainment paving the way for his entry into politics as a popular figure who did not mince his words or bend the truth to score a point. By the age of forty five he had achieved a record in devolved government that had clearly identified him to all who cared as a potential leader of the country, and one to be relied on and turned to, to lead the nation through the maze of issues clouding the emergence into total independence.

The barman raised his hand in greeting.

'Mr McLeod. Please. Over here, if you will.'

Gus turned and greeted his old friend, smiles and "hellos" reaching down the bar from others standing around. He gave a general wave of his arm in salute.

'Gus. How are you?'

'Fine. Fine. I was wondering the same about you. Fiona tells me you are overworking, too many long nights in the office, and not enough rest. Take care. Casualties in your line of business are all too frequent.'

'At least we tend to drop dead less often than journalists, if only because there are fewer of us!'

They laughed together, the mood relaxing instantly, a drink placed in his hand and an hour of good hearty eating and socialising to look forward to.

'Fiona suggested it, in fact. Said I should drag you out of the office, take you for a long walk; "on a lead if necessary" was how she put it.'

'Ah, the lovely Fiona. If only I had more like her around me. Always wanted a daughter, but never had the luck. More's the pity.

But enough of this rubbish. What's the news? Did you read Jackson's announcement? What's he up to? Eh?'

They moved off to the table by the window, still talking. At the bar the sense of loss was tangible. Away from the immediate shoulder-to-shoulder of the crowded bar, they sat quietly in conversation, giving no hint or clue to the curious onlooker of the content or tone of their exchanges. After some time they returned to the subject of the Jackson announcement.

'It's a mystery. Why should he choose now, of all times, to announce a resumption of manned space flights? I suppose they still have a long way to go before they reconsider a landing on Mars; so, the Moon is still their only training ground. Their claim to be testing equipment is plausible I suppose, and that bit about being there to welcome the *Caliban* crew with an interstellar handshake was damn good copy. Made the front pages around the world. Whether they can achieve it in time is questionable.'

Gregor, surprised, looked up as he replied.

'Unless of course, it has been planned for some time, as I suspect it has.'

'No. I don't think it's been in the pipeline long. I had a word with a friend of mine in the Pentagon last week. His view, for what it's worth, is that they're going hard at it, all funding made available to NASA to go for a landing before Christmas. Jackson, it seems, wants to end his first term with a "spectacular", and the Moon shot seems to be his way of saying goodbye, if you can believe it.'

They ate in silence for a few minutes, Gus pouring wine freely into both glasses, the friendly long founded familiarity between them, the easy relationship apparent to all around. Gregor began again.

'Do you for one moment believe that there is any substance whatsoever to the popular claims flying around everywhere these days that they never in fact landed on the Moon; that they failed in the end despite all their efforts? Now, don't think for one moment that I doubt them. I was around then as well. But, consider if you will ...'

'Now, hold on there. They *definitely* made it to the Moon.

*Nobody* disputes that. The evidence is simply too overwhelming. Everything stacks up. Why should they have lied? It would eventually have had to come out if there had been any funny business. You couldn't keep that kind of thing a secret for long, and it would only be a matter of time before somebody else landed on the Moon. The fact that we will be the second nation to make the journey is hardly ground breaking news either. The fact that we are a tiny state paying for it ourselves, certainly is.'

Gregor was thoughtful.

'Let us suppose for one moment that they failed to reach the surface.'

He held up his hand at Gus's protest.

'I said, just *suppose*. Let's imagine for one moment that, for one reason or another, they could not land, found instead that they had failed in their mission and needed a way out. I imagine that manufacturing the evidence would be all too easy. Wouldn't it?'

'I suppose so. It's been done before. Every bloody film maker in the world has built a Moonscape at one time or another. But you're surely not...? A great nation like the United States would have nothing to gain from such a deception. It would be an enormous risk. The Russians at the time might just as easily have turned their attentions to a Moon landing instead of building the Mia space lab. It makes no sense.'

'No sense at all. I agree. Unless they had failed their administration, and their president, and decided to opt for silence.' Gus looked up, suddenly aware that the subject had moved on from hypothesis to statement of likely fact, and that Gregor was serious.

'Gregor. Come on. Be realistic.' Gus looked at him with a mixture of incredulity and amazement.

'Hold on. I am not saying they *didn't* do it. What I am asking you is this. If you were told that proof existed that it had all been faked would you, sitting here now, shown the facts, believe it or not?'

'You're asking me if I believe in Hiroshima or the battle of Hastings or ... These things are undisputed for heaven's sake. What proof? It would need to be damn convincing proof!'

'Yes. I know. But just suppose. Just suppose I proved it to you incontrovertibly. No doubts remaining. No room for error. Would you be able to accept it, rejecting your previous firmly held views on the Americans having landed on the Moon?'

'Gregor. Come on; you're beginning to sound like those ravers who believe the world is flat. But ...'

He hesitated, considering the options.

'I suppose ... if the proof was sufficiently strong and tested; shown to be accurate and irrefutable ... then, I suppose, that conversion to the truth would be fairly quick.'

'Exactly! You see? You would be swayed. You would accept the proof after testing and weighing up the argument. Your earlier solidly held views would be dismissed out of hand; rejected as fallible. Am I right?'

'Yes. In essence you're right. But where are you leading me, where is this thing going ...?'

' ... and if I could convince you that the Moon landing was a set-up could I just as easily persuade you that, say, Hiroshima had also been manufactured?'

'No! Certainly not. The facts surrounding Hiroshima are just too terrible to dismiss. It effectively ended the Second World War for Christ's sake.'

Gregor stopped him, bringing the discussion down to a quieter level, leaning forward, eagerly pursuing his argument.

'And you'd be right. Because it *can* be researched. It happened *here*, under our noses and not out there in the furthest reaches of space. Because it can be checked out. The evidence is all around us. The test after test that followed; the cold war race to develop weapons of mass destruction, all the result of the success of the first atomic bomb. The truth cannot be contested. Am I right again?'

Gus looked at him long and hard. This was a rare glimpse of a Gregor McLeod he had only seen once or twice before.

'Yes.'

'But the only proof I could offer you of events on the Moon would be photographic essentially in nature. Yes? Anything I had to show you would be, by definition, images, recorded pictures or sound recordings that could be readily manufactured. Am I right?'

'I suppose so.'

'Even recordings? Television footage? All images that *could* be faked? Yes?'

'Yes. OK. But what are you getting at?'

'Do you have anything at all to offer, other than recorded images and transmissions to convince me that the Americans landed on the Moon? Do we have anything by way of artefacts that tells us that they were successful?'

'There are the Moon rocks, widely distributed to universities and research centres around the world.'

'…and shown to be no different from rock formations found here on earth. Am I right?'

'Possibly. I don't know. I've never been inclined to look into it in any great depth.'

'So? As a newspaper man, what can you give me other than generally accepted views and beliefs to show that the Americans landed on the Moon? Not a great deal, I imagine.'

Gus was silent for a bit.

'Is it important? Are you trying to tell me you know something I *don't* know? Is that why we're going to the Moon? Why would anyone go to the length of manufacturing enormous masses of evidence in support of a Moon shot that they could simply have avoided, by just walking away. They didn't have to go to the Moon after all. They could have announced a cancellation. Disappointing I suppose, but practical.'

He paused again, looking at his old friend, recognising that behind the smile was a question that needed answering.

'But, I suppose they felt that they had to go on. Kennedy, as we know, had virtually staked his Presidency on it. I can still, to this day, see him giving assurances that they would do it; that they would succeed. And everybody had to go along with it, I suppose, after the assassination. Time was short. They had to succeed. The pressure on them to get it right must have been enormous. Under the circumstances … if, and I stress *only if*, they saw failure looming, I believe that somewhere along the line someone *might* have made the decision to get the cameras rolling, setting up the evidence; just in case…'

Gregor waited for him to finish, then leaned forward with a wry smile on his face.

'Mr Simpson. I hope you're not trying to convince me that the Americans never landed on the Moon? If so, you will have just spoiled a very pleasant lunch.'

They were still laughing as they separated on the pavement outside, Gus returning to the office and Gregor heading off to a meeting with his lawyers. For the remainder of the afternoon Gus Simpson sat deep in thought, the conversation with his old friend still fresh in his mind as he questioned whether or not the First Minister of State had any immediate plans for getting into the film business, or whether in his advancing years he was simply preparing the ground for yet another of his intricately configured manoeuvrings.

# 15

Nathan Jackson listened carefully as he was briefed on developments at Cape Kennedy and at other centres across the country where the components for the Moon shot were being prepared and assembled. With the approval of the House of Representatives now assured, his plans for allocating funding to the newly resuscitated programme for manned flights were now firmly underway, all systems at "go", and his hopes for a landing on the Moon ahead of the Scottish launch apparently supported and strengthened by the latest reports reaching his desk from everyone concerned with the project.

Now seated with Tom Sherman and Sam Cavanagh from NASA, Arnold Denham, his National Security Advisor and Joe Skinner from the C.I.A., Dale Johnson, his Secretary of State, the Under Secretary of State, Elmer Franklin, and Joe Levin from the Pentagon, he was at ease surrounded by America's finest. Sam Cavanagh was wrapping up the session.

'So there we are Mr President. We have taken your instructions on board, and we are now pushing as hard as we dare to affect a lift off for the Moon by November 27th. Plans are well advanced in all sectors, staff have been recruited and we have secured the services of men and women who have established expertise in the field.

'We are, as you know, currently building the new descent vehicle which we will use to land on the surface of the Moon, carrying with us all of the necessary bits and pieces ...'

At this he paused, coughing slightly as if embarrassed.

' ... all the artefacts that we require to ensure that ...'

At this juncture, he was interrupted by Jackson, leaning forward over the desk, his face serious, hands clasped in front of him.

'What you mean to say is, "to plant the essential evidence", don't you?'

Sam Cavanagh managed a weak smile, the rebuke causing untold pain to already stretched nerve endings in his neck and lower back. He wriggled in his seat.

'All I am saying is we are on target to carry out your instructions, which hopefully, will result in America placing a man on the Moon again,'

At this, he noticeably bit his lip. Jackson was staring at him, shaking his head.

'I, of course, mean placing a manned vehicle on the Moon by the end of November.'

He struggled to a close, the effort showing on his sweat lined brow, his hair damp and his skin pale.

'Gentlemen, I am heartened by what I have heard here today. I remind you, all of you, that we must not fail. Tom, I want you to report to Dale here on a daily basis. He will inform me if anything requires my attention. That is all. Thank you.'

The assembly rose to leave.

'Oh. Franklin, and you, Dale. Please. If you don't mind? Give me a moment longer of your time.'

The two men sat down again. Outside in the corridor, Paul Burke stood to one side as the members left the Oval Office. As the bodyguard appointed to Elmer Franklin, he was no stranger to the White House.

Seated around the desk, Jackson turned to Franklin.

'Franklin. I believe that you have been briefed this morning on the reasons for our particular and rather sudden interest in returning to the Moon at this time. I understand that it came as a great shock to you. I can only say that I was also shocked by the news. I trust that you understand the need for this matter to remain strictly between us and the others who were here just now. No word must leak out, to anyone. Is that understood?'

'Yes Sir. That was made clear to me. On that other matter we discussed ...' He paused, uncertain of how to go on.

'As you know I did not personally travel to Scotland. Instead, the two agents who accompanied me to London visited the place after arrangements had been made and were treated most kindly. Our Ambassador in London and the new Consul in Edinburgh were very relieved that permission for the visit was so readily granted. As you are aware from my reports to you, they were shown around the establishments in question, and they made no secret of their general interest in the programme. They confirmed to me that the Scots are indeed heading for the Moon in November and look certain ...'

At this, Jackson held up his hand.

'Yes. I've read your reports. What concerns us now is the success of our own mission. We must be sure that we are there in place to welcome them when they arrive. If,' he added, 'they manage to find the landing site. If, as we are led to believe, their launch date is behind our own we will have no problem. Our concerns would however begin to surface if, for any reason, our plans were to be delayed. With this in mind, we want you to return to Scotland to monitor their progress first hand. Take your agent with you. You will be contacted by Joe Skinner in the event that we have a fresh mission for you to undertake. Stay there until we contact you.'

He was looking away, choosing to avoid eye contact, failing to clarify his meaning, preferring instead to leave the ambiguity to speak for itself, the echoes of it causing drums to resound in Franklin's fevered head.

He continued, distracted, his mind seeking the solution to the problem that he so badly needed.

'You see, Elmer, we are uncertain if we can get our act together sufficiently early to achieve lift off with any certainty of success by November. We need more time. Oh, I read the look on your face. Yes. I know. I have read your report. But this is a dangerous time for our great nation. I believe that any means at our disposal should be used, and will be used to achieve our ends.'

Elmer Franklin straightened his back, as he began to fear the worst. He nodded unhappily.

'So you see if it should transpire ... technical hitch or some other contrivance ... many a slip between cup and lip ...'

Franklin had stopped listening. Jackson paused again, unsure if the look of horror on Franklin's face was a reliable indicator of his ability to mastermind so delicate an operation.

' ... find some way ... something along these lines. You know the sort of thing. Your man must surely ... and in the end reflect suitably on this great nation of ours allowing us to ...'

He hesitated again, unable to wind up his monologue or finish the sentence.

'... to lead the way.'

Dale Johnson was speaking at the same time.

'We have tried to ascertain if any of their subcontractors are associated with any American suppliers. If so, we could perhaps have exerted pressure on them to affect a delay. We found nothing. So, as you will realise we are truly in a jam.'

He began thumbing through the flimsy report.

'This Fiona McLeod? She is the niece of the First Minister, I believe?'

'She is. And her father is director of the project. The agent, Paul Burke, had the opportunity to meet several of the leading project managers and directors during his stay. It is not inconceivable that he could affect entry for a second time either by invitation or by ...'

He left the word unsaid.

'... to arrange something.'

His voice tailed off, his knees and his hands now shaking visibly.

'One other thing,' said Nathan Jackson.

'You must see Ryder again, taking the agent with you. Spend time in England. Take a break. Visit your daughter. Give your man some time off. No great rush. But do it! Explain to John Ryder that we got it wrong and that we regret raising the issue as we did. Explain to him that we are resuming manned flights with a view to conducting essential scientific experiments in space all aimed at placing a crew on Mars by the end of the decade. Whilst you are there, get up to Scotland. We can arrange a formal invitation if it helps. Offer them every assistance. Your agent can act as liaison officer between NASA and their directors. Meet with their First Minister. Talk with him. Discuss cooperation. Meet his boffins. Try to keep us informed on a daily basis. Do I make myself clear?'

With this, he nodded to the others and exited the room. They both stood, Franklin turning slowly to look at Dale Johnson.

'A shooting war might have been easier in the long run,' he said, still shaking.

Rab sat in the back of the limousine surveying the scenery as he was whisked away from Queen Street Station and over to Pacific Quay, where fame and fortune surely awaited him. Susan's attempts at repairing the damage caused by years of neglect and a general failure to observe even the mildest forms of personal hygiene, had resulted in a Rab Nicol who smelled of rose water, carbolic and new leather. Looking down at his feet, the new shoes smiled back at him. Tight but shining fair. The two hours sitting on the edge of the bed, while his jacket and trousers were laundered and pressed was surely time well spent; his T-shirt now a sparkling off-white on his hairy chest; a bath and fresh underwear resisted but adopted.

At the mention of a haircut, Rab had drawn the line.

'Always dae it masel', Doll. Never been tae a barber's fur years. Canny stand the chit chat an' the aftershave. Drives me mad. Honest, it does!'

Not to be outdone, determined to see her new man decked out for his leap to stardom, the scissors came out and an hour later Rab faced the mirror in a confrontation of wills, his true self struggling to relate to the shining schoolboy innocence that returned his scowls.

'No. Honest. It's great. Naw really. It's great. Whit ah've always wanted. Aye, yer a dab hand wi' they scissors, so ye are.'

Sneaking a further betrayed glance at the mirror an hour later, Rab was less incensed.

'Efter a' doll, if ma public wishes fur me tae appear on telly, who am I tae challenge ma fate? Change may well be a necessary evil at this time in ma career.'

And so saying, they had departed for the "Skite" to refresh themselves before the evening performance.

Sitting now beside him, excited and proud, fat Susan watched as the limo deposited them at the front doors. The chauffeur rushed round to open the door.

'This way, Madam.'

'Ma name's Rab. Aye, Rab Nicol. Ah'm expected. Ah've tae be on the Kirsty Monroe show at eight o'clock. Aye. Yer right. Sorry.'

The porter at the reception desk eyed them warily. Used to

dealing with oddballs and freaks he immediately classified them as unemployed New Labour. Phone calls were made. They waited.

'If you will just follow the gentleman ...'

The director led them into the hospitality room, the drinks handed around, the other members of the panel sizing them up warily.

'The name's Nicol. Oh aye? Is that a fact? Nae kiddin'? Member o' Parliament no less. Ah see. No. Nae problem, hen.'

He was led off to the make up room, grinning and waving goodbye to Susan as he went.

'Make up. Make up? Whit next. As a matter o' fact, ah wisnae expectin' that like. Real fillum star stuff this! Aye. Jist stick it oan me hen. Never you mind. Making me look like Cary Grant, so ye are.'

The studio was large, the packed audience grouped in a half circle, the members of the panel and the hostess seated on sofas and easy chairs, appearing relaxed, professional and dutiful. Rab was ushered into a place between the Honourable Member and the blonde reporter. Across from him sat a familiar face whose name he had forgotten, his public school accent adequate identification in the short term. Near him Murdo Sinclair sat in conversation with Kirsty Monroe.

Rab was entranced. The lights, the cameras, the crowds. This was the life. No more hanging around in scabby pubs for him. His audience demanded something better. Still grinning from ear to ear he waved at the rows of faces recognising the small support group from the "Skite", feeling the rich weave of the studio furniture under his hand, hearing the familiar voice of the show's hostess, completely overwhelmed by the aura of high profile show business buzz that had suddenly descended on him.

'... so tonight we hope to allay those doubts in open discussion on the subject of America's flights to the Moon, both past and present, what this means for Scotland's entry into the space era and for the future of manned journeys to other parts of the solar system. As well, we will be showing you some recently uncovered footage of the early landings which should erase for all time the fanciful notions that are often expressed that America never quite made it to the Moon.'

There was general laughter around the studio, the camera men exchanging grins and quiet in-house signals with each other.

'... so there we have it, experts from all walks of life gathered together tonight to answer your questions and give their opinions on whether or not Scotland should be embarking on manned flights and inevitably on the age old question ... "is there anybody out there?" Before we move on to your questions let us remind ourselves once more of that historic moment when Gregor McLeod announced to a stunned House that Scotland seriously intended to reach for the stars.'

The studio quietened and darkened, the huge split screen showing mixed images over the voice of Gregor McLeod announcing his intention to place men on the Moon at the end of November. The shots of *Caliban* sitting under wraps in North Uist and the views of the first landings of the prototype vehicle in Uzbekistan were followed by the Saltire on the side coming into view. The audience broke into spontaneous applause as the clip ended.

'James Brodie from Stirling. My question concerns the timing of the whole thing. Just because we can do it, is this any reason for going to the Moon at this time? Like Everest, the Moon has already in one sense been conquered, I mean ...'

'Mr Sinclair?'

Kirsty Monroe was inviting Murdo to respond for the panel. Rab's face was filled with wonder, the realisation that he was rubbing shoulders with the truly informed beginning to dawn on him. The small step from "the Skite" to the public arena had become a giant leap from running off at the mouth to assembling his thoughts into meaningful statements. Waves of nausea began to roll over him, the blushes he was experiencing and the truth of his predicament sending noticeable tremors coursing through his body as he wriggled uncomfortably, dreading the pointing finger that would fall on him ... when?

'Well, we can't begin to make comparisons with the conquest of Everest or any other event for that matter. This adventure for Scotland marks a time in our history when, in effect, we will see the culmination of centuries of engineering development, the end product of enquiring minds, a wish fulfilled in a sense. We should all see it as a great achievement, as a step forward for science and learning. The flight in itself is less important to my mind than the years of success in defining for ourselves the problems associated with space exploration, and the methods that we have used across a wide range of disciplines in many fields of science and engineering to resolve the many, many problems that we have had to face in maturing our plans for developing fuels and rockets that would fulfil our original agenda of competing in the field of satellite launch technology.'

The words were ringing in Rab's head. The ease with which the other speakers engaged with the audience and each other, his isolation as he sat quietly like some schoolboy outside the headmaster's office, as yet uncommitted, dreading the moment when the ground would open and he would be swallowed up. For a second he questioned the existence of a hell designed for blaggards and liars, seeing himself caught in consuming fires.

'Malcolm Bailly, from Glasgow. Does the panel not agree that the Scots as a nation have always been the last people on earth to blow their own trumpets, and that this expedition, with its high profile and world wide publicity only serves to paint a picture of a small country with a very high opinion of itself, showing off to the rest of the world in a quite shameful way? Would it not be better all round if we had stuck the money into something quieter and altogether more positive, such as developing an international soccer team that might one day make us all proud in a way that we can all relate to?'

There was loud laughter and applause from the audience, the panel seen to be joining in the merriment.

'Mr Paterson, perhaps you might care to *field* this question given your days in Premiership football.'

'Thank you. Scotland *does* deserve a better football team. I couldn't agree with you more! What she does *not* deserve is this philandering and riotous behaviour from those in charge up at the Rock. Whether or no' we qualify fur the World Cup this time around is really neither here nor there. What *is* important is that we should

159

all recognise that the money invested in this crazy expedition could have been better spent in setting up sports centres and in improving the stadia that we have inherited around the country. We failed as a nation to attract the last World Cup in two thousand and ten, because we could not achieve even the basic requirements as laid down by FIFA for hosting the competition. It was a disgrace which thankfully we have now began to address. If the Scottish Socialist Party had been in charge at that time, I can assure you that...'

'Thank you Mr Paterson. And now, the lady in the pink top? Yes, you. Your hand was raised?'

Fat Susan leaned forward her face bright and suddenly intelligent, her Southern States accent immediately receiving hushed attention.

'I have a question for Mr Nicol. Your speaker earlier this evening, MSP Mr Johnson, was very insistent that the evidence of the success of the Americans in the late sixties in landing on the Moon was so overwhelming as to warrant dismissal of any criticism on the grounds that such criticism was the work of cranks and attention seekers. *If* that evidence is so overwhelming, why is it that the general public around the world are becoming increasingly aware of the current popular outpourings of disbelief, aided and abetted by some of the most informed men in science, that the claims of the Americans that they successfully landed on the Moon are at the very least open to considerable doubt? Does Mr Nicol believe that there is any charge to answer on the issue of whether or not the Americans landed on the Moon?'

'Mr Nicol ... ?'

Kirsty Monroe was sensing the heightened interest of the audience, that tell-tale quietening of the room hinting that here was a question of real interest to the majority of the audience. At the same time her disquiet with the selection of Robert Nicol as suitable material for contributing anything worthwhile to a televised debate on her weekly show was beginning to surface.

'Mr Nicol ... ?'

Rab was in a trance, her words reaching him through a red coloured mist, the studio lights blinding him, his discomfort shrouding his situation. Startled, he heard only the final few words of Susan's question, his mind racing to catch up with the debate, the terror he was now feeling beginning to take over his reason, the fight he was facing in quelling the rising Guinness beginning to occupy most of his conscious efforts. He heard his voice emerging from somewhere on the sofa beside him as he turned his full attention to the reply. Struggling to master his feelings, fighting the drowning suffocation, he suddenly surfaced, the craft that had seen him through years of subtle wheedling and scrounging forcing its way to the forefront of his conscious being, leaving him instantly aware, in command of himself and coldly focused on the importance of his appearance on this, a network presentation that would give him the opportunity to have his case heard and judged by all. Stretching, his head held high, his face serious, his composure now evident he reached for the script in his head that had been so thoroughly honed in the back room of the "Skite".

'The question is very interestin' and it is one I have thoughtfully considered fur some time now. In ma opinion the Yanks did not land on the Moon.'

At this there was an immediate response from the audience. This was what they had been waiting for, an entertainment that defied the balanced logic of the panel, leaping the boundaries of commonsense and soaring off into the wide open spaces of speculation, improbable science and dubious half truth.

'If we consider a' the available evidence and the many articles that huv been dedicated tae the subject, it is clear tae me that they never made it tae the Moon. Fur wan thing, the photies they took were obviously faked. They were too perfect. The position o' the sun in some o' the fillums they showed was wrong. The double shadows under the lunar lander ... Fur Christ's sake, it's obvious that somewhere along the line there has been duplicity and evidence o' a cover up no' tae mention ...'

At this point, Kirsty Monroe interrupted him.

'Well, if I can pause you there for a moment Mr Nicol, perhaps we could just take a look at some recently released footage by NASA that followed that first historic landing and which clearly shows from a fixed camera set up on the surface, the L. E. M. and the astronauts going about their business shortly after descending from the lunar lander.'

All eyes turned towards the large screen, the Moonscape clearly seen, the harsh light, the darkened sky, the strange sharpness of the images, the slow deliberate movements, the muffled exchanges between the astronauts, the placing of the flag, and the silent eeriness all too apparent to the audience in their cosy surroundings. Their attention was riveted to the screen. It faded and stopped. All eyes returned to Rab.

'Very interestin'. But it only confirms much o' whit ah huv been sayin'. The double shadows, the sun up there when it should huv been doon here... It's jist as ah said. Tae me, an' it's only ma opinion, that tells us nothin'. An' another thing. Where were the stars? We're telt that frae the Moon the lack of atmosphere allows ye tae see every bloody star in the sky. Did any o' you see any stars?'

He turned slowly to address the panel. Looking distinctly uncomfortable, they were not lining up to reply to him. Heads were turned away, some appearing to be giving his proposition due consideration, others pleading disinterest and dismay.

'So tell me. Where are the stars? And if we look again. Look at their gloves. The size o' bloody footballs. Try takin' a photie wi' gloves like that. Ye couldnae feel a red hot poker through gloves like that.'

The film had been rewound and was being screened again in the light of the direction the debate was taking, the director beginning to sense controversy, seeing the ratings rise as the audience began to fall in line behind the T-shirt with the fancy hair do.

'... an' another thing. Look at the flag wavin' its wee heid aff, and not a breath o' wind tae help it. An' look. Look there. Ye see? See they shadows. The shadows on the rocks and the shadow cast by the big man there; they're goin' in two different directions. But there can only ever be one source of light up there. Our sun!'

He turned to the audience in disbelief, they responding to him in similar fashion.

Rab was now in full flight, standing, in his mind back once

more holding the floor at the "Skite", his talent rising, his ability to conjure the questions, to phrase the obvious and challenge the probability, all emerging in an easy flow of furious rhetoric that took over the debate turning the panel into helpless observers, demoting them to the level of the punters in the audience.

'So. Ah ask yees all again. Where are the stars? Gone? Painted oot? Buggered aff fur a cup o' tea? Naw. Gone tae bye-byes maybe? An' the flag, it's *still* waving in the wind.'

He paused again, half turning, giving the audience his quizzical look.

'And, I wid remind yees all that in zero atmosphere there can *be* no wind.'

Rab was enjoying himself, Kirsty Monroe desperately trying to regain the initiative, the director restraining her, allowing the piracy to continue for as long as it captivated the imagination of the audience.

'Mr Nicol, perhaps we could have an opinion from Mr Sinclair on the issues you have raised. Whilst your views are obviously popular, they do need analysing and we are not equipped here this evening for an in-depth technical analysis of the film or the many contentious issues that you have raised.'

There was a round of fierce applause as Rab sat down, smiling but still floating, the experience exhilarating, the applause rewarding and warming. Fat Susan was beaming. The few supporters from the "Skite" were on their feet.

'More. More.'

Kirsty Monroe was pleading for silence, Murdo Sinclair trying to ease himself into the debate, but struggling against the general level of chatter that was turning it into something approaching a political rally.

'Well, of course, we are all familiar with the conspiracy theory surrounding the Moon shots, we have all seen the documentaries and heard the endless arguments expressed from Hollywood on the probability that the Americans failed in their many attempts to land on the Moon. What I can tell you, is that *we* will succeed, and I have no doubts at all that we will find evidence of the American landings when we get there. All such conspiracies hold and grip the attention of the public at large from time to time. And, sad to say, the rumours are easy to come by, the dissemination easy to effect. Of course, without such rumours, life might be very dull. I believe that we, all of us initiate a search for such denials in order to enliven our existence, to confirm to ourselves that we do not believe everything that we read or everything that we are told, and to underline and reinforce our views that we are all, thankfully, curious and inquisitive beings.'

'Aye. Too bloody true. But can you answer the questions? Where were the stars? Why is there two shadows fur everythin'? Ye see, people are bound tae ask these questions. An' don't forget, when Kipper knickers said that the earth wisnae in the middle o' the solar system, they burned him fur his trouble. But everybody at the time knew that he wis right. Instinctively. So they did. The very dugs in the street knew that he wis right. Ye know … ,' he said, controlling his emotions,

' … sometimes, the truth can be starin' us a' in the face, an' we're no' capable o' seein' it.'

Murdo was smiling, the others huffing their displeasure at being so artlessly upstaged.

'Mr Nicol, Rab. I cannot give you the answers that you require right at this moment in time, but I will make a point of checking out the facts. When I have the answers you will be the first to know.'

'Right on, Jimmie. That's fine wi' me.'

The audience were off again, encouraging the debate, longing for Rab to come back with more of the same.

'So before we wind up the show for this week, may I take this opportunity to thank the members of the panel and you the studio audience for being here this evening. We wish you a pleasant evening, and remind you that our show in two week's time will continue this evening's debate with First Minister Gregor McLeod and his brother Hamish, the director of the installation at North Uist. Until then, this is Kirsty Monroe bidding you all goodnight.'

As Rab rejoined Susan and the regulars from the "Skite", there was no doubt in their minds that the final score reflected game, set and match to their champion. In the control booth, the director made a mental note to contact Rab about appearing on the next show.

Back at the "Skite" in Edinburgh, the euphoria continued, the pub jammed with punters, the late licence intended to maintain service until their hero returned to the cheers of his faithful followers. Intent on revelling the night away, they were secure in the firm belief that their mentor had yet again demonstrated the power of common sense over academic learning, to a record audience, at that very moment jamming the lines into the switchboard at Television Centre demanding tickets for the next show. As far as Rab was concerned, it was unlikely to ever get any better.

# 16

Gregor McLeod sat with his Cabinet in the conference room adjoining his office. The meeting was well into its second hour, as junior ministers and secretaries entered and exited, feeding the ministers with data and reports. As usual, discussions were informal and frank, opinions freely expressed, offence seldom intended or taken. Having risen in the ranks together, they knew each other well, some having served in previous administrations before jumping ship to join the swelling ranks of the Independence Party.

The sudden announcement by Gregor of the voyage to the Moon, had taken a few of them entirely by surprise. Gregor had spent many patient hours massaging egos and bolstering the self esteem of those among them who felt that they should have been consulted. With explanations given, and apologies registered, reputations restored and attended to, the discussions had now settled on the subject of the forthcoming elections, the focus centering on the publication of their revised manifesto for the coming term.

'Not that we ever stick to any of it. Publishing a re-jigged manifesto is a waste of Party funds. When did we ever really fulfil our promises? I'm not saying that I disagree with the way we operate; it just seems so utterly unnecessary for us to promote ourselves given the popularity of the party at this point in time. If we don't walk this election, I will resign for all time to come.'

John Mason, the Minister for Health and Safety, sat down to loud laughter and cries of ...

'Resign! Resign now!'

Gregor looked down the table, amused but saying nothing, his mind on other matters. For most of the morning, he had been focused on the way ahead in deciding how much to leak and when to the men and women in front of him. Harry Millar, life long friend and party activist from their shared years together at university; Margaret McIver, Minister for Transport and the Environment, and a strong party member for as long as he could remember. All of them good workers, independently minded, contentious and difficult on occasion, but united in their lifelong commitment to total independence for Scotland.

Fierce argument within his Cabinet had followed his surprise announcement to the House on the coming launch; an announcement that had shocked his closest colleagues and had almost split the party, salvaged only at the eleventh hour by his pleading and coercing, his ability to demonstrate good cause, and by his overall authority in matters that had come to be identified as part of his personal crusade for the betterment of Scotland and her peoples.

Inevitably, they all recognised that in working alongside Gregor McLeod, there was no place in their coalition for petty squabbles or grievances. Under Gregor, life simply and irrepressibly went on. Notwithstanding their continuing support for his announcement, he knew that all too soon he would have to bring them on board to share his burden and shoulder a share of the responsibility for his proposals; proposals which could backfire dramatically if he failed to carry them through to a conclusion. For the moment, they knew very little, his closest allies choosing to wait, knowing that it would all come out in the course of time.

John Mason was off again.

'We will carry the country and you know it. They all know it's a foregone conclusion. The polls put us too far ahead, even with months to go. And with the success of these latest launches and the Moon landing to add to our long line of credits, who is there at present, who could begin to dent our record given the increased public awareness, not to mention the expansion in education and health?'

Gregor sighed.

'Nevertheless, we must continue to remind our fickle populace of the wonders in store from our party. Let's give them the revised manifesto, get it out of the way and get back to dealing with the things that matter. I tell you all now, that I will not spend a day longer than absolutely necessary in canvassing and electioneering, unless it goes along with a good dinner at the end of it.'

They all laughed. Gregor's reputation for looking after himself on electioneering tours was all too well recorded.

'Don't you worry, Gregor, we'll see to all of that.'

Margaret McIver had seen it all before, accompanying him on many a despairing haul across the country. But that had all changed with the leadership appointment of the man at the head of the table.

Gregor leaned forward, and they all listened.

'If we do win, I will go forward, but not for long. I want, in truth, to hand over to some of you younger bloods. I think it is time for me to put my feet up and get some fishing done.'

He stilled their protests with his hand.

'We couldn't be stronger as a party. There are enough of you who believe in what we have come to stand for to ensure that we will continue to survive, and to lead this country forward. How you arrange it is for you to decide. I know that you will decide well. I make no recommendations. There are no favourites in this Government. No teacher's pets.'

The reference to the opposition's political in-fighting caused laughter and some head shaking. Margaret McIver said it for all of them.

'We will miss you. Let's hope that you'll have a change of heart.' Gregor stood.

'That's for the future. No need to remind you all to keep mum about it in the meantime. I have a twelve thirty, and I have kept her waiting long enough. You will have to excuse me. Take your time. I will try to meet you all for lunch at one fifteen. Until then.'

He picked up his files and left the room, his secretary indicating on the way through to his office that his next meeting was overdue, and that his guest had arrived. A moment later, the door opened and Sally McIntosh put a tentative head around the doorway, unsure of her bearings, recognising the man behind the desk, his arm raised in greeting, motioning her forward. She closed the door and approached the desk. Meeting the First Minister was not usually included in the course of an ordinary day's work. He stood as she approached and they shook hands, she sitting and he coming around the desk to sit opposite her.

'Sally, this is our first meeting although I understand that you have been with the Ministry for some months. I thought we might have a little chat since there is something on my mind that you might be able to help me with. They tell me you are qualified in international law, highly qualified as well, I hear.'

He smiled, as her curiosity began to build.

'I don't recall seeing anything ...' she began.

'No. I haven't committed anything to paper. Not yet. I thought a quiet chat would be better, before I go as far as writing down what I have in mind. No. This matter is rather delicate and before I say anything to you, I have to tell you that it may ultimately involve you in exercising your considerable skills, setting you against some very heavy players on the international stage. It may also involve you in substantial travelling. Oh, don't worry, I have no doubts in my mind that you are eminently qualified to take on this task or I wouldn't be asking you. At the same time, this business is of the utmost importance and when I've finished briefing you over the course of the next few days, I will want you to consider very carefully what you're getting into, and whether or not you will want to do it. Incidentally, you will not be working alone. You'll have the necessary support when the time comes.'

She sat, intrigued by his statement.

'You see, for some time now I've had an idea that has recently been fleshed out and is coming along nicely, an idea that is both controversial and ...'

He paused before continuing, stroking his chin, unsure of whether or not to go on, to commit.

' ... likely to backfire on all of us as well.'

He watched her face, she showing no signs of concern, waiting patiently instead for him to go on. Nevertheless, he was certain that her mind was racing, although her eyes remained steady and her composure undisturbed.

'Before I bring you fully into the picture, there are several answers I require that concern you in your role as international lawyer. When I have the answers to these questions, we may take the subject further, but for the moment I would ask you to keep this between us. No other soul will be told. Is that clear?'

She nodded in agreement, searching his face for some

indication of his intentions, finding nothing there other than a concerned kindness.

'You see, some time ago, it occurred to me that ...'

An hour later they were still talking until the telephone interrupted.

'Gregor here. Yes. Ah. Lunch. I had forgotten.' He leaned across to her. 'Have you had lunch yet?' She shook her head.

'Tell Nancy to lay a separate table for two at the end of the dining room away from the pack. I am expecting a guest for lunch.'

He laughed and closed the line.

'Now where were we? Oh yes ...'

Taking her gently by the arm, he led her to the private lift and together they went down to the Ministers' dining room at the third level. Watching her enter the room, the Minister for Education watched with great interest as Gregor led her to the corner table, placing her chair under her, talking all the while. As they lunched, the room gradually emptied until they were alone. With her head reeling from the briefing, Sally McIntosh began to realise that her life would never be quite the same again.

'So I have to ask you. Will you be willing to go forward?'

Unsure of the total extent of the commitment and recognising that at every turn the possibility of failure would be ever-present, she hesitated for the briefest of seconds before answering.

'I think I had already committed to the idea before you so generously bribed me with lunch. When do we start?'

Early morning in the Scottish Lowlands, the dawn beginning to appear, the clouds along the horizon, deep red tinged and custard yellow. Sprawled across the lush meadows the scattered buildings of the Rosewell Institute were pale shadows against the dark sky. Here and there, security lighting illuminated an area of activity, vehicles appearing then retreating as the test area was prepared.

Sitting in the conference room and surveying the scene outside, Murdo Sinclair was entertaining his visitors. Gregor, Hamish, Gus Simpson and Fiona McLeod sat around the table, talking and drinking warm rich coffee, the aroma drifting down the wide corridors and lifting heads in tiny offices, where men and women in white coats prepared their computers in readiness for the seven o'clock test.

Gregor stood and moved to the window. The large doors to the main hanger were now opening and the test bed was being rolled out, the *Moonraker* sitting low like some athlete's discus, polished, sleek and beautiful. Six metres in diameter and three metres high at the centre she could carry two operators in comfort, the tiny cabin designed to simplify the layout of controls, the emphasis placed on order, simplicity and function. Around the lander, men were conducting final checks, ensuring that this, the final test, would be as near perfect as was humanly possible.

'Murdo, it looks stunning. Such a beautiful craft.'

Gregor turned towards him, smiling. They all moved over to the window, the security lights fading, the sun just beginning to appear through the trees that surrounded the site. Away in the distance the high wire fencing could now be seen.

'Yes. She is beautiful.'

Murdo was pensive, looking out to where the safety nets were being slowly raised into position.

'When you think how far she will travel as a passenger, making one relatively small journey down to the surface and back into orbit again, you really have to ask yourself if the millions we have spent are invested wisely ... Oh, I know. She can be used again. But I've yet to hear anybody around here talk about a *second* trip.'

'If everything goes according to plan, one trip will be all we'll need.' Gregor slapped him on the back.

'After that, you can go every weekend if you like. So, cheer up. This is your big day. And if it all goes well, I'll buy the lunch. When do we meet up with the crew? Which one of them will take her up?'

'Well, in fact, one of them, probably Sandy, will lift her up and the other will control the landing. We are programmed today to rise to around three hundred feet or so, then descending slowly, attempting to hover gently over the test area, until final touch-down. All in all, it will be a real test of the craft's ability to remain stable at all times. The hovering exercise is particularly important, since we may need to pick our spot carefully when we land on the Moon.'

The door opened, and the two test pilots, Sandy Martin and Colin Millar, entered the room. Murdo introduced them, the jovial atmosphere intensifying as they stayed for a coffee before making final preparations for the test. Gregor stood.

'Sandy and Colin, we wish you the very best for the test today, and when the big day dawns, I know that you will be carrying the hopes and prayers of the Scottish people with you. Murdo tells me that you could not be any better trained than you are at present. Whoever is finally selected to make the descent in the *Moonraker* will make history too as he sets foot on the Moon. But it's more than that. It represents the culmination of years of hard work, testing the skills and abilities of the men and women of this country to the limit, proving to ourselves and the rest of the world, that we are a force to be reckoned with. A force for good. Again, I wish you both, on behalf of your Government, a safe journey into space when the time comes.'

Colin replied for both of them.

'Well, as you will realise, we are both elated at the prospect of the journey. To have got through the course and to be finally selected is, well, after all the years in training… it's beyond our wildest dreams. We are ready. We know that. And we've discussed the question of "who goes first" when we reach orbit. We both agree that it is of no importance to either of us. We, both of us, have a job to do and we're proud to be associated with the programme. At the end of the day, a safe return is all I hope for.'

'Amen to that.' said Gregor.

Fiona led the way as they prepared to go to the bunker to watch the test. Murdo made his excuses, and the visitors were shown down to the viewing room on the edge of the landing area, the monitors around the room relaying the progress of the *Moonraker* from every conceivable angle. They sat as they waited, Fiona explaining everything to Gus, looking now towards the lander, as the men around the machine completed their checks and the three figures made their way to the door of the craft.

Gus Simpson was busy taking notes, his first experience of the innards of the Rosewell Institute promising good copy for his next feature. He and Gregor sat together, as eager as the rest for the test to begin. Suddenly a speaker on the console crackled into life as a commentary began to fill the room, the exchanges between the craft and the control centre being relayed to the visitors. Then they heard the faint murmur of the engines starting, the noise rising to a steady pulsating whine, the voices becoming more difficult to hear, and the excitement building around the Institute as everyone held their breath, waiting for the moment of lift off. Overhead, the helicopter monitoring and recording the ascent, sat ready to rise with the craft as it began its slow journey up and through the low cloud cover.

The steady voice of the controller was now directing the operation. They heard the countdown until the final seconds as the *Moonraker* lifted smoothly off the test bed and rose slowly, climbing above the buildings, until finally disappearing from view. They turned then to the monitors, continuing to observe the climb. Gus Simpson was entranced, he and Gregor, talking excitedly, noting the slowing of the ascent and the marginal side slip as the craft hovered high above the ground before beginning its descent again.

Returning to the viewing windows, they heard it approach, seeing the underside of the craft as it hovered ten feet above the sandy floor of the area. For a moment or two it was stationary, then it slipped to the side and everyone held their breath. From the speakers on the consoles, the strains of the Blue Danube waltz began to fill the room as the *Moonraker* dipped and weaved for a full minute in time to the music, laughter being exchanged between the controllers and the pilot.

Then it was down and a burst of applause came from those watching. They were led off to the hanger to greet the pilots, Hamish waltzing down the corridor with Fiona until the music stopped. Gregor was thinking.

'Success at last. The landing was now on. There were no further obstacles to overcome. With the *Caliban* almost ready he could give the order any time now.'

Hamish caught his eye.

'Feeling better? I thought so. If we are not ready now, we never will be. That was a remarkable demonstration. They've come a long way in three months. From six feet to three hundred. Not bad going, all things considered.'

He and Gregor exchanged smiles, content, both knowing that their plans were maturing well. Together they walked through the long corridors heading towards the hanger, the others trailing behind.

Climbing down from the *Moonraker*, the three stood on the sand shaking hands, well pleased with their efforts. As their flameproof visors were removed, Gregor was surprised to see Murdo Sinclair lead the others towards the hanger. As they came nearer, Hamish reached for Gregor's arm.

'I received a memo from him. It seems he feels that he qualifies to lead the launch crew on the day. Having seen him waltz I am sure he will have mastered the tango by the time they are ready to lift off.'

They exchanged smiles, everything passing between them unaided by words, their only concern, the success of the project.

'It's probably just as well. We would have had to bring the crew in on the objective sooner rather than later. If Murdo is to be at the helm, then it's time we brought them all fully into the picture. Let's have lunch tomorrow at the office. Make sure they are both there. There is someone else we need to take on board as well. I'll make sure she's there too.'

They stood side by side as the staff of the Rosewell Institute lined the great hanger, a steady beat of enthusiastic applause driving the starlings out into the open skies as the crew, the Minister and the Project Director walked confidently back into the hanger.

# 17

At one o'clock in the morning, the "Bletherin' Skite" was packed out, the beer flowing as the party atmosphere surrounding Rab's victorious rout of the panel members on the Kirsty Monroe Show entered its dying hours. Susan and Rab were in their usual seats, jackets discarded, the heat stifling, the glasses filling as they were lauded by all and sundry eager to share in their moment of glory. The more ardent punters and fans formed a protective ring around their leader as they probed him for the inside view of the show and its aftermath.

'Yes. It's true. I was approached by the producer regarding my part in next week's show. I telt him I would be in touch through ma agent. As far as ah'm concerned I learned nothin' tonight that I did not already know. As a matter o' fact I found the entire experience tae be a bloody waste o' good drinkin' time.'

A goodly cheer arose from the ranks of the faithful.

'Hi. Rab. That bit where the Sinclair guy wis contradictin' ye. When he said that he could explain yon thing aboot the shadows. Whit did he mean?'

Rab lowered his glass and considered the question.

'It wid seem that the fact that there *appears* tae be two sources o' light, is, in his mind, easily explained. He wis sayin' that it is entirely due to the perspective on the wide angled camera lenses that they wir usin', the distortion creating a false impression o' distance, resultin' in the picture that ah showed yees all.'

At this, he held up his hand.

'I am still not convinced. The shadows are too distinctly different, not only frae each other, but frae ither shadows roonaboot. In ma humble opinion, the evidence indicates a fraud and a cover up.'

The listeners edged forward, sensing another night of argument and dissension on Rab's pet subject of NASA's fraudulent claims of having conquered space, of having reached the Moon.

'There is another thing that ah wid like tae bring tae yer attention.' Holding a photograph in front of his hairy chest he raised one eyebrow to look at his followers.

'Here we see the astronaut comin' doon the ladder, dae we no? Now observe. Ye can see every detail o' his suit, ah'm ah right? Yes?'

He looked around for confirmation, nodding eventually.

'Yes. He is clearly in strong light, strong light which is evidently comin' frae *behind* him. No? Yes, he is! Now look here, in front o' him. What do we see?'

Again he paused for effect, waiting for several minutes while necks craned forward, looking for the truth they had missed.

'Well ah'll tell yees all. We see the darkest, blackest bloody shadow imaginable. Do we no'? Just look at it if ye will. Is that no' somethin'?'

His audience were staring at the photograph, the pub silent, the aura of Rab's presence filtering into the furthest recesses of every dusty nook and cranny.

'How is it, that he is perfectly visible but we can see bugger all o' the ship aroond him? Surely this bit here should be in the sunlight as well. If it's in deep shadow as we clearly see here, that must mean that the light is behind the ship. How else can ye huv a shadow here ... but no shadow ... here?'

A murmur of approval at this revelation which smacked of pure detection filled the room. Those who had failed to get the point now turning to their neighbours for explanation, determined not to miss a single word of the story unfolding before them. Fat Susan nodded wisely, a developing authority in her own right on the subject of her country's failure to reach the Moon.

'Fur ye see, here we huv further evidence if ever we needed it, o' the duplicity o' the Yanks in claiming tae huv been the first men on the Moon.'

He adopted a studious, thoughtful expression as if reconsidering his analysis, then seemingly well pleased with his interpretation, he returned to the subject with renewed interest.

'Could ye just run that past us again Rab? Some o' us got a wee bit lost somewhere along the way like.'

Hanging his head apologetically, his stupidity exposed, the punter received a friendly pat on the head from Susan for his trouble.

He returned her comforting gesture with a half smile full of further apology.

'Not at all. It's ma pleasure tae make sure that I huv carried yees all wi' me so far.'

He began again.

'Ye see. If he is standin' in the light, see ... here, an' the background which is the front o' the descent module is in darkness, it should only be from his own shadow. But the whole front o' the thing is in darkness. Either the photie is retouched, which I doubt, or the shadow is cast frae a light source behind the lander. It's the only explanation. Dae ye see now? The whole scene should be in bright sunlight. It's as obvious as the Moon itsel'.'

'Oh aye. I see it now. S'obvious as you say. S'no possible.'

They exchanged friendly smiles.

'Aye. Ye're bloody right it's no' possible. Ye wid huv tae be some kind o' bloody conjurer wi' theatrical effects burstin' oot o' yer bag tae come up wi' a picture like this. An' ah huv nae doubts that that is exactly whit happened. The whole thing wis orchestrated by Hollywood. It's bloody near perfect.'

He suddenly paused again.

'But ... like the other pictures ah showed ye, they are faked. Nae question o' that. I am convinced that here we see the evidence o' a cover up o' monumental proportions. A cover up that has had the best brains in this world questioning an' questioning the evidence before us, trying tae arrive at some explanation that wid give the benefit o' the doubt tae the Yanks tae support their erroneous claims o' havin' been the first men on the Moon.'

He held his hand aloft, turning slowly to look at the room.

'They failed.'

A shout went up, then spontaneous applause, initiated by Fat Susan, her hands beating against each other in frantic time, sending her affection out to her new found love in waves of passionate applause. Rab ignored the tumult, the cries of:

'More. Give us more'.

Again, his hand lifted graciously into the air. From the bag under the table another print out emerged, the descent module shown sitting in front of a rugged Moonscape, a gentle hill rising in the middle distance behind it.

'Now observe.'

His finger pointed out the various elements of the photograph like some nursery teacher instructing four-year-olds, the cat sitting squarely on the mat.

'Here we huv the descent module. An' behind it - this nice wee hill. OK? So far so good. Now this wan ...'

Reaching down to extract another print ' ... wis taken on the day efter this wan. Or so it says.'

He produced the second photograph, the backgrounds apparently identical, the descent module clearly prominent in the one but missing from the second print. The crowd were enthralled, leaning forward, the air in the pub stifling, the darkness and poor levels of lighting causing many of them to edge closer trying to see the images, trying to hear the dialogue that was the focus of everyone's attention.

'Now it is claimed ...' He paused again, waiting for perfect silence.

'... that this one wis taken the day after this one, an' after the astronauts had moved a mile or so up the road away frae the descent module. But what dae we see? What is this, I ask yees all? Is this, or is it no' the very same wee hill?'

All eyes were switching from image to image, Rab holding the photographs aloft nearer to the light.

'If we believe that it is the same hill...where the bloody hell has the descent module gone? Buggered off on holiday? Gone fur a leak maybe? Changed its digs? Ah don't think so.'

He put the prints down in front of him, all eyes again on his face as they awaited the unfolding of the plot.

'No. Ah don't think so. If ever we needed proof o' the fabrication o' evidence surroundin' the claim that the Yanks landed on the Moon, here we huv it. A module that hops aboot like a kangaroo, first it's here and now it's no'. Some kangaroo. Some module. Of course, no doubt there is a scientific explanation. Maybe somebody got the bloody dates all wrong. But the date is on the printouts! The dates are part o' the very pictures themselves. Unless of course ...'

He looked up smiling smugly,

'... unless of course the pictures were doctored, after, or maybe even *before* the event.'

A roar of approval could be heard several streets away as Rab made his way to the bar, Fat Susan in attendance, the slaps on the back and the many expressions of congratulations surrounding him on all sides as he found space against the worn counter, the staff hanging on his every word, his followers watching his every move.

'Aye. Two pints o' Guinness please. This lecturing fair develops a drouth so it does. Mouth's like the inside o' a parrot's cage.'

Charlie Smith leaned over to him.

'Ye hud something else tae dae last night, Rab? Ye weren't in, ah noticed. Place wis hoachin' as well. Everyone wis very disappointed. Everybody wis expectin' ye like. Whit could ah tell them? Wis very embarrassin'.'

Rab appeared to notice him suddenly.

'Oh yes. Ah'm sorry if ma absence created any kind o' a stooshie. Ah wis otherwise engaged. Bein' interviewed by reporters if ye must know. Very interestin' it wis. Insisted, they did, that ah huv a few bevvys wi them efterwards in the lounge o' the George Hotel. Ah'm sure ye'll understand. Ma time's no' ma ain at the moment.'

'Oh aye. Sure. No problem. It wis just that ... well ... ah suppose ye made up fur it tonight. That wis great. Ye really hud them goin' wi that stuff ye were sayin'. An' we saw ye oan the box as well. Ye were great. Made us a' proud. Ah notice that ye never mentioned the pub, though? Widnae be a bad thing if ye could. Maybe just drop a word here or there? Maybe next week? Will ye be daein' a show fur us *tomorrow* night?'

Rab was disinterested. With his arm around Susan and a night of drinking and loving ahead of him, he had other things on his mind.

'Aye,' he said absentmindedly, 'It's possible. Ye could try talkin' tae ma agent here tae fix up one or two dates between now an' the start o' the Festival. Ah do believe that there are a few spare evenings when we could accommodate ye at the usual rates. We're no' sure if the American tour should be squeezed in before the Festival or just efter. This hectic lifestyle is surely goin' tae be the death o' me, so it is.'

# 18
## Letters to the Editor - The Scotsman

*Dunrovin - Dalgety Bay*
*July 2011*

*Sir,*

With the opening of the new underground Garden Mall reinforcing the attraction of Princes Street as the destination shopping area within the City Centre, is it not time for the city fathers to reconsider the ban on commercial vehicles operating within the Inner City Limit, thereby allowing traders in other areas of the city centre some relaxation on delivery times and parking restrictions, especially during the very busy Festival period?

It has been amply demonstrated that the times allocated for kerbside deliveries place undue stress on shop owners and businesses that depend heavily on scheduled deliveries arriving on time. Recent experience of delays caused by the extended "pedestrians only" timings within the Inner City Limits will ultimately lead to closures and possible decamping of major brands to Leith and elsewhere in search of an easier life.

The automated delivery system to the Garden Mall shops and the ease with which shoppers can move between the Princes Street outlets and the underground shopping are much admired, but do little for the traders in Rose Street waiting at five o'clock in the morning for vans that fail to qualify for access because they are running five minutes late on an already tight schedule.

If the decision makers on the Rock spent more time addressing these issues and less on flying to the Moon and back we might all find ourselves with fully stocked shelves and many more satisfied customers. As it stands, the easy option of higher priced shopping in the Mall by far outweighs the cheaper prices on offer for goods that are stranded somewhere outside the Inner City Limits until the early hours of the following day.

*L. Moffat*
*Goods and Chattels - Rose Street*

Rose  Cottage, Dunbar.

Sir,

Is it not about time that we put this Moon nonsense into perspective and cried foul on the current notion that we are all firmly behind the latest adventure by the ruling party in power?

Am I the only voice to be raised in questioning the absurd amounts of money that have been poured into the venture to date?

Money that could have been directed towards finding cures for some at least of the many diseases that continue to plague our communities?

In tackling the issue of AIDS and cancer head on, we were able to demonstrate that given sufficient funding, a cure could be made available for almost any illness.

I would respectfully suggest that the ministers responsible tour some of our less-favoured hospices to see for themselves where the money might have been directed, with a surer hope of doing some good in the long term for those unfortunates confined to institutions that have waited too long for the handout that would have made all the difference had it arrived on time.

R. Mercer SRN


"Orion",
Blackford Hill
30th July 2011


The recently televised debate on the subject of the Moon raised the issue of whether or not the stars would be apparent to the astronauts from the surface of the Moon. As it is on earth during the hours of daylight, stars fade from our sight due to the fact that they are too dimly lit to compete with the enormous strength of the sun's rays. So it is on the Moon.

One other point raised is, however less easily explained. It does raise some doubts as to the veracity of the evidence as portrayed on some of the photographs allegedly taken on the surface at the time. The almost total lack of convincing shadows on adjacent surfaces is hard to equate with the amount of strong light beaming down on to the subjects within the frame. One might have expected a very *clear and sharp edge to any shadow being cast, and thereafter transferred, to the photographic image. Unhappily we saw no such confirmation on the pictures shown, despite conditions being exactly right for shadows to be clearly outlined against the immediate side of the L. E. M. If any of your readers can offer an explanation, I might yet stand corrected.*

> J. Mason
> Photographer
>
>> *The Manse, Gogarburn*
>> *August 1st 2011*
>
> Dear Sir,

*At the risk of sounding peevish, I do feel that we should be questioning the worth of the proposed Scottish manned flight to the Moon when judged alongside the lack of benefits deriving from America's earlier journeys into space.*

*Despite considerable time spent on contemplating the question I have failed to find even one item of positive benefit that addresses the many pressing problems surrounding us in the world today. And even if we do solve the so-called riddle of the universe, will it make as better people in the long run?*

*Will we suddenly find goodness in our hearts? Will we suddenly strengthen our resolve to live the decent life, caring for our neighbours, families and friends, while at the same time returning to our faith, seeking the only true path to enlightenment; an enlightenment that has no need of fiery chariots blazing trails across the universe in search of the truth?*

*I very much doubt it.*

> *Rev. J. Milligan*

>> *August 1st 2011*
>> *Balmoral Hotel*
>> *Edinburgh*

*As a visitor to your country, hoping to enjoy your International Festival, I feel that I must write to congratulate Scotland and her people on having achieved the ultimate goal of independence. Above all I must say how much I appreciate the many changes that are now evident around your beautiful country. Returning from a visit to friends in Dunfermline the other night, we were struck by the awe-inspiring view of the new Parliament building sitting so proudly and so beautifully* atop the famous skyline of Edinburgh's ancient castle. Whilst I am aware of the contentious issues surrounding the construction of this masterpiece and without wishing to enter into the debate in any way, I must applaud the decision to construct this magnificent building at the very heart of Edinburgh. The view of the two structures so complementary and so beautifully floodlit on a dark evening, standing majestically on their craggy base, will live in our memories for many years to come.

Dorothy Carnegie. - Chicago

Floodgarry, Tain.
August 4th 2011

The dubious benefit of having a high speed monorail connection to Perth and Inverness must be seen in the light of those of us "unfortunate enough" to be living anywhere north of the Black Isle, "deprived" of the "opportunity" to make the return journey to Edinburgh in under thirty minutes. Contrary to the views expressed by Mr Stewart (Letters page, 2nd August), if I ever felt the need to reach the drinking capital of Scotland in such a great hurry, I would certainly give full priority to having my head examined first.

Rev. J. Stevenson

Thirlestane Ha'
Gullane
6th August' 2011

As a retired architect I am appalled at the complete lack of sensitivity displayed by this administration in condoning the destruction of the city skyline by the introduction of the new parliament building on the Castle Rock. I make no direct criticism of the building per se, but only question the wisdom of erecting so massive a structure over a well loved monument. This action serves only to boast and brag of over-achievement at a time when Scotland has justifiably established her rightful place in the world as a nation of thinkers and movers, who have no need to blow their own trumpets in such a loud and ostentatious manner.

The argument that we must discard the trappings of haggis and sporran in favour of a more forward looking approach to ourselves and our society at large is surely faulted when we begin to surrender the physical grace of a much loved city to the frivolous designs of some of our more fanciful designers. Presumably, we can look forward to neon Coca Cola adverts appearing soon on the Disgrace of Edinburgh *with similar horrors inflicted on the Scott Monument as our city hurries to achieve the dubious distinction of becoming the Las Vegas of a once Bonnie Scotland.*

*J. Pringle Smythe*
*Architect, Rtd..*

*Rutland Sq., Edinburgh*
*6th August 2011*

*The debate surrounding the new Parliament building continues unabated. Hardly a day passes without some criticism or another flooding the pages of your newspaper with ill-informed judgements on the architectural, aesthetic and even the morality of erecting a thirty storey sky scraper on the site of one of Scotland's best loved monuments.*

*Whilst it remains the case that the skyline is now changed forever, we must view the resulting architectural unity with a more progressive eye, mindful of the designer's intentions in coming to terms with a difficult site, the demands of an informed client and the sensitivies of many Scots at home and abroad who have expressed the concern that their beloved city would be disfigured for centuries to come. Not so.*

*What we have instead is a harmonious marriage of two complementary structures both interwoven into a sculptural entity creating its own very interesting interplay of spaces and volumes subtly reinforced by the structural, tracery-like, elements that serve to lift the great mass of the Parliament building, enabling it to float easily above the ancient walls of the Castle ramparts.*

*When seen at night from Princes Street one can only marvel at the richness of texture and tone, the colours blending so carefully with the natural rock face, the old walls and the new landscaping creating a picture book image surely serving only to inspire the very many who pause to stand and wonder at a work of art surely seen as representative of the very best that the profession can offer at the present time.*

*R. Bartholemew-Thistleswaithe. (Technician)*
*President,*
*Royal Incorporation of Architects of Scotland*

# 19

In downtown Holyrood, somewhere between the ancient gravestones of Greyfriar's Kirkyard and the plusher new rise buildings of the West Port, Rab lay asleep, sprawled across the mattress with fat Susan implanted into the crumpled sheet beside him. Around the room, the evidence of a disordered lifetime of drinking and drifting was plainly seen in the chaos of old furniture, sagging chairs and dusty drapes. Here and there, touches of concern were sadly misplaced among the piles of newspapers, books and rows of empties.

The fading paintwork and the coloured shawl draped around the lampshade were the only signs of some earlier, brave attempt to hide the cracks in the peeling wallpaper. At eleven o'clock on a bright morning, a single dust-laden ray of sunshine began to creep over the disorder on the dresser, touching the crimson of the plastic flowers and showering the room with a pale, warm glow.

Somewhere above them, a radio blared into life. Saturday morning and the sounds of freedom echoed down the worn treads and over the torn lino on the landings. Across the tiny hallway, the disordered kitchen cried out for help, the sink overflowing with plates and cups, the worktops littered with the evidence of an addiction to fast food and Chinese takeaways.

Somewhere on the common stair, the clatter of impatient feet filtered through the doorway, dogs began to bark somewhere in the yard below and the steady rise in the noise of children playing and screaming cut through the walls, until with groans and complaints, Rab heaved himself upright. Suddenly coy in his nakedness, smiling shyly to himself, struggling against his hangover, he was all too aware of his new-found matrimonial responsibilities in the generous shape of Susan, still asleep, still fat, and still out of the game beside him.

In the tiny yard below, the sounds of the traffic rattled over the cobbled streets. In every corner, the throng of tourists took advantage of the first truly bright day of summer. There was a promise of heat in the air. On every billboard and available surface, posters proclaimed the Festival of Festivals. With a thousand shows and thirty times as many performances, the pubs and cafés overflowed into busy streets heaving with tourists, theatres were booked solid for performances, exhibitions and concerts filling the corners of the vast city with music and laughter.

Down on the High Street, "The Skite" threw open its shutters letting the sunshine stream in as far as the third floorboard from the stone step by the door. Charlie Smith was sweeping and hosing down the floor, the water running out over the dusty pavements into the drier dust of the gutters carrying the debris and glaur of the previous night's partying. On the flaking wall near the window the grinning face of Rab Nicol smiled back from the new posters around the bar.

## An Evening with
# Robert Nicol
### Scottish Man of Letters

Beneath the angelic image were selected quotations from the dailies and other dubious journals:

*"With his unerring eye for detail, he exposes the curious myths and the half truths surrounding some of our more entrenched beliefs."*
(The Scotsman.)

*"His ability to analyse the facts and uncover the truth is all the more astonishing ..."*
(The Daily Record.)

*"If Rab Nicol is right then we are all of us wrong ..."*
(The Daily Express.)

*"Now has a loyal following of supporters always eager to cheer him on to further embarrassing disclosures about a period of American History which was, up until recently, taken for granted."*
(Playboy International.)

*"A walking encyclopaedophile."*
(The Evening Post.)


*"With Rab Nicol keeping an eye on things we need look no further for a champion to challenge authority and reveal the conspiracies lurking behind the corridors of power ... "*
(The Anarchist Times.)


*"Another fine evening's entertainment full of sound and fury, deserving of much wider public awareness."*
(The Caterer & Licensed Victualler.)


*"As innocent as he is gullible, Mr Nicol is nevertheless in his element among all too familiar surroundings ... "*
(The Guardian.)


Charlie Smith was hardly concerned with what the papers were saying. With business booming, his only worry was the irregular appearances of the rising star, 'the nutter wi' the natter' as Charlie, more often than not, referred to him.

On the pavement outside, brightly coloured tourists peered uncertainly into the dark abyss, unsure of their fate should they venture inside to probe the secrets of these ancient drinking dens. The roar of denim and the glint of cameras recoiling from the nosegay of dead beer and stale air was a regular event each summer as the street played stony host to the timid passing trade, light meters denying their rising thirst as the prospect of buying a beer and still failing to take a picture ensured their hasty departure.

But this year was different. Already the word was spreading; "The Skite" was the hottest show in town. Rab Nicol was the hottest property on the street. As unpaid secretary, Charlie was taking messages and summonses from far and wide; his man in serious demand from news hacks, radio presenters and television producers. With Rab signed up for the three weeks of the Festival, Charlie was assured of a packed pub every night.

Back in the flat, Susan sat waiting for Rab, the awful reality of her surroundings bearing down on her. Something would have to be done and done quickly.

'Hey Doll. A'right, then? Welcome tae the sin bin. Everythin' OK? Aye. Sorry aboot the breakfast.'

He grinned sheepishly.

' ... an' the promise o' champagne. Never touch the stuff. Dinnae like the bubbles ...'

He was laughing.

'Trouble is ... ah never huv time tae dae any cleanin'. Ye ken how it is. Busy life. Just hectic. Never stops.'

Susan smiled back at him, blinded by love.

'Time fur a wee heart starter. Eh? D'ye want tae try some?' The half empty can of stale Guinness was lifted and drained. He moved around the room shaking cans in search of further surprises.

'It's the aliens,' he said. 'They sneak in here efter ye're asleep and drain the bloody lot.'

Satisfied that it was dry, they left the crowded apartment.

'Time ah checked oot the phone calls and the bookings. Must drop intae "The Skite" fur a second or two. Just tae check up on things. Business first ye know.'

They hurried out into the hot summer morning, the crowds heading for the pavement cafes and bars in the Grassmarket, the street traders and buskers adding to the general excitement they felt as they headed up the hill towards the pub.


They entered "The Skite", the place already filling with locals and tourists alike. Charlie Smith was in discussion with someone at the far end of the long bar. He gave a quick nod in Rab's direction and Rab felt his hand gripped warmly, eyes still half blinded from the dazzling sun, he was aware of a presence, a person of substance, shaking his hand and leading him to the corner table. They eyed each other warily as Rab's eyes adjusted to the gloom. The sports jacket was rising now, ushering Susan and the drinks into a seat beside them, his manner persuasive but unpatronising, the smile fixed in his handsome face.

Charlie said,

'Bloke here wants tae interview ye.'

'Rab. Nice to meet you; finally managed to track you down. I hope you don't mind ... '

He was looking into Rab's face, sensing the beginnings of a distrust of the clean shaven, heavily built Latino with the faint aroma of cigar and dry martini hanging about his person.

'I just wanted to say how much I enjoyed watching the show the other night, the way you got through to the audience. It was great.'

Rab's mouth hung open, curiosity tweaked, a sixth sense warning him of trouble ahead.

'Oh aye. The Kirsty Monroe interview. Aye. Ah think she's great. It went well. Nae problem. Canna remember fur the life o' me which night it wis ...'

'It was an eye opener for me. You've obviously studied the subject. Where do you get your facts?'

Rab was drinking, thinking,

'Oh, here an' there. Ye know. A wee bit o' this and a wee bit o' that.' He shrugged, laughing but still guarded.

'Well, you were just fine! You raised a few issues I hadn't considered before. It was really interesting. You might be surprised to know that there is a number of folks, who like you, find the whole thing a bit suspicious. Many of us find it hard to believe that they ever succeeded. Too many inconsistencies; too many questions unanswered. You see we've been taking an interest in the American claims of Moon landings for many, many years.'

Rab glanced up quickly.

'Who's "we"? if ye don't mind me askin'?'

'Oh. I'm sorry. The name's Frank Nelson. I'm a reporter. Look. I work for The Washington Post and cover the scientific features. I'm over here to cover the Moon shot. As I've said, you're not the only one asking these questions. There are many others out there all saying the same thing. Believe me. Years ago, I got pulled into this business through an old buddy of mine, Jack Duggan. He worked for a spell with NASA.

'He used to question things as well. Did him no good. Eventually, he reached the point where his continual research led to him being fired as head of public relations. Jack found himself on the scrap heap at the age of forty-two and decided to write a book listing his misgivings on the whole story of manned trips to the Moon.

'At that time I was a fellowship student with a fascination for space travel. I was hopelessly hooked on the whole thing. I loved every minute of it, until I started doing some research work for Jack. Before too long he had me convinced that there was the very real possibility of a serious cover up within the space administration reaching to the highest levels in our government. After a few months, I became as curious as he, asking the sorts of questions that you yourself raised on Saturday. As I Iistened, I decided I'd like to interview you and maybe do an article for the Post.'

Rab sat, his shoulders down, his face peering into his stout, his attention focused as never before, as he began to recognise that there were other punters out there as well, like minded people who were in it for more than just the loose change.

'And the book ... ?'

At this Frank Nelson turned serious.

'Well, I know that it was well on the way by the time I had to get back to London. From time to time he would send bits over to me for an opinion. Mostly stuff I had already researched. Then one day he called me. He was having trouble finding a publisher. Every door was closed to him. He asked me to source a publishing house in the United Kingdom. That was the easy part. So I called him and he promised to bring the book over. Two days later, I learned that he had been killed in a hit and run in New York.'

Susan suddenly broke into the conversation.

'Oh. I remember now. June, 1998. I remember it well. He'd been on a lecture tour of the state colleges and universities and he was scheduled for an appearance at U. C. L. A. the following fall.'

They both looked at her in surprise.

'I'm sorry. I hadn't realised that you're an American. So you were at U. C. L. A. ?'

'Yeah. I did three years majoring in European History.'

Rab's face beamed in open admiration.

'Aye. Good fur you, doll. History, eh? Whit next.' He squeezed her hand affectionately.

'So sorry, Ah should have introduced ma partner and research assistant.'

They all smiled politely, Susan drawing her chair closer to the table.

'Yeah. I remember. He wrote to us outlining his lecture. I'd forgotten about it.'

'What happened tae the book?' asked Rab.

'We have no idea.' He indicated an envelope lying by his side.

'As far as I know these copies of his notes and photographs are the only things that remain. His sister found nothing in the apartment. Not a scrap of evidence that he had ever begun the work. I'm pulling it all together again for my articles.'

He sipped his drink. Rab leaning forward now, wholly engrossed, the suggestion of skulduggery adding a layer of intrigue to the cover up. Nelson began to pull stuff out of the folder placing it in front of them. Rab's interest was on the rise. He began to sort through a wad of clippings and notes interspersed with photographs.

'This is a copy of an article Jack wrote several years ago when he first began to take an interest in our space programme. These others are all from magazines with a broad scientific readership. They mostly say the same thing. Some of these photographs ... '

He began to offer them around, Rab and Susan studying them intently, unaware for the moment of the National Security Numbers stamped on the back.

'... were sent to me by my friend at the time. Others kept arriving years after he had passed on, and many years after our last manned flight took place. Whoever was sending them had an agenda it seems. But when I had had time to study them, I was shocked by the realisation that much of what Jack had been saying all those years ago was, in all probability, nothing short of the truth.

'I quickly came to the conclusion that the whole thing was a set up. The very words you used the other evening. I thought your remark about Copernicus was also to the point. We've been seeing and believing what we want to see and believe for far too long.'

He looked up, his manner less determined, his tone quieter, the change in his manner becoming more apparent the deeper he went into his story. As they pored over the items Rab's interest intensified, his initial resistance to Frank Nelson subsiding as the documents went from hand to hand, his questions being answered, explanations and more questions flying between them as the shadows crept into the bar. Behind them, the strong light of the midday sun faded suddenly, as it sank behind the chimney pots on the tenements on the opposite side of the High Street.

At the end of two hours, they were still hard at it. As Charlie Smith drifted over to the corner, he could not help but notice that the Guinness had been moved to the next table, the glasses hardly touched as the rising star struggled to take in a surcharge of information lifting him from the status of talented amateur to the elevated heights of informed conspirator.

'So there we are, Rab. If you can make use of these copies, continue the good work - spread the word far and wide. Do you mind if I get a shot in before I go?'

He snapped off a couple of frames. As Frank Nelson left the bar with handshakes and smiles again fixed in place, Rab sat down looking at Susan who stared back in wonder at the folder in his hand containing material that guaranteed their future as informed pundits on the ever expanding list of questions surrounding the lunar landings and the certainty of the cover-up of a lifetime orchestrated by the most powerful nation on earth.

'Holy shit !' said a wide eyed Susan.

'Aye. Right enough, doll.' said a pensive Rab.

'What did he want wi' ye?' asked Charlie Smith.

'Fuck off,' said Rab politely.


Elmer Franklin sat in the spacious waiting room outside the First Minister's office. Across the room, Paul Burke stood by the door enjoying the view through the broad sweep of glass that opened onto the city below and the mist covered mountains in the background. Ever since leaving Washington, the joy at the thought of returning to Scotland had stayed with him during a long week of meetings and endless late shifts in London, staying close to the Assistant Secretary of State as he weaved and shuffled through a heavy calendar of diplomatic dinners and social functions.

Along the corridor at the end of the room, a parade of secretaries and officials carried endless papers to and from the Minister's office. Running ten minutes late, Gregor had already emerged once to greet his guest, offering profuse apologies for some last minute business, his door left open as Franklin calmly waited to be admitted.

Waiting with him, the junior commercial attaché from the American Consulate sat quietly, legs crossed, his document folder on his lap. Gregor's secretary came walking towards them.

'The Minister apologises once again for the delay in receiving you and asks you both to follow me.'

She led them off towards the large doors and they entered, the great booming voice of Gregor McLeod filling the rooms and corridors until the doors closed and peace returned once more.

'Mr Franklin. This is indeed a great pleasure. I have of course met with several of Mr Jackson's aides including Mr Johnson. As yet, I have not had the pleasure of meeting your President although I did have occasion to speak to him last year on other matters. Please, be seated.'

They sat down, Gregor joining them in front of his desk, his secretary offering coffee as they exchanged preliminaries. Franklin surveyed the office, the magnificence of the view creating an immediate impression no less than the rugged charm and honest appeal of the man in front of him.

Franklin made the first move.

'Let me reassure you, First Minister. The pleasure is entirely ours ...'

Gregor interrupted him.

'Please, my first name is Gregor, and with respect to

politicians and diplomats everywhere, I usually insist on dealing on first name terms with everyone who walks through that door. So, Elmer, let us begin. I received your very courteous letter and due to the shortness of available time, I had my secretary call your office to confirm our meeting. Welcome to Scotland. I hope your stay here will be a pleasant one. We Scots tend to pride ourselves on our hospitality. I have arranged lunch here today and there is a formal dinner, I believe, tomorrow evening in your honour. I trust that these arrangements do not conflict with other plans you might have made in the interim?'

Elmer was pleased.

'That will be most suitable, Gregor. I am very anxious that we use our time together wisely and that our intrusion into your busy schedule will not place undue stress on your administration. I convey Mr Jackson's best wishes to your government and his congratulations on your having achieved independence as a nation. Our President claims Scottish ancestry of course and he regrets that in all his many visits to England he never quite made the journey out of London to visit your beautiful country. For the moment, I am mixing business with pleasure, being on an extended vacation. I think you may know that my youngest daughter now lives in Oxford. It is so long since I had time to look around, meet the grandsons and just put my feet up for a while. But it won't last.'

He laughed, the other sharing the joke.

Gregor watched and listened, his ability to respond to protocol tempered with a distinct humanity that invariably broke down the usual reserve of visiting dignitaries from a number of countries. Casting his mind back to an earlier occasion, he saw again the look of shock on the face of his secretary as she had entered the room, after a night of heavy entertaining, to find the area strewn with empty vodka bottles and three snoring Russians asleep on different chairs as the sun streamed in through the windows.

Elmer was speaking and Gregor realised that he had not been paying due attention.

'... so as you can imagine when news began to filter back to us of rocketry, joint ventures with the Russians and launches from

Uzbekistan we were naturally worried. I flew over in fact, to meet with John Ryder in July this year, as I am sure you are aware, to take his opinion on the matter. We regret now that we did not use the diplomatic channels newly opened to us to contact your government directly, but as you will understand, we were more familiar with the personalities and procedures in place in Westminster than here in Edinburgh.'

Gregor nodded sympathetically.

'Yes. Yes. We quite understand. We have regular contact at all levels of government with our friends down south and of course we share a joint defence strategy. In other matters we are also close ...'

He paused, a twinkle in his eye.

'... except of course on this business of our proposed trip to the Moon. We felt that this was one item that we should keep to ourselves. We all know of course that the spin off from actually reaching the Moon will not bring direct material benefit or financial gain; but as a small nation, the fact that we are able to undertake the venture and hopefully succeed, is surely worthwhile in itself.

'We also have new fuels coming on line which we believe will ultimately replace petroleum products once we get the costs down. The fact that we have a *clean* fuel on offer to other countries to market under licence is also something that our chemists are justifiably proud of. To our minds, anything that assists in cleaning up the world has to be good for all of us. Already, we have been approached by a number of conscientious countries all eager to reduce their dependence on fossil fuels.'

Elmer reflected on the long list of countries currently in line to sign up to produce the new fuel. The total dependence of the United States on fossil based fuels must not, however, be allowed to cloud his meetings, he decided. Elmer took up the conversation.

'We are well aware of the technological strides that you have made and we are of course interested in sharing with you, as we have in the past, our own advances in medical and scientific matters. It is thanks to the development and research work carried out here in Scotland that the development of vaccines for a number of infectious diseases and in particular AIDS has practically eliminated the need for the administering of expensive drugs. We are ever hopeful that you will continue to work with us on any advances in areas where we can make progress, particularly in your new field of rocket fuels. This is one area we are particularly interested in furthering with you.'

Gregor smiled courteously.

'Of course. Of course. As I have said, we are almost ready to begin discussions with several countries worldwide on erecting production plants and in discussing the best way forward in converting and replacing their outmoded machinery, cars and petrol dependent vehicles ...'

He paused.

'... and we also believe that this new fuel will be most beneficial once we have resolved the problems related to making it widely available for use in airliners. It is passive and extremely safe ... and,' he added, '... environmentally friendly.'

Elmer was anxious to continue.

'I might add that President Jackson is most anxious to assist you in any way we can. If there is anything at all that you need, any way that we can be of help...'

Gregor appeared suitably grateful. Glancing at his watch, he pressed the intercom on his desk. Relieved, Elmer saw a reprieve at hand from entering a discussion on the one subject that he had no immediate plans to debate; America's role in global warming.

'Grace. Please find out if everything is prepared. Mr Franklin and I would like to enjoy a light lunch on the terrace. Yes? Good. The usual arrangements. Thank you.'

They all stood. Gregor led the way to his private lift, Paul Burke falling in behind, ever watchful, ever present. The prim commercial attaché eyed him warily. Paul wondered absentmindedly who his daddy might be.


Late afternoon, and Gus Simpson sat hunched in front of his monitor reviewing his copy for the next day's edition. Here and there he made minor adjustments dismissing the spell-check option as unnecessary and time wasting. With five minutes to spare he pushed the right buttons and rolled out a hard copy for reading as he enjoyed a well deserved pint in the pub across the street.

### 'Moonraker Trials Successfully Completed – Moon shot on course for November lift off.'

'Yesterday the Rosewell Institute announced the successful conclusion of a year of testing on the lunar lander which will carry two of our astronauts to the surface of our nearest neighbour in the solar system. As we witnessed the predawn preparations for the final test yesterday morning, the full extent of the dedication of the crew and support staff at Rosewell became all too apparent as the latest chapter in the development of Scotland's commitment to space travel was unveiled for the privileged few.

'At first light, under low cloud cover, we watched as the *Moonraker* was unwrapped, beginning a series of ascents and descents which were conducted with skill and precision by a crew of three of our finest young men. On the thirtieth of November, they will be hoisted into space on a journey that will see them traverse the universe on a round trip of five hundred thousand miles in the course of eight days. Whilst it is as yet uncertain who will command the crew, or who will ultimately be selected for the honour of being the first Scots in space, we are certain that they will carry the good wishes of all for a safe journey and a successful conclusion to a feat of enterprise and endeavour, which has seen this tiny nation take second place only to the might of the United States in the race to place men on the surface of another planet.

'Yesterday the mood was jubilant, as the *Moonraker* touched down after lifting to a height of three hundred feet, settling back to earth in a flawless performance, the craft controlled in the final moments of the landing back to the precise spot on the ground from which she had lifted off twenty minutes earlier. Clearly the need for sensitive handling will play an important role in the final moments as the craft drops slowly to the surface of our rocky neighbour, ensuring that the crew are able to negotiate the terrain in search of a suitable flat landing platform.

'In the press release prepared by the Rosewell Institute, the Director, Murdo Sinclair stressed the wish of the committee that the landing site should be as close as is feasible to the original site selected by NASA all those years ago. Mr Sinclair clearly does not join the ranks of those who dispute the claims of the Americans that they successfully conducted a series of lunar landings in the seventies, and hopes to return with photographs of the Scottish crew standing alongside the original lunar lander, before beginning a short series of experiments on the surface.

These have been designed to investigate a number of issues that have kept scientists guessing ever since the original Moon rocks were successfully returned to earth. At the same time it is intended to circumnavigate the Moon before returning to orbit, possibly landing in the polar regions, an area long considered as the most likely spot to look in the search for evidence of the presence or otherwise of water on the Moon's surface.

'It is unlikely that the journey will reveal much more than we already know about the composition of the Moon, nor is it likely to throw up new evidence on the origins of the universe itself. In the long run, it will almost certainly dispel the conspiracy theories that have done so much to damage the credibility of the United States of America as the pioneers of space travel, given that so many informed scientists have expressed scepticism that the voyage was even remotely feasible given the state of our knowledge at that time.

'We trust that Scotland will not be dogged by the same show of scepticism in the decades to come, once the Saltire has been planted alongside the

Stars and Stripes, as she strives to demonstrate
to the world at large that the justification for
undertaking the voyage is less important in the
final analysis than the action itself; an action
which places our nation once again at the hub of
scientific matters in an increasingly competitive
world. When one considers that, as Scots, we are
a minor player in world scientific matters we
must surely be allowed to take some small pride
in an achievement that has been undertaken for a
fraction of the cost of earlier flights, due in no
small part to the advances that have been made in
design and research into friendly fuels that may
one day transform the world we live in.'

Folding his copy into his inner pocket he closed down his computer and waited for the process to end. On his desk, the phone rang abruptly disturbing the empty office.

'Mr Simpson. My name is Nelson. Frank Nelson. I'm over here to cover the conference and the press briefings on your space programme. I was wondering if you could spare me some time? If we could perhaps meet up for a chat? I'm with the Washington Post. Yes, that's right.'

There was a brief exchange as credentials were established.

'Yes. Right again. John Hopper is still there. Yes. Still holding on.'

They laughed together, contact established. Gus thought for a second or two before replying.

'Look. I'm going off now heading for the pub. Where are you?'

'I'm quite close by. Yes. Staying at the Balmoral. I'm about a block away from there right now. That's right. OK. I'll find it. No. Don't worry. Say in fifteen minutes time? Great. I look forward to meeting you. So long for now.'

As he closed the line he crossed to the news stand on the corner to take fresh directions.

'Tell me, did you ever hear of a restaurant ... a bar ... around here called the Doric? Is it far? Do I need to take a cab?'

Standing on the pavement, the standard performance of arm waving and pointing went on for several minutes before Frank Nelson strolled off in what he hoped was the general direction of his rendezvous with Angus Simpson. Heading down towards Market Street he lifted his eyes to the graceful spans of the North Bridge, the towers of Cockburn Street rising before him, the floodlighting on the Castle and the parliament building dominating the skyline to the west. Under his arm, copies of the documents that had so stunned Rab Nicol earlier in the day were protected from the light drizzle by an old brown envelope with a Virginia postmark.


Gus watched as the figure appeared at the top of the steps and turned into the tiny bar area. Unmistakeably, a Yank. From the broad shoulders and the clean cut looks, the fifties haircut and the badly fitting jacket he was every inch the suburban American. Stepping into the line of fire, he smiled the length of the bar extending his hand as the other strode forward, avoiding the crush of office workers and fellow hacks, politicians and regulars jostling for service in the narrow space.

'Hi. Nice place. Took the tour in finding it, though. Must have passed it a couple of times until I enquired at the pub next door.'

Gus laughed in sympathy.

'What can I get you? Beer? Scotch? What?'

'Bourbon; if they have it.'

Gus stepped towards the bar, emerging minutes later with drinks for both of them. He motioned him towards a table. They sat casually taking in the scene until Gus tilted his glass in salute and sampled the malt.

'So, you're with the "Washboard"? Used to know several of your correspondents quite well. Met up with a few of them when I was gallivanting in foreign places covering wars across the world. Nice to know that John is still hanging in there. Jesus. He must be nearly seventy now.'

'Seventy this year. Lost his wife couple of years back. Knocked the stuffing out of him for a while. But he came back as fierce as ever spoiling for a good story, and getting it.'

'So far, so good', thought Gus.

'How is the short guy who used to handle the camera for him? They always worked together. Sam something or other?'

He thought for a minute.

'You mean Sammy Kevorkian? Still going strong. Still drinking like a fish.'

Gus relaxed a little more. Frank Nelson was checking out just fine.

'So! What, if anything, can I do for you?'

He looked up smiling, as two more glasses were delivered to the table. Gus tipped the dregs of his whisky into the fresh glass, adding a drop of water.

'Well, I read your piece a while back at the time the launch was officially announced, and I *had* thought of stopping you at the first press conference, but you were surrounded one minute and the next you had disappeared. Of course I am over here from time to time, covering the period between now and November. My third visit as a matter of fact. America is abuzz with the story and the daily handouts make damn easy copy. They can't get enough of it over there. Frankly I'm running out of angles, hence the call to the Scotsman. I tried to arrange an invitation to the preview last week at Rosewell but was locked out. If there is anything I could use for tomorrow's late edition I would be delighted to hear of it.'

Gus grinned.

'It's true, security was very tight. I counted only a handful of foreign journalists. The rest were locals, mainly representing the majors. Your old countryman from Newsweek was there. He always seems to get a foot in the door one way or another.'

'Oh I know how it is. There's always an angle to play. But tell me something. Everywhere I go there is so little fuss being made here in Scotland. It's seems that it's no big deal. Everybody is carrying on as though flying to the Moon was an every day occurrence! I listened in to that debate the other night on STV and apart from the Nicol guy everyone was calmly discussing the whole issue as if it were a train ride to the seaside. I remember the near hysteria in America in the seventies every time anybody went into print or even mentioned NASA. Over here it's very different. I can't quite believe the difference.'

Gus laughed.

'Don't let them fool you. Everybody is cock-a-hoop about the whole thing. It's just that we Scots tend to hide our feelings a bit better than most. Not that you would know it. But when you know where to look and how to listen, the true nature of the beast shows through.'

'You didn't get much of a chance during the televised debate. It seems the script was highjacked by Nicol and his supporters in the audience. I caught up with him today. He claims to have a show on at the Festival picking up on all the loose ends left by NASA in the seventies. I must say I enjoyed his performance. The audience loved it. A natural! Seems he was invited back for next week's show as well.

'I fed him some old stuff today that I thought might spice up his act. Spent an enjoyable hour this morning talking with him and his lady friend. He gave me enough quotes to fill a couple of good columns and I got a couple of good shots to send back.'

He pulled a smiling bubbly face out of the envelope holding it up for Gus to see.

'Oh him. Yeah. I remember him. Took his shoes off halfway through the show and nearly gassed the starlet on my left.'

They both laughed, Gus looking again at the sagging features and the unshaven face of Robert Armstrong Nicol, Man of Letters and full time slob.

'You say he's performing? Holy shit! I don't believe it. Most of the stuff he trotted out had all been aired before, surely. There was nothing very new about his claims. We've all heard that conspiracy stuff before. After a while it gets tedious.'

Frank Nelson gave a sigh, shrugged and smiled as Gus continued.

'As an American you must get sick and tired of hearing it all? Three weeks ago I sat here at this very table with someone who should have known better and debated the whole issue all over again. In the end, he bloody nearly had me convinced that the Moon landings of the seventies were a mirage. I had to revisit the whole story to remind myself of the events as they unfolded. As it happened, it came in useful as a refresher course just prior to the Kirsty Monroe show. I was quite pleased that I had taken the trouble to check it out in the end.'

Gus walked to the bar and returned five minutes later with more drinks.

'Hey. At least, let me offer to pay. I thought you'd gone to the john. I didn't call you up to bum drinks off you all night. I'll tell you what. After this one we could drop into the "Skite" for an hour and listen to Nicol. I have a standing invitation and I'll buy the rounds.'

Gus was pensive. But he *was* intrigued. Returning through the crush at the bar his eyes had made contact with his number two on the features desk, a brief shake of the head and a vacant shrug confirming the fact that nobody at the "Washboard" had ever heard of Frank Nelson.

'Sure. Could be amusing. I remember wondering why a guy like that would be remotely interested in the history of the NASA landings. Let's go.'

Striding down the High Street heading for the "Bletherin' Skite", Gus wondered just where the evening might lead. One way or another he was determined to see it through to the final curtain. Once a newsman; always a newsman.

A light drizzle had begun to fall again as the welcoming lights of the "Skite" came into view, the roars of applause echoing through the narrow doorway into the darkening night; somewhere in the steamy interior the mangy lions were fifteen love up on the bevvied Christians.

# 20

Mark Brander, White House Press Officer, stood at the dais fielding questions on a variety of domestic and international issues. For the fourth week running the focus had returned to the issue of the Space Agency's return to manned flights to the Moon. Too young to have experienced the heady days of NASA in the sixties and seventies, he had nevertheless come a long way in responding to questions on past performance and the whole argument for and against the futility of further manned exploration of the solar system.

'Lisa Hewat. New York Times. Would we be right in assuming that the government's current proposal to place men on the Moon ahead of the November mission by the Scots is being given priority over other projects that were in hand prior to Mr Jackson's announcement, and is it not the case that there is widespread pessimism among the workers and scientists down at Cape Kennedy that the job can be finished in time for a November launch?'

Mark Brander straightened, his body language clearly defensive, the thin smile on his face failing to conceal the anxiety that he always felt when reassuring the press that everything was on course and running along just fine. He understood enough about the present administration to know that no matter how positive the public utterances were, the reality was seldom as assured, nor was the end result guaranteed. His feedback on progress to date was less than encouraging and his private thoughts on the matter were constantly held in check.

'Good morning Lisa. Nice of you to show up occasionally.'

There was laughter; Lisa Hewat was an infrequent attendee at White House briefings.

'First of all I'm assured that progress is on track and I know that the President is receiving regular briefings on the work as it continues. Of course, the precise date for the launch has not yet been set. This will depend on weather reports in the final analysis, but the window, which we have, will allow us a three-day margin either side of the twenty sixth of November. As far as morale at the various establishments is concerned, I am unaware of any problems in that area. What I can tell you is that the injection of support into the industry has put a few smiles on a number of faces of late. The subcontractors and their hundreds of suppliers do not share your view of low morale, nor have they experienced any pessimism that we have been able to detect thus far.'

There was general laugher as he turned towards the next questioner. So far, so good.

'John Galbraith, Los Angeles Times. Mark, we, some of us at least, were over at the press conference in Edinburgh last month and we came away with the distinct impression that the people over there are very serious indeed about their plans for exploring the Moon and possibly further afield in the years to come. This new fuel of theirs is a major advance in chemical engineering and as far as we could determine, their project borrows very little in terms of aeronautics or instrumentation from either the Russians or ourselves.

'Since we Americans are largely dependent for this latest shot on technology that derives from our trips during the seventies, are we not in danger of losing out to a much smaller nation in terms of advancements in design development and fuel technology?'

Mark Brander fingered his cuffs and pinched his tie.

'Size isn't everything, as you are well aware, John.'

There was sustained laughter, Brander having a ready wit and ability with words that had marked him out as a journalist of distinction some years earlier.

'It is true that the Scots are a minor player on the world stage but they helped found this great country of ours and as pioneering explorers they were the ones to write up the early guide books. In addition, they pioneered engineering in all its many forms. It is now forty odd years since America first set foot on the Moon, and we should not have been surprised by the announcement that the Scots, or anybody else for that matter, intended to repeat the exercise. As for losing out, we are currently negotiating with Gregor McLeod to produce his new fuel under licence. If it is everything it is cracked up to be, we won't be far behind for very much longer. We maintain good relationships with the Scots and we have maintained our consulate in Edinburgh with a view to developing even closer trade links with the independent Scottish state. Next?'

The boom microphone swung easily to the next participant, the pecking order in the first hour fairly well established, the questions already screened for bouncers, the essential easy flow of the televised briefing the first priority.

'John McGrory. Scientific American. I wonder at this time if the administration is aware of the rumours flying around, some of them widespread, that this latest trip to the Moon has more to do with getting there before the Jocks do for more spurious reasons. Whichever way it pans out, the President has set a race in motion between ourselves and the Scots which, however unintentional, is now focusing world attention on our efforts to catch up with their programme; a programme which started five years earlier. Do you not agree that we have little to gain from competing at this time in an event where we could so easily fail to get there ahead of them?'

'I doubt very much if the President sees it quite that way. The timing of the return to manned flights so close to the announcement by Gregor McLeod is entirely coincidental. We have no notion of competing or of winning. The remark by the President that we would be there to welcome them, was not intended to provoke any response or stimulate competition and the whole issue 'who goes first' is hardly relevant in the present circumstances. Let them get on with it. After all, we *were* the first to venture into space and *succeed* despite popular myths flying around to the contrary.'

Mark Brander was tiring of the line of questioning.

'May I just make one further point?'

The microphone swung back to the journalist, his first words lost to the room.

'… and the persistent rumours that have dogged our manned missions are as strong today as they were forty years ago. Isn't it the case that this latest Moon-shot and the eventual handshake on the surface is little more than an expensive fly swat to crush the rumours once and for all time that we did not land on the Moon?'

There was a burst of loud laughter and calls for the speaker to sit down. John McGrory was well known for his controversial views on the Moon landings and his frequent interjections into otherwise stuffy debates had more than once seen him silenced by the Chair. Mark Brander appeared amused.

'Mr McGrory. Mr McGrory. John, John. I can see that the only way we are going to convince you, is to send *you* to the Moon. May I add your name to the training programme? You, above all people, should know that this administration has nothing to hide and nothing to gain from rekindling an interest in manned missions. In addition, we have no use for conspiracy theories or cover-ups of any sort. Next?'

'Ken Regan, ABC News. Mark. Good morning. Do you have any comment to make on the Scottish claims that their vehicle is capable of making the journey without booster rockets, eventually returning through the atmosphere to make a conventional landing?'

Brander would have preferred to get off the subject of the Moon shots, but to have steered them away would have ensured a determined reluctance to fall in line.

'Well. We have not been favoured with a technical handout but you have all seen the clips that were released at the press conference. What I *can* say is that our best men have considered the claim and are dubious at best that the vehicle has the performance characteristics claimed for it. As far as we are concerned we are still many years away from developing a shuttle that could withstand the journey into deep space, orbit another planet and be back in time for dinner. But we shall all just have to await events as they unfold and trust that Scottish hopes pinned on the *Caliban* will see a safe return for their astronauts in early December. Next?'

'Mr. Brander. Good morning. Phil Westwood, Washington Post. Your administration is currently under severe pressure to sign up to the July '08 amendments to the Kyoto Protocol. Is there any possibility that the President is now inclined towards reaching a settlement on emission levels given that his tenure in office could shortly expire?'

Brander took a deep breath and sighed audibly.

'We have made our position on global warming clear to all concerned. We do not believe that global warming is the direct result of high carbon dioxide emissions into the atmosphere. And ... before ... before ... you all get too excited, I have here the latest report that clearly shows that the debate is far from closed. We do concede that the world would be a fresher place altogether if we could simply stop emitting gases into the atmosphere, but at the present time this administration is disinclined to return to the table this fall with any further concessions to world demands for a major reduction in CO2 emissions.'

'But surely the President's recent speech to Congress gave assurances that the whole issue of global warming was being studied seriously and that a policy statement would shortly be issued? How soon can we anticipate any shift in position towards a recognition that in the eyes of the world, we are putting profit before an overwhelming body of work that suggests that we are slowly, but surely poisoning the planet?'

Mark Brander fixed his eye on Phil Westwood.

'I would ask you all to read the report which we copied to you in the press handout. From it, you will see that a number of issues have been addressed and disposed of by some of the finest brains available to us. On the evidence available to us, we foresee no immediate shift in our position *vis a vis* global warming. Gentlemen. Ladies. Thank you for your time. Good day.'

And with that, he collected his notes and left the podium.


Down in the press club, the cocktail bar was thronged with journalists and reporters, most of them familiar figures on the news circuit in Washington. Here and there, introductions were being made, old acquaintances checked out and new faces noted for future reference.

Phil Westwood of the Washington Post leaned against the bar facing the crowd. As the elder statesman of the press core he attended every call, maintaining a watching brief on several administrations over a career spanning fifty years. Beside him, the equally seasoned face of Ken Regan of ABC News looked on.

'Another day, another dollar! Eh, Ken? How did you find it?

Usual pile of shit.'

'Oh I don't know. He came clean on a number of things. I ditched the press handout of course, and I don't exactly see you burdened down with any additional paperwork.'

They laughed, old hands, if not exactly old buddies. Phil reached behind him groping for his glass, his wrinkled neck and stiff back a legacy of rough sleeping over the years and an ounce of lead from the Vietnam War.

'Did you notice? He used the term "cover-up" twice. Once when he needn't have said anything, and again when he could have said something else. Did you notice? Anything going on that I should know about?' He half turned as he spoke, not expecting an answer. Then he was off again.

'Heard a whisper the other day that things are a bit touchy up at the palace. Rumours of heads shortly to roll; that kind of thing.'

He resumed sipping his martini, the other non-committal, staring ahead and ignoring the babble of the crowded bar. Tucked in the corner at the end, they were in a rare sanctuary under the potted palm, an area of the bar that they both knew well.

'Seems that this latest little adventure is breaking all records for fund allocation without so much as a chitty in the petty cash box. Budgets Unlimited Incorporated. That's what they're calling the Treasury Department now. No expense spared.'

They were silent for a while, the other still saying nothing, the format a well rehearsed overture for a session of drinking and soul baring that would see them in place at lights out time.

'Yeah. Heard there was a bit of a panic going on. Nothing hard as yet. Nothing printable.'

'No! There never is.'

'Terry Lockhart called me yesterday.'

'Oh yes?' There was a sustained pause as the implications of a rare call from their contact at the F.B.I. were digested.

'Seems someone has had enough; wanted to talk to him about something unusual that happened a couple of weeks back, over on the West Coast. L. A. no less! He pointed the finger obligingly in the right direction. It took a bit of digging, but my man eventually got to it. Seems that some little model-maker up in Studio City was approached through some shady third party to kit out a full size replica of the lunar module from the sixties right down to the last detail.'

Westwood had a puzzled look on his face.

'You remember the L E M? It was the descent vehicle on the Apollo eleven mission? Sure, you remember.'

Phil nodded absentmindedly.

'So?'

'Well it seems that this little guy is handed a substantial down-payment but he never gets around to completing the order. Story seems to have been that some studio or other was doing a movie about the Moon landings in the sixties.'

'Oh yeah?'

'Except that ... as far as we can ascertain nobody in the business is doing the life of Neil Armstrong just at this moment in time.'

'Ahuh!'

They were silent for a few minutes before Ken Regan turned to order two more martinis. Reaching out he grabbed the only remaining nuts and olives left on the bar, moving them within easy range of his arm and out of reach of anyone else's.

'Yeah, couple of days later, this little guy takes fright. Seems a pile of drawings had just arrived to help him build the thing. Not just *some* drawings, but four hundred and thirty two of the fuckers to be exact; in six boxes. Right down to the last lightweight nut and bolt.'

At this, Phil Westwood spun round, his glass halfway to his lips.

'What?'

'Yeah. All dutifully stamped and approved with big National Security numbers printed all over them. So the little guy rings his friend, an ex cop employed up at the studios in security. He takes one look at the stuff and calls the F.B.I. ... Before they can get into the act ...'

'Don't tell me. Somebody walks in and removes the bloody

lot.'

They sat again deep in thought, a jaundiced look on the face of Ken Regan.

'No leads I suppose?' asked Phil.

'None so far. I have a guy down there now. The model maker couldn't help. He couldn't add much to the bare facts. He had done work for a couple of the studios in the past; clearly not involved; just happy to be sitting on a fat cheque wondering if it will be cleared or not and clearly confused for his trouble.'

They sat in silence nursing their drinks.

'Who the fuck would have wanted an obsolete piece of kit like that? A museum or a school somewhere maybe? Could be a number of things; somebody needed it. Somebody with access to the drawings that were around at the time? It wouldn't warrant a second look nowadays. Out of date by fifty years.'

Phil Westwood was trying to attract the attention of the waiter behind the bar.

'There's more.'

Leaning towards him, bringing his face closer to his ear;

'Somebody it seems found the time and the inclination to torch his workshop two nights ago. No evidence of any connection of course. Luckily, he was not at home. Otherwise ...'

Phil Westwood showed no sign of surprise, no indication of conclusions drawn, betraying nothing of the interest he was taking in this seemingly off-hand conversation. To an outsider they might have been discussing the weather or the Yankees performance of late.

'What did the police report come up with?'

'Not sure they even filed one. It's only just happened. Worth checking the records I suppose.'

Phil drained his martini, signalling to the bartender who reached for the empties.

'Play it again, Sam.'

He stood to fetch his wallet from his hip pocket fending off an intruder who was showing distinct signs of optimism in pushing between them to reach the bar.

'Why not move along, son? Get yourself a nice milkshake

somewhere else ...'

The offender sloped off and Phil Westwood edged closer to Ken Regan to close the gap and bolster the defences.

'Are you suggesting that there might be some deeper reason for the turn of events? Is there more?'

'I'm suggesting nothing of the kind. For the present that is. If however we dig anything up, I will be in touch.'

They drank quietly, the familiarity between them heavily disguised, each tending his own space and to all intents and purposes, ignoring the other.

'Makes you think, though. Who the fuck would have a call for a replica of the L E M ? Some transport museum perhaps? An overseas space agency redecorating their entrance way? Whichever way you dress it up, it makes no sense.'

'I'll place a couple of calls to a guy I know. I might just catch him. Keep my place warm. Won't be long.'

Draining his drink, Ken sauntered off to find a phone in some quiet spot where he could tap into his rich background of informers and people "in the know" who might be able to help. Phil ordered another round of drinks. How many had he had? Four? Five? What the hell! Another four months and it would be Christmas.


Gus Simpson found a place at the bar, making room for Frank Nelson to order up the pints of Guinness. The place was jammed, making service around the bar all but impossible. Carrying their drinks, they fought their way through to the archway between the two rooms finding a refuge large enough to stand and enough shelf space overhead to park their glasses. All eyes were on the figure of Rab Nicol sitting at the end of the room his sweatshirt stained and damp, the perspiration running down his back, his face glowing like the fires of hell. Even with the windows thrown open the heat inside the pub was unbearable.

Rab waved to Frank Nelson, nudging fat Susan who waved in turn. Frank shouted something to them, which was lost in the din.

'Tomorrow morning and his face will be beaming out from

every newspaper in America. I syndicated my story and the interview I had with them. Not a bad piece if I say so myself.'

Gus turned to him shouting to make himself heard.

'Don't tell me that the Washboard is running anti-American propaganda? I would have thought that *his* opinions on the lunar landings would find little sympathy with readers of the Washington Post.'

Nelson laughed.

'You'd be surprised. I even persuaded them to do a full spread on a friend of mine who spent most of his adult life debunking American claims of reaching the Moon. The stuff I handed over to Nicol there this morning was mostly copies of his early research. Remind me to tell you about him sometime. But not in here.'

The lighting had suddenly changed and a surprising hush fell over the crowd. The Tartan Messiah was about to speak. Someone at the back began to push forward through the crowd, drawing loud protests from the punters.

'Hey. Bugger off! Stop shovin'. Gi'e it a rest, Jimmy! Sit the fuck doon!'

Rab's finger was raised and all eyes were immediately focused on him. Frank Nelson nudged Gus on the arm, his amusement clearly showing. As they looked around them, the faces of the faithful were lifted in anticipation, awaiting the pearls of wisdom that would soon descend to enlighten their minds, leaving their spirits raised and their pockets lightened by the price of a few drinks.

'Hello. Welcome to the only packed house, night after night, at the Fringe of the Edinburgh International Festival. But first, an apology. Tomorrow night there will only be two shows due tae the fact that me and ma wee doll Susan here will once again be travellin' through tae Glasgow tae appear live on the Kirsty Monroe show fur the second time. Now Ah hear some o' yees askin',

' "Is the TV show more important than pleasing the good folk here at the Festival in Edinburgh" Well ah'll tell yees all. The answer is No! An emphatic No! But ...' - a wide grin and a cheeky expression to emphasise the point - '... the bevy is free and the money is a helluva lot better than sittin' aroond here chattin' tae you lot!'

At this the crowd applauded wildly, boos and cheers and good-natured barracking flying across the room, the atmosphere charged, their attention unwavering.

Gus Simpson was uncomfortable wishing himself out in the cool night, eager to seek a friendly pub with a less dedicated following. Frank Nelson on the other hand was plainly enjoying himself.

'The man's a natural. The way he handles them. Amazing.'

Rab was once again lifting his hand for silence. The crowd stilled immediately.

'Friends, tonight I will take you on a further voyage of discovery uncovering yet more of the vital proofs that ah huv been showing you over these past weeks; proofs which in themselves have shown you the undisputable truth about the failure o' the United States o' America to land as much as a flecky budgie on the surface o' the Moon. Tonight we go one step further, bringing ye yet further proof, if ever ye needed it, that the Yanks did not set foot on our nearest neighbour in the solar system. Not only that, but further disclosures about the conspiracy of silence that has surrounded the biggest cover up in history will be made here tonight in this humble hostelry for the very first time; at nae extra charge, ah might add.'

A cheer went up and Gus found that he was smiling despite his earlier objections. Frank Nelson was standing quietly against the wall nursing his pint amused by the proceedings. Rab was off again picking up on some point made at some earlier time.

'No. What ah said wis that the photographs were faked *before* they even took aff. If they *did* take aff. For I am now inclined to believe that not only did they fail tae land on the surface o' the Moon but ah huv every reason tae believe...'

He paused, and stood waiting for the moment to begin.

'... that they never left the orbit of the earth at any time.'

At this, there was an immediate hubbub, the noise rising as the master's words were debated. Rab was trying to make his voice heard.

'... for I believe with the aid of evidence that has only recently been placed before me, that they never got any further than making a few birls around the globe. Fur if we think about it for just a wee minute, what dae we huv in the way o' convincin' proof? Nothing. From the very moment that they shot themselves off intae space until they splashed doon somewhere in the ocean, they were OUT OF SIGHT. So, what do we huv other than a load o' taped conversations an' a few reels o' fillum that look as if they were shot through the bottom o' a damp jeely jar?'

Rab paused, looking around at the faces. Somewhere in Gus Simpson's head a feeling of déjà vu began to take over while the memory of Gregor's excited voice in the Doric three weeks earlier came flooding back to him. The First Minister was not the only one off his trolley, so it seemed.

'… fillums that could huv been made anywhere … on earth! And … if we look closely at these fillums, what dae we see? Well. Ah'll tell yees all. We see close up shots o' the surface o' the Moon as they are comin' in tae land. We see them skiffin' ower the surface just before they land. But … where are the shots o' the Moon taken when they were in orbit? Where are the long shots taken as they were getting' closer tae the Moon? Where are the shots o' the lander separating from the orbiting vehicle? A tricky manoeuvre ah wid tend tae think and somethin' ye widna want tae miss. An' where are the records of the descent o' the lunar lander as she says "Bye, bye" tae the orbiting vehicle?'

Again he searched their faces for a response, finding none.

'Yees don't know, so ah'll tell yees all. They don't exist. Now … if ye were goin' tae somewhere as wonderful as the Moon fur the first time ever in the history o' mankind, wid ye no' think tae take a couple o' approach shots as ye're zoomin' in just tae stick up above the kitchen sink fur the weans tae look at?'

Somebody yelled out, 'If ye've got a fuckin' sink,' and the laughter broke out across the room. Rab took up the challenge.

'Never you mind son, we'll pass the hat fur ye before we throw ye oot. Fair enough? Ye see, there are so many wee bits and pieces o' missin' evidence that set ye thinkin'. Did they run oot o' fil-lum? Ah don't think so. Were they too busy driving the buggy tae pay attention tae takin' pictures? Ah don't think so. And another thing ah wid ask yees all tae consider ...'

His pause, and the expression of anticipation mixed with a questioning look forewarned the punters of some further gem in the offing.

'Last week when they showed us the module liftin' off frae the Moon ... did ye ever see anythin' mair like a bungee jump in reverse? Wheech! It wis gone. Now, ah'm no expert, but that seemed tae me tae be a bit contrived. An' nae dust cloud. Nae disturbance whitever! Amazing. Absolutely amazing.'

Gus turned to find a further drink being pushed into his willing hand as Frank Nelson reclaimed his place against the wall. The room was cooler now, the sun long since gone and the fine drizzle that was falling bringing the temperature inside down to a bearable level. Gus looked at his watch. Gone ten thirty and a heavy day ahead tomorrow. And he still had to eat something. At the door, it was a case of "one out, one in". The place was crammed to the rafters. Gus looked around trying to find the attraction. Why anyone in his or her right mind would choose to suffer the lack of basic comforts was beyond him. But Frank Nelson appeared to be oblivious to his surroundings. Gus decided to grin and bear it until a suitable opportunity to detach himself presented itself. Rab meanwhile had hardly faltered.

'So what do we huv here I ask myself?' In his hand he was holding a photograph, which Frank Nelson instantly recognised as one of the bunch he had left with Rab earlier in the day. A sly wink in his direction acknowledged the fact. Nelson did not respond.

'So! Whit dae we see. One of a bunch o' photographs released at the time o' the landings in the seventies. Which one, I cannot say for sure. An' when ye look at it, there's nothin' unusual or special that springs tae mind. BUT... Take a closer look. Whit dae we see?' Rab was holding the photograph at arm's length, circulating it in a wide semi-circle that gave no opportunity for close examination.

'No? No? Well ah'll tell yees all. Ye see these wee lines that criss-cross the photie ...'

Again he proffered the image to all who would look ...'

'These wee lines are register marks or *calibrations* ... ' he uttered the word as if adding it to an already overstretched vocabulary, '...  which are incised into the lens to allow distances and heights to be calculated when looking at the picture. Dae ye follow me? Whit ah'm saying is, the lines are there on the camera and ye canny rub them oot! They're fixed behind the lens, so that no matter whit picture ye're takin' ye always end up wi' the lines in front. OK, so far?'

There was considerable nodding and chattering, immediately stilled as Rab continued.

'But what dae we huv here? Some o' the lines seem tae huv been rubbed oot! Now is that no' the bloody limit? A camera that thinks fur itsel'. Ye see here, this wee line disappears behind the lander, while this wee line is oot in front o' it. Now, since a' the lines are on the lens they should *all* be in front o' any image that's photographed. Is that no' the case?'

Rab had handed the photograph over to Susan who was circulating with it among those closest to the throne. Gasps of understanding and appreciation not shared since Columbus failed to fall off the edge of the world were heard rolling around the bar as those in front passed the news to the unbelievers in the rear.

'Now THAT my friends is whit ah call proof of a fix up. Doctored photographic evidence so badly done that it had tae huv been done in a great hurry. Mark you, it wid take an expert tae huv spotted it.'

Another sly look in Frank Nelson's direction expressed grateful thanks, a recognition of the academic standing of equals in a shared quest for the truth. Rab was quietly basking in the waves of adulation sweeping the bar. As the photograph was passed back, Nelson got hold of it. Offering it first to Gus he smiled.

'Already studied this one many times, many years ago. Look, see here. And here! It's obvious when it's pointed out to you.'

Gus Simpson was sceptical. Maybe the proof *was* there. But proof of what? And if a photograph could be doctored one way, it could just as easily be doctored to prove something else.

'Were these checked out by experts?' he enquired. Nelson nodded emphatically in reply.

'I have copies if you want them, and a lot more besides. Here, look at your leisure.' He handed the brown envelope to Gus.

'Thanks. I'll let you have them back. I can't see the Scotsman going for this lot. But you never know.' He stuck the envelope under his arm. He would take a closer leisurely look at them and get an opinion. He knew just the man for the job. Rab was off again having retrieved his photograph.

'Where did ah get it? That wid be tellin'. Sorry. Ma sources o' intelligence are protected. Always huv been, always will be.' A further sly grin in Nelson's direction.

'But what ah can say is this. There are plenty more where this one came from, I'm tellin' ye, boy!'

Gus motioned to Frank Nelson indicating that a retreat from the bar was in order. Rab had moved off to get a drink promising to continue his discourse within a few minutes. Nobody moved, drinks being ordered and handed around with practised skill over the heads of those sitting on the floor.

They struggled towards the door and out into the bustling street, sounds of revelry coming from the many restaurants along the Royal Mile. At eleven o'clock on a damp summer's night during the Festival the city was just coming to life.

'I know a small bar where, around about now, we might just find a seat. I'd like to take a look at this lot in peace. It's not far. Guaranteed to be quiet until around midnight.'

They strolled up the High Street taking the scenic route to the Tron Church. Five minutes later they entered the Royal Oak and to the quieter strains of an acoustic band they settled in the corner of the basement. Gus withdrew some of the material that Nelson had given him. At Gus's suggestion, Frank returned from the bar with the drinks. Gus was already reading the clippings and thumbing through the pile of photographs and printouts.

'And you say that this guy Duggan spent twenty years of his life researching this stuff. Unbelievable. There can be no doubt surely that the landings were for real? There is simply too much riding on the whole thing. For a country like America to even contemplate a cover up on this scale would surely be unthinkable? Christ. I remember watching the whole thing as a boy. I was completely spellbound. I can't believe that anyone ... I mean, who in their right mind would begin to believe this kind of crap?'

Frank Nelson was smiling but his expression became serious. 'Why not suspend your scepticism for just a moment or two and read on?'

Gus looked at him, his expression ridiculing any suggestion that he might be somehow swayed in his beliefs.

'Don't tell me that *you* too believe this shit?' He shrugged as Nelson elected not to reply. Bemused, he continued to scan the articles as Nelson returned his attention to the singer. After twenty minutes he put the material back into envelope.

'I promise to give it my undivided attention. Tomorrow. But I would ask one favour. If you don't mind, I would like to pass some of this stuff on to a friend of mine. I told you he recently brought the whole subject up at lunch and I had a hell of a job persuading him to hold on to his sanity. If this lot doesn't convince him he's wrong, nothing will. It'll only be for a day or two. How long are you here for?'

Nelson waved his hand in agreement.

'I have no immediate plans to go back provided I can keep the copy flowing from this end. You pass me something I can work with on the *Moonraker* tests and I will answer any queries you might have on any of that stuff. But to answer your question. Yes, I do believe the conspiracy theory and what's more I can prove it. Believe me, Gus, they never got within a mile of landing on the Moon's surface - one reason why I am so interested in the upcoming launch.'

Gus stared in disbelief at Nelson, unsure if he was winding him up or not.

'Let me hear you say that one more time.' he said.

'There's no need. It's all in there. And when your guys get to the Moon we'll all know for sure' came the sober reply.


Earlier that same evening, Gregor McLeod and his guests were assembling for the civic dinner in honour of both the Under Secretary of State of the United States and the American Consul and his wife. Standing now, waiting to enter the great hall, they chatted amiably, each holding prepared notes for their formal after-dinner speeches. They waited for the moment when the head usher would signal that the guests were assembled and seated, awaiting the entrance of the guests of honour. Gregor led the way. The assembly rose to greet them as they took their places. A moment later the anthem 'Flower of Scotland" rang out from the small band of pipers standing at the side of the hall. Then they stood respectfully motionless as the anthem of the United States of America was played in turn. As the last notes faded, the gathering took their seats and the festivities began.

The banqueting hall was impressive, the great tables arranged to allow a clear view of the top table where Elmer Franklin sat flanked by Gregor McLeod and his inner cabinet. Seated alongside him, Margaret McIver, the Minister for Transport, was busy pointing out the various celebrities and dignitaries around the room, many from the opposition benches, others prominent in one way or another in business. Behind the top table the wide curve of the full height glazing framed the view of Princes Street from the West End to the clock tower on the Balmoral Hotel, the festive decorations and the floodlighting of the buildings adding to the colour and the magic of the finest street in Europe.

Below in Princes Street Gardens, the Ross bandstand was thronged with people as the Scottish Symphony Orchestra prepared to play. In the background, the crowd strolled along the parade, the lights and shop fronts of the subway shopping mall with its restaurants and clubs an established Mecca for the hordes of tourists streaming into the city from all destinations for the Festival.

Elmer Franklin turned to Gregor McLeod, obviously enjoying the evening and the party atmosphere.

'Gregor. I must say, you Scots certainly do know how to throw a party. I am very impressed. Your chauffeur today very kindly gave us a wonderfully detailed running commentary on the places of interest we visited. I became completely engrossed in the tour, the history of your country and the wonderful warmth that we encountered everywhere we went. It has been a truly momentous day for me, and now, with this dinner and the overwhelming kindness that you have shown us, I can only thank you most sincerely for everything you have done.'

Gregor laughed and responded in like manner.

'You are most welcome. As you know, you are the first American statesman we have had the honour of receiving and we are delighted that you have been able to spend some time with us these past few days. I trust my invitation to a round of golf at St. Andrews still attracts you for Saturday afternoon?'

'Of course. Of course. I wouldn't miss out on that for the world. When I tell the President that I had the honour of partnering the First Minister of Scotland at the home of golf, I feel sure I will be sent into exile at the earliest opportunity to one of our less civilized outposts. He plays a good game as you probably have heard. I understand Minister Mason will be part of the foursome ... and your Minister for Education with whom I had a very interesting meeting this morning.'

Gregor interrupted him.

'I have gone one better. We will be playing with two of Scotland's finest professionals, both of them eager to meet you, and both ex-members of the Ryder Cup team. Afterwards we might very well introduce you to some other Scottish celebrities in the form of the finest of our Scottish malt whiskies.'

Eyebrows were raised a fraction as they both laughed, the hospitality cutting through the usual fog of protocol that so often resulted in polite exchanges and political correctness.

The meal was superb. Gregor's insistence on the finest fare being prepared at all times had extended to the staff canteens and coffee kitchens throughout the Rock to the point where the ministers' dining room was at serious risk of receiving a Michelin star and the queue for official "invitations" to lunch far outstripped the ability of the chefs to cope with the ever increasing numbers of visitors.

Soon the lights dimmed and the coffees and liqueurs were offered around. The Master of Ceremonies duly called for order and Gregor rose from his chair. Softly, from the concert platform below, the sounds of Rachmaninov began to filter through the glass wall.

'Honoured guests, Ambassadors, Ministers of State, Ladies and Gentlemen. On behalf of my Government, my Cabinet and Leaders of the parties in opposition, my thanks are due to you all this evening for taking the time to join us in welcoming our esteemed guest, Under Secretary of State Elmer Franklin, who has graced us this evening with his presence. A short while ago he was thanking me in no uncertain manner for our hospitality and congratulating me on the kind attention he has received *and* for the extensive running commentary offered today by my chauffeur as he escorted Senator Franklin's party around the city visiting various centres of historical and cultural interest. He'll be happy to know that I have since sacked the said chauffeur who talked far too much anyway.'

A roar of good-humoured laughter greeted this remark, knowing full well that Gregor had rarely ever fired anyone in a long lifetime of public service. He continued.

'This is a rare occasion tonight for us, coming together as we have to honour the representative of the United States of America, Under Secretary of State, Elmer Franklin.' A short burst of enthusiastic applause was heard as he continued.

'At the same time, we of course extend the welcome, as always, to our good friends the American Consul and his wife Mr. and Mrs. John Willmott.'

A further round of applause followed.

'John is a frequent visitor to the Rock as many of you will know, more often than not seen as a guest in the Minister's dining room, which leaves all of us wondering just how bad the food really is over on Charlotte Square.'

He paused, and waited for the laughter to subside, exchanging a quip with John Willmott before moving on.

'Tonight we have shared an excellent dinner and I extend my thanks on behalf of us all to the chefs, kitchen and service staff who have made this evening such an enjoyable affair.'

There was a spontaneous burst of applause as Gregor poured a large dram handing it personally to the Master of Ceremonies with a quiet word of thanks.

'Now before I propose the toast to our honoured guests I want to take this opportunity to say a few words of welcome to Senator Franklin. It has been a great personal pleasure for me these last few days making your acquaintance and I am pleased that we hold so many opinions in common on the current state of the world at large. I would also like to take this opportunity to thank you for your tact and consideration in that not once did you refer to us as "English". Clearly there has been some careful coaching going on behind those shutters up on Charlotte Square.'

Gregor paused for a ripple of laughter, the guests enjoying the performance.

'I only wish that we could have found the time to explore the many other issues that concern us; issues which jointly face our two governments in the areas of climate change and protection of the environment, together with a host of lesser, related topics. Time unfortunately prevented us developing these discussions. I should point out however that over eighteen holes this weekend at St. Andrews I shall be making hay on my favourite subject whether the sun shines or not.

'Here in Scotland we look forward, as you are aware, to developing cleaner and better fuels for our transportation systems with the fervent hope that we are contributing, albeit in a fairly minor way, to the drive to clean up our planet for future generations to enjoy.

'I am pleased to announce, that today, we took the first steps towards making our research available to the United States in the fervent hope that within a few years, we shall all see a significant reduction in the levels of noxious gases polluting our atmosphere.'

There were loud cheers and applause, Elmer Franklin joining in enthusiastically.

'In return I have impressed on Senator Franklin the need to convey to President Jackson the urgency of the many appeals made by world leaders for America to recognise that, if the world's leading industrial nation turns its back on the scientific facts regarding global warming and all that that entails, we can hardly expect less well-heeled nations in the third world to comply with existing targets.'

Elmer Franklin was exchanging rapid side-glances with the

Consul who, in turn, was inwardly surprised at the direction that Gregor's speech had begun to take. It was with considerable relief that they noted the swing away from environmental issues to the proposal to reach the Moon by St Andrew's day.

'As we all know, both the United States and our own small nation will shortly be heading for the Moon, the Americans landing there ahead of us by a matter of days. When President Jackson proposed the first interstellar handshake between our two crews, we felt that the gesture, so simple in itself, yet so far reaching in terms of symbolising the long years of friendly cooperation that have always existed between our nations, would mark a milestone in man's continuing search for peaceful cooperation between nations. We look forward eagerly to this historic meeting and hope to mark the occasion here in Scotland with a public holiday and countrywide celebrations.'

A round of warm applause followed this announcement.

'I would ask all of you to rise and toast the continuing good health of our special guest here this evening. I give you, Elmer Franklin.'

The assembly rose and settled again as Elmer prepared to respond to the toast.

'First Minister, Ambassadors, Ministers of State, Ladies and Gentlemen. You have honoured me tonight with your best wishes and your splendid hospitality over these past few days and for these things I thank you from the bottom of my heart. For those of you who carry a sense of justice, I should add that I have since spoken to the First Minister and he has promised that his chauffeur *will* be reinstated as of tomorrow morning.'

There was loud applause. Gregor joined in enthusiastically.

'But, to digress for a moment, some of you might be aware that in June this year, news began to reach us across the pond of dark deeds and curious alliances being formed which, I can now admit, caused a fair degree of apprehension among those of us responsible for maintaining security in all its many forms. When news of your advances in rocket science and your satellite launch programme became known, talk of advanced fuel, technological successes and cooperation with the Soviet Space agency, we were frankly alarmed. Fortunately for all of us Gregor McLeod does not appear to be maturing plans to take over the world.'

Laughter and applause.

'But nevertheless we saw fit to take the perceived threat, as we saw it at that time, seriously enough to dispatch our agents on a fact finding mission to gather what intelligence they could about this possible danger to global peace and stability. With arrangements duly concluded between the Embassy in London, the Consulate here in Edinburgh and at the invitation of your own First Minister, it was arranged for two of our agents to be flown in to inspect and report on the facilities at North Uist as being the quickest way to dispel the rising fear being felt "in certain quarters"; fears that might have sent our greatest carriers heading for the Hebrides, Marines put on full alert and Congress recalled to debate the growing threat of nuclear attack by a hitherto friendly nation.'

He was smiling broadly as he painted the picture of Scotland under imminent attack, causing a few smiles and a few shaking heads to comment under their breath about neutrality and peace on earth, goodwill towards men.

'After several days of silence from the two agents we were almost ready to send out a second party to find them, when they were duly returned to us quite the worse for wear.'

He shook his head as if recalling the state of the two agents concerned.

'After a week in the company of Hamish McLeod and the inmates of the Covenanters' Inn up on North Uist ...'

Here there was loud laughter.

' ... they were finally handed over and immediately flown for emergency treatment to a detox clinic in Maryland.'

There was further loud laughter and general applause as the notion of two well-trained agents falling into bad company on North Uist. Elmer continued.

'I have to reassure you that one of them ...'

Here he was interrupted by further laughter.

'One of them has now been pronounced fit for a return to

duty, provided ...'

Prolonged laughter.

'... provided he seeks counselling and enlists part time with the Salvation Army,'

Elmer was having trouble getting to the point.

'... while the other has been awol in downtown New York ever since escaping from MP's somewhere en route to Langley, Virginia.'

At this, there were loud guffaws of laughter not least from Gregor and the top table. Elmer held up his hand.

'So, the C.I.A. is currently being sued by one wife, the other agent is learning to beat the big drum and shout Hallelujah! while our President ...'

Further laughter ...

'... while our President is again happy and reassured having placed Hamish McLeod and the inmates of the Covenanters' Inn at the top of the list of America's most wanted.'

Further loud applause and merriment.

'I might also add that the only fears felt by Congress at the time were related to the possibility that there might have been a halt on whisky imports into the States, if hostilities with Scotland had ensued, a threat infinitely more terrifying than impending nuclear attack.'

Through the rising wave of laughter, he raised his glass in the direction of Hamish McLeod who responded with an angelic smile and the merest of bows to all and sundry.

'But, let us be serious for a moment or two. You are all aware that there never was the slightest possibility at any time that we considered your satellite programme a threat to world peace. We never doubted that the excellent relations and family ties that we have nurtured over the centuries would in the end prevail.'

In his mind, he recalled Nathan Jackson's defiant briefing to him two months earlier.

'We are now truly happy, and I know that I speak for President Jackson at this time, that, at the end of November we shall reinforce that fraternity with the first ever meeting on another star between two nations who have throughout their history shown determination and resolve in upholding the virtues of democracy and freedom for all men, irrespective of colour or creed.'

He continued.

'Many of you may already know the publication, but some years ago I happened to pick up a book printed by one of our university presses. The book sought to list the one hundred people in the history of the world who, through their actions, inventions or deeds had exerted the most influence on the development of mankind. As I recall, the first in line was the Prophet Mohammed. Again, hardly surprising considering the vast areas of the world dominated by Islam over the centuries. The second was the great Englishman, Sir Isaac Newton. The third, as I recall, was the Chinaman who invented paper. Hardly surprising again. I will not bore you with the remaining ninety seven.'

There was loud laughter and some cheering.

'What *is* unusual, however, is that out of the total of one hundred, five of them were Scots.'

There was a general murmur of surprise at this statement.

'Yes. Five. When one considers that as Scots, you represent less than an eighth of one percent of the world's population, this has to be a truly amazing concentration of talent. Of course the book represented one man's opinion. But I do feel, that having met your charming First Minister, that if the book is ever edited and republished that the number I have quoted might easily have risen in the meantime to six.'

There was further applause and sustained laughter.

'Ladies and gentlemen, It is with great pleasure that I propose the toast to Gregor McLeod, the Scottish people and to this great nation, Scotland.'

Standing just inside the partition that screened the view into the banqueting kitchen and within close reach of his V.I.P., Paul Burke continued to monitor events as they unfolded, constantly scanning the many guests around the great hall for even the slightest glimpse of the lovely Fiona with the clear green eyes and the golden hair.

# 21

Ken Regan had returned from placing his calls and resumed his place at the bar. Phil Westwood hardly acknowledged his presence except to thumb in the general direction of the last round ordered, the chill on the martini long since departed and the nuts long since consumed. Around them, the throng of reporters was still going strong, the crush at the bar hardly reduced by the fact that the press call had been over for hours. Again, the protocol between them was re-established as they each sought the isolation that one can only feel by occupying a stool at the bar in a busy cocktail lounge. After a few minutes, Phil Westwood spoke.

'Well? Anything?'

Regan did not reply. Pushing the warm martini to one side he called out to the bartender.

'Manuel. Hit me again. Yeah. Over here.'

They sat in silence for a while, Regan obviously preoccupied. Around them, the crowd was becoming louder, the younger element, some of them on their first assignments, held the floor. Phil and Ken retreated further into the corner, the potted palm all but concealing them and blocking their view of the room. Unseen by the two of them, Mark Brander had made an unexpected entry into the room. The atmosphere changed immediately as he passed through the crowd, nodding to left and right, before heading to the end of the bar. Ken Regan noted the change in noise level and nudged Phil Westwood.

'As good a time as any to catch the son of a bitch.'

Ken Regan shook his head. 'Would do you no good and you know it. That bastard couldn't come clean in a tower full of Chinese laundries.'

'I just spoke to Somerville.'

'Oh yeah?'

'Yeah. He was on the defensive alright. Said very little as a matter of fact.'

They sat, still apart, each in his own world, but drinking together. 'Funny thing ... though,'

There was the sudden sound of broken glass and shouting as the crowd applauded the spilt drinks, the atmosphere becoming boisterous as the afternoon wore on.

'Yeah?'

'You know what he's like? Fucking old woman. Told me to get lost.'

'So?'

Mark Brander had seen them across the room. Phil waved absent-mindedly and Brander stayed where he was, unsure of whether or not to join them.

'So?' Phil Westwood enquired, more emphatically this time.

'There's some panic on. That much is for sure. The story of the lander stacks up. How, I don't know but he didn't deny it. There's more.'

He sipped his drink looking around for more olives and finding none.

'... Seems there's talk of the administration having egg all over their fat faces. No. He wouldn't say any more. But I could tell. The bastard was hiding plenty. Shit. But whatever it is, it involves NASA and this latest Moon shot.'

They sat again, each holding a personal wake for the role of truth in government. Phil leaned across the bar and called the bartender over.

'Manuel. Please ask Mr. Brander if he would consider joining us for a drink.'

Ken Regan looked across at Phil Westwood wondering what was to come. A few seconds later, a freshly showered and smiling Mark Brander offered a limp wrist to both of them.

'So. What are you two old foxes cooking up this evening? Whose chicken run is in the firing line? Eh?'

Phil Westwood looked him straight in the eye; long experience of sizing people up had given him an almost supernatural ability to suss out the lies that had regularly been served up over the years in dealing with politicians and spin doctors alike in various administrations. As the orange juice and soda was placed on the edge of the bar, and at the precise moment that Brander was leaning over to pick it up, he felt a sudden vice like grip take hold of his testicles, his body pulled until he was face to face with the veteran reporter, his heels clear off the floor, his face contorted as the survivor of many a conflict whispered into his ear, still smiling, but with a voice that was icy clear.

'Just tell me what the fuck is going on with the current cover up over this Moon shot and I will return you to your boyfriend in one piece. Give me any more of the crap you were handing out today and I swear I will tear these perfumed nuts of yours out of your miserable body.'

A few minutes later, as the White House Press Officer hurriedly left the bar, Ken Regan smiled for the first time directly at his old friend.

'He's right. He *could* have you for assault.' As their eyes met and as hilarity erupted between them, they both knew it would never happen. Moreover they were now within an inch of cracking the best story of their long careers in journalism.

'Manuel,' Phil shouted. 'Get your butt over here and to hell with the rest of these assholes.'


The lakeside was beautiful, the water sparkling as the sun danced on the tiny ripples caused by the ducks as they moved about on the water's still surface. At lunchtime, they tended to congregate around the small cobbled jetty that sloped steadily into the bed of the lake. Lunchtime and the area was all but deserted. As Sam Cavanagh crossed the broad swathe of lawn and moved on down the hill towards the water, he could already see the distant stooped figure of Tom Sherman toiling along the pathway, past the boathouse and beyond to where the tall cedars stood shading the pathway encircling the lake. Far off in the distance the traffic on the streets of Washington's diplomatic quarter could be faintly heard.

'Tom. How are you? How's the flu? You feeling better?'

The other shrugged. Despite the warm August day he was wrapped against any sudden change in the seasons.

'I'm fine. Just fine. Age. Just age. I tell you. When it catches up with you, you can start counting the days. Maybe the weeks.'

They laughed as Sam Cavanagh indicated the park bench bordering the path and facing the little jetty.

'Mallards. Don't often see them this late on. Used to feed them regularly when Jessica was alive. How she loved her ducks. There. See there? The grey geese? Now there's a sight for sore eyes. They are late as well.'

They were seated now as Sam opened his lunch tin. 'Your favourite piece of pie. Knew you would like that.'

He smiled.

'Mustard?'

'No. No thanks. Heartburn if I touch the stuff. So, let me hear it. Any problems? No sudden summonses in the middle of the night?'

They were laughing now.

'Not that I know about. We are still in business. Seems that the show will be ready to roll as we agreed by twentieth or thereabouts of November.'

He paused as the old lady with the dog turned to feed the ducks on the jetty; the sudden squawking causing them to lift their heads, stilling conversation. On an impulse she turned around smiling.

'If I take him too close to the water the ducks will fly, then he will get excited and bark.'

She smiled again, tethering the dog to the waste paper bin beside their bench. 'Now sit!' she commanded, adding apologetically, 'Only until I feed my friends', shuffling off out of earshot. The dog settled and Tom threw the piecrust to it.

'We are well ahead on the modifications to the ship. Everything is running smoothly with the lunar lander and the rovers. I had a look at the drawings we had prepared back then for the lunar rovers we used in the studio shots. How you got away with it is anybody's guess. This time around, the things will have to work. The tests have gone well but I can understand why we found it difficult to control them back then. Things have certainly moved on.'

'What about the crew? Will they go along with it? Have they

been fully briefed yet? Who else will need to know? You'll have to come up with a damn good cover story in case of any leak.'

Sam Cavanagh watched the ducks jostling for position, diving to retrieve pieces of crust thrown to them.

'Yeah. We've got that covered. We know who we want to do the business. They are working on it right now. Just don't ask, right? In any case, we have bigger problems to contend with. The suits *will* have to be remade. Boots, protective linings, everything. It's a nightmare. We've rehearsed the whole thing of course. That side of it is going well. The tests are all on schedule too. Everybody is working flat out. We are back in the space race and that is what counts after all. I just wish we weren't so rushed. Some of the gear is obsolete and we really ought to have spent some time developing new solutions.'

They sat quietly, contemplating the serenity of the quiet pond in front of them, the willows touching the water on the far side, the stillness of the scene a far cry from the activity back at base. After a bit, Tom Sherman began buttoning his coat, indicating that the meeting was at an end.

'One slip up and the world's press will pounce on us,' he said quietly. They stood to go, facing each other.

'When do you next have to report back to the Palace? Did I hear you say Wednesday?'

'It'll be Thursday now. I'm up in Chicago at the press conference on Tuesday and Wednesday. Look, I am going to tell them it's a goer. I have no choice. You'll just have to press on and do your best. We can't afford to lose this opportunity. I'm sure you are already painfully aware of the alternative.'

They shook hands each turning away and retreating back the way they had come.

Down in the boathouse the agent dropped his headphone on the table. He called through to the back room.

'Tell Rover he can take the old bird home now. And next time, find a spot without those fucking ducks. I'll have to clean this mother up for hours before I can use any of it.'

Sitting silently beside him the second F.B.I. agent was wondering if the targets could possibly have been alerted to the surveillance. Either that, or they were conversing in a carefully prearranged code. As it stood, he utterly failed to see how this latest conversation related in any way to the previous taps they had collected. Might be a good time to kick the whole thing back to control. Let them sort it out.

By the time that they had collected their gear, the old lady was back at H.Q. working out in the gym, while Rover slept peacefully in the corner of the kennels dreaming of chasing fat mallards and sleek grey geese across wide expanses of open green pasture.


Later that evening as Sam Cavanagh was catching the late night news broadcast, his phone rang. 'Yup! Oh! Yeah. Yeah?' There was a click as the scrambler snapped in. 'Tom. We're OK. We can talk. We did well today. They'll be running around trying to figure out what the hell we're doing.'

He laughed.

'Are you sure they were there? I saw nothing.'

'Sam. The dog! The bloody dog was wired.' He was off laughing and coughing again, his wheezing coming down the line as if he were in the same room.

'Christ, Yes. The dog. Why didn't I spot it? So much for all that training. Look, keep in touch. Everything *is* O.K. We're nearly there. I'm planning to go over in about ten day's time. Call you soon nearer the time. Bye.'

And he was gone. Reaching for his beer Sam wondered just how safe his line really was. He was slowly reaching the conclusion that the safest route lay in trusting nobody.


Gregor picked up her report for the third time and studied it again. Sally McIntosh sat opposite him at the conference table watching his reaction to two weeks of dedicated work.

'Has anyone else seen this yet?' he asked.

'No. As we agreed I am preparing the work at home in the afternoons and this is the only current draft of the document.'

He turned a few pages and continued reading. Suddenly he stopped,

'I'm sorry. I have of course read it earlier today. It's good. It's very good in fact. I cannot fault it. If everything works out as we have discussed, this should prove to be the ideal blueprint for the biggest heist in history.'

He was smiling.

'Coffee?' He held the pot of Columbian Blue towards her sending the aroma temptingly across the polished teakwood table.

'Yes please. As you know, I am a decaf freak, but this stuff you have is worth the odd shake and tremor.'

He raised a fresh cup from the buffet and brought the coffee to her.

'Tell me something. I told you at the outset that this new assignment might involve substantial travelling. How do you feel about commuting from Washington back to Edinburgh once a week for extended weekends? Say three and a half days over there, the rest of the week here. It'll be hard on you. But, as you know, the assignment should be all over bar the shouting by the New Year. Before you rush to answer ...'

He held up his hand.

'I have said it will be no picnic. You will be working long hours and there is a lot to get done before the launch. You would be working out of the consulate building, which has been ready for some time. I haven't seen it, but I am told it is well equipped and has secure lines. The latter I somehow doubt knowing the F.B.I, hence the need for de-briefing at regular intervals. We would provide you with a secretary of course and a driver. No need for a bodyguard,' he added, 'just yet.'

He saw only the fleetest of smiles cross her face at the mention of personal security.

'If you need some time to think it over ...'

She stopped him.

'First Minister, sorry, Gregor, I thought we had gone beyond the stage of committing to each and every stage of this venture. I told you I was in from the start. If we continue like this I might start having second thoughts. Don't give me that choice. Let my commitment suffice. When do I travel?'

He grinned from ear to ear.

'Hold on. Hold on. We are just starting. You already know most of what is required of you, and *that* we will keep firmly to ourselves *pro tem*. That also goes for the new Ambassador.'

Now he saw a look of surprise cross her face. Not yet a poker player, but getting there.

'Yes.' he said. 'We can't activate the Consulate without appointing a Consul at least. He will have to be accredited and all the formalities taken care of. Initially that will fall to you. Something to cover your role on arrival, so to speak. Thereafter, you will hold the post of Liaison Officer between the Consulate and other Government representatives, dealing of course with your counterparts within the U.S. State Department. At the same time, I will have you officially approved as Press Officer and Protocol Advisor.'

He watched her face for some reaction seeing nothing.

'So! What do you think? Can you handle it?'

She faced him squarely across the table.

'Of course I shall do my level best. But you already know that much. I just wish that I shared your confidence in me to carry out the task ahead. Sometimes when I weigh it up ...'

He was smiling again as he approached her, extending his hand. 'Enough of this mutinous talk. To lunch. To lunch.'

And for the first time ever, he suddenly burst into song waltzing her around the table and dancing her smartly through the foyer to the door of the tiny lift. His secretary gave him a pitying look and shook her head

'If they only knew,' she said quietly, to which Gregor roared.

'Oh, they will, they will,' as the lift doors closed behind them.

Standing there, giggling like school children in the sudden stillness of the confined space, suddenly aware of the great strength of the man beside her and catching a first glimpse of his humour, of barriers suddenly being removed, she instinctively reached out to straighten his tie, regretting it immediately, removing her hand quickly away and averting her eyes as he, still grinning, looked down on her.

Stepping out into the lobby, he led her gently to the quiet end of the dining room. They ordered lunch and she broke the silence.

'May I ask the identity of my new boss? Who will be the new Ambassador? Do I take my orders from him or directly from here?'

He was still smiling, his plans transiting smoothly from concept to reality aided by the courage and vision of the woman sitting across from him.

'First things first. You will be provided with a clothing allowance. Get yourself some stuff that will turn their heads. In Washington you will be up against the hostesses who are hard work at any time. You need to take them on. As for taking orders you will appear to take them from the Consul. In reality you will be working directly for my inner Cabinet and myself. This will be made clear to the Consul, but I do not anticipate friction on that score. It will be explained to him, but one thing you must know. He must never be a party to our little pantomime; is that clear? He must be able to remain in place irrespective of the outcome.'

'Of course. That is understood.'

He was talking again, his ability to switch topics and blend answers with questions slightly troubling and confusing.

'You'll like the new man. I looked for a woman initially but there was no one I could imagine in place who would be robust enough to serve us during the difficult times that lie ahead. No. I feel that Rod Cameron has the drive that the job requires. I had a short meeting with him this morning. He is prepared to move, family and all, to Washington so, to all intents and purposes it's a done deal. He leaves in one week's time.'

He saw the look that had crossed her face.

'Is there a problem?

'No. None at all,' she replied. 'Where will I be staying? Has that been discussed?' she asked tentatively.

'Yes. The residence is vast. Too big, even for *his* family. You will have two rooms at the outset on the upper floor. Your office will be next to his on the first floor. I left the arrangements to Rod. If you have any doubts, please let me know once you are settled in. Now, is there anything you wish to ask me?'

She thought for a minute weighing up the need to disclose her recent attachment to Rod Cameron and decided against it.

'I am sure that whatever arrangements have been made will suit me very well,' she said amiably.

'Good', he said. 'Let's eat. I have to leave for Glasgow after lunch to appear on the Kirsty Monroe show. Why not join me? I know a great little place near the Concert Hall for a late supper after the show.'

'Why not?' was all she said. But somewhere, deep within her, a familiar chord had been silently touched.


Kirsty Monroe was enjoying herself as she steered the debate on this, the second show given over to Scotland's entry into the new era of space exploration. And for the moment, her old friend Gregor McLeod held the floor.

'It is difficult to be precise on exactly when our decision to go for the Moon landing was made. Oh, we had toyed with the idea once we knew that it was possible and yes, I freely admit, that we were all surprised at the pace of developments, realising the many technical issues that the team had to face in constructing a shuttle of this nature. Of course we worked very closely with our friends in Russia ...'

Kirsty interrupted him.

'I was going to come on to that question in a moment or two. But meantime, if we can just see the clip of the trials conducted earlier this year in Uzbekistan ...'

There was a brief pause as the monitor rolled.

'There!' she said.

The screens were portraying a view of the earth from a much higher orbit than normally seen from earlier orbiting vehicles, the horizon and the curvature of the earth clearly visible, the big blue marble sitting serenely in space; the lonely planet. There were gasps from the audience. She turned to Hamish.

'Can you tell us what is happening here? We seem to be a long way from earth. Is this the prototype of the same ship that will carry our astronauts to the Moon?'

'But of course. Here, you can just see the edge of the western seaboard of the United States. And here, an unusually clear view of the Antarctic ice cap. As you know we developed the *Caliban* in collaboration with the Russian Space Agency and the early tests were conducted over there.'

As he spoke, the monitor was displaying the re-entry of the vehicle and the breathtakingly beautiful views of the earth as the craft decelerated and prepared to land.

'With the new fuels we are able to reach much deeper orbits and, as we now know, there is nothing preventing us from going to the Moon every weekend if the fancy takes us!'

He looked around at the audience as they shared his laughter, his wit well known to the general public.

Kirsty Monroe was off again.

'And here we see the descent ...' The clip drew to a close as the craft touched down and ran off into the distance, the thrusters reversing to slow its progress.

Hamish spoke.

'That was all several months ago. The latest model now being readied at North Uist is a much larger version, modified to carry the extra payload of fuel. Of course we have made minor variations to the satellite hold to accommodate the *Moonraker* descent vehicle, but, all in all, the two ships share the same technical specifications.'

Rab sat entranced, his only contribution to the programme being his occasional outbursts of applause. Another speaker was on his feet from the audience.

'Can anyone tell us how the *Caliban* will begin the journey? Presumably the lift off is conventional then settling into orbit before spinning off towards the Moon?'

Kirsty Monroe was pointing at Murdo Sinclair. 'Mr. Sinclair, perhaps you could field this question. Murdo?'

'Well, *Caliban* will be wheeled out on her cradle to the end of the runway and slowly lifted to a vertical position, where the fuelling masts and the support services are already installed. The countdown period is around four hours from the time that we batten down the hatches. As you said, we will take off and enter an orbit from which, after final checks have been conducted, she will begin her powered trip to the Moon. On her return, she will make a gradual re-entry deploying the fins and wings to make a conventional powered descent on to the new runway that has recently been completed on North Uist. It's all terribly simple.'

There was applause and laughter as he shrugged before sitting down again.

'You certainly make it all sound very simple but I suspect that there is a great deal more to it than that,' said Kirsty Monroe.

'Can you tell me something that has troubled many of our listeners ever since the announcement was made? Inevitably, they all come back to the same point, despite their admiration for the project and their great pride in the technical achievement. Simply put, they all seem to want to know "why"? Why repeat the voyages of the seventies, given that the Americans did all that there was to do on the Moon, except perhaps establish the presence of water?'

Hamish looked at Gregor, who motioned him to respond. Gathering his thoughts for a moment, he paused before replying.

'Well, whilst it is true that America has led the way in space exploration, it all happened a very long time ago. I daresay that, if we hadn't discovered the properties of our new fuel and established its use in rocket propulsion, I doubt very much if the idea of going to the Moon would ever have occurred to us. Not even to Gregor here.'

He laughed, the audience joining with him.

'But with the realization that the *Caliban* was capable of being adapted, and when the possibility of deep space travel was first suggested, the dream of many of us at Rosewell has been to see this country undertake a voyage to the Moon, to demonstrate to ourselves and to the world that the initiative and commitment to underwrite the mission were alive and well in an Independent Scotland. And let us not forget, the great advances that have been made in avionics, in space telemetry and in the general field of digital instrumentation, and above all, the new fuel - all areas of potential commercial spin off which will undoubtedly earn enormous sums for the treasury in the years to come. Like all great undertakings, this venture will, prove to have significant benefits for all of us as time goes on.'

There was a round of applause as a member of the audience rose to put the next question.

'Simon Taylor, from the State of Nevada. I have a question for the panel and in particular for the First Minister. Does the panel consider that there is any conclusion to be drawn from the announcement by President Jackson that America intends to reach the Moon a few days ahead of your own landing, and does anyone on the panel see any link between recently published reports suggesting that we did not land on the Moon in the sixties and the apparent sudden urgency of NASA to send men back to the surface?'

Rab was straining at the leash as Gregor McLeod turned to reply. Out of the corner of her eye, Kirsty Monroe was aware of the impending volcanic eruption, recognizing that sooner, rather than later, she must involve the Nicol man in the debate. For the moment, however, she put the question to Gregor.

'Well, again, I doubt if it has any significance. But one thing I am sure of. We intend to land within a short distance of that historic first step on the Moon and I fully expect to find all of the earlier artifacts in place just as they were abandoned all those years ago.'

He paused, a twinkle developing in his eye.

'On the other hand, if, as you suggest, there is nothing there to find, we shall all have to think again.'

Rab was applauding wildly.

'Good for you, son. You tell 'em.'

'Mr. Nicol?' Kirsty was calling on Rab to respond, his attention still focused on the First Minister.

'Mr Nicol? What do you make of all this? Will we find the original site sitting there just as they left it? Will we find the descent module, the trails of footprints running all over the surface, the golf balls lying around at close of play?'

Rab's angelic face took on a serious expression. 'I have made ma position very clear on these issues,' he said. 'In ma humble opinion, the Yanks never made it doon tae the surface. I firmly believe that the photies they took were all homegrown and the cameras they had strapped tae their chests were just window dressing. Ah can tell yees all. When we get tae the Moon it wull be a first fur Scotland.'

There was loud patriotic cheering, Gregor and Hamish hugely amused and applauding loudly. But Rab was off again.

'Earlier on today I presented photographic evidence tae the producer, Mr Thomas that clearly shows that fur whitever reason, the Yanks had a' their photies in the can, *before* they even took aff!'

Further wild applause.

'If indeed, they ever *did* take aff! Fur what dae we have in the way o' concrete evidence? A few photies, a handful o' rocks frae some crater, an' a few reels of faded fillum?'

Kirsty Monroe was once again forced to regain the initiative.

'Before we come back to you Mr. Nicol, perhaps we could ask someone on the panel to reply to these issues?'

She was motioning for Rab to be seated, he grudgingly conceding.

'Mr. Simpson. You are the features editor of the Scotsman and you have written extensively on the current project. How do you respond to the accusations levelled against the Americans of skullduggery and cover-up over their many Moon missions?'

Gus was tugging his ear looking perplexed. This was not the question he had been expecting. He coughed nervously.

'I have heard all of the current arguments and I must say at the outset that I firmly believe that the Americans landed fair and square on the Moon. The possibility of a cover up is just too awful to contemplate. Believe me; it could never have been sustained for all those years. But I will concede that, if we examine the evidence as it stands, that there is very little, other than photographic or audio recordings of the event. And it is precisely because the evidence is, in a sense, so fragile, so easily fabricated, that the dissenters can have a field day, highlighting the various anomalies that have been researched over the years. And, let us not forget, even if the photographs *were* prepared ahead of the launch, I feel that we should remember the situation at that time, the super powers locked into the cold war, Russia breathing down America's neck, the Cuban missile crises and the whole miserable race to be the first in space.'

'Mr. Nicol?'

Rab was on his feet.

'So ye're prepared tae concede that the photies were faked? Ye accept that they could never huv taken photies that were in perfect focus, hampered as they were by their divin' helmets? So. Ah huv tae ask ye. If they could've faked some o' the evidence, why not the bloody lot? Tell me that, boy!'

There was loud supporting applause from the audience; the panel greatly amused, Gus Simpson unable to reply, waving his hands in defeat.

On cue, two photographs had appeared on the monitor and Kirsty Monroe was inviting Rab to comment on them. Having rehearsed the explanation several times over during the earlier part of the day, Rab began his exposé of the lunar landscape and the appearance and subsequent disappearance of the L. E. M. from the one location, the same backgrounds being compared, and the dates on the photographs clearly showing at least a major anomaly in the photographic evidence.

'So just how can anyone say that they are goin' back tae visit the site, when a' the evidence o' these photies shows that they never made it? How can the lander be in one photo but no' in the same location the very same day? It seems tae huv moved. Not once, but twice. Gone fur a walk, then toddled back again. Is that no mystifyin'? Is it no obvious? The photies *huv* tae be fakes. They were never near the Moon. There is no other explanation.'

He sat down. Across the room Gregor watched the monitor, clearly excited by the account of the wandering lander.

'Be that as it may, Mr. Nicol, but surely, even if we concede that the photographs have been interfered with, the tampering with the evidence could have been carried out at any time over the past forty years?'

'Aye, darlin'. Ye're maybe right. But take a look if ye wull at the back o' the photies.'

The monitor was now showing a view of the reverse side of

the photographs, Rab's hand clearly seen holding the item up to the camera. 'This stamp on the back is official. And this number here is a "National Security Number" used only on items with a classification that restricts their circulation and distribution.' There was immediate murmuring from the audience, the panel becoming curious and involved.

'Now, of course; the number and the stamp could also be a fake. But somehow I don't think so. In fact ah huv every good reason fur believin' these photies tae be the genuine article.'

This with a big wink at Gus Simpson who sat, his face a picture of innocence, determined not to be drawn into further confrontation with Rab Nicol. Out of camera range, Gregor was deep in conversation with Hamish, his brother nodding in agreement.

And so it was that after the programme ended, that Hamish McLeod, scholar and man of science sat face to face with Rab Nicol and fat Susan in a booth in a nearby watering hole, ample supplies of Guinness decorating the narrow table between them, as Rab, flushed and exhilarated after a further excursion into the field of television journalism, poised on the threshold of his new career, fêted and fawned on by men of letters, sat holding court and discoursing at length on the facts as he saw them, aided and abetted by the photographs and articles given to him by Frank Nelson earlier in the week.

# 22

Friday lunchtime, two days later, in The Doric, and Gus Simpson watched as Gregor McLeod studied the photographs and assorted press cuttings, observing the intensity with which he read the handwritten notes, referring back to this photograph, or that article, his food abandoned and his wine glass untouched.

'Gregor. Eat something. We can do this later.'

Gregor looked up, distracted.

'Yes. Yes. What do you make of this lot? Why are these photographs so special? Is what he is saying factual in your opinion? Who is this guy?'

Gus raised his hands.

'That's a good question. He claimed at the outset to be working for the Washington Post, but I had Paul check him out and nobody there has heard of him. I was going to ask you to run a check on him.'

Gregor looked up.

'Is that a fact,' he said absentmindedly. 'When can I meet him?'

Gus was taken aback.

'Are you sure you want to? Most of this shit has all been peddled before. There's nothing really new in there. I had a look this morning.'

'But you say that your media man confirmed that the photographs were not retouched? Correct?'

'Yes. But...'

Gus hung his head, refusing to concede that the photographs might contain some sinister evidence.

'There *are* discrepancies on some of them that can only be explained by digital enhancing or ... possibly by creating overlays or whatever. If it's been done digitally then that would be proof enough that someone had edited them. I have asked him to let me know what he finds. He will do further tests. If there is anything ... I will certainly let you know.'

Gregor folded the papers back into the envelope, handing it

over. Gus was fingering the envelope.

'Did you catch the postcode?' Gregor looked again, nodding.

'Were you thinking of running a feature on this lot?'

Gus laughed.

'I might, but my editor would certainly have some views on that. Somehow I don't think so.'

He paused, seeing the look on Gregor's face.

'Why do you ask?'

'Gus. Listen to me. If you run a series of articles on this little lot I will give you first call on every news story from here till eternity. You can have first access to the stuff that comes back from the Moon as well. Think about that.'

Gus looked at him.

'You couldn't. The other dailies would crucify you. A Scotsman exclusive. Never!'

'You have my word. As the stuff comes back, day-by-day, the Scotsman can handle the syndication. How does that sound to you? And ... if you can spread this stuff over a week ... ?'

Gus glanced up.

'But why?' shaking his head, clearly bemused. As he looked up, the tall figure of Frank Nelson was crossing the floor to greet them. Gregor looked at Gus.

'Frank. Hi. How are you? You found the place again? Just having a mid-day breather. Eh? Let me introduce you to my friend and colleague Gregor McLeod. Gregor, this is Frank Nelson of the Washington Post, the guy on the other end of that envelope.'

Gregor rose as Gus pulled up a third chair.

'Take a chair. Have a drop of wine.'

He signalled for a glass as Frank and Gregor exchanged pleasantries.

'No. No. We weren't discussing anything serious. We never discuss business over lunch. Gregor, as you surely know, is First Minister of the Scottish Parliament and the one whom you heard making the introductions at the initial press conference.'

'Yes, of course. It's a pleasure.'

They shook hands again, sizing each other up. The waiter

arrived interrupting the introductions.

'Yes,' he said, 'I mentioned to Gus here that I spotted the two of you at the opening conference and later on at the reception. Tried to make contact but when I looked around you had both disappeared. I only recently tracked Gus down through the Scotsman.'

The waiter was hovering, proffering the menu.

'No. No thank you. Nothing to eat. No truly. I already had a late breakfast.'

Gregor was thumbing through the photographs trying to locate one or the other.

'So tell me Mr. Nelson, do you really believe the claims behind these articles Gus has been showing me? He tells me that you are firm in your assertions that ...'

Frank Nelson interrupted him.

'As sure as I am of sitting here. I won't go into it now, but there is serious room for doubt on all counts. Have you studied the stuff in there?'

'No, not yet. But I would like to. I am also trying to raise this young man's interest in running some articles on the subject in his column.'

'Oh. You should ask me to do that. I write them in my sleep.'

They laughed. He looked sideways at Gregor. 'And I am not alone. You know, there are people quite close to our highest levels of government who secretly harbour the same concerns. I know. I have spoken to many of them. My good friend Tom who lives over at Sherman Oaks has a high position within NASA and even *he* is a secret convert to the idea. He believes that there are many good men and true who support the view that the American government has been misleading us all for generations on the achievements of our space agency in the sixties and seventies.'

He was looking straight at Gregor as he spoke, his manner easy, his voice casual.

As he continued talking, Gregor was watching him intently.

'And when did you last see your old friend?' he asked quietly.

The other paused before replying,

'On St Stephen's day I think it was.'

Gregor had turned away, his attention apparently diverted. Pushing back his chair, he sat now with his hands on his thighs, looking around the room anxious to be gone, but nevertheless observing the protocol that the occasion demanded. This was the Gregor that Gus knew well. Always restless, forever moving on.

'Gus,' he said eventually, 'Why don't you bring Frank over to my office this afternoon after five and we'll see if we can get to grips with this material here?'

Gus looked at them both. At some point in the conversation he had missed a beat. Somewhere along the line, something had passed between them in the few minutes when he had been distracted by the waiter.

'Fine,' said Nelson. 'What if I meet Gus here at, say, four thirty? Would that suit you?'

'Fine by me,' said Gus wondering where he had lost the plot. Somewhere between the fish cake finale and the coffees, Frank Nelson and his old friend the First Minister had bonded. As he strolled off, Gregor turned to Gus and leaning forward said,

'I doubt if there is any need to check him out and it might be best not to probe too deeply into his story.'

Gus began to object.

'But, why not run the check?' Gregor slugged the last of his wine.

'Because I just did,' he said evenly.

As they stepped out on to the busy pavement, Gregor pulled Gus gently by the arm.

'Gus. When you've collected him, bring him over to my office and then find some excuse to leave us alone for half an hour. Can you do that?' Gus looked confused, a wan smile and a shrug his only reassurance.

The cocktail party at the American Consulate in Charlotte Square was in full swing, with guests assembled from other embassies and the business sector, together with a representative selection of ministers and members of parliament from the various parties swelling the ranks and adding to the mêlée. Elmer Franklin stood chatting with Gregor McLeod, Hamish and his daughter Fiona, as their hostess, Joan Willmott, moved around the room ensuring that everyone was catered to. And in the background, discreetly, Elmer's shadow, Paul Burke surveyed the gathering.

'So! Who won?'

John Willmott, the Consul, had joined Gregor and the Assistant Secretary of State. Elmer bowed graciously towards Gregor.

'He did. And well deserved too.' He laughed loudly, clapping Gregor on the shoulder in congratulation.

'I never get the time. You know how it is? This travelling around ruins your handicap. The champagne before the match didn't help much either. But, thank you again for an excellent lunch.'

It was Gregor's turn to return the bow.

'You are most welcome.' Gregor excused himself and drew Fiona away from the gathering.

'When do you go back?' he asked. She looked at him, surprised by the abruptness of his question.

'Why? I was intending heading off on Monday morning?'

He was thinking.

'Can we meet sometime over the weekend?' He hastened to add, 'It'll only be for an hour at most?'

She smiled before replying, 'Of course. But, I do wish you would all stop worrying; we are bang on schedule.'

It was his turn to smile.

'No. It's not that. It's something else. I will be travelling back with you. We have some very special guests arriving on Monday night. Is the guest wing unoccupied? If it's easier we can talk on the chopper.'

She shook her head.

'There's no need. The airport is fully operational now for night landings of all sorts. I'm flying in on the Cessna. There's room for all of us. As for guest accommodation, we can manage something. Just tell me how many.'

He thought for a moment.

'I think I would still prefer to brief you here before we leave if it's all right with you? As for numbers, five, possibly six at most.'

'I'll call you in the morning,' she said, wandering off once more into the crowd.

Standing apart, by the buffet table, head and shoulders above most of the room, Paul Burke had already exchanged greetings with the lovely Fiona, who was maintaining a discreet distance from him while he remained on duty. From time to time a coy smile would be directed across the busy room, and as the party with Franklin drifted into the adjoining room, she detached herself from the crowd and stood alongside Paul for a moment as he moved to take up a better position inside the door.

'I would offer you a drink but ...'

She smiling, looking up at him briefly.

'Orange juice be alright?' They laughed.

'I'm a free man after ten o'clock,' he said quietly. 'The local agent takes over then.'

Whispering now.

'By ten, I will be ready to kill for a drink.' She reached out and lifted a glass from a passing tray. Sniffing it, she tasted it and handed it to him.

'Sorry.'

'I tried to call you on the number you gave me but all I got was your switchboard,' he said. She was looking around the room avoiding too much eye contact with him. Nearby a party of secretaries from one or other of the other embassies were making no secret of their appreciation of his slim figure and dark good looks.

'Cheers,' she said. 'No. That's right. I came down on Friday afternoon. I fly back on Monday morning. As you can imagine we are panicking to finish everything on time.'

There was a tantalizing pause before she added with a slight catch in her voice,

'But I knew you were here, of course.'

She turned to look at him briefly, feeling her pulse begin to race as he leaned forward to talk to her.

'If you're free at ten?'

He left the question hanging as she quickly brushed the hair away from her face where his mouth had passed close to her ear. As she suppressed the urge to reach for his hand, the blushes rising on her cheeks, she felt her arm being held as Joan Willmott interrupted them.

'Fiona, do excuse us, may I introduce you to ...'

And she was off, her mind in a spin, an apologetic backward glance, which she was not sure he had seen, his attention being diverted as Franklin moved towards the large windows.

In the minutes following, she failed to hear most of the conversation, responding mechanically, smiling and nodding, stealing a dozen glances across the room, oblivious to the chatter and the laughter as she tried to control the rising excitement she was feeling. She was sure that she could feel his eyes on her back. The sun streaming through the tall windows was a reminder that the evening was still young. Faintly, above the noise, a chiming clock somewhere in the house struck seven. Outside the arriving cars and departing taxis reminded her that the party was not, as yet, in full swing. Only another three centuries to go.


Gregor's meeting on the Friday with Frank Nelson had been productive, if unscheduled. At the end of an hour they had stood, shaking hands. Gathering up the file from the desk between them he closed it and moved over to the safe in the corner to secure it.

'How long will you be around?' Gregor asked.

'I'll be in Miami by tomorrow night,' he said. 'I leave this evening, direct to Boston. My meeting is on Sunday morning. I haven't said anything about leaving to Gus by the way. Not that it matters. I'll have an early drink with him this evening then make my excuses.'

He paused, turning on the way to the door.

'How much does he know by the way?' Gregor was leading him instead towards the inner office and the private lift. He thought for a moment before replying.

'He knows that you're not with the Post; as far as the other issues are concerned? Nothing really. At the present time, my own cabinet knows even less than he does. I sometimes wonder just how many people *are* involved. I can assure you that, for the moment, everything at this end is stitched up tight. Let's keep it that way. Shall we?'

They smiled at each other as the lift arrived, Gregor leading the way. 'I'll show you down to the basement exit. It will take you straight on to the Castle approach. I've warned security. You should have no problem.'

The lift doors opened and they stood in the dimly lit hall, the security officers standing back as the two men made their way to the great doors. Gregor turned.

'It goes without saying that if we succeed in this venture, that we will have achieved something of great significance and importance to all of us. I want you to convey my total commitment to the outcome to all concerned, and in particular to Tom Sherman and the others. Now go quickly, and God speed.'


Edinburgh, on a warm September evening, the sky still not dark at ten o'clock, the streets of the capital city alive and bustling with crowds making their way between performances, filling the pubs and restaurants, the hi-jacking of the city centre by the throngs of tourists set to continue for the remaining week of the Festival. Overhead, swallows and swifts darted across the slow dimming blue of the sky.

In Charlotte Square, the last limos were leaving the steps of the American Consulate, the chandeliers still sparkling on the first floor, the front door opening and closing as the guests departed. Paul Burke crossed the busy square and found the basement steps leading to the crowded wine bar. Fighting his way through the crowd he ordered a whisky, retreating five minutes later to the only quiet spot in the corner from where he could keep an eye on the entrance. The ice in his drink was disappearing fast, the heat oppressive as he struggled to remove his tie and loosen his collar.

'Undressing already, are we?'

Fiona stood beside him, taking the glass from his hand as he struggled with his tie, a broad smile on her face. He looked down at her as, over the noise, he pointed to the glass in her hand.

'Yes please. A glass of white would be nice.'

He began to ease his way through the crowd moving towards the bar, but she stopped him.

'On second thoughts ... Let's move on. You will be hours fighting your way through this lot. I know just the place at this time of night.'

She pulled him gently by the arm as he hesitated. Then her hand fell easily into his and together they left the bar and climbed up into the noise and rattle of the busy street. They strolled quietly down towards Princes Street, leaving the traffic behind them. Towering over them as they rounded the corner, the ancient castle and the slender towers of the new Parliament building were floodlit against the darkening sky. Along the length of the street, cafes and restaurants spilled over onto the wide walkways, the activity and noise rising from the basement courtyards where the shopping, cinemas and theatres on the Garden Mall provided a second level of busy pavement traffic, covered cafes and bars fronting on to a tree lined avenue. They took the escalator to the lower level, pushing through the crowds and walked along under the trees listening to the music from the bandstand, the arena packed with people, the atmosphere heady with the scent of flowers and rich with the hint of Havana cigar.

They stopped under the canopy of an open bar, the smell of frying seafood filling the air around them. As the crowd thinned they found two seats at a table near the bar and ordered a bottle of wine and a plate of mixed fried fish.

'These are delicious. Try it. Go on. Try the squid.'

She poured the wine while he tentatively sampled the fish.

'It's very good. Wow! Let's get some more. I'm famished. I've had nothing since lunchtime. These are terrific. I think I told you that I grew up in Maine and was practically weaned on fish.'

Suddenly she was deliciously happy, the moment of certainty

in the embassy suddenly remembered. Looking at him she realized how little she knew about him, the need to get to know him better suddenly pressing. He saw the serious look on her face and mistook it for something else.

'What's the matter?' he asked, his expression concerned.

'Nothing. Nothing at all.'

She was smiling at him again and he relaxed. She stood now and moved to the bar calling to the bartender, ordering a further plate of fish.

Overhead a burst of fireworks shook the air, the detonations resounding across the valley and echoing off the buildings on the street opposite. Almost immediately there were more massive explosions as the night sky was illuminated sending showers of colour out over the city. As he took the plate from her hands she leaned over the table, feeling his hands reach out to encircle her face as he tenderly kissed her mouth. Overhead the sky was ablaze with greens and reds, the white light showering the area with powerful shadows, the acrid smell of gunpowder drifting on the light breeze. From the bar the familiar strains of an old sweet song began to filter through the noise, competing hopelessly with the fanfares booming out high across the night sky.

But for Fiona McLeod, these were dwarfed by the beating of her own heart and the surges of emotion from deep within her being, where fireworks of a very different kind were remaking her soul and lifting her to heights that she had never known before; while the squid grew cold and her heart took flight forever.

# 23

They stood in the dimly-lit control tower looking out into the night sky, as the last traces of sunset turned to midnight blue, the stars appearing clear and high, the Moon not yet above the horizon. Around them, the quiet discipline of the air traffic controllers continued, as the exchanges between the approaching aircraft and the tower reached them across the carpeted room.

Quite suddenly, the fading outlines of the tiny hamlet below and the beaches beyond were thrown into sharp relief as the runway lights were switched on, the glow reflected in the still sea as they ran straight and true through headlands and over beaches, suspended over the water from time to time, ignoring the natural topography of the rocky shore. Then they saw the aircraft quite clearly as the landing lights came on and the pilot made the final turn onto his approach.

Gregor, Hamish, Sally McIntosh and Fiona entered the lift and went down to the reception area. Gregor put his arm around his niece as he led her towards the doorway.

'Tired?' She nodded in agreement.

'Just a bit.'

They watched as the plane drew to a halt, the great engines stilled, as the steps were rolled out.

'Have you met him before?' she asked suddenly.

'Yes. Just the once, but it was a few years back. You'll like him. And don't be fooled by his appearance. Beneath the frail exterior is an intellect to be reckoned with. He's a very special person. You'll see.'

Gregor moved out onto the apron with Hamish at his side and strode forward to greet the new arrival, as the doors of the aircraft slid back and the sole passenger emerged from the interior. From the reception hall, Sally and Fiona watched as the introductions were made, Gregor leading the frail figure back towards the building, pausing now and again to point out the features of the complex, eventually entering the lobby where further introductions were made.

'Miss McIntosh, our legal advisor, Fiona McLeod, my niece

and Project Manager, meet Mr Tom Sherman from NASA.'

They all shook hands, Gregor leading the way towards the runabouts.

'Tom, we must apologize in advance for the rather cramped conditions in the guest wing, but we will do our utmost to make you and your crew as comfortable as possible during your stopover. If you feel up to it, we can either meet this evening or tomorrow early ...'

Tom Sherman stopped him.

'The sooner, the better, Gregor. Give me just twenty minutes to freshen up and we will make a start. Just lead the way.'

As Fiona escorted him away, Hamish looked at Gregor, the silent exchange between them saying all that was required.

'This close.' Gregor was thinking. 'We are this close.'

Standing apart from them, Sally McIntosh saw the wild, broad-grinned, excited look on the faces of the two men, as they linked their arms in hers, feeling a sudden rush of tenderness towards them both, knowing that they were risking everything in their desperate bid to save the world as it gradually sank towards an uncertain future.


The following morning, Gregor and Tom Sherman strolled slowly along the beach, walking on the hard-packed sand, the tide receding and the early morning sunshine dancing off the flat calm of the ocean. Here and there, strands of brightly coloured kelp lay half buried in the sand. Their meetings over, agreement reached, Gregor was buoyant, aware that in these closing weeks they were as close as they could possibly hope to be, success within their grasp and an end in sight for the years of patient investment in a shared dream.

Tom Sherman was also happy; happy and relieved. The unscheduled private charter, details carefully concealed, had been a risk but one well worth the taking. Now, with the realisation that everything was running to plan he was confident that they would succeed. Knowing the extent of the problems facing the Jackson administration and with the distinct possibility of success in sight, he was convinced that, between them, they now held all of the cards. Knowing that the *Caliban* could begin its journey as early as the middle of October was a clincher. All it would need would be a week; ten days clear at the very most. After that ... Tom Sherman had often pondered the consequences of failure, of early exposure of their plans, of the fall from grace and the cover up that would inevitably follow. With the certain knowledge that the F.B.I. had begun to take an unexpected sudden interest in his movements, he would have to be doubly careful. But at least, the outcome either way would, by definition, be a quiet affair he had decided. No accusations of treason or plotting to bring down the government. No sir! No pointing fingers and no punitive action taken against the conspirators for fear of the revelations that would surely engulf the Presidency and the government's top advisors. At his age he had no fears for himself. He had achieved his goal, delivered his dreams. NASA was once again a hive of activity, funding assured for the next five years and the dust being blown away everywhere by the urgency to reach the Moon.

What he was doing was good and necessary, the time for reasoned argument and dutiful persuasion long since gone. It was now time for the showdown. A showdown without fanfares of any kind; a mere rumble of heavy thunder that would reverberate for a short time within the confines of the Oval Office, contained and silenced, buried thereafter for eternity, denying the truth forever.

Gregor watched him, knowing that he was deep in thought, never doubting for one second the sincerity of the man nor his commitment to the task in hand. A frail body supporting a brilliant intellect. With men like Tom Sherman on board, Gregor knew that it would all come right. Sometimes, all it took was the will to change things for the better.

Standing on the dunes overlooking the beach, Fiona McLeod and Sally McIntosh watched as the two men ended their stroll and began to head back towards the road. Now that both had been made aware of the task ahead of them, realizing the risks involved and desperate, above all else, for it to succeed, they were accomplices and conspirators in an undertaking that would either make or break them in the weeks ahead; an undertaking that, of necessity, carried with it a vow of silence that could never ever be broken.

Nathan Jackson was a worried man. Sitting now with David Berkhoff, head of the F.B.I., Arnold Denham, the National Security Advisor and Dale Johnson, he studied the files that they had placed in front of him minutes earlier. David Berkhoff was talking.

'So you see, Mr President, these reports span the last two and a half months and represent many hundreds of hours of surveillance in gathering and assembling the information that we have set before you. You will have seen that what started out as a routine operation tracking a drug trafficking network, threw up some very revealing items of conversation that alerted our operatives to the possibility of something going on that we felt should be brought to the attention of the C.I.A. It was at that point that we both began to take an interest in the affairs of the gentlemen concerned. I must stress that there may be a very simple explanation for their frequent meetings and for the tone and subject matter of their conversations.

'As you will see my agents were sufficiently intrigued to extend surveillance over a period of weeks ending with the latest meeting between the parties last weekend. The references to the upcoming Moon shot and the many references to NASA all appear to be fairly innocent. The highlighted items are less easy to explain and seem to suggest some unexplained involvement of the two men concerned with some other scenario, involving yourself and the White House. The many references to programming and progress down at Cape Canaveral, talk of the lunar lander and information received by us of security breaches relating to ongoing work connected with the Moon mission, have led us to believe that there is a conspiracy of sorts on the go, which may reflect on National Security in the long run.

'As we felt it to be important and since it seemed to relate to matters outside our brief, we passed the dossier to the C.I.A. to see if it flagged up any responses from any of their on-going security investigations.'

He paused as Jackson continued to listen, still warily scanning the report.

'We are fairly certain that the people concerned are unaware that they have been targeted. There is however some room for doubt as the last few conversations between them seem to have been encoded in some way, the many references in their talks contradicting and even denying earlier statements made to each other over the past weeks. Whilst it may all appear to be fairly innocent, the many references to yourself and the White House, NASA and the on-going programme for the launch ...'

Jackson held up his hand.

'David, I express my thanks to you and your department for bringing these reports to my attention, and for involving the C.I.A. We will of course look into the matter and keep you advised. If there is anything that concerns your bureau I will, of course, get back to you. Meantime we need to study this thing and ask a few questions ourselves.'

He stood proffering his hand to the F.B.I. Director, as Dale Johnson reached for the report. Jackson was ushering David Berkhoff out of the office with his thanks for a job well done. He returned to the desk and sat down, his expression thoughtful as he tried to come to terms with what he had just read.

'Arnold. The references in these early reports are very worrying, very confusing. It looks as if there has been loose talk along the way. Tom Sherman and Sam Cavanagh have been party to our many conversations and, above all, they are party to the one little secret that we have no wish to see leaked from this office. I made it clear to all of you that what we discussed that day would go no further than these four walls. I want you to call off the F.B.I. and set up your own surveillance. How Berkhoff and his boys got on to it we will never know. But clearly they have. We must get to the bottom of this thing. If there is something going on ...'

He left the sentence hanging.

Arnold Denham was now thumbing through the report, watched by Dale Johnson who sat deep in thought. After a moment he addressed the President.

'Sir. These briefings you have been getting on progress towards the November launch?'

Jackson looked at him, a confused expression on his face.

'Yes?'

Johnson went on.

'May I suggest that we ask Arnold here to check them out? Verify the essential facts. Look into the contracting side of the launch to make sure that everything is as they say it is. Reading between the lines of this report, I get the feeling that there is something going on here that needs closer examination. The last thing we want is any kind of a delay that might affect the launch date.'

At this Jackson shifted uncomfortably in his chair.

'You don't think for one minute that any of that is in doubt?' He was nervous now, searching for reassurance. Johnson looked at Arnold Denham who had closed the report and was ready to voice an opinion.

'There is a great deal here that needs looking into. I don't know what it means. Yet! But I will. Whatever is going on I will find out. Meantime, may I suggest that we say nothing to anyone? We must close down the F.B.I. involvement immediately. We don't want them going too deeply into this thing. If word should get out due to some unfortunate slip of the tongue, and news of our little secret should ever become known ...'

He paused, a serious look on his face.

'My gut feeling is that both Tom and Sam are utterly loyal. How on earth they came to the attention of the F.B.I. we'll probably never know. I doubt if there is a conspiracy going on, but I would put my life on the line that security surrounding this business is tighter than a gnat's piss'ole. That said, I cannot guarantee that it will always remain so. There are already too many parties to the conspiracy. With contracts let to dozens of firms across America in support of the November launch, with any number of potential leaks looming it will be a miracle if somewhere along the line somebody somewhere doesn't drop a mention or two ...'

Again Jackson held up his hand.

'Let's hope that you are wrong. But on the other business, I believe you have a valid point. I want you to report back on progress at our various establishments connected with the manned mission. If there is a snag that could adversely affect our programme that we are currently unaware of, I want to be the first to know. Is that clear? There is enough loose talk flowing around in the media at the moment to fuel a thousand conspiracies. All in all, it is making me very uncomfortable. All this talk in the press of a race to be ahead of the Scots is very troubling. As I understand the current situation from Franklin, the Scots are still looking for a window at the end of November. As long as that remains the case we have a good chance of recovering the situation. If that should change for any reason, I will need to be informed. Meantime, I expect to hear from you, Denham within a few days. We must not suffer delays of any kind. We must not fail.'

'Hi! I'm looking for Mr. Regan.' There was a pause as the other end of the line effected a transfer, a contact made and the operator came back on the line.

'Yes? Whom did you say you want to speak to? I see. Mr. Regan. We have two Mr Regans. Which one do you ...?'

'Just gimme the ugly, syphilitic, tap-dancing one.'

Ah! You mean Mr *Ken* Regan. One moment please. Who shall I say is calling? Mr Phil Westwood. Thank you, caller.'

There was a further pause until the familiar voice of Ken Regan came on the line.

'Good morrow, sport. You're up early.'

'Hi! You old soak. Where've you been? Thought that you might have popped into the club last night. What are you doing for lunch? Yes, today.'

The conversation swung to the other end, then back again.

'I've been speaking to an old friend of mine about our recent enquiries. Very interesting. I've got something I want to run by you. Something big.'

There was a further pause as arrangements were made.

'Right. Twelve thirty. And don't keep me hanging around like last time. What was that? Yeah. Up yours, too.'

# 24

Gus Simpson sat opposite Gregor at the long table overlooking the Edinburgh skyline. In front of them the photographs were strewn across the hard polished top. In his hand he held a magnifying glass, which he now passed to Gregor.

'It's here in this corner. Look. Just there.'

He watched as Gregor focused in on the object.

'Try holding the glass further away. Not too far. There. You see?'

Gregor peered uncertainly at the photograph, raising his eyes to smile across at Gus, and then resuming scrutiny of the details. After a moment or two, he picked up a second photograph.

'And you say that he managed to conjure this out of this?' He was waving both photographs around in the air.

Gus looked at him, a serious expression on his face.

'At first, I accused him of pulling my leg. Then he took me through it. Step by step. By straightening and then enhancing the image on the mirrored visor he came up with this.'

Gregor laid the images down, staring across the room.

'So. Finally we find out that there might be some substance to the rumours after all.'

He looked at Gus who was trying to look uncommitted. He tilted the photographs towards him again peering through his half lenses, first at one, then at the other.

'Of course you know what this means? If these are genuine and your man seems to think that they are, then they cast real doubt on their claims of ever making it to the Moon. If they were committed to faking the photographs, then why not the voyage itself?'

He picked up the photographs again.

'This is a remarkable bit of detective work. What was his reaction when he showed you the images?'

Gus looked at his old friend.

'He thought that I had set him up. He thinks now that somehow, I faked them. It's highly specialized work apparently. Somebody would have to know what he was doing and it's out of my field entirely. Of course, as he said, with computers these days, anything is possible. At the same time, he is doubtful if they have been doctored in any way but it's hard to tell of course. For myself, I don't know what to believe.'

Gregor stood and moved to the window.

'You know Gus, when I asked you if evidence could be found that would prove once and for all that the Americans never made it to the Moon, I never for one moment expected to be shown something like this. Could he be wrong?'

Gus shrugged his shoulders for the hundredth time.

'Gregor. I'm telling you and showing you what he found. No more. No less. He didn't doctor the photographs himself - that much I do know! He is just as puzzled as I am. In his view, the photographs are genuine. Genuine fakes, of course. But convincing until you look hard at them. As I said, he reckons the possibility that someone added the images to the visor to be highly unlikely. Which means of course that somewhere, on earth at that time, there was a very detailed stage set wired to produce just this kind of image and a photographic studio somewhere that burned out the half tones giving these prints their high contrast.

'Somehow or other, they failed to pick up the image on the visor. When Frank Nelson first pointed it out to me I was sceptical. I still am. It was too easy. I'm still trying to figure out what he's getting out of the whole affair.'

Gregor laid the prints down in front of him knowing precisely what Frank Nelson hoped to get out of it and wondering if he'd had a hand in doctoring the images.

'Would the Scotsman print these do you think? Would they risk the controversy?'

He looked at Gus hopefully.

'I haven't run them passed the editor yet and I have asked my man to keep mum about it until I clear it upstairs. But yes, I think they would go for it. Interest is high with the launch coming up. Everybody is talking about the trip. They can't get enough of it. Frankly, I still can't believe it. Having listened to you, then Frank Nelson, not to mention that bloody lunatic Nicol down at the

Skite…'

He was shaking his head in disbelief. Then they were laughing.

'Still not convinced?' asked Gregor with a chuckle.

'You still think they went to the Moon? Still a believer?'

Gus looked down at the detail of the visor worn by the astronaut as it reflected the scenery around him, the familiar Moonscape with the lunar lander clearly visible in the background. Just what a nineteen sixty-eight Chevy pick-up was doing on the Moon was beyond him. Around it a collection of casually dressed men clearly watching what was going on in front of them. In the background the unmistakable outlines of low lying buildings and desert scrub. But there was no doubting it. As the astronaut had turned in his heavy suit, his mirrored visor had picked up the images around him distorting them out of all recognition. Until today, when the computer imaging had slowly focused in on the incidentals, straightening and enhancing them until even the number plate on the truck was clearly visible.

Gregor took him by the arm.

'Gus, my boy, you have just made an old man very, very happy and that's worth a lunch in the minister's dining room any day. The champagne is on you, of course. Now, about Hiroshima …'


That evening, unaware of the recent conversions to his cause taking place up on the Rock, Rab sat in his usual place surrounded by the usual crowd. In the other corner a busker, ever bashful, ever hopeful, had unslung his guitar and was quickly told to "fuck off" Fat Susan sat with her head leaning affectionately against Rab's shoulder, his pint of Guinness in his hand as the stream of chatter and infectious laugher continued undiminished. As usual the pub was full, on this, the last night of the Festival, the streets packed with tourists and locals congregating in the centre of the town awaiting the finale of three weeks of music, culture and assorted drivel. And as the city romped and played on a chilly autumnal evening, the sky darkened and the fireworks roared up into the clear sky.

Although several blocks away from the source, the noise from the Castle Esplanade was deafening, forcing Rab to wave his hands in surrender until the *burrach* was over. On the wall behind him, an assortment of framed photographs had appeared showing Rab with this celebrity and that celebrity, Rab on television and Rab on the make. And nestling between the photographic tributes, a large flat screen monitor. Below, the video spoke of technical innovation invading the "Skite".

Again the place was packed to the roof, the crush around the bar raising the temperature inside, the windows flung open in a vain attempt to clear the smoke and disperse the smell of urine drifting up from the toilets below. A final crescendo of explosions signaled the end of the display and as the noise settled and the acrid smoke drifted down the High Street, Rab returned again to his exposé of the greatest cover up in history.

'Friends, Romans and shoplifters, tonight we can promise you further spectacular revelations about the subject that is closest tae ma heart. The Moon. The lonely Moon that still awaits that first footfall to land on it. A Scottish foot no less. For as ye all know, it was not an American foot. Ah'll tell yees all. For in November when we land on the Moon, it will be a first for Scotland. Be sure o' it. We will be the first men on the Moon. And ... I hear yees all say. "How can he be so sure?" So, ah'll tell ye.'

He reached down to lift his brimming glass to his lips, taking a generous long pull, his eyes clouding over at the experience, smacking his lips and smiling broadly, replacing the glass as he looked around the room.

'Yes, for tonight I shall reveal, for the very first time, the true extent o' the shameless cover-up perpetrated on a gullible world in the seventies by our friends and neighbours across the Atlantic.

'And ...'

He held up his hand.

'You shall see further evidence; if ye ever needed tae see it, o' the amazin' stupidity o' the Yanks. Stupidity that is hard tae credit, when ye consider how much they spent on fakin' the whole thing - just so that we could uncover and reveal the facts tonight, as we explore the murky past of American claims o' huvin' landed on the Moon.'

There was a loud round of applause as Rab paused in his delivery. Behind him the screen flickered into life as Fat Susan held the remote.

'Observe. Now this here shows the L. E. M. or lunar lander as she appears in most o' the photies that we huv a' seen time an again. Except ... that this one lets us see a close up o' the feet doon here at the end o' the legs.'

'Aye Rab,' somebody shouted, 'That's where ma feet are as well.'

There was loud laughter and good-natured barracking as Rab smiling broadly, gave way to the crowd.

'Sorry tae hear about yer broken leg, pal' he said. 'An' if it's no' broken now, it soon wull be if ye dinne shut up.'

He paused, as once again the pub erupted with shouts and laughter.

'To continue. If we look here ...'

He was indicating the shiny polished pans under the feet.

'If we look here ... carefully, jist what dae we see? Any ideas. No? Well, as usual, ah shall jist huv tae tell yees all. Now, remember this! They had jist landed. Right? Motors and jets and things blazin' away as they slowly landed on the dusty, yes, on the *very* dusty surface o' the Moon.'

He looked up at them his face vacant, his jaw hanging, a retard struggling with some insurmountable problem.

'Yees don't see it. Ah knew it. Ye're lookin' but ye're seeing nothin'. Look at the pans here. Not a speck o' dust anywhere.' Incredulously, he looked around at the punters.

'Ye see? How can ye drop doon on tae a powdery surface like the Moon and keep yer pans shiny? An' don't forget the jets blowing everything all over the place. Surely ye wid expect *some* o' the dust tae rise up and cover the feet at least? And wi' nae air and very low gravity, how long dae ye think the dust wid hang aboot? An hour maybe? A day? It is ma contention that after they created the first big stour on landing, that it wid take a day at least fur the dust tae settle.

In ma humble opinion, the pans should huv been half buried. And another thing. If their jets were roarin' away as they landed, where the hell is the crater you wid expect tae find under the lander?'

The picture changed and an astronaut came into view, the mirrored visor, the cumbersome backpack, the heavy footwear and the massive gloves.

'An' look here. This guy has been hoppin' aboot fur at least an hour, and look here ...' Rab was pointing at his boots.

'Not a speck o' dust tae be seen. His helmet is as clean as a whistle. Is that no' remarkable? Now. Ah'll ask yees all. Is that no' the bloody limit? Dae they really believe that we're half as daft as they think we are? No. I don't think so.'

'Tell us, Rab. Dae ye no' think maybe they tidied up before they took the pictures? Took the washin' line doon like? Pit the weans' toys away. Ye ken what ah mean.'

'That's right, Rab, they've maybe shoved the empties under the bed.' Rab held up his hands as the laughter and backchat flowed across the room. After a minute he turned back to the screen.

'Now,' he said, 'for something completely staggering.'

A quick murmur of anticipation ran around the room. On the split screen two images had appeared, one showing the lander against the lunar background, the other, the same view but without the lander.

'Now, here we see something truly amazing. As far as ah know the Moon is lifeless. Naebody lives there. No' even the Man in the Moon! Ah'm ah right? Yes? Right. So what do we see here? In this one ...' pointing to the screen, ' ... we see the Lunar Lander just before she does her big bungee jump headin' back intae orbit. At least, that's what we're supposed tae believe. And in this one, taken wi' the camera they left behind, we see nothin'. The lander's gone. Buggered aff fur a Jimmy Riddle. Now look closer. Spot the difference. For there is a difference and it's no just the fact that the lander has disappeared.'

Rab stood back as everybody studied the split screen. In the outer room, the punters around the bar and the bar staff were following events closely. All eyes were riveted to the screen. Fat Susan watched their faces waiting to see if anyone had spotted the glaring blunder that had evidently escaped the attention of the censors at NASA. Rab moved forward.

'Look here' he said. 'See the footprints on this one, *before* they left.'

The photograph showed a confused series of footprints and tracks made by the astronauts as they had moved around the site. In the harsh light, each print was perfectly defined and clearly visible on the photograph. Rab was enjoying the moment as the crowd leaned forward, peering at the screen but unable to spot the difference.

'And now see this other one,' he said quietly. 'If any o' youse can tell me how this extra footprint got there *after* they had buggered off, ah'll buy the next round… for everybody!'


Phil Westwood sat opposite Sam Regan in the corner alcove in the restaurant, a place they both knew well from their early days as hacks on the same publication, at a time when the world was younger and the world of politics was a private club for statesmen and gentlemen. Around them the fading billiard table baize on the walls hosted a hundred or so framed photographs of various, transient personalities who had come and gone, raising the reputation of the tiny restaurant for a week or so before they both settled back into obscurity.

Well into their fourth martini, Phil Westwood was in earnest conversation with Ken Regan, their privacy protected by the partitioned booths that ran the length of the restaurant. In front of them, the remains of their meal indicated a reluctance to eat, while the empty glasses told a different story.

They sat apart, digesting the information that Phil Westwood had charmed from the files of a friendly agent - one given to losing regularly at the poker table, lying to his wife, dependent on regular handouts passed under the table in a diner not a block away from where they sat. Ken Regan looked across at his old friend who sat with a bemused smirk of disbelief.

'It's too big. We could never run it. And it will never get

airtime. That's for sure! But what the hell do we do with it? I'm fucked if I know. And if the Jocks make it to the surface and the balloon goes up, what then? There has to be another way. There has to be.'

He picked up his glass.

'The stupid bastards! Of all the cretinous options open to them, they had to go for the one that brought the glory and the quick returns. God above, what have they done?'

They sat in silence for a while. Phil Westwood sat half turned in his seat, his knee up on the chipped leather of the aging benches staring vacantly across the room, his arthritis dulled for the moment by the gentle buzz from the alcohol. Ken Regan stirred into life.

'I still can't believe it. I still can't see how they thought they could get away with it. How in God's name did they keep it quiet? I never doubted for a second … Of course. We don't know for certain … ' He paused for a moment.

'One thing's for sure. It knocks giant fucking holes in my belief in the democratic process. Where were truth and decency hiding all this time? And as for patriotism …'

'So just how patriotic are you, Ken? How patriotic are you feeling right now? Tell me. Go on. When you were over there covering the mayhem of Vietnam and Iraq, dodging the shit, did you ever think for one minute that after a lifetime in reporting you'd be sitting here like a patsy, being lied to by your government, and duty bound to protect the rotting corpses of their phony schemes, having to shore up their damned lies for fear of bringing this great country into worldwide disrepute?'

He turned away, a look of disgust on his face, the quiet exchanges between them becoming ponderous with the realisation that the story had to be kept under wraps.

'I'll tell you something else.' Phil Westwood was leaning forward earnestly, keeping his voice down and his delivery low key.

'According to Andrews down at the Cape, they are hell bent on bringing everything on line as we know already. But, from what he's been telling me, the programme to build the transport module and modify the lander has been on-going for the last year. The talk of panic is just that, talk! So it's clear that somebody down at NASA gave the go ahead to mount a launch long before the word went out from the White House. He reckons that somewhere within NASA, somebody has been developing his own agenda. If you think about it for just a minute, the announcement to return to manned flights was just too sudden. No foreplay whatsoever. It's the first time within living memory that announcements like that have not been leaked well ahead of time to the media. It smells now, and it smelled at the time.'

He signaled for another round of drinks before returning to his point.

'It's still only guesswork, but if you ask me, I think somebody's feeding the White House a line - exerting pressure to suit his own ends. If there is any truth in the story and the whole thing *was* a pitiful sham from beginning to end, it still doesn't explain the fact that the programme to launch the latest manned mission seems to have been started as far back as February 2008. Andrews is convinced that the order didn't come from the top. Somewhere within NASA, the story must have been kept quiet for years. If the announcement by the Scots triggered the sudden rush to get back into space, and we now know why, it would seem to indicate some prior knowledge of the whole story being blown apart, unless ...'

He paused, the possibility that the twist in the tale had yet to be revealed turning over in his head. Ken Regan looked up expectantly.

'Yeah?'

Phil Westwood appeared to be weighing up the thought that had occurred to him.

'Unless the whole thing is a pack of lies and the White House has bought into it, unable to verify one way or the other the truth about the early missions. Knowing full well that they could never risk the possibility of exposure ...'

He paused again.

'What if, somewhere along the line, the Jocks had given advance warning of their intentions to somebody over here; somebody who, knowing the truth one way or the other, had recognised the danger of doing nothing ...'

Ken Regan was watching him intently, saying nothing, his own mind racing with other possibilities, all of them found wanting for lack of confirmation of any kind. But what he had just heard was too big to have started life as a mere rumour. This had the steadying ring of truth about it. Nobody invented this kind of shit. It was all so improbable, so utterly unbelievable, so utterly unexpected. This thing had been buried so deep that it had survived administration after administration, a time bomb that had suddenly become career threatening, needing to be smothered, covered up with lies; lies which could never be let loose. He spoke quietly, the other listening as the waiters moved around them, familiar with the lunchtime working sessions of the press, sessions that stretched their shifts and shortened their free time. Ken looked up as Phil Westwood reached for the tab.

'You'll have to be careful. This is big. You sure as hell can't file it. And as for asking questions ... You can't. I suggest we bury the whole thing for a day or two and wait. But what you've told me confirms what we already knew. There is a massive cover up going on. Of that much we can be certain. And if NASA doesn't get to the Moon before the Scots do, we'll be left sitting here on our asses watching as the biggest news story in history unfolds before us, and we won't be able to do a damn thing about it.'

Ken Regan was staring into space, detached and in his own world of endlessly likely explanations. When he did speak there was a trace of mischief in his eyes and a marked new resolve in his manner.

'Don't be so sure about that. There's still plenty we can be getting on with. But you're right, and yes, I will be careful. This thing is big enough to kill for, and I have no intention of missing one beat. But if you ask me, I think we've been digging around in all the wrong places. If the answers exist anywhere, I think we'll only find them by looking in the right place; and that place is clearly over there in Bonnie Scotland.'

The bright Autumnal colours were scattered over the sidewalks as the trees gave up their leaves, cushioning the sounds of cruising traffic as the early arrivals hunted for parking spaces in downtown Washington. Frank Nelson sat wrapped against the chill air under the awning of the tiny café. The morning sunshine began to warm the sidewalks sending dappled shadows across the terrace and onto the table where he read, for the third time, the leader by Phil Westwood in the columns of the Washington Post.

Under the heading, "A Time to Reflect" the piece was a thinly disguised attack on the Jackson administration for resuming manned missions, ending with a call for answers to the many charges of irresponsible philandering in the dying days of his presidency. The general tone was hardly critical, given the normal levels of cynicism and concern usually found in editorials when discussing the Moon mission, but it was the final paragraph that stood out as ill conceived, hurriedly put together and possibly salvaged from an earlier rejected draft that had intrigued Frank Nelson, as he read between the lines, aware for the first time that a leak had occurred. Turning again to the final paragraphs he read,

When one considers the current difficulties facing the present administration, the ever deepening gulf between the social classes, the on-going threat of global terrorism, the inability of the United States to come to terms with her lack of international popularity, not to mention the constant international pressure being applied for the United States to adopt the terms of the Kyoto agreement, it is indeed strange that, at this time, so much effort and expense is being lavished on rekindling interest in an adventure that is "yesterday's news" for the majority of Americans. Is it not just possible that this sudden interest in returning to our barren neighbour at this time has more to do with arriving there ahead of the Scots to make sure that our house is in order, at a time when the average American retains serious doubts concerning the truth surrounding those earlier missions?

Could it be, as some have suggested, that in the heady political atmosphere of the sixties surrounding the court at Camelot that the price of failure was just too awful to contemplate. That what we saw and heard (and were led to believe) was no more or less than the secondary, fallback, agenda drawn up to be presented to the American people in the event that the mission failed to accomplish its goal, of placing an American astronaut on the moon ahead of the Russians and within the time remaining to Richard Nixon in office?

With the American public still in mourning for the most popular President this country has ever seen, is it not also possible that the failure to reach the moon and accomplish the task proclaimed by John F. Kennedy would have been a tragedy too far for most Americans to bear, at a time when the nation was crying out for a sign that the times were indeed a-changing?

As Frank Nelson lowered the paper he was a worried man. If the news of the cover up was about to break, he would have to move quickly. Somewhere along the way the Washington Post had picked up a thread of the story and had launched a fishing trip. Within days the affair might start to unravel. If the Jackson administration was exposed and the cover up revealed ... Checking his watch, he reached for his cell phone and dialed a number that would interrupt Gregor McLeod as he wound up a meeting with his cabinet.

Two hours later after much debate they had come to a decision. As they trooped out, Gregor reached for the telephone on his desk.

'Ah. Hamish. How are you? Fine. Everything is just fine. We are all just fine. But we do have a small problem. I need to talk to you all. Can you get Murdo and Fiona here tomorrow morning? Can you make it too?' There was an exchange from the other end.

'Murdo is over there with you I believe. Yes. That's good.

No. No. Not now. Tomorrow. It will wait. But be here early. Make sure everything is set tonight. Have the plane made ready. Yes. Yes. I would have come over there but my schedule is tight. Fine. OK. See you all tomorrow.'

As he closed the line, he crossed to the sideboard and poured a stiff dram, then moved over to the window and stood watching the busy bustling thoroughfare below until the day faded away and the lights of the city transformed the night with ten thousand twinkling stars.


Tom Sherman had read the editorial as well. He considered for a moment placing a call to Scotland, but knew instinctively that there was no need. The contingency plan covered all eventualities and Gregor would react accordingly. But this changed things. Time was no longer on their side. As the car dropped him at the White House his thoughts were elsewhere, other than on his upcoming meeting with his President.

As he entered the lift and then made his way down the broad corridors to the Oval Office his mood lightened with the realisation that the moment had arrived. There would be no more waiting, no more subterfuge. With luck, he could foresee an end in sight, perhaps within weeks, perhaps only days. His encoded message to Scotland in the early hours of the morning would leave no doubt in Gregor McLeod's mind that the time was fast approaching for the last act of their conspiracy to be set in motion. From now on, he would have no part of it as the onus for success was transferred to the broad shoulders of the First Minister of the Independent State of Scotland.

The marines on duty came smartly to attention as he was ushered into the inner room. Then he was being greeted by the President, shaking hands with Dale Johnson, Joe Skinner, Arnold Denham, Sam Cavanagh and Elmer Franklin as he muttered brief excuses for his late arrival. Nathan Jackson was already returning to his interrupted conversation he had been having with Sam Cavanagh as Tom Sherman noted the blue FBI files lying on the desk in front of him.

' ... so it would seem that for the moment, we have a potential launch date ahead of the November 20th deadline that we set previously. If we can improve on that by a couple of weeks as you seem to be saying, then we surely don't have a problem; do we?'

There were smiles all around as he turned towards Tom Sherman.

'So, Tom - how are things going down at the Cape? From your reports it would appear that we are bang on schedule as far as the subcontractors and suppliers are concerned, and Sam here assures me that the ship is already being fine tuned for the trip.'

He looked enquiringly across, a certain hesitancy and lack of eye contact apparent in his manner.

'Well sir, we have done well; very well in fact. We have had a wealth of good fortune in that much of our earlier design work was easily resurrected, the many components that were so carefully stored for possible future use, the expertise that has lain dormant all these passing years ... All in all it has been a remarkable four months of dedicated endeavour by the finest workforce I have ever had the privilege of serving. I believe that we can all be proud of what we've achieved.

'Of course the final pieces of the jigsaw are not yet in place. The telemetry is still lagging behind and our computer link-up has yet to be fully commissioned, but I don't believe that these minor hitches will, in the long run, delay us in any significant way. As Sam has indicated we are fairly confident that we can advance the launch window by as much as two, possibly three weeks giving us ample time...'

He paused for a very brief moment choosing his words with care.

' ... To take care of matters at our destination.'

At these last words, a nervous shifting of feet and a range of minor chest complaints were duly noted.

'So, as you see sir, with all of the parts coming together and with the flight deck in last minute training, I remain confident that we will sail forward towards a November launch and be there and back before the Jocks have even begun their final checklist.'

At this, Jackson interrupted.

'That would miss the point entirely, Tom. Of course, we all know that our justification for going in the first place is to be there to tidy up the site, but we need to get there just ahead of the competition, and only by a matter of a day or so.'

There were further rapid eye movements around the room at the reference to the need to plant the evidence. He continued unabashed.

'... and to record the first ever international handshake between our two countries on the surface of a distant planet. The value of such a deed cannot be overstated when one considers the implications for future generations of this ... '

At this, he appeared to be running out of words as Dale Johnson stepped into the breach.

'... This bold and heroic step by the most technologically advanced nation on the face of God's earth.'

They were beaming at each other now, coffee cups circulating and Jackson relaxing noticeably as the reassurances he was hearing began to brush away the spectre of failure that had haunted him over the previous four months. Sherman had begun again.

'One thing *does* concern me however. It would appear that our little secret has somehow been leaked to the press. The editorial by Phil Westwood in today's Post is very worrying. No doubt you have all read it?'

There were brief glances exchanged around the room as Sherman looked directly into the eyes of his President.

'I suppose it was all too much to hope for.'

He began shaking his head despairingly.

'But at least we *are* within a few short weeks of reaching our goal ... after which, the press of the world can say what they like. The proof will be *shown* to exist and the doubts and suspicions now widespread in many areas that we have something to hide can all be shown to be unfounded.'

He looked around the room at each man in turn, smiling benignly, his expression frank and open, not a hint of duplicity to be gathered anywhere. Jackson was fingering the files on his desk, his earlier intention of confronting Sherman with the F.B.I. surveillance now hanging in the balance. He needed this man to continue on board. But there was now no doubt in the President's mind that the frail old man in front of him was deeply involved in a dangerous game, somehow inextricably linked to the success or otherwise of the impending Moon mission.

The reports reaching him over the past weeks all indicated that the work at NASA had been commissioned a full eighteen months in advance of his directive to plan it. For the moment he had no inkling of why, only that it appeared to suit his plans very well. The speed with which components and spares had materialised without fuss were inextricably linked to the records of enormous expenditure and dubious money laundering now being uncovered, all pointing to a hidden agenda that shed a very different light on the facts as they had emerged. Exactly where it was all leading was unclear, as Jackson looked first at his Secretary of State, then at the others in turn, wondering who in God's name he could start to trust in an increasingly complex scenario, the likes of which he had never previously encountered.

Deciding at the last minute not to subject the old man in front of him to an in-depth interrogation by the C.I.A., he would nevertheless step up surveillance on both him and the senior staff at the space agency, in the fervent hope that somewhere along the line a clue might surface to point the way to a rational explanation for some very dubious goings on.

# 25

At about the same time that Nathan Jackson made his decision not to arrest the Director of his Space Agency, Sally McIntosh was entering her offices on the first floor of the Scottish Consulate on a sunny tree lined avenue not a stone's throw away from the White House. Already settled into her new post and enjoying it immensely, her days had been filled with official functions and her nights with a round of parties that had robbed her of much needed sleep, added to which the several return trips to Edinburgh, over the past six weeks for debriefing, had taken their toll on her normally robust constitution.

Her intermittent work-related involvement with Rod Cameron had developed cautiously, with few opportunities arising for their previous involvement to surface or interfere with her workload, a factor for which she was increasingly grateful. As she made clear her intentions never to get involved again, he in turn seemed to respect her wishes, even giving her a wide berth in situations where they were alone or by necessity drawn into each other's company. Only on one occasion had he attempted any intimacy, after which he had been left in no doubt whatsoever about her need to continue resolutely with the separation.

On occasions she would be invited for dinner with his family and close friends in the apartment on the second floor, an invitation she could not afford to refuse, but which never failed to raise her heart beat or to remind her of her previous feelings for him, more often than not whilst deep in conversation with his wife or playing games with his children. She had steadfastly refused to share his office and in line with her instructions from Gregor had instead furnished and prepared her own suite of rooms on the upper floor, using one bedroom as an office where she could work comfortably well into the night.

On several occasions in the early days of settling in, he had knocked on her door, but receiving no encouragement to enter, had gradually appeared to lose interest until their exchanges became random and infrequent. She suspected that his instructions included a brief to leave her alone to pursue her role as Press and Liaison Officer within the Consulate, a job that had little to do with the waiting and watching for the signal that would start the cycle of negotiations for which she had been preparing.

As she began to organise her in-tray and waited for her computer to boot up, she opened her diary to check her schedule. Turning absentmindedly to her e-mail she began to read the messages that had arrived over night. In an instant she was fully awake, her mind beginning to race, her composure ebbing away as she read Gregor's ominous message:

"Happy St. Stephen's Day".

She had work to do. Taken by surprise at the speed of events, her heart still racing, she drafted a brief reply and set off down the corridor to the secure room from which her return transmission would be sent.

Turning the key softly in the lock, she pushed open the door, expecting to find the room in total darkness. By the light of the desk lamp, sprawled in the chair behind the desk she could see the square frame of Rod Cameron, his head thrown back, as, oblivious to the world around him, his hands cushioned the tousled head of his blonde secretary as her mouth bobbed around enthusiastically on his dishevelled lap.


Gregor sat them all down at the conference table; Hamish, Murdo, Fiona and two members of his inner cabinet, Margaret McIver and Harry Millar. Gregor came straight to the point.

'As we all know our plans for the launch of the *Caliban* have always been flexible to within a day or two of the 30<sup>th</sup> of November. However recent developments now mean that we may have to review our plans for a St. Andrew's day launch. I remember you telling me Murdo that the optimum date for the launch would be earlier, in the first half of October. Is that correct?'

He looked across at Murdo who was consulting his files before answering.

'Yes. That is correct. Sometime between the 13th and the

18th October would be the most propitious date for the launch, weather permitting of course. But, as I've already said, the fuel burn is no longer part of the equation. At an earlier time I would have recommended an optimum window for a launch as the only opportunity to minimise the travel distance and optimise the trajectory. But with our new motors and the developments in fuel technology, provided that we are within a day or two either way, the exact date of departure is immaterial. If we are early into orbit, we simply hang around before blasting off for our target. If, on the other hand we are late, then we would have a helluva lot of chasing to do.'

They laughed.

'So you would suggest that anytime between the 13th October and the 18th would present the best window of opportunity?' Murdo looked at him, a smile on his face, the unexpected always the expected where Gregor McLeod was concerned.

'Are you asking me if we *can* launch between these dates or are you telling me that I must? As you know we have only just completed the final trials and despite excellent reports coming back I would like to have had at least one orbital flight and a return landing before we make the final push for the Moon. Otherwise, all systems are at go. We have a full check-list of positives in every sector and theoretically we could launch tomorrow.'

Gregor was thoughtful, weighing up the situation, aware of the risks, yet mindful of the developing situation in the States.

'Fiona?' She looked at him and sighed.

'I already know what's coming. I felt it this morning as soon as I walked in here. You want an early launch for reasons you can't fully disclose. Well ... as far as the project is concerned; everything is ready. The crew is well rested and have been on stand-by for the past six weeks. Their suits fit like gloves and the life support packs are faultless. If you ask me, I could give you no good reason for delaying the launch if you are determined to go earlier rather than later.'

Gregor looked at his brother, who sat listening intently. his hands on the table and his head lowered.

'Hamish? How do you feel about going early? You've heard

the opinions. Do we go now or risk the whole adventure being blown sky high in the American press? As we now know, there has been a leak, and it is clear that the Jackson administration will be coming under severe pressure in the coming days to confirm or deny that there has been a cover up. Of that we are certain. I received word yesterday and there is no doubt that the word is out. If we are to succeed we must not delay. What do you think?'

Hamish lifted his face, his eyes bright, and his face serene.

'Well now, well now. So that's how it is?'

He raised himself slowly and considered the options for a moment before replying.

'We have already risked much, not to mention the heavy investment involved. If there is a serious risk that we will be overtaken by events, then we must act now. Since we are going to do it sooner or later, let it be now.'

Gregor looked at the faces around the table inviting comment. Margaret McIver spoke first.

'Gregor, my old friend. As you know we are firmly behind you in this adventure. Ever since you declared your intentions, we who know you have had faith that you would succeed. We will not stand in your way in this matter. I also speak for the others in the Cabinet. They wish you well. If we fail, and God forbid that we should, you will know that we support you completely in this cause. Those of us who have watched you and who have worked with you, know in our hearts that you do not risk your reputation and everything that you hold dear, for your own selfish ends but for the future of generations still to come. You have our blessing in this venture whether you succeed or not. And ... may God protect Murdo here and his brave crew when the time comes.'

Gregor was touched by her remarks. He then looked directly at Fiona who returned his gaze with unfaltering affirmation.

'Can we go at the end of the second week in October?' he asked her. She smiled at him her eyes misting over as she spoke.

'Yes.' She said, visibly moved and unable to continue.

Gregor nodded his assent before continuing.

'In order that you are all kept fully informed, I will bring you up to date on the developments which have, in a sense, forced our hand on the date of the launch. For you, Fiona, it will mean an earlier departure date for Washington. Your accreditation is already underway and will be ready by Tuesday. I would ask you to contact Sally and make arrangements with her to stay at the consulate. For safety reasons you will arrange for the non-executive staff on North Uist to return to the mainland in groups for well-deserved R and R. What excuse you give I will leave to you. As far as giving out an explanation of the early launch is concerned, we can let it be known that we are intending to run a test orbit prior to the main launch. At the last moment we can inform, on a need to know basis, the key personnel who have to be in the picture. Does that seem a sensible way forward?'

Fiona nodded in agreement.

'As for you, Murdo, I leave it entirely up to you when you advise the crew of the departure date. But there can be no phone calls home.'

Murdo sat quietly, aware more than anyone else that the time had finally come.

'I understand that you may wish to captain the flight yourself and in this matter you have our blessing in whatever you may decide. The entire journey will be your responsibility, the selection of crew and the precise departure time will be yours to decide also.'

He turned to his Minister for the Environment.

'Margaret. I would ask you to ensure that suitable letters of apology are issued to our many invited guests ...'

He paused, his hand raised.

'But only after the crew are safely on their way.' She smiled at him as he continued.

'Hamish, I rely on you and Murdo to make sure that Air Traffic Control is advised of the launch eight hours ahead of the time and no more. Television crews will get even less warning.

'So there we have it. In two weeks' time we shall all be standing in the bunker at North Uist watching the preparations for the launch and listening to the countdown begin. We must now maintain complete secrecy about these discussions. I want a complete news blackout on the island and I will make sure that the regular press briefings continue as usual to ensure that we do not raise suspicions.'

As the morning wore on, the last of the autumn leaves fluttered from the trees as a chilling wind began to blow in from the north. As the sky darkened, the heavens opened and the storm blew loud gusts of rain and wind against the tall windows of the room. Gregor rose and switched on the lights, watching as the heavy drapes slid noiselessly into place, closing out the gathering storm.

A week later as Fiona McLeod boarded the transatlantic flight from Glasgow Airport heading for Washington, Ken Regan was stepping down from his overnight flight from Boston on to the tarmac at Edinburgh. Carrying just an overnight bag for an indefinite stay, he checked his pockets for passport, credit cards, press card and wallet as he wandered out of the terminal building and headed for the taxi rank. On his way into town heading for the Balmoral Hotel, he consulted his address book and placed a call on his cell phone, realising it was still quite early on a dull overcast Tuesday morning. After a brief pause he was connected.

'Gus Simpson speaking.'

The familiar voice instantly recognisable, as memories of sharing the last bottle of Ksara in a cellar in the ruins of downtown Beirut came flooding back.

'Tell me, Mr Simpson, if I give you a hundred dollars for half the fare, will you share a cab with me across town as far as the airport?'

There was a momentary pause, then a chuckle at the other end.

'No way. Get your own arse shot off, Regan.' They were laughing now.

'Where the hell are you?'

'I'm in Edinburgh for God's sake. Came over to find out what the hell is going on with your Moon mission. Say, how about grabbing some breakfast? I just got off the plane. I'm just about to find out if my half-witted secretary has booked me in or not.'

The conversation switched to the other end.

'It's the Balmoral. Yeah! OK. OK. Give me some time to check in and I'll see you in the lobby in, say, half an hour. OK. Bye. Bye.'

As the taxi pulled up at the kerb, the billboards on the news stands read,

### U.S. Moon Photographs are fakes
### Caliban to verify U.S. Landings

Standing as the doorman tried to take his satchel, he mused in front of the billboard. Maybe the answers would be found over here after all.

Gregor slouched as he sat by the window deep in thought, his hands clasped in front of his face, his elbows buried in the soft leather of his armchair. Since arriving at eight o'clock that morning he had poured himself a coffee which still lay untouched on the table beside him, scanned the newspapers for a brief moment or two, and then moved into the deep chair that had held him captive these past three hours.

In the outer office, his secretary knew better than to disturb him. Having caught a whiff of the intense atmosphere emanating from his office over the past few days, she knew when to leave well alone. There would be no fussy intrusions to tidy his desk and no casual exchanges between them until his mood had run its course. With the telephones muted and his direct line diverted, he was free to do what he did best when facing so many problems. In the end he would emerge relaxed and confident as always. Of this, she was certain.

For Gregor, it was a time for reflection. There was very little he could do now to alter the course of events as they were predestined to unfold. In two short weeks, the last act of his carefully laid plan would be acted out, drawing on players who had no notion of their role in the affair and who would have no sight of the final curtain. If he succeeded, his private satisfaction at the outcome would be reward enough. If he failed, he would be discredited and run out of international politics forever.

In fairness to his party, he had played a lone game. So very few of them had even the slightest inkling of his plan. To have involved everyone would have been tantamount to declaring his hand. It had to be this way. There was no fit option that guaranteed their protection whilst involving them fully. And they could never be told. History would never record the achievement. There would be no valid document stored for generations for future scholars to marvel at. In time, the voyage of the *Caliban* would go down in history as an absurd gesture by an over-endowed government with a capricious sense of its own importance. There would be no fanfares, no cries of "well done", nothing other than the satisfaction shared with the chosen few who would know that, in the end, they had succeeded in bringing about something of everlasting value; something that could never be measured in cash or kind, but something which would benefit every man, woman and child on the face of God's earth.

He stirred as the ache in his arms caused him to stretch. Glancing at his watch, he stood, seeing the cold coffee staring back at him. He walked to his desk where the morning papers were scattered around. Gus's editorial had been 'to the point'. The exposé of the Moon photographs and their beginnings on terra firma all but discrediting the American claims of having reached the Moon.

But what if anything, would they find? In his own mind he remained convinced that the American claims were the true account of things. It was absurd to believe otherwise. But on the other hand, there were so many loose ends, so many inconsistencies, so much room for doubt.

Well, they would soon know one way or the other. Either way, it was immaterial. The script was already in place. The deck had already been dealt. There was no going back. The seeds of doubt, so carefully sown over these past few months had either germinated or not - Gregor thought he would know when the time came. But he would have preferred a face-to-face encounter. To face your adversary across a table was one thing; to have to play poker for the highest possible stakes with an opponent at the other end of a satellite link was quite another. Hamish had said,

'You will know if we've won from the moment he opens his mouth to speak.'

And Hamish knew a thing or two about presidents and their like.


Seated in the corner of the dining room of the Balmoral, Ken Regan and Gus Simpson reminisced over a hearty Scottish breakfast, the black pudding and fried haggis deftly exiled to the edge of Ken's plate while they ordered a further pot of coffee. Soon, the room began to empty until they remained alone in the corner, the rain drumming on the vaulted cupola and the ever present musak filtering through the muted din of the waiters clearing tables.

Gus sat with one elbow on the table listening intently to his old friend. Ken Regan was talking, his expression one of controlled concern, his rapid discourse, initially disjointed, beginning to form a pattern and indicate the direction the conversation was taking. That feeling of *déjà vu* that had become so familiar of late, was beginning to surface in his mind as Regan began to voice concerns over the cover up that he sensed was closely tied in to the sixties Moon landings and the current Scottish mission.

'So you see, depending on your ability to suspend logic, it all adds up. You guys announce you're off to the Moon and, lo and behold, we have to get there first. And we will it seems. I am reliably informed that NASA intends to launch on the 26th of November and will be there ready and waiting with whatever kind of shit it is that you guys cook up for breakfast.'

This with a final disgusted shove at the remains of his breakfast. He was off again.

'Some of us have been sniffing around for some months now and we know for sure that the White House is rattled. NASA has been on round-the-clock for the past six months. Whispers of a cover up are rife. The F.B.I. is all over the plant down at the Cape.

The Johnson Space Centre in Houston is crawling with cleaners who have never handled a brush. And people everywhere you go are asking the same thing - Was there a cover up, for whatever reason back then? Did we or did we not reach the Moon? Was the whole fucking shebang a box of tricks? And if so, *why* for Christ's sake?'

Gus looked at him unsure of whether or not to get back on the carousel. His many arguments with Gregor over the past weeks and the photographic evidence splashed across the centre pages of most of the dailies all adding to the strength of the rumour that was now achieving some dubious credibility. The more he thought about it, the more convinced he became that Gregor held the answer; some confirmation of the truth that he had, thus far, refused to share with his old friend. He looked at Ken Regan, surely as jaundiced and worldly-wise as any journalist alive.

'Tell me honestly. No shit! Do you think there is any truth at all in the stories being thrown around? Is there any basis for believing that the whole thing was a fabrication from beginning till the end?'

He waited. The journalist was staring into space. At length he spoke.

'Believe me when I tell you that of the many stories I have covered over the years, they all had a rosy beginning, a cosy middle and inevitably a muddy ending. This one has been top-to-toe in shit from start to finish. Nothing hangs together. There is very little floating to the top that makes any sense any more. It's out there. The story is out there. That much we know for sure. But, pinning it down ...

'If it is, as I suspect, the biggest fuck up in American politics since time began, a lie so big that it has remained buried for fifty-plus years, then I seriously doubt if anyone alive would dare to go to print on it. Be that as it may, if it turns out to be the case, and God help us I hope it never does, that we fabricated the whole fucking issue from the launches to the landings over and over again, I can only hope that Nathan Jackson finds the courage from somewhere to stand up and explain to all of us why it ever had to happen.'

# 26

Under a clear sky, on the apron at North Uist, the recent arrivals were taxiing to the stands, whilst the planes carrying the press corps and observers from a number of countries circled overhead in the dark awaiting their turn to land. Since mid-afternoon the centre had seen a steady stream making their way though the terminal. Away from the main runway the helicopter pads were busy as a line of choppers was waved down to safe landings only metres apart, their rotors slowing as their passengers were bussed away to the relative quiet of the hospitality lounges.

Still some distance out over the sea, Gus Simpson pointed out the coastline of the island to Ken Regan as the pilot began his descent and they swooped in, avoiding the main flight path where light aircraft and a couple of wide bodied carriers were being rapidly shepherded to a halt on the new apron. Below them, the snow white beaches and the wash of the ocean reflected the full Moon as they slowed, turned and manoeuvred the last few feet to a gentle landing a stone's throw away from the edge of the water.

Away to their left on the man made peninsula thrust out into the North Atlantic, the *Caliban* stood at her moorings, her silver hull and blue Saltire clearly visible. On board, last minute checks were carried out to a multitude of fragile systems that would govern the performance of the great machine as she reached for the heavens and beyond. Overhead, the stars were clearly visible against a dark sky.

Unnoticed by the horde of press men and visitors, the unmarked transit vehicle carrying the three astronauts exited from the side of the terminal building and began its journey down the service road towards the lifts that would take them to the flight deck. Once there, they would be settled and monitored for the extended pre-flight check that would see them ready for the launch shortly before dawn.

Gus Simpson and Ken Regan began to make their way to the edge of the apron where a fleet of cars stood waiting to ferry them to the terminal building. Still stunned by the deafening roar of the arriving aircraft they passed into the relative calm of the main building and headed for the bar.

'My turn, I think. You bought the last one twenty five years ago.'

And he was off, pushing his way through the crowded area leaving Gus to size up the gathering. All around him there was an air of expectancy, nobody quite sure of the reason for the hastily summoned press conference but nevertheless impressed by the organisation behind their assembly and transportation to the space centre within hours of receiving the initial invitation.

Here and there, familiar faces and television support crews were hastily checking equipment and boxes, the early arrivals now relaxed and waiting patiently, some drinking and chatting, all of them wondering what was to come. Ken Regan returned with the drinks, raising his voice to make himself heard.

'The crowd up at the bar are all saying the same thing. The launch is tonight. For some reason or another they have brought the date forward. Seems that everyone on the base was given just two hours' warning. Personnel are being called back from leave and once the last plane is down, they reckon the island will be sealed tight. So much for Jackson's hand of friendship on a distant star. So much for yesterday's press conference. Eh? Not a bloody mention!'

He laughed.

'So, whatever it is, we could be here for the duration. I only hope you told the wife. Cheers!'

He wandered off to speak to a group of American journalists, leaving Gus wondering why he had not been given a hint by Gregor of the new arrangements. True, they had been out of touch over the past week but thinking back, there had been no indication that anything was amiss. Whatever was behind the sudden change of plan, it had to be something big. The hype surrounding the launch date had been trumpeted around the world for weeks. Celebrations to coincide with the lift off had been planned in a hundred venues across the globe. If this was the big one, then something major must have prompted the decision to launch ahead of the carefully prepared country wide celebration on St. Andrew's day.

Standing quietly alone in the noisy concourse, sipping his

whisky, Gus wondered how his old friend was feeling, knowing in his heart that whatever was behind it, Gregor McLeod would have all the loose ends firmly under control. With syndication of the material coming back from the Moon promised to the Scotsman there was nothing to worry about. Any questions he had remaining would surely be addressed at the press conference. Just how many whiskies ahead that might be was anybody's guess.


Phil Westwood came on the line just before midnight, causing Ken Regan to quit the bar, stepping out into the cold clear night. Beyond the runway, framed by the dark night sky the *Caliban* shimmered in a blaze of light. Throughout the evening, personnel had been ferried to and from the ship, alerting everyone to the distinct possibility that the launch was imminent.

'Yeah. It's me. Bought a kilt yet? No? How're yah doing'? Thought I might catch you just before bedtime. Yeah, I got your e-mail. What's up? Where are you?'

'I'm at the Space Centre on North Uist. Yeah! Middle of the fucking Atlantic. I got here a couple of hours ago. You should see this place. It's enormous. And ... they seem to have brought the launch date forward by six weeks. Nobody knows why. We are expecting a press briefing any minute now. First we all knew about it was six o'clock this evening. Since then nothing.'

'Surprise, surprise. Say, did you read my article? What do you think?'

'It was risky. It should rattle a few cages. No knocks on the door as yet I don't suppose?'

'No nothing. But the other dailies are picking up on it for sure. Two of the networks were discussing it here this morning. The balloon could be about to go up. So far, no denials from the palace. What do you think?'

'Shit! I've no idea. Just wondering if it has anything to do with the sudden panic over here. There *is* something going on here but I can't quite put a finger on it. You know, we might be much nearer the truth than we ever could imagine. I've been talking over here to one or two folks and the idea of a conspiracy surrounding the earlier landings is widespread. The newspapers are full of it. For Christ's sake, everywhere you turn ...'

'Well, you know my views. I am convinced that the cover up is real enough. The more I think about it, the angrier I get. At least we should know one way or the other, quite soon I imagine. But keep me posted. If you can get something over to me it would be much appreciated. We have someone over there as you know, but keep your ears open just the same. As soon as it's confirmed, call me. I might make the late editions. Then I'll place a call to Mark Brander, if he hasn't already heard, and listen to him shit himself.'

They laughed. Hurrying back into the warmth of the concourse, he caught up with Gus Simpson as he entered the main lounge where the press briefing was just getting underway.

The programme faded and was replaced with the news announcer.

'We apologise for this interruption to the scheduled programme this evening in bringing you some breaking news. We understand that a press conference is underway at the Space Centre on North Uist where it is expected that the First Minister, Gregor McLeod will shortly make an announcement. We cross now, live, to the centre where the statement is about to begin.'

The camera panned around the spacious lounge returning to the view of the *Caliban* seen through the panoramic window and clearly visible to the assembled crowd. On the podium, Gregor and Hamish stood flanked by several members of his cabinet and top aides from the Space Centre. Slowly, the noise subsided as Gregor approached the microphones.

'Ladies and gentlemen of the press; my thanks are due to you this evening for accepting the rather sudden invitation to join us here at the Space Centre. Some of you may already be aware that shortly before dawn, the *Caliban* will lift off on her maiden voyage into orbit prior to launching herself towards the Moon.'

There was an immediate rise in the noise level, several of the reporters interrupting with questions even as he raised his hands to still them. Cell phones were immediately produced and there was a modest rush of people heading for the media room to file their stories. Gregor waited before proceeding.

'We have a press statement ready for issue. Let me first of all apologise to those of you who would have preferred longer notice. Unfortunately, that was not an option. You will see from the statement that there were a number of issues prompting this move, not the least, the very real possibility of major solar flares projected for the original date of departure at the end of November. Clearly we could not risk the lives of our crewmen at such a time, added to which the optimum launch time has always been between the twelfth and the sixteenth of October.

'I have to admit that the rather fanciful notion of choosing St Andrew's Day for the launch was my own very unscientific view of how things should be done, but fortunately for all of us I was persuaded otherwise. Now, we all recognise that preparations are well advanced for country wide celebrations in November, not to mention the plans broadcast by the American administration for a timely handshake between the respective crews on the surface of the Moon. I should point out, however, that, to date, we have had no firm proposal from the Americans on exactly when they intend to launch.'

This was followed by bursts of raucous laughter.

'What I can tell you is that November 29th and St Andrew's Day on the 30th will still be public holidays in honour of this historic moment. Ladies and gentlemen, our hospitality is on offer. We trust that we can make you all comfortable in what promises to be a long night. We will shortly hear the countdown begin. The commentary will be broadcast in the lounge at thirty minute intervals to keep those of you who are still standing informed. Once again, I thank you all for coming. We now invite you all to join with us now in a short word of prayer for a successful outcome and the safe return of our young astronauts.'

As they stood quietly while Hamish led them in prayer, the first announcement over the public address system drowned out his final amen.

'Lift off minus three hours and thirty minutes.'


Mark Brander heard the subdued buzz of his cell phone almost immediately. Easing himself away from the brawny arms of his handsome partner, he was instantly awake, reaching for the hold button as he left the room, struggling to locate the arms of his dressing gown.

'Yes; Brander speaking. Who is this? Reuters? Jamie, how are you?'

A pause.

'Do you realise what the time is? OK. OK. Just give it to me.'

He stood for a moment as the news was relayed to him, and then he sat down slowly.

'Shee ... it! When was this dated? What time do you have on the message? Holy shit! Have you received anything by way of independent confirmation?'

Pause.

'No. What the hell are they playing at?'

Pause again.

'There was nothing earlier to suggest ... Yeah? OK, thanks anyway.'

He closed the line debating whether or not to raise the White House. Twenty after midnight. He flicked the television set into life and scrolled the channels searching for CNN.

Excitedly, Scottish newscasters reported the moments before lift off and the spectacle of *Caliban* thrusting skywards on a mission that might unwittingly destroy U.S credibility for centuries to come. After a moment or two of indecision, he opened the line and dialled.


'Hello Space Centre Control. This is *Caliban* calling. We receive you loud and clear. All systems are presently at go. Our orbit is confirmed as 1245Tf at altitude 55.46 exactly. How do you read me?'

'We read you as positive on all counts. All systems are at go. You are cleared to leave orbit at 10:21:25 hours as planned. We will give you further update at 08:00 hours. God speed, Murdo. Switching transmission channel; changing in eight seconds' time ...'


As the *Caliban's* engines roared into life and the great hull lifted effortlessly into the pale dawn over North Uist, Rab sat entranced surrounded by the enduring patrons of the "Bletherin' Skite". Their long night vigil ending, the doors were opened to the dark, damp, cobbled street that had witnessed many a historic passing, but nothing to compare with the majesty and the awe-inspiring beauty of the *Caliban* blasting off into space.

'When will we ever see the likes o' that again, I ask ye? Did ye ever see anything sae bonnie? Wis that no' truly wonderful?' Rab Nicol was elated, his eyes wide, a look of sheer excitement filling his face.

'Aye, right enough Rab, that wis great. I never thought that I wid live tae see the day...'

'Just imagine; the Moon an' a'.'

'Aye, that's right Rab, ye'll ken soon enough now.'

Charlie Smith laid the fresh pint of Guinness in front of Rab.

'Aye, soon enough.'

Rab looked at him quizzically, sensing the unspoken jibe behind the seemingly innocent remark.

'Hey you. Ba' face. Aye you.'

Charlie Smith was avoiding even a suggestion of eye contact.

'Are you insinuatin' by any chance, that ma claims that the Yanks never made it tae the Moon are about tae suffer a wee setback like? Are you trying tae tell me something maybe?'

There was silence now along the length of the bar.

'Naw, naw! Ah wis only saying that any wee notions that might be hingin' around tae the contrary, could maybe be ironed oot in the comin' days, seein' as how we'll soon be there tae kinda verify everything an' a'.'

Rab was incensed, anger rising, shoulders squarely set, his jaw thrust towards Charlie Smith as the publican searched the faces of the faithful for some glimmer of support. He found none.

'Well, ye ken what ah mean. Seein' is believin', efter a' is said and done. It's no' that we dinna believe ye, Rab, it's just that it's kinda hard tae swally some o' the stuff ye've been tellin' us.'

At this point, the atmosphere in the tiny pub chilled as all eyes turned to the master. Charlie Smith had paused in his mopping up as the import of his last remark dawned on him. Desperate to retrieve the situation he moved quickly along the bar.

'Now, dinna get me wrong, Rab. I'm a fervent believer tae. Truly. Ah think ye've been right all along It's just that ... well, some o' the lads, well ... we've been talkin' like, an' it seems tae us ...'

Rab turned on him, concern written all over his features, recognising for the first time the possibility that he might in the end be proved wrong about everything. What if he *was* wrong? The thought was suffocating. Somewhere in the back of his mind a tiny voice was sounding the alarm. His mouth was dry, his throat clogged, his head beating as the betrayal he was feeling began to settle over him. His eye still fixed on Charlie Smith, he laid the palms of his hands on the soggy bar to still a minor tremble that had started somewhere in his lower regions and was threatening to reach his lower lip. The bar waited for his reply with baited breath.

'See you, ya wee piece o' shite, I have personally gone on record as havin' put ma considerable reputation on the line on this matter and I remain confident that in the end I shall be proved right. When we get tae the Moon I shall be vindicated. Of that much I am sure. And when that great day dawns on Friday morning and oor gallant men send back the historic message, "There's buggerall here tae find ... ", I shall personally request that you and yer gang of doubting bastards get in a straight line doon the middle o' this bar tae pay due homage and ceremoniously kiss my erse!'

Around 1.00 am in the morning the telephone rang by Tom Sherman's bed. In an instant he had moved the call into his study where he took his time reconnecting the line to hear Mark Brander fluttering at the other end. Being unaware of the departure of the *Caliban*, it was with genuine surprise and concealed delight that he reacted to the news.

'Mark, I can only say that I am at a complete loss for words to express my disappointment. We were so close to finishing. Tell me more.'

'Yeah, word came through to me from Reuters that they had called the date forward. It has taken everybody by surprise. There was no warning at all. It's a mess. At any rate the President has scheduled a meeting for 11.00 a.m. tomorrow morning and has asked that you be there. I should warn you that he was practically apoplectic when I had finished talking with him. Heads are sure to roll over this one. Any notion of getting there ahead of the Scots is now lost I suppose? He is bound to ask.'

'Oh. It's out of the question. Unless of course they fail, which God forbid. This leaves us all in a very embarrassing position. I wonder if the President recognises the magnitude of the damage this could do to our diplomatic standing across the world. It will be catastrophic!'

Mark Brander was breathing heavily down the phone, the realisation beginning to dawn that few, if any, would escape the purge that was bound to follow.

'Well, we must come up with something. I mean, there has to be something we can do. We can't let him go down carrying the can for Kennedy, Nixon and those conspiring bastards who set this whole thing up in the first place. Tom, we are desperate. Please come up with something. He is threatening to cancel the NASA programmes and a whole lot more besides. I have never seen him this way.'

There was silence for a moment or two before Tom Sherman replied, his tone measured, his voice calm and hopeful.

'Well,' he said at last,

'It looks as if we will have no option but to open immediate and direct negotiations with the Scots. At our meeting tomorrow I will suggest that we approach their consulate here in Washington to advise them openly of our little problem. I have met their First Minister on two occasions and by all accounts, he is a fair-minded type of a guy. I shall be happy to initiate discussions with him on a one to one basis in the hope of achieving an understanding of the delicate nature of our predicament. At a time like this, we may need a little help from our friends.'

The audible gasp from the other end of the line gave no hint of how this suggestion had been received. Mark Brander, kneeling on the carpet sat back on his heels before rocking forward and putting his forehead to the ground in front of him. Close to tears, it was all he could do to stammer thanks into the handset.

'God bless you, Tom Sherman.'


They sat in a semi-circle around the desk, half turned in a contest between respecting the presidential presence whilst viewing the large monitor vying for their attention across the room. On screen, the minutes leading up to the launch of the *Caliban* were being replayed on CNN. Sherman sat together with Dale Johnson, Joe Skinner and Arnold Denholm. Sam Cavanagh and Elmer Franklin sat in muted conversation with Mark Brander, a sheaf of printouts in his hand, as he appeared to be quietly briefing them on the most recent news updates. Behind the desk a restrained Nathan Jackson fidgeted and frowned as he glanced across at the screen, his face serious, his discomfort barely held in check.

The President interrupted the proceedings with a petulant cough that brought everyone to an immediate state of alertness.

'We all know why we are here. The situation is threatening to get out of hand. I can see no way forward that gives us an even chance of digging ourselves out of the biggest hole in history. Gentlemen, I confess to being terrified of the outcome. I now look to you for suggestions on how we can mitigate the damage that will be done if our claim of having landed on the Moon all those years ago is shown to be a pile of shit. With our manned missions to Mars already condemned to the dustbin of history, how do you imagine our failure to reach the Moon in the sixties is going to play out with the American public? They will crucify us in the coming elections!'

As he spoke, he had raised himself halfway out of his chair, his body leaning towards them from behind the desk, pleading, imploring. He sat down again mopping his face.

'Old Tom here is of the opinion that we should negotiate. For myself, I believe that it is a touch early to start talking to the Scottish government until we are absolutely certain that we are well and truly caught. After all, they may not make it as far as the Moon, or ... let's face it ...'

He paused, looking away to the far corner of the room.

'They could fail to land safely, in which case ...'

At this, all heads were lowered in respect for a brief moment.

'There again, Dale has suggested that we brazen out the disclosure claiming that we gave false co-ordinates for the landing sites at the time. Equally possible, but less sustainable in the long run.'

A few sniggers followed this disclosure, followed by a further bowing of heads. He turned towards Sherman, unable to look him in the eye.

'Right at this moment in time, and this concerns you, Tom, I have decided to abort our little plan to reach the Moon. You will advise your personnel at Mission Control in Houston and at Cape Canaveral to cease work immediately. I will not spend one cent more on this business. I see no value or gain in compounding a felony that was never of my making in the first place. Let history be my judge.'

Tom Sherman gave a resigned shrug.

'As you wish, Mr President. I should however point out that we are within a few weeks of being ready for the trip. Who knows? The situation might not be entirely lost. Anything could happen. They might yet get into difficulties and need our help. The game is still not won, nor is it lost. They have no prior experience of space travel and could very easily land themselves in a whole heap of trouble. But, be that as it may, we have to face up to the fact that they may very well succeed. If that happens and they do manage to land safely at the coordinates we gave out in the sixties, then we will be faced with one helluva problem.'

He allowed his message to sink in, watching each face in turn as they were reminded of the gravity of their collective situation. In the background, the commentary from the television rumbled on, several replays of the launch bringing home to everyone the need for some resolution of their predicament.

Jackson rose suddenly to his feet slamming his hand down on the desk, his eyes ablaze.

'We'll nuke the bastards. We'll blow the whole fucking lot of them to kingdom come. Godammit, we could even ...'

His rhetoric ran out as he caught the sudden fear across the room and the wide eyed look of utter disbelief on the face of Dale Johnson. Crestfallen, he sat down again. After a moment or two, the silence in the room reached breaking point.

'If I may, Mr President.'

Sherman was on his feet, half turning, his manner conciliatory, his tone gentle as he addressed the gathering. He moved to silence the broadcast. The screen darkened and fell silent. For a moment he gazed out of the window before turning towards them.

'I've been thinking.'

He paused, head bowed as he appeared to be weighing the options. They turned to him, upturned faces glowing with half baked anticipation, frowns turning to unconvincing smiles of encouragement, their desire to be done with the agony of indecision and frustration lending weight to the glimmer of hope they were so eager to invest in the slight figure of Tom Sherman. A mischievous smile began to develop slowly on his face.

'Do you know something? I don't believe that the situation is half as bad as we are making it out to be. Let us examine the facts. The Scots brought forward their departure date, knowing that we were within an inch of a launch. I have to ask myself the question, why? Why indeed?'

They were looking at him now, hanging on his words; each man in the office with a reputation carefully crafted over many years of service in politics; each one wary and nervous, afraid for their futures and desperate for an exit that would clear them of the remotest connection to the conspiracy.

Tom Sherman continued pacing slowly around the room, studying the worn carpet, his hands clasped behind his back.

'They knew! Godammit, the whole world knew that we had offered the hand of friendship to their crew, that we wanted to be there to greet them on their arrival. Why would they blow such a chance to demonstrate generosity of spirit to a watching world? The only two nations to reach the Moon? I find it inconceivable that they would not welcome an opportunity to exchange a handshake with our crew, the first such meeting on a distant star.'

He paused again.

'Unless of course they had a very good reason. And the more I think about it, the more convinced I have become that they have such a reason; *and* an agenda that will be unfolded in the coming days. I know this Gregor MacLeod. He is an honest man. Whatever it is that he has up his sleeve, there is no doubt in my mind that there will be a rational explanation for his behaviour.

'If his team land successfully at the Sea of Tranquillity in the next few days I imagine that they will be far too busy to even notice the absence of any evidence of our previous visit. And even if they do land on the button, what would they be looking for? The remains of the descent module? The flag? A maze of footprints? A couple of runabouts? Some forty-year-old golf balls? Small targets by any measure to my way of thinking.'

In front of Jackson, the F.B.I. reports on Sherman and Cavanagh lay in their blue folders, gathering dust and crying out for attention. Sherman continued,

'No. I believe that when they find no evidence of us having been there they will simply conclude that they have landed wide of their target. God knows, the Moon is hardly their own back yard.'

He smiled wryly at his fellow conspirators, they in turn appearing to relax as a modicum of comfort began to seep slowly into their tortured souls.

Then Jackson was on his feet, his expression one of desperate expectation, leaning forward over the desk, his hands waving, his body language signalling hopeless defeat.

'But what if they move to the other sites? For God's sake we claimed to have tootled around covering half the surface area between Apollo Eleven and Apollo Nineteen. They wouldn't have to move very far. We are supposed to have left tracks and gear and Christ knows what behind after every sortie. How in hell's name do we get that kind of shit up there before they start poking around in years to come?'

The others looked crestfallen, their recent optimism dwindling sharply at the thought of the Scots wandering over a virgin Moon, slowly coming to the conclusion that they were the first to land there. Tom Sherman considered the issue, the smile still fixed on his face.

'Mr President, friends, let us not lose heart. I feel we are making much too much of this issue. Sure, we could end up being crucified by the world's press. But I don't believe that it will go that far.'

Straightening now and standing again in front of the great windows he was the magician at the party, smooth and unruffled, working desperately to conceal the artifice.

'No. We are far from being exposed. All of this is mere conjecture. There is nothing, absolutely nothing at present to lead us to believe that our little secret is not safe for a very long time to come.'

He smiled broadly, every expression riveted to his own. Across the room there were audible sighs of relief and not a little laughter.

'But to return to the point I wanted to make. I believe that the Scots simply want to demonstrate yet again their independence. Nothing more; to show to the world that they need nothing from us, or from any other nation for that matter; to let everyone know that they have achieved something truly astonishing; and above all, *to do it alone*. We were simply presumptious in assuming they would go along with the hand shake bit. And ... '

He paused, looking at each face in turn,

' ... they were simply too polite to state the fact.'

He waited, watching their reactions as they listened to his words. There was a murmur of approval and some nodding of heads.

A wry smile appeared briefly on the President's face.

'And something else too. Let us remember that they will surely have their hands full at the moment. And, let us not forget that they have yet to confirm that they intend to head for the *exact* co-ordinates that we gave out in the sixties. I wouldn't mind betting they will be so relieved to be down safe and sound *anywhere* on the surface, proclaiming their success to the world and equally desperate to get home to earth, that they won't find the time to wonder why they haven't found us.

'If there *is* an agenda that threatens our position we shall know about it soon enough. Gentlemen, I propose that we do nothing for the moment. Instead I suggest that we await the outcome over the next few days. If nothing happens we will have time aplenty to plan our strategy for restoring the reputation of this great country of ours.'

Then quietly,

'Let us not forget that we still have an agenda to return to the Moon in any case to set our house in order.'

At this, there was more discomforted shuffling of feet.

'At any rate, I *would* suggest that you resist the temptation to see our plans as being hopelessly aborted. Shutting down our magnificent effort at this stage may be seen as a sacrifice too far. But let us be wary. We have no idea what the next forty eight hours will turn up, but I believe that we should be ready for any eventuality, whether it be to answer the call to mount a rescue mission or simply to monitor the progress of the *Caliban* as she carries out her mission. In this way, we shall remain fully informed and be better able to counter anything they may throw at us.'

With misty eyes and not a little hand wringing out of sight beneath the desk, an agitated Jackson nodded his assent, uttering a quiet, 'So be it.'

Aboard the *Caliban* all was quiet. The soft light from the banks of controls lent a cosy reassuring warmth to the small space. While the others slept Murdo peered out at the distant stars seeing an increasingly beautiful vision of the Moon as they closed the distance to their target. The vastness of space and the eerie impenetrable blackness, the clarity with which the universe was unfolding around them, the sharp focus of the hanging star clusters and the utter silence that enfolded them reminding him of the sheer wonder of their journey; a journey that had started only thirty six hours earlier in the breaking dawn of a perfect day on a perfect world.

On the monitor in front of him, the image of the earth glowed like some pale blue paper lantern surrounded by a chilling mantle of darkness. The constant awareness of the isolation from familiar surroundings tinged with the utter uniqueness of the situation, the monitors recording staggering speeds of 5000 feet per second and the knowledge of the great distance already travelled in the space of a few hours all added to the dream-like quality of the experience.

Thus far their journey had been uneventful, the daily televised transmissions to base being the high point of their day. Taking turns at resting, their tasks made routine after years of simulated practice, they were frequently astonished at the degree of normality with which they viewed their situation. Already the Moon was bigger and growing by the minute; the seamless motionless movement of the *Caliban* hiding the fact that in less than a day and a half they would enter lunar orbit and begin preparations for the descent to the surface.

Exactly who would go and who would remain behind to control the great ship was one of the many questions on Murdo's mind as he gazed out at the heavens. All in all it was a matter of little consequence to him whether or not he actually set foot on the Moon. Of the three astronauts, he was possibly the most qualified to command the *Moonraker* as she made the risky descent to the surface. Still day dreaming and not a little tired himself, he decided to postpone the decision making until after they had settled into orbit and made their calculations for descending to the Sea of Tranquillity.

# 27

Early evening on a dull October day, the last of the autumn leaves clinging hopelessly to the bare branches of the trees, Gregor McLeod strode through Prince's Street Gardens, nodding and smiling to passers-by as he made his way to the American Embassy in Charlotte Square. A cold wind tugged at his coat as he tightened the warm scarf around his neck. His great mane of white hair, forever in need of tender loving care, blew over his face as he struggled to reach his cell phone. Never one for an addiction to gadgets, he paused, as he always did before deciding which button made the desired connection.

Relieved, standing squarely in front of the Ross bandstand he heard the early morning traffic on the streets of Washington playing gently in the background as Fiona's voice rang out loud and clear.

'And a very good morning to you too. How are you both? Well, I trust?' They laughed.

'We are fine. The Consulate is just wonderful. Very posh. Very comfortable. Settled in here without a hitch. I am standing on the balcony of the kitchen overlooking this great city *and* the sun is shining, so what more could a girl ask for? Yes. We are both delighted with the news. Yes. Stayed up to watch the whole event. It was magnificent. The whole place is buzzing. I am so happy for all of you.'

Gregor smiled, charged with a deeply felt happiness tinged with a degree of apprehension for the final outcome.

'Careful. We are not there yet. Many a mile to go I'm afraid. But I am confident. So far there have been no glitches. The reports coming back are all positive. Of course, the press are killing me with demands for regular televised updates which, thus far, have been denied them. They want to know why we are maintaining a partial signals blackout.'

Fiona interrupted him.

'It's the same over here. We have practically shut down the phone lines. A single recorded statement is all anyone ever gets if they ring in. We have been pestered for interviews and it is nearly impossible to get out of the Consulate. The crowd outside stopped the traffic after the announcement of the launch. Since then it's become much worse. The guards do their best but I think we will have to give out a brief statement later on today.'

'Yes. Do that. Give them only the bits we prepared. Everything is on course and I have no doubt that our moves will play out exactly as we discussed. I hope everything is ready? No last minute nerves? Good. Let's keep it that way.'

'Sally and I went over our notes again last night. Don't worry. The Oscars are already spoken for. We won't let you down.'

'I never for one moment believed you could. I am having dinner this evening with John Willmott and his wife. I have no doubt that the touchy subject of our early departure will be high on the list of ... No. I don't think so. Everybody is still at the guessing stage. No. I'm fairly sure of that.'

'Give our love to everyone. Take care. Enjoy your dinner. Talk again soon.'

And with that the line closed, Gregor again undecided if the green or the brown tag silenced the beast. Suddenly faced with the immediacy of the next critical moves he had a brief moment of mild panic as the thought of failure swept over him. Never. They would succeed. All of the ground had been well prepared. There was no turning back now. No last minute hitch to warrant a cancellation. But what if ... Buttoning his great overcoat, he strode forward, his giant steps and swinging stride an indicator of his positive mind-set as all thoughts of "what if" were swept aside.

Less well protected from the bitter wind and the darkening skies, but equally well disposed to inner doubts, Rab Nicol and doll Susan shuffled aimlessly along in the opposite direction heading for the "Bletherin' Skite". In a few minutes time their paths would cross, each in his own way playing for stakes they could ill afford; each with a reputation built on credibility and a strong belief in their respective charters. For Rab, the last few days had been hell on earth, exemplified by the rise of the opposition led by that arrogant, ignorant bastard Charlie Smith. Slowly but surely, the following of fervent supporters was dwindling and dividing down a line, those for and those against.

'How do you know fur sure, eh? Tell us that! How can you be so bloody sure a' the time? What gives you the right tae tell us that your way is the right way? Do you think the Yanks would huv wasted a' that money on a pile o' shit?'

'Gi'e the man a chance. You tell them, Rab. Show them the photies again. Whit aboot the footprint? Tell them, Rab.'

'And another thing, Rab. You've still tae answer the wan big question. How come, if Scotland has found the technology tae make the trip, you are still convinced that the Yanks didnae do it? Aye - go on. Answer that one, if ye wull.'

'See you, Rab. Yer talkin' through yer erse. America's the biggest, richest country in the world. They poured money intae the thing fur Christ's sake. There is no way that they could've failed. Aye go on if ye wull. Tell us, Rab. Tell us.'

Walking in silence, fat Susan sharing the agony and the uncertainty, they brushed shoulders with Gregor as he approached the steps leading to the street. With heads lowered, each deep in thought they failed to notice the great man as he pursued his own thoughts on the very same subject to the only possible logical conclusion; that success based on careful preparation and years of hard work was the reward that would rightly come his way.

At that very moment, Rab raised his head towards the sky, a fierce determination entering his being as he resolved to fight to the bitter end, holding fast to his beliefs; beliefs that would either see total vindication in the coming days or total destruction of the only thing in his entire shabby existence that he had truly made his own.


Gregor and the American Ambassador entered the quiet study overlooking the windswept gardens of Charlotte Square, the great fireplace and log fire framed by comfortable leather armchairs and soft lighting from a pair of rare Ming pottery vases converted into table lamps. Sitting with a generous dram each, they relaxed in each other's company as they had done on many previous occasions.

'I didn't want to raise the matter at dinner for obvious reasons, but Joan and I will shortly be heading back home for a while. She is naturally upset at the recall as you can imagine. We have been here longer than most postings that I can remember.'

He sighed deeply.

'And of course, she has made many friends here. The pace of this place suits us. We have never been happier. All in all, it will be a wrench.'

Gregor was looking at his old friend with mild concern tinged with sincere regret.

'We will miss you of course. Where is it to be? Tokyo? Havana?'

'You never know. Postings are the best kept secrets. I could speculate but I have never been right. Not ever. It could be anywhere. Or they could just pull me back to a desk job in Washington. You never get told until the last goddamned minute. It's one of the things you have to live with in this line of business.'

He raised his glass towards Gregor.

'Enough of my problems. I give you a toast. To the *Caliban* and a successful conclusion to your venture. Let's hope that they all return to us safe and sound.'

'Amen to that.'

Gregor responded raising his glass, sinking deeper into his chair as the warmth from the fire contributed to the overall feeling of well-being and creature comfort.

'My turn I think. My thanks are due to Joan and yourself for a wonderful dinner. You do realise of course that your new chef will be poached just as soon as you leave?'

They laughed together.

'How soon do you think? Months or weeks, perhaps days?'

'Some months yet I guess. They rarely bring you home to the East Coast during the winter. Spring I imagine. More than likely. There again, it could be anytime. I am due to fly home at the end of this week. I have to tell you that I am certain to be pumped for anything I can give them on your Moon shot. The traffic over the past months has doubled in volume, mostly down to your announcement and this talk of an interstellar handshake. I *was* due to make you a formal offer on that subject, but of course you have short changed us by heading off sooner than expected. Is it true that you were forced to bring it forward? Sun spots and the like? I saw the reports, but we all thought it odd that the decision to leave early was not advertised.'

Gregor smiled, savouring his dram.

'Well, it's partly true. In truth, we were ready and I decided to keep the momentum going. November would have missed the optimum window for the trip. Murdo Sinclair was raring to go. The other pilots had known for some time that the launch was imminent and nerves were beginning to set in. I looked at the psychological profiles and the long range weather reports for this week and decided to go for broke. I think I made the right decision. Apart from some flutters at the launch, their pulses have slowed down to normal over the last twelve hours.'

They laughed.

'Rather them than me.'

John Willmott sat forward, eager to press home the questions he had held back during dinner.

'Gregor; let me ask you this. Is there an agenda apart from the voyage itself? I know it has nothing to do with the hysteria filling the tabloids at the moment. You and I, any reasonable person for that matter, knows for sure that there isn't a grain of truth in the assertions that we faked the Apollo missions. We hear from Washington that even our dear President hasn't been above asking the same sort of question. We here at the Embassy can hardly believe some of the garbage served up these days disguised as news.'

He was smiling but his voice held a hint of concern. Gregor was smiling too as John proffered the decanter of malt.

'Aye, I must admit, neither can I, although I do have to admit to a vicarious pleasure in reading the stuff. But it's certainly not very friendly. America always seems to be the butt of somebody's resentment. Of course it's nonsense. No right minded person gives it a moments thought. If you want the truth, we are all a bit upset that our serious work in building the *Caliban*, developing the fuel, the technology and everything else is being overshadowed by the absurdity that we are going to dig up some evidence of some dastardly deed or whatever on the Moon.

'No. I can assure you that we are not looking for anything of the sort. We are making the journey essentially to demonstrate our enormous achievement to an indifferent world that would have difficulty locating Scotland on a school atlas. It's a reaction, in my own mind, to the centuries of seeing ourselves as the under-dog; that irritating appendage at the end of the British Isles; the tail that the dog forgot to wag. For as long as I can remember I have wanted to see this country exploit its full potential for the good of its people, to see our nation lift its head and feel that pride that comes from knowing that the job has been well done. It's many other things too, but you've heard it all before from me and now is not the time for sermonising. It's late and we both have a full day ahead of us tomorrow.'

As they wandered down to the hallway John turned to him.

'Gregor, it's been a pleasure as always to see you. I will always treasure our times together.'

Then, with a twinkle in his eye.

'Before you go, let me ask one final thing of you. In the event that your guys fail to find any evidence of us having been there first, you *will* let me know?'

Then he was off down the steps, shaking hands as their laughter echoed through the great house.

'Come what may,' Gregor was thinking with genuine regret, 'I hope to God we do.'


The call came through shortly before midnight. At his bedside, the house phone beeped quietly, the signal that the call required his attention. John Willmott got out of bed and walked the length of the upper corridor to take the call in his study. The smell of fine whisky still hung in the air.

'Yes, Simon. How are you? Fine. All doing well. You've received my message? Oh, good. Yes ... I had a very pleasant dinner this evening with our friend and as far as I can tell they have almost no interest in anything connected with the Apollo landings. They are simply flying the flag. No. I am certain of that.'

'Well, John, the administration up on the hill is sure as hell panicking over something. We can't forbid them to land at the old sites, now can we? Short of telling them the area is toxic or off limits for any number of reasons I don't see what we can do ...'

'I wonder what we're hiding for Christ's sake. It makes you think.'

'No idea.'

'I think that it's all too late. They will be down there in a matter of hours. A bit late to be thinking of recalculating orbital paths or looking for new landing sites don't you think?'

'I don't know anything about that kind of thing. Never been too interested. I only found out that they were on their way a few hours ago. Seems the papers here are full of it. I never get told anything stuck down here. I never get to meet regular people. I am only allowed up to street level once or twice each week.'

They laughed together.

'Look. Seriously, I think I'll tell them that we have had a chat and simply report your findings. If they want to take it further, that's up to them. I don't think we can help.'

'Fine. Call me if you need anything further.'

'Oh. Hold on. One thing more. Is there anything to suggest that their descent vehicle is capable of exploring the surface? Somebody needs to know I guess.'

'I have no idea. I can ask the question of course. Let me see what I can find out. We had a press pack handout some time ago that gave a few technical details. Somebody around here is bound to know.'

'OK. I'm off home. See what you can do.'

'Bye.'

'Okay. Bye for now.'


'Well sir, it seems we can now be certain that they will attempt to land in the shadow of the Eagle; bang on the button, they reckon.

They claim to be unaware of the fact that they will find diddley when they get there. Willmott reckons they have nothing to hide and fully expect to find everything just as we claim to have left it.'

Mark Brander paused in his summary of the recent incomings from Scotland. Nathan Jackson looked at him distractedly seeing his years of effort about to slide into the abyss as the threat of exposure loomed before him. Dale Johnson had a fleeting image of the Titanic going down, chaos raging and the dark cold waves pulling him down.

Brander waved his messages again.

'They will enter orbit this evening in about an hour's time. In the early hours of tomorrow they will separate and ...'

He paused as he caught a look from Johnson that stopped him.

'Yes, thank you, Mark. We have the picture for now.'

Johnson, suffering now, just managed to catch the final fleeting moments as the stern disappeared beneath the waves. Beneath his feet he was certain the carpet was ebbing and flowing.

Jackson was beaten. The anxiety that had kept him awake for the last two nights was beginning to take its toll. He waved his arm in the general direction of the New England dresser behind him.

'Dale. If you would be so kind. I believe a drink might be in order at this juncture. Stiff ones; please.'

'There is just one further thing Mr President.'

Brander paused, looking at Johnson who was preoccupied fixing the drinks.

'It has been confirmed that they *will* be exploring the surface in their lander on the second day of the mission. I fear that any hope that we might have entertained that they would assume that they had simply missed the site is now lost. We have the transcripts of their transmissions from the *Caliban* so we are fairly certain that this is the case.'

The President, slumped in his chair, lifted his head for a moment.

'Then I think we must conclude that nothing short of a miracle is gonna stop the sons' o' bitches from blowing the whistle on us. We are finished. Mark, first thing tomorrow make contact with their Consulate and talk to ...'

Brander interrupted him. 'I'll get on to the Consul immediately, sir.'

'No. Don't do that. Talk to green eyes. The niece. The one who told me the grass needed cutting. Send her the usual warm congratulations. Through her, we can keep a channel open back to Scotland in case we have to talk to Gregor McLeod in a hurry.'

Dale handed over the drinks.

'Scotch, all right?'

Unaware of the unintentional irony, he missed the pained expressions that passed over their faces.


Gus Simpson sat in the press gallery as the Ministers' Question time rolled on. Hardly surprisingly, the focus of the questioning was targeted at the voyage of the *Caliban* and the various progress reports that had been presented to the House. Margaret McIver held the floor. As the Minister for Transport and the Environment, it was she who had the ultimate responsibility of passing on the updates being relayed nightly from the ship.

' ... and I can assure the members that not only are our boys in good health but they are also in high spirits and carrying out their duties in every respect, as the responsible trained professionals that they are. I am told that they breakfasted well and have since changed their socks.'

Nobody laughed.

'At present, they are only a few short hours away from preparing to orbit the Moon early tomorrow. Once settled into a confirmed orbit, they will rest for several hours before two of them will then transfer to the cargo bay and entering the *Moonraker* E. T. vehicle.'

She was reading from the speech prepared for her earlier.

'After ensuring that relays between the two vehicles are working properly and that systems on board are functioning normally they will begin separation from the *Caliban* at approximately 12 noon our time on the morning of Friday the 21st of October. Thereafter they will remain in orbit until such time as they initiate the descent procedures for landing, it is hoped, in the Sea of Tranquillity at the precise spot made famous by the American astronauts in 1969.

'Their first sortie to the surface will take place at approximately 1500 hours on the same day. It has not yet been confirmed how long they will stay on the surface but they have a programme to complete. As we know, the time they spend on the Moon is not limited in that their survival packs can be serviced and ready for re-use within a few hours at the most.

'I am happy to report that to date the journey has been uneventful. We are hopeful for the remainder of the journey and the safe return of our astronauts. I will now take questions.'

Harry Millar, the Speaker of the House, motioned to one of those who had immediately risen to their feet.

'Mr Speaker, we thank the lady Minister for her welcome report, and I am sure that I join with everyone here in wishing success to our brave boys, but is it not the case that we and the public are still being kept in the dark, given the very scant coverage that this mission is receiving? Surely the on-board cameras are capable of transmitting images of the ongoing work of the crew, as well as the wonderful views received last evening of the Moon, as they draw closer to their goal. We would welcome fuller coverage of the event at any level, given the enormous world wide interest in the voyage. I might add that I have received several complaints from members of the press that information on progress is in very short supply.'

Gregor McLeod conferred with Margaret McIver and rose to reply.

'I must agree with my honourable friend that the images we are receiving are indeed wonderful, and I can assure him that we will be covering the descent and the extra-vehicular programme as it unfolds. I must however report that for all our undoubted skill in getting thus far, our ability to control some irritating minor glitches to our cameras, and the radio links back to base are causing concern. The crew are working on the problem, and I am confident that they will have things back and running for tonight's broadcast.

'In the meantime, may I take this opportunity to thank all those concerned with the success of the project? Without their dedication to duty and their skills in a wide field of endeavour, we would not now be about to celebrate the successful realisation of the voyage of a lifetime. Mr Speaker, I believe that we all have a great deal to feel proud of at this moment in our country's history.'

Gregor sat down to loud applause as a sealed transcript of an e-mail was handed to him. Having read it he folded it and placed it in his pocket. From the consulate in Washington it simply said,

```
Contact established with our friends. Seems that
somebody wants to parley. Sally & Fiona.
```

Up in the gallery, Gus noticed the passing of the note and the serious look on the face of Gregor McLeod. Clearly it was time to press him for a heart to heart, now that he had established the true credentials of one Frank Nelson, environmental activist and man of many parts.



The phone rang in the hallway. Fiona handed the receiver to Sally as she came out of her room.

'Hello. Yes. Sally here. Oh!' She turned to Fiona. 'It's for you.'

Taking the phone she heard the voice of Rod Cameron.

'Hi. The call came through to my apartment. I'll transfer it. Hold on.' She heard the line open then his voice at the other end.

'Paul, how are you? It's been ages. I tried reaching you last week when I arrived but as usual nobody would say where you were.'

'Yeah. I've been on the move. Just flew in from Singapore. I was there for four days. Helluva journey. Glad to be back.'

'Wonderful. I got in ten days ago; been working ever since. You heard the news. The *Caliban* is in orbit around the Moon.'

'Yeah. I managed to get the in-flight news. Carried me straight back to Bonnie Scotland. So ... How are you? How long are you over for?'

'Well ... that's a bit complicated. I usually fly back once a week but I am here now until I complete my task.'

'Ahuh! And do you get time off for good behaviour? I just happen to know a great little fish restaurant?'

'Why? Where are you? I thought you were based in New York?'

'No, I'm working out of Washington; have been for some time. Matter of fact, I passed the Consulate on the way to the airport a week ago and wondered if you were here. So; what's it to be? Lunch or dinner?'

She laughed.

'Whatever suits you. My time is a bit tight at the moment but dinner should be O.K.'

'Right. That's settled. I'll pick you up at eight. Yes, tonight! If that suits you? O.K. Fine. Eight o'clock it is.'

# 28

Friday lunchtime, as Rab and fat Susan walked into the "Skite" and ordered drinks, all eyes were fixed on the television screen. Somebody nudged him in the ribs.

'Hi Rab, huv ye heard? They're saying that they've lost contact wi' the *Caliban*. The news has just been on. That guy that's been doing the regular announcements says that they've been trying since one o'clock to talk tae them but it's nae use. They're no' answering.'

'Is that a fact?'

'Aye. That's right enough, Rab. Looks bad. They had just opened the doors fur the *Moonraker* tae dae its stuff and then phut! Nothin'. The guys at Mission Control are goin' daft. The big space special tonight is maybe cancelled.'

Charlie Smith shouted down the bar.

'See you, Rab Nicol. You're the jammiest bugger in town. Just when it looked as if we were goin' tae get tae the bottom o' this affair, yer mates up at Television Centre huv pulled the plug on us. Did you huv anything tae dae wi' it like? Huv ye been havin' a wee word wi' yer pals oan the *Caliban* maybe? Huv ye been talkin' again tae yer wee man in the Moon?'

The pub erupted with laughter.

'Aye. Go on. Tell us Rab. Whit huv ye done?'

Rab ignoring the jibes, sipped his beer contentedly, seemingly thoughtful and distracted, his eyes missing nothing. A friendly punter touched his arm.

'Aye Go on, Rab. Can ye no' tell us what's happenin'? That producer lassie was oan the phone an hour ago asking tae speak tae ye. Wanted a quote no less. Charlie told her ye were retired frae the business o' screwin' the Yanks. Told her yer secretary had been paid off an' had buggered aff tae Spain. Can ye believe that? Disgraceful! Ah think ye'll be proved right in the end. Ah've always said, Rab knows best, so he does.'

'Aye. Thanks pal. I know ah'm right. It only takes brains and a bit o' education. That's what's missing wi' this lot. They ken buggerall aboot anything. Ah'm tellin' ye boy.'

Charlie Smith was off again, egged on by the regulars at the other end of the bar.

'Huv they no' asked ye yet tae go an' sort it oot Rab? You wi' a' yer experteese. Few weeks ago, they were crawlin' all over ye fur yer opinion?'

More wild laughter filled the pub.

Incensed, Rab cautiously cast his eyes around the walls. Gone were the posters advertising his nightly slot. In the corner, the busker with the guitar was struggling against the noise. The place seemed different. Gone was the promise of nightly adulation. Instead, the faithful few returned his cheery grins with half hearted smiles and reassuring pats on the arm.

'Never you mind Rab. We all think you're right. Wait an' see. Then we'll wipe the smug grins aff their faces. You'll see.'

All eyes returned to the broadcast. The replays of the earlier reports from the *Caliban* were abruptly interrupted as the news announcer prepared to make a statement. An instant hush fell over the crowd.

'Good afternoon. This is the Scottish Broadcasting Corporation. We can now bring you some breaking news. As you will be aware, Mission Control lost contact with the *Caliban* at approximately one p.m. today, shortly after the cargo bays were opened in preparation for the release of the *Moonraker* descent vehicle into orbit. We know that two of the crew members had already completed their transfer to the *Moonraker* and Mission Control assures us that up to that point everything was proceeding to plan. Problems with the radio and television transmissions had been noted earlier on in the voyage but it had been hoped that the repairs that had been made had resolved the problem.

'I should add that we have no evidence to suggest that the *Caliban* has suffered a mishap, or that there is anything to fear for the safety of the crew. At this point in time we have a signals failure which Mission Control is trying to resolve. If we have anything further to add to this bulletin we will interrupt this afternoon's programmes to bring you an update.

'Just to recap. In about ninety minutes from now, the

*Moonraker* was due to make the descent to the surface of the Moon. The likelihood is that we will not now be able to bring you these pictures, but we can only hope that the situation will be resolved before too long. Our science correspondent informs us that it is highly unusual for all relays on board to fail simultaneously. The possibility that this indicates a major systems failure on board the *Caliban* cannot therefore be discounted. We will bring you further news as it develops.'

Fat Susan could not be consoled.

'Rab. They could be dead. They're just not telling us. Isn't it terrible? I wonder what happened.'

'Naw. Naw. Take it easy, doll. Have faith in Mission Control. They always huv a back up. You'll see. By tonight, they will be back on the box as large as life. You'll see. Honest.'

In trying to comfort her however, Rab was not convinced. This was maybe too convenient. Convenient certainly for him, *and* convenient for anybody else determined to hide or cover up the truth. Suddenly Rab saw the whole thing. A conspiracy! A cover up! Jesus Christ Almighty, a cover up! That bastard Gregor McLeod hand in glove with Nathan Jackson to keep the whole thing under wraps. Wrapped up nice and tight.

Rab's face tightened with anger. Pushing along the bar, Rab stood in front of Charlie Smith. Taken aback, he retreated as far as the optics shelve unsure of how to deal with this new, determined Rab who had cleared a space for himself around the bar like some prize fighter preparing to swing. Turning to address the rabble like Christ berating the money lenders, Rab adopted his old arrogant stance, ignoring Charlie Smith as he prepared to speak.

'Ye see, you lot. Aye, you lot. Ye're blind. Blind and stupid. What huv I been tellin' yees all for the past four months? Tell me what. Huv yees learned nothin'?'

He paused, that old snarl returning as he searched their faces.

'So. Yees don't know. Well, as usual, I will huv tae tell yees all. Does it no' occur tae ye that this wee mishap is maybe laid on fur oor benefit? Is it no just a wee bit too convenient?'

'Whit dae ye mean Rab? Ye've lost us. Whit dae ye mean?'

'Hold on, boy. Just you hold on, boy, and it will all be made clear. First things first. Dae we honestly believe them when they tell us that their systems are no' working? Not just one system, mark you, but the bloody lot? Is that no' just a wee bit too convenient? Is that no' just a wee bit funny?'

He held up his hand to still the protests. Charlie Smith with head bowed was furiously polishing glasses.

'Huv I or huv I not pointed out tae yees all the extent o' the conspiracies surrounding this whole Moon thing? How many times huv I asked ye tae look at the facts and no' the fiction? Go on, how many times?'

'Aye, right enough Rab, ye've said it a' b'fore.'

'Right. And now what do we find? The *Caliban* is just about to reveal all, when in steps Nathan Jackson and his buddies and says,

' "Hold on, ye canna dae that. Exposing us wid be a mortal sin, like Celtic playin' fur a draw."

' And Gregor McLeod says,

' "Are youse telling us that you've got something tae hide like?"

'And Jackson says,

' "Aye, too bloody right, fur we never landed on the Moon."

' Then McLeod says,

' "Help ma Boab! Is that no the bloody limit!"

'at which point they all shake hands, call off the troops, and decide never tae tell anybody the truth, fur ye see ...'

He paused, his eyes narrowing, the pub falling silent as never before, every eye focused on the magician.

'Ye see, they are a' part o' the same bloody conspiracy.'

The uproar that followed could be heard a mile away as Rab sauntered back down the length of the bar, retrieving his pint and getting a big hug from an adoring Susan. A minute later, a timid Charlie Smith edged still closer.

'Will ye be back in tonight, Rab, by any chance?' he whined.

'Like fuck I will.' said Rab, with an arrogant toss of his angelic head.

Nathan Jackson sat listening intently as the voice of the controller at Mission Control in Houston was relayed down the telephone to the Oval Office. They gathered round the small speaker, the President preferring the handset which he held close to his ear, forgetting for the moment that the call was on conference mode. Having waited patiently through most of the night, listening in to the infrequent exchanges between the *Caliban* and Mission Control on North Uist, Dale Johnson, Tom Sherman and Sam Cavanagh listened as the news confirmed that all contact with the *Caliban* had been lost some two hours earlier. He checked his watch. It was eight thirty a.m.

'Yes sir. As far as we can tell they have lost all contact with the ship and the *Moonraker* E .T. vehicle. We are convinced that despite regular calls going out from Scotland, no return messages have been transmitted. We can be certain therefore, that the link between the *Caliban* and their home base is temporarily lost.'

Tom Sherman posed the next question.

'Is it likely that their ship has perhaps suffered some accident or do you think that this is simply a communications failure?'

'We can't know for sure, sir. But it is most unlikely that all systems would fail at one time. They would surely have back-up relays which in the direst emergency would allow them to talk to home base. In unusual circumstances, such as an accident that wiped out normal relays, they would activate an emergency beacon that would transmit a signal at regular intervals for anything up to a month. Thus far, we have detected nothing of the sort. It is highly irregular and we are slowly but painfully coming to the conclusion that this may well indicate a major setback to the project.'

'Thank you, Colonel Sanders. You have been very helpful. Please call us if you receive further news or if contact is re-established.'

With that, Jackson closed the line as Mark Brander entered the office.

'Mr President. I have contacted the Consulate here in

Washington and they can add little to what we already know. The transmissions ended abruptly and there was little or no warning that the systems were about to fail. They are still upbeat, refusing to concede that there may have been a catastrophic accident. They did however give out that there had been an earlier problem with their antennae, but nothing on this scale was anticipated.'

Nathan Jackson was silent for a while exchanging subdued but meaningful looks with Tom Sherman. At length he spoke to his press officer.

'Given the current situation, Mark, I would suggest that you hold off your meeting with them. This would not be the right time to intrude as I am sure you will agree. No. We should hold fire for a day or so until we either hear that they are safe, or ...'

At this point he hesitated, unable to bring himself to express his feelings as a confusing mixture of sadness tinged with overwhelming relief fought for ascendancy in his tired brain.

'Tom.' He was turning towards Sherman, his manner offhand.

'Your people are still on course to fly to the Moon I hope? You haven't ... ?'

He paused as Tom Sherman nodded in turn.

'Have no worries sir. I can have a team on the Moon within four weeks from now if needs must. We were nearly ready to roll as you well know. Everything is on stand-by for an imminent departure date. You only have to say the word.'


Aboard the *Caliban*, Murdo Sinclair was too busy monitoring the progress of the *Moonraker* as she prepared to leave orbit and descend to the surface to worry about how things were being read back on earth. Since deliberately breaking radio and television links with home just as the *Moonraker* was preparing to break free of her moorings, he had been fully engaged monitoring the procedures of the crew of Sandy Martin and Colin Millar as they went through the systems check on board the descent module.

From his elevated vantage point he watched as the *Moonraker* hung in space some fifty metres in front of him, awestruck as the changing reflections from the curvature of the domed roof showed the slight pitch and roll of the craft as she maintained her orbit alongside the *Caliban*. As they entered their third complete orbit, the *Moonraker* tilted and on cue side slipped away to port descending under power towards the Sea of Tranquillity.

As he listened to the well rehearsed dialogue of the two pilots on board he could tell that everything was going according to plan. In four minutes time they would begin to slow the descent and lower the *Moonraker* to rest on the silvery grey surface. They would have ample time to select the best spot, avoiding large boulders and seeking out an area of relative flatness.

Murdo waited, confident but fearful, remembering the tilts and sudden sideslips that had nearly ruined the tests back at Rosewell. Suppressing the wild urge to contact them, he instead carried out a routine check of the vital systems on board the *Caliban*. All was well. For a few minutes longer, with time seemingly suspended, he waited motionless until he heard the voice of Colin Millar calmly counting off the last few metres of the descent. Then it was over. He became aware of the silence that confirmed that the engines on board the *Moonraker* had been cut.

Then Sandy Martin broke his silence.

'Murdo. We have landed. All systems performed perfectly. We have shut down the main engines. Our fuel burn was less than expected. We will now begin preparations for the E. T. to take place at 1600 hours. Colin is checking the recordings of the descent. All the pictures are safely in the can. The descent went like a dream. Slower than we expected. Absolutely amazing. We can't believe that we are actually sitting on the Moon. It's fantastic!'

'Great. Well done to both of you. Pity that the folks back home are not able to share it with us. Tell me, how is the view from where you are?'

'We are panning the cameras around as we speak, and it is just as it was on the simulators. Bright, very bright and grey. Not a chestnut tree in sight. I can see the low ridges over on our right and, yes, the group of boulders and the long rise in the background. In the foreground mainly small rocks and stones. We are level and stable. I can just identify the crater B3 in the distance. I think we may have rotated some ten degrees or more just before final touchdown. The anchors have been deployed and we can see the ends of the arms are firmly in place. Oh, and it goes without saying that you were right as usual; a bird in the hand *is* worth two in the bush. Over and out.'

Ten-thirty and a hint of winter in the air. The sky not quite dark, the bright city lights spread out before them. Across the Firth of Forth the lights of the Kingdom of Fife were reflected in the dark water. From somewhere close at hand, the smell of wood smoke and a hint of fine cooking reminded them that they had not yet eaten. Standing on the Castle Esplanade, Gregor turned his collar up and prepared to move off. Gus Simpson fell into step beside him and together they walked briskly in silence, slowing as they trod the narrow cobbled street leading to the Royal Mile. Once in the High Street they headed instinctively down the Mound in the direction of the Doric.

They climbed the stairs to the bar finding it unusually quiet.

'Here. Over here. This will do. Let's see if they can do us a sandwich.' Gus wandered off to set up the drams leaving Gregor to order.

'I've ordered a couple of omelettes. OK with you?'

Gus nodded, lifting his glass.

'See what I've got. A couple of nice big ones. The Arran. Cheers.'

He was reaching for his cell phone.

'I was thinking of calling in to see if there has been any news. You never know.' Gregor motioned him to sit down.

'Gus. Relax for a moment. I am going to share something with you. You can't however use it.' He glanced up and Gus nodded slowly in agreement.

'There is nothing wrong with the *Caliban*. All her systems are working perfectly. They cut off contact because it was pre-arranged. It's a case of no news being the best news in every sense of the word.'

He laughed quietly. Gus looked at him saying nothing, his expression betraying nothing of what he was feeling.

'This is between us as I have said. The lads are safe. The *Moonraker* should be on the surface by now and all we have to do is wait. There never was a problem. Suffice it to say that we have a very good reason for doing what we're doing. All I will say is that this and the final outcome has been planned for a very long time. It's all part of a much wider picture as I am sure you've guessed.'

Gus waited, wondering if he was going to hear the whole story or just as much as Gregor McLeod was prepared to divulge to a close friend.

'It has been a great strain, but I feel now that we are winning. These last few months have been very worrying. Just seeing them blast off like that on Tuesday morning ... I had to question my motives all over again.'

'But Gregor, what of their families? Colin Miller is married and ...'

Gregor held up his hand, determined not to be overheard. Then quietly,

'They have been told enough to reassure them that everything is going well. I spoke today to Sandy's father. I think I convinced him that they were all safe and sound and asked him to say nothing for the moment to the press.'

'Christ! Half the dailies will be printing obituaries right at this very minute. I hate to think what tomorrow's headlines are going to say. You're still doing the press conference tomorrow morning?'

Gregor nodded. 'Yes. I am.'

'And I suppose this is where you tell me that Frank Nelson is wrapped up in the business as well? Where does he fit in? We know he has a long history with Greenpeace and Friends of the Earth. You haven't denied it so far. Am I right?'

'He has had a role to play. His motives are beyond reproach by the way. Your friend's description of him as a poodle terrorist is not so far from the truth. If only we had more like him.'

They sat in silence, Gregor tired and drawn, Gus eager to

press home the questions that had troubled him over the past five months.

'Gregor. It has been obvious to me, knowing you as I do, that you have been up to your neck in something big. From time to time I have had an inkling of where you were headed, but each time I was proved wrong. Or so I thought. Until now. I won't press you, but I am choking with curiosity.'

Gregor looked at him placing his hand firmly on his shoulder.

'Gus, you know I love you like one of my own. I treasure our friendship. But this one has to stay with me. It's a story I'll carry to my grave. But ... I believed that it had to be done and I damn well made it happen. Gus, play it down if you can. Soften the words. I don't want people getting depressed or losing heart. But I can promise you one thing. The *Caliban* will contact us very soon, and I want to make sure that you are there. Get a good night's sleep and tomorrow, after I talk to the press, we will fly over to North Uist. I've had the plane on stand-by since I got back. A night or two in the Covenanters is just what I need right now.'

Gus was smiling. The thought of relaxing at the Covenanters a contradiction in itself.

'Gregor, we won't be sober from the minute we arrive. That's the *last* thing you need. Believe me.'

'And when we break radio silence and the *Caliban* comes on line? Are you sure you would prefer to miss it? No? I didn't think so. Put the next round on expenses. I'll have the same big ones again, and remember, not a word to anyone.'


Gregor stood impatiently hovering around the dais chatting to Hamish and getting sidelined into discussions with various people around him. The conference hall was already half full when the ushers announced that the doors were closed and the press call could get under way. For the last hour the atmosphere in the foyers and around the building had been gathering pace as rumours flew and guesswork replaced fact as the newsmen did their best to forecast the outcome of the voyage of the *Caliban*.

'Ladies and gentlemen of the press, we bid you welcome.' Hamish had advanced on the microphones and had decided to get things moving.

'We thank you again for coming and trust that we will be able to field your questions for you in a meaningful way. You see behind me the experts who I am sure have much to impart, although I understand that there is still no direct radio link established with either vehicle. We are of course concerned and as ever we are all praying for a successful outcome of the project, and the safe return of our lads.

'Now if those of you still wandering around like lost sheep can find a seat, we can make a start. Thank you.'

'Janet Holmes, Daily Mail. Hamish. Do you have any update at all that you can give us that would indicate that this is no more than a communications failure? It is now more than twenty four hours since the last contact was made. Is it not just possible that the *Caliban* has suffered some catastrophic accident that precludes any possibility of further contact?'

'I can only repeat what I have already said that we all share some concern at this time for the outcome of the trip. But I hasten to add that this does not mean that we believe that all hope is lost. What we have is a communications failure. It was a problem after the first day and it got progressively worse, the further from earth they travelled. We tried, as you know to realign the antennae, which we all think must have suffered a mishap at launch. I can only add that the tests carried out prior to lift off indicated that all was well.'

'Nial Smith, the Guardian. I understand that there was some urgency in getting the launch date brought forward? For reasons which, thus far, have not been corroborated by the astronomers we have consulted. As I recall, talk of sunspots and solar flares was given as the reason for changing the date of the launch. Can the First Minister now tell us the *real* story behind his decision to launch ahead of time? Did this have anything to do with ducking the invitation of the Americans to rendezvous on the Moon?'

Gregor stepped forward to take the question.

'Yes. I can tell you that solar activity was one of our main concerns at the time and in fact we now believe that our current difficulties with communications may very well be due to the early start of the solar activity we referred to. As for avoiding the Americans and refusing to shake their hands, all I can say is that no contact was made with my office, nor I believe with any other department within the government to co-ordinate such a meeting. For myself I can't believe that it would have contributed very much to international affairs and as far as I know our boys were not carrying a set of tiddlywinks with them.'

Gregor nodded towards the next in line.

'Corin Dougall. London Evening Standard. There is a report circulating that some low frequency exchanges have been monitored on the Moon that may very well have originated from the *Caliban* and the *Moonraker*. It would seem that these were timed sometime around two-thirty this morning. Can you confirm or deny this report?'

'As far as I am aware I know nothing of this. But let me say I will be delighted to have confirmation if indeed this is the case. It's true that the two ships retain a limited intercom capability, but I doubt if this would be capable of being picked up from as far away as earth. Next?'

'Janie Parker from the Telegraph. Are you aware of a headline in one of the New York dailies claiming that NASA would be prepared to mount a rescue mission in the event that such a mission could be launched to guarantee the safe return of your astronauts? And do you think that the time has now come to start thinking about such a rescue?'

Gregor smiled.

'I have said that we remain confident that the mission is alive and well, and we, all of us involved with the project, do not accept that the time has come to start counting our losses. If, on the other hand we hear nothing over the course of the next twenty four hours, then, and only then, will we start to re-appraise our position and begin to accept the possibility that something may have happened to the mission. For now, we have high hopes of a safe return for our boys. I would ask you all to share with us the confidence the team has for a successful outcome. We leave the doom and gloom for others to consider. We want no part of it.'

From the back of the hall Ken Regan gave up trying to activate the microphone in front of him as he stood to address the platform.

'Hi. Ken Regan, NBC News. First Minister. Let me first of all congratulate you and your government on a truly spectacular feat. I sincerely hope that everything turns out for the best, as I am sure it will. First Minister, I don't know how closely you have been following newscasts over where I come from, but it seems that an awful lot of people are speculating that when your boys eventually land, whenever, they could be in for a bit of a surprise. I understand that the bookmakers are currently giving two to one against the chances of finding any evidence of an earlier American mission to the Sea of Tranquillity'.

Laughing now, he continued.

'In the event that your crews fail to find anything, will you be talking directly in confidence to the American administration or will you simply publish and be damned?'

Still smiling broadly, he sat down. The noise in the hall rose as they turned to identify the speaker. Gregor, also clearly amused, waited until it was quiet.

'Mr Regan. We all thank you for your kind thoughts and good wishes. I have previously made it clear that my government do not share the views of the pundits who forever seek to decry your country's great achievements with the Apollo programme. We have no doubt that American astronauts were the first true pioneers who led the way into space. To believe anything else is absurd and petty. As for publishing our findings, we intend to make everything available just as soon as we can for the benefit of all. We simply regret that the pictures we promised of the landing and the first E. T. on the Moon have been denied you.'

'Just one further point, First Minister. If I was to tell you that I have recently been persuaded by the failure of the American administration to present convincing arguments to support their claims of having landed on the Moon, would you at least concede that the possibility could exist?' Gregor was smiling broadly.

'Mr Regan. If I thought for one minute that you were serious and that the possibility *did* exist, and that a Scot was about to be the first man to set foot on the Moon I would be overjoyed. For the moment you will appreciate that we have our hands full coping with the real issues demanding our attention, which leaves us with little or no time for chasing rainbows. However I suggest you hold fast to your beliefs for the next forty eight hours, until we can prove to you, one way or another, that you are mistaken.'

'Or maybe not, as the case may be,' came the thundering reply as the microphone suddenly became live and the people of the press were overcome with laughter.


As they approached the warm lights of the Covenanters' Inn the rain beat down on them as they left the car and dashed the last few yards to the front door. Once inside, the warmth and the atmosphere were in stark contrast to the storm outside, the waves thundering up the beaches and the spray being thrown against the windows of the tiny inn.

'We just made it here in time. Another half hour and we would have had a problem getting down. That must rank as the bumpiest flight I've had in years.'

Gregor was already at the bar. Gus parked himself on a stool still shaken from the second time lucky approach to the airstrip.

'Gregor, it's yourself. My, my. We are indeed honoured tonight! And Hamish. Oh, I see trouble ahead. And flying in this weather; have ye no fear? Have ye no sense? The devil himself is sheltering on such a night. Come away in and make yourselves at home.' Lachie was already handing out drams and dispensing the water.

'Here, this cures all. Drink it down.'

They moved closer to the fire, Gregor shaking hands and exchanging greetings with the locals, as Hamish led Gus to a corner seat.

'I've never been keen on flying machines myself. If the truth be known I'd sooner swim across.' More whisky arrived on cue as

Gregor joined them.

'I've just spoken to one of the controllers from the base. He reckons the pilot we flew in with is certifiable. But, we are here now. A few more of these little beauties, some good food, and we'll be ready to catch the evening news. I'm told that there is a clip of an interview with Nathan Jackson, and Sandy Martin's father has been talking to Kirsty Monroe. I hope he sticks to the story. Sunday's papers are going to be interesting as well.'

Around the room, the locals kept to themselves well aware of the current situation with the *Caliban* and anxious not to be seen to be concerned; for the moment. In trying to glean any information by reading the faces of the First Minister and his guests, they were at pains to be discreet; a fact for which Gregor was duly grateful.

# 29

In Houston, at twelve minutes after midnight, a bleary-eyed Colonel Pete Sanders leaned over the console while his operators juggled with the signal.

'It has to be them. The interval is right. Good God, they must be alive. This is fantastic.'

A listener at the end of the row of monitors called out.

'Over here sir. I have them loud and clear; intermittent but ... yes there it is. Listen.'

The Colonel moved quickly to his side.

'Switch it to broadcast.'

There was silence except for a faint low pitched hum. They waited. A full eight minutes elapsed. Suddenly the reception cleared and the voice of Murdo could be heard trying to reach control on North Uist.

'This is *Caliban* calling Mission Control. This is *Caliban* calling Mission Control. We are in orbit around the Moon at a height of 64 nautical miles. The *Moonraker* initiated powered descent at ...'

The transmission broke up. Another few minutes of waiting, then ...

'*Caliban. Caliban.* This is Mission Control on North Uist. We read you loud and clear. Where the hell have you boys been? Over?'

Further transmission delay.

' ... and both vehicles are performing well. We are safe and well. Touchdown was completed on schedule. Our first E. T. was timed at 16.23.54. We have repaired the antennae. We will advise revised transmission schedule to you. Meantime please confirm the following. Latitude degrees north 0.6875.'

Pause.

'Longitude degrees east 23.4333. Do you copy?'

'*Caliban* we copy. But please repeat longitude degrees ...'

This time the break in transmission lasted for a full twelve minutes. Then a two second spell of conversation and all was quiet again.

'We've lost them, sir. They might have switched frequencies

again.' Colonel Peter Sanders moved to his desk and picked up the phone. 'Get me the White House. Yes, I know what time it is. Just do it!'

At one thirty on Sunday morning, Lachie MacDonald tapped lightly on the door of Gregor's room; then louder for a second time, before entering the darkened room. He leant over the bed and gently shook the sleeping figure. Gregor awoke instantly.

'Lachie, all these years of friendship and I never suspected a thing.' They laughed.

'Behave yourself man, you're still drunk, I'm thinking. Listen. I couldn't sleep. They are saying on the wireless, from the SBC no less, that they have heard from the *Caliban*. Is that not wonderful news?'

Gregor had already rolled over and was settling to sleep.

'Thank you, Lachie. Aye, it's great news. And thank you for telling me. Now go back to bed before people start talking about us; if they haven't already done so. For God's sake, think of your reputation, *and* mine. Away with ye, man.'

Fiona McLeod lifted the coffee pot. 'More?'

Paul Burke shook his head. 'No thank you. Too much gives me indigestion.' He smiled across at her, reaching for her hand.

'When do you have to leave?'

'It's Sunday. I'll go in later just to check on things.' she said. 'I usually get in week days by eight thirty. Shall I clear up?'

Paul, distracted, shook his head and motioned for her to listen. He had already turned up the sound as they sat listening to the news on television.

'... and since then there has been nothing further. The signal, just to repeat for the benefit of our new viewers, was intercepted by Mission Control in Houston at six o'clock Eastern Time this morning. It would appear that the crew are still experiencing difficulties with transmission but at least we know for certain that they are alive and well. From what we can gather, the *Caliban* is in an orbit above the Moon while the *Moonraker* has made it down to the surface. She is in touch with the mother ship but does not have full broadcast capability at this time. As far as we can tell, there have been no televised pictures beamed from the surface although we understand that the crew are currently trying to repair the equipment. So where does that leave us this fine Sunday morning?

'I have with me Mr Sam Cavanagh, a senior analyst at NASA who has been reviewing what we *do* know about the trip thus far.

'Sam. Tell us, if you will, what you think has been happening out there in space? Why did they lose contact? And do you think the disaster, that we all assumed, is now a thing of the past?'

Sam Cavanagh and the interviewer began watching footage of the earlier transmissions.

'Well, we don't know for sure but whatever it was, it sure as hell blacked out the pictures we were all waiting to see - of the Scots setting foot on the Moon. I don't know if they managed to record anything before they lost power, but I do hope so. They seem to have had a problem with their antennae. We had a similar problem, you may recall, on one of the early Apollo missions and it sure as hell screws things up.'

'But what of this morning's broadcast, short as it was?'

'Well, it was clear but intermittent, which would seem to indicate some kind of power failure somewhere. It's really hard to tell. But, thank God they are alive and well, and let's face it; they don't need a radio to get back home.'

They laughed together.

'No, I don't suppose they do. But another thing; what do you make of the question they were asking? The latitude and longitude they were quoting?'

'That's an easy one. These are simply the references, the co-ordinates if you like that we agreed upon for the original Apollo eleven landing site. We understand that they intended to land at the same spot. Why they want them confirmed I can't imagine, but no doubt we will find out in time. Let's hope that they are lucky with their next transmission, which I believe they said would be at 19.00

GMT.'

Paul turned off the set, leading her gently back to the quiet of the bedroom.

'I doubt that they can be transmitting sir. We've been all over the ether and there's no word from them. If they said they would try again at nineteen hundred hours it's just possible I suppose that they have suffered another failure. We will continue to monitor the previous wavelength and hope they come back on. But right now …'

Pete Sanders nodded.

'Call me if you find them. I need sleep. But call me immediately if you get anything.' Turning now, addressing the rest of the room: 'Got it? Anything at all.'

He wandered off, unsteady on his feet to find a couch in a corner and a much needed rest.

Nathan Jackson was beside himself with anger mixed with despair, some guilt and a scattering of fear. Since early morning the reports reaching him of the *Moonraker's* successful descent had been inconclusive. Instead he had been given scraps of intelligence that had failed to give a clear picture of the situation, leaving him with the distinct impression that he was being protected from the truth. The lack of contact with the *Moonraker* was disturbing. Turning to Tom Sherman he voiced the question that they all knew was coming.

'Tom, If they've located the site then they must know for sure? Why don't they say something?'

Sherman, his expression graver than usual, looked at Jackson and wondered for an instant how a man of his discredited capabilities could ever have risen to the noble rank of President of the United States of America. Dale Johnson was waiting for him to state the obvious but, unable to look Tom in the eye stared blankly at the carpet. Mark Brander was fiddling with his cufflink as if he hadn't a care in the world.

'Well, sir. There may be several explanations all of which are worth considering. My own view however, for what it's worth, is that they are confused.'

'Confused? How? In what way confused?' Jackson asked nervously.

'Well, it seems to me that having landed at the site expecting to find the descent vehicle, the flag and the remains of our visit, they have found nothing. They have therefore queried the co-ordinates to make sure that they have landed on target. Which means, of course, that they will very soon come to the conclusion that there is nothing there to find.'

Jackson uttered a stifled cry covering his mouth abruptly to still the noise, slumping back into his chair utterly defeated. For some minutes nobody spoke. Then they looked up as a secretary entered the room and handed a paper to the President. He read it slowly by the light of the lamp on his desk, then staring ahead into the uncertain future, he said,

'Gentlemen. There has been a further contact. The transmission lasted for only a minute apparently. The transmission was encoded. It has taken some time to get it. The message is timed at 1800 hours G.M.T., four hours ago.'

He handed the note to Tom Sherman. It read,

```
We have now completed a second E.T. which lasted
for a period of eighty five minutes. During this time
we extended our surveillance of the areas B and D
progressing out as far as the low hillock at 34.22.
Our return path has taken us out as far as a large rock
in area E. In all we have covered a large area of the
immediate terrain on all four fronts. We have visual
for a distance of one thousand metres on three hundred
and sixty degrees. We are at a loss to explain the
lack of evidence of any previous landing by any other
nation. Over.
```

Tom Sherman looked up, seeing the look of wide eyed desperation on the face of Nathan Jackson.

'I think the time has come Mr President for us to take the

initiative and contact the Scottish consulate. I would suggest that we try to meet with them before they go public with this news. I am now convinced that we have no other option.'

Sally McIntosh listened as Mark Brander proposed that they should meet. Expressing surprise, she agreed to attend a meeting in the White House Press Office at 10.00 a.m., Monday, the following day. Closing the line she picked up the transmission just in from North Uist, reading again the message which she would carry with her to the meeting.

```
Attention. - S. McIntosh - Press Liaison
Priority. - Highly Confidential.
```

We are receiving transcripts from the Caliban relayed from the Moonraker which seem to indicate that our astronauts have thus far failed to detect any signs of any previous visit by the Apollo missions to the area we are surveying. Our recent exploration of the other sites claimed to have been visited during the later missions are also devoid of any signs of previous disturbance. We have checked and agreed the coordinates given and we are certain of our claims. There is now no doubt in our minds that the American Apollo missions did not land on the surface of the Moon. It seems to us that Scotland may very well lay claim to having been the first nation to have reached the Moon.

Clearly this will need to be discussed with the Americans. Advise your intentions for apprising the White House of our findings. We must assume that they are already aware of our exchanges. Proceed with extreme caution. This information is classified.

```
Regards
Gregor McLeod - First Minister
The State of Scotland
```

'And ah'm tellin' yees all, there is no doubt at all in ma mind, that right at this very minute, oor gallant Gregor McLeod and that eejit Nathan Jackson are cookin' up a story tae tell the world that nothing's changed and that everything on the Moon is jist as the Yanks left it a' these years ago. Of course, they're no' goin' tae tell us right away. Oh no! Ye see; they wull huv tae decide how they are goin' tae break the news tae us; gentle like.

'Then they are goin' tae huv tae *massage* the story tae make sure that we canny spot the joints. Oh yes! Huv nae fear, I am sure that when we're eventually told the story, it will be wrapped up in fuckin' Christmas paper and delivered doon the chimney by bloody Santy Claus.'

'Rab. We've still heard nothing. Dae ye really think they're playin' games wi' us? Why can they no' tell us whit's happenin'? Ah think Gregor McLeod should jist tell the world that there's nothin' there. Tell everybody that we were first. Aye, right; first tae reach the Moon.'

Shouts of approval filled the pub as the crowd gathered around Rab, pressing forward against the bar, intent on missing nothing.

'Of course they're playin' games. But, ye see, ye huv tae understand politics, so ye dae. Dae you think that Gregor McLeod can jist say whit he likes? No! He bloody well can't. Ye see, he has tae consider the *stability* o' the world when it comes tae a decision like this. If he was tae tell everybody the Yanks are a shower o' lying bastards, whit dae ye think that wid dae fur us? Nothing.

'No. this thing has tae be handled very carefully. Ah'll bet that right now he's wonderin' how he can score one up against the Yanks. Ye see, that's how it works. He says this, then the other bugger says that, then they agree tae trade. Then they a' agree tae differ an' say the same thing; then they shake hands and naebody gets hurt. That's how it'll end up. You mark my words boy! They'll be kissin' an' cuddlin' each other before the week's finished; the shower o' bastards!'

# 30

Introductions concluded, Fiona and Sally sat across the table from Mark Brander, Tom Sherman, Elmer Franklin and Arnold Denham, the National Security Advisor. The atmosphere in the room was superficially pleasant with a distinct undercurrent fraught with concern and unease. Mark Brander and Tom Sherman began talking at the same time, each retreating in favour of the other before Sherman eased himself to the fore.

'Miss McIntosh, Sally, Fiona, our thanks are due to you this morning for agreeing to this little chat. First of all, let me repeat the congratulations of this administration for your wonderful success in journeying to the Moon and we are all hopeful that your brave men will return home safely to their loved ones. As you know we confirmed that our listening stations intercepted various broken transmissions received from the *Caliban* and we are now certain that the crew are alive and well.

'Presumably, you too have been concerned that your level of contact with your crew has been less than you'd hoped for, but as I say, we all thank God that our earlier worries that the crew might have been lost have been allayed.

'Nevertheless we do retain some concerns. There is one particular aspect of your voyage which we need to discuss with you.'

There was a sharp intake of breath from Mark Brander, clearly concerned lest the introduction to the real point of the meeting should be broached without the spin that he would normally have favoured. Sherman looked directly at Fiona before turning to Sally.

'You see, for some time now, we have been wrestling with a problem which we inherited from the administration of Richard Nixon in the seventies. To come straight to the point, yesterday we intercepted this.'

He handed over a copy of the transcript from the *Caliban*. Sally passed it to Fiona without reading it. Looking straight at Tom Sherman she opened the file in front of her and laid the message from Gregor in front of him. Instantly, the other two leaned towards him to read it. When they had finished, Sherman folded his hands in front of him and raised his head to look at Sally.

'So, Sally; where do we go from here on in?'

He turned his head, as Fiona took up the question.

'I think Mr Sherman that we can, as you say, "cut to the chase". We were in touch with Gregor McLeod last evening and he is most concerned that none of this should in any way be leaked at this time. We must insist on this before we move ahead.'

She looked at each of them in turn. The men exchanged glances until Sherman nodded slowly. Sally noted the relief that clearly showed on the face of Brander. Fiona retrieved the message and deliberately folded it back into her file. She laid both hands on top of the folder.

'We do have one or two questions that need answering if you gentlemen would care to help us before we go on. We require some basic reassurance that we have not mis-read the present state of affairs. Can you please confirm our understanding of the current situation: that your space agency never at any time landed men on the Moon?'

She looked at each face in turn, their expressions cast in stone.

'In addition we need confirmation that the images you published at the time were generated here on earth, and that this secret has remained buried until now?'

She looked at them again, one by one. Arnold B Denham was clearly disturbed, appearing reluctant to confirm or deny anything.

'We can't get into that area just yet, young lady. I don't give a damn what these messages say. We have our national security to consider and a number of other things as well.'

Tom Sherman turned to him with a pitying look before continuing.

'Regrettably, that is the case, Miss McLeod.' He held her gaze, the seconds ticking by. He looked away, shrugging his shoulders in a gesture of concession. After a moment or two, he continued.

'This is not the time or the place for explanations, but I do feel that some apology is called for, although why I feel this way, or why it should be necessary, I am not entirely sure. I do know that we are all,' (he gestured towards his associates) 'we are, all of us here, blameless, and I can assure you that we're as disturbed by this turn of events as you must be. The decision to initiate a cover–up was made long ago and it now falls to us to find a way out. You can understand how this might threaten the present administration and reflect badly on the policies of the United States.'

Fiona took up the theme, a hint of sympathy creeping into her voice. Remembering the meeting between Gregor and Tom Sherman on a lonely beach not too long ago, she was finding it hard to play the role of hang-man.

'Mr Sherman, we are not here to demand explanations or to try to understand why this has happened. Instead I would suggest that we consider what actions we might initiate to ensure that we move forward in as positive a manner as possible. Had we known the true circumstances, we would have avoided this confrontation by simply landing elsewhere. As it stands now, we can hardly just walk away.

'However, we fully understand the need for your government to conceal these facts and we do recognise the damage that could be done to America, not to mention the free world, if the truth was to be revealed. On the other hand I cannot see Scotland joining this conspiracy as a willing partner. We have always dealt with world issues in an honest and even-handed manner. Neither do I have a brief at this time to negotiate an agreement that would cover our joint interest in suppressing the facts. I am instructed to listen to you and to report back to the cabinet in Edinburgh.

'This is a very difficult situation which, in the end, can only reflect badly on all of us. It is a dilemma that is not going to be easy to resolve. If Scotland agrees to conceal the truth, it might return to haunt future generations in ways that we cannot now foresee. But I doubt if Gregor McLeod has reached any conclusions since receiving the news and we cannot be at all sure how he will react.'

Elmer Franklin was showing signs of genuine distress as he leaned towards Fiona, his arms outstretched as if to embrace her, his eyes pleading with her for an understanding of their position.

'Fiona, my dear. I have met your uncle as you know, and I feel sure that he will understand the gravity of our situation. This is a painful time for all of us and I am sure that if our positions were to be reversed, we would quickly come to the conclusion that we couldn't see an old friend discredited by actions that took place nearly half a century ago. I ask you to reason with him and ask him to assist us at this difficult time.'

He had half risen from his seat as he had been speaking and now sat down again, casting apprehensive looks at his colleagues. Arnold Denham was clearly disgusted, his body language denying his part in the proceedings. Sally appeared to be considering the options and the suggestion that she approach Gregor for help.

'We will of course be talking with the First Minister this evening. I am prepared to suggest that it would be churlish of us to adopt anything other than a positive attitude towards your situation at this time. I propose that we convene again tomorrow at the same time, and that until then we keep everything that has passed here between us strictly under wraps. In the meantime I shall give serious thought to drawing up a document that gives my government the security it will need if we agree to go along with the idea of suppressing the truth about this whole affair.'

She stood up, the meeting clearly adjourned. Arnold Denham remained seated.

'I should add that in all my experience of Gregor McLeod, I have never known him to underwrite a lie or to walk away from making a painful decision. He is the most honourable man I have ever had the privilege of serving. All in all, we may be in for a tough time ahead in the coming days. Gentlemen; thank you. Until tomorrow.'


Gregor McLeod listened carefully as he was given the report on the meeting in the White House.

'OK. Sally. Let Tom drive the issues. Then, depending on how they react, tell them that I'm prepared to discuss the matter directly with Nathan Jackson. We can either do it the easy way on the phone or put it to him that he is welcome over here to sew the whole thing up. I am sure the Covenanters would be delighted to prepare a small welcome for the President of the United States. OK. Until then. Take care.'

'Rab. Rab. They're on the way home. It's jist been confirmed. It was on the news. They'll be here on the 29th. Aye, Saturday morning. Is that no' great? They made it sound as if they were jist catching the bus hame.'

'Aye. Thanks pal. Great. Huv they said any mair aboot whit they found? Huv they sent back any pictures? No? Nothin' Eh?'

'Naw. They never said. Jist the one statement, and a repeat o' the same shite they've been showin' a' week. They're comin' hame. That wis a' they said.'

The next day Sally and Fiona were ushered into the meeting room. Dale Johnson came forward to greet them. Standing at the far end of the room Tom Sherman was in conversation with Nathan Jackson. Seeing the President in the flesh came as a surprise to both women. He came forward.

'Ladies. My thanks are due to both of you. This is a great pleasure. Please be seated.'

Jackson sat opposite Sally. To his right, Tom Sherman smiled and chatted with Fiona as Dale Johnson moved into place beside the President. Clearly the importance of the meeting had moved up a notch. The slight tremor in Sally's right arm was matched by the anxiety felt by Fiona at the prospect of dealing directly with the power behind the United States of America.

'Sally. My people told me about the meeting you had yesterday and, bearing in mind the sensitivity of the current situation, I decided to chair this little get together myself. Tom here has told me that you will have discussed the issues with your First Minister and we're all very anxious to hear his views.'

He coughed nervously, his voice tired from lack of sleep.

'We recognise the impossible demand that this places on your government and we are of course deeply aware of the difficult decisions you will face in coming to terms with ... our little problem.'

He was affable, charming and courteous to a fault, the tiny twitch at the corner of his right eye and the bags under both signs of developing stress. Sally took a deep breath before beginning, keeping her manner relaxed, returning the steely blue gaze of the President.

'Well sir, I have talked with the First Minister and as you can imagine he is deeply troubled by this whole affair. As he pointed out, this is *not* something that he can take to his Cabinet. It's much too close to home for him. He feels that it will jeopardise his future leadership of Scotland, and create an unbearable burden that he would have to carry for the rest of his life. In effect you are asking him to sign up to something, which could in the long run, reflect very badly on the integrity of our country in our dealings with other nations. In other words, whilst he recognises the close relationship that we share, he is disinclined to underwrite the biggest lie of the twentieth century ...'

Across the table, Nathan Jackson was slowly turning a pale shade of green.

'... bearing in mind that, however useful our compliance might be for the United States, it will bring little or no direct benefit to Scotland, and may even be prejudicial to relations between our two countries in the future. If news of our little arrangement were to leak out at any time, we would be forced to join you in maintaining a lie we simply could not sustain. He is however prepared to meet with you to discuss the matter as you see fit. However, I should warn you; Gregor McLeod's advice to your administration is to publish and be damned. He wants no part of it. I'm sorry.'

There was a stunned silence around the table. Jackson, mouth open, sat in a trance. Dale Johnson, his head down, was covering his bitter disappointment. Only Tom Sherman continued to smile, holding his gaze firm as he addressed the two women.

'Could I suggest that there may be a situation here that might be influenced by some inducement, some political gain perhaps? Or ...'

He paused as he noted the polite but stony lack of response on their faces. Sally looked directly at Sherman. There was a longer pause before she replied.

'As you are aware we have had plans in place to draw up agreements between Scotland and a number of other countries including your own, to share in the development of our new fuel. The benefits of adopting it are obvious and the results have been shown to your various agencies over the past few months. You will also know that Scotland has worked tirelessly to develop it with a view to reducing the world's dependence on fossil fuels.

'The United States of America is the world's biggest consumer of these fuels and up until now, you have persistently refused to sign up to international agreements on pollution reduction, with the result that projections for reducing the effects of global warming set out in the last century show that they have risen rather than fallen over the past decades.'

She was watching his face, he sitting as if hypnotised and powerless to move.

'If you, Mr President, were to review your current problems, weighing them against the overwhelming evidence of the effects of global warming on this planet, then I suggest that you would very soon come to the conclusion that the problems you are now facing don't amount to a hill o' beans when weighed in the balance against the survival of the planet.'

Turning to Tom Sherman, Sally's anger was just beginning to show through the veneer of efficiency.

'Mr Sherman, if you seriously believe that we can be bought, have the good grace to make it worth our while. Sign up to the Kyoto protocol and we can perhaps live to talk another day.'


Jackson was beside himself with anger, pacing the carpet and mopping his brow. Sitting and turning in their chairs as they tried to keep him centre screen were Sherman and Franklin. Brander was mixing martinis. Since leaving the meeting room, the President had ignored them in favour of a personal tirade against everything and everyone and against smart-assed women lawyers in particular. His special displeasure was directed at Sally McIntosh who had shaken hands with him and indicated, in no uncertain terms, that time was not on his side.

'I can assure you, Mr President, that when our crew returns on Saturday 29th we will be expected to hold an immediate press conference. Unless we receive confirmation from your office at that time that you accept the terms laid out in the draft memorandum I have given you, we have instructions from Gregor McLeod to announce that we were unable to detect evidence of any previous intervention on the Moon by any other nation. If it gets to that stage, then you must bear full responsibility for the consequences of your actions. You, in effect, will be leaving us with no option.

'If however you decide that you are in a position to give your word that the United States will sign up to the Kyoto protocol then I feel sure that we will be able to accommodate your every wish. It's all in there and I suggest that you take some minutes to read it.

'Good day, Mr President.'

And with that they had left without a backward glance.


Gregor and Hamish were in no rush to hurry back to Edinburgh. On this, the third day of their escape to North Uist, Gus was beginning to realise that they intended to remain there until the *Caliban* had returned. With the hospitality at the Covenanters threatening to disrupt his liver function he was beginning to wonder if he could last the pace. Having breakfasted at noon, he looked up as Gregor entered the tiny dining room, his white hair dishevelled, his mood buoyant. He sat down beside Gus.

'Gus! It's the early bird that catches the worm. Can you pass the toast? Tis better to give than to receive. Please pass the butter. He who pays the piper calls the tune. Is there any damned way we can turn that pitiful musak off?'

Gus laughed in spite of the hangover.

'Gregor, where do you get your energy from? Hamish is the same. He was bloody well running along the beach singing his head off before he finally went upstairs at four o'clock this morning. Even then, he was banging around for ages before he settled down. Lachie tells me he slept in the chair in his room. Didn't make it to the bed.'

Gregor was laughing.

'Untidy wretch! This is the only place that he can get away with it. Sober, he's fairly reserved; well, on Sundays at least. I'll get some more coffee.'

He wandered into the hall to raise the waitress while Gus looked out through the tiny deep set windows at the machair, the sea now calm and serene. The day would be perfect. Time to get his copy into the office. Gregor returned at that moment leading a very subdued Hamish. They sat down, Hamish afraid to lean forward, tending to slide into the chair. Holding his head he was muttering to himself.

'Ah, the good Lord giveth us whisky and lo! He taketh away our good sense. Gregor, pour me some coffee for the love of God. No man should have to suffer like this. I'm going to speak to Lachie about serving us so much liquor. Is there no limit to that man's stupidity?'

Gus and Gregor both looked on with wide grins on their faces as Hamish struggled to butter his toast. Unshaven, bleary eyed and still wearing the same shirt that he had arrived in, he caught Gus's eye, a wry smile lighting up his face.

'Aye. And to make matters worse, my daughter arrives tonight from Washington, and that will mean an immediate halt to the festivities. Be warned both of you; I will not tolerate tale-telling once she arrives. If anybody asks, we've just arrived from Edinburgh and haven't touched a drop in days.'

Gregor placed a plate of porridge in front of him.

'Try this, Hamish. I'll need you in good form for tonight. We're expecting an unexpected arrival this evening. It seems that our prayers have been answered and that we'll soon be offering our hospitality to the great Toom Tabard himself.'

Hamish looked up, as Gregor's words began to dawn on him. He dropped his spoon, pushing the plate away from him. His eyes met Gregor's as a slow grin developed on his face turning to a roar of laughter as he leapt up and jigged around the room. Gus looked on in amazement.

'Sit down man. You'll do yourself an injury.' Gregor was leaning back his hands folded behind his head, a huge smile on his face. Hamish came and put his head very close to his brother's.

'You've got him!' he exclaimed.

'He's coming here. The saints be praised. When did ye hear? How? How in God's name ... When does he get here?'

Gregor pulled them both in close, his arms extending round their shoulders.

'He was pretty well forced into accepting our generous invitation. He'll touch down at eight thirty this evening. Now, not a word to anyone. We keep this to ourselves. Gus, I'm sorry; pictures only at this stage. I gave my word. This visit is strictly social. No interviews and no press. In time you can use them. Just make sure the backgrounds remain anonymous.'

Gus looked at them both, searching their faces for some sign of explanation.

'Who? Who are we talking about? For Christ's sake just tell me.'

'Why, Gus. You haven't guessed? Who else but Nathan Jackson, the most powerful leader of the most powerful state in the world?'

Gus was stunned but Hamish was wagging his finger.

'No. Not tonight. Tonight, Gregor, that tag will be tied to *your* tail.'


At 35,000 feet aboard Air Force One, Sherman sat back in the deep leather armchair nursing a coffee as Jackson and Franklin prepared for their upcoming meeting. Having already decided that the options open to them excluded any clear way out, they nevertheless remained determined to negotiate to the bitter end and salvage what they could from the encounter. The President turned to Sherman.

'Did you get a chance to look at this pile of shit? Not only is she insisting that we sign up to Kyoto but she wants a fucking public apology made to Friends of the Earth, Greenpeace and every other bunch of fruitcake activists on the face of the earth.'

Mark Brander tried to calm him, placing a drink in his hand.

'... and as for this bit; she insists we desist from drilling within the Arctic Circle. Is she completely mad or what?' He threw the agreement across the cabin. Then, summoning a degree of control, he turned to Tom Sherman.

'Tom, I'm sorry. This business is driving me insane. I am not getting at you. Your proposal to update the film clips we made in the sixties is a good one. I am sure that we can set the whole thing up and running again in a matter of days and release them to the press. We will need access to the stuff they brought back, however. I'll leave you to deal with that aspect of the negotiations.'

Tom Sherman interrupted him.

'If I may sir, I would propose that we do *not* make any use of their film material. It could prove to be controversial and we know how nit-picking those damned conspiracy theorists are once they get going. No. I would suggest that we set up the whole thing again in the studio. We have the equipment after all. The model of the L. E. M. is ready, the old suits; in fact everything we need to produce a damn' convincing scenario. The original set is still under wraps so we won't have to do too much to it.

'I will talk to Gregor McLeod about flying his guys over to use them in the sequences. We wouldn't even have to go to the Moon at all. We have everything we need within our grasp to do the job right here. Don't worry, I'll make sure that we cover ourselves. Gregor has already said that he failed to get any images of the site. So ... I don't see a problem. But we need to sign him up to never releasing any footage in the future. We need everything stitched up nice and tight. That way, we buy time until we can get around to setting our house in order. I see us actually getting to the Moon within three to four weeks.'

Nathan Jackson was becoming agitated again.

'That doesn't help us short term. We need to release stuff to the media by the weekend. You'd better get on to it now. The deeper we dig ourselves into this mess the less I like it. We are completely at their mercy. For God's sake, they could blackmail us from here to kingdom come if they wanted to. It's intolerable. It's extortion of the worst kind. It's plumb dishonest for Christ's sake. If it wasn't for the fact that they have got us by the balls, I'd have ordered the marines to go in.'

Tom Sherman gave him an old fashioned look that said it all. As Air Force One passed over the Pole heading for North Uist, Sherman set his chair to recline and decided to try to get some sleep. All in all it had been a tough couple of days. Notwithstanding the stress, he was looking forward to meeting Gregor again, finding some quiet corner, and pumping his hand in congratulations for a job well done. Glancing across at Jackson he wondered if he, Sherman, would survive long enough to be of service to the next president in line.


Some two hundred and sixty miles ahead of Air Force One, and unbeknown to the President and his merry men, Fiona McLeod relaxed for the first time in days. With the ultimatum delivered on target, she had travelled to Dulles Airport immediately to ensure that she caught the flight to Edinburgh where the Cessna would be waiting to ferry her to North Uist.

Having tippled on a prime bottle of chilled champagne in the first class accommodation, she was in high spirits. Moments later, she felt a slight touch on her arm as the stewardess said,

'Miss McLeod? The captain sends his regards and has asked me to pass on a message received in-flight some minutes ago. The message apparently was received from Air Force One.'

Fiona unfolded the note. It read;

```
'See you tonight in the Covenanters.
Mine's an Arran.
Love P.'
```

# 31

Hamish said,

'We should have considered a red carpet. Jesus! It makes you wonder just how many incumbent Presidents of the United States of America have made it as far as North Uist. I hope he hasn't packed his golf clubs.'

Gregor was watching the sky.

'They're late. The tower says that the winds will have delayed them. Hamish, give the tower a call and see if they've heard anything.'

He turned to Gus.

'When was the last time you shook the hand of a President?'

Gus shook his head.

'Never, but there is always a first time, I suppose.'

They walked together towards the stairs.

'Gus, I've told you very little about this meeting but I know that you are aware that I'm playing tonight for big stakes. A President like Nathan Jackson doesn't get on his bike at a moment's notice unless it's important. He is coming here because he has no choice.'

He glanced up at Gus.

'How does that strike you?'

Gus shrugged before replying.

'Gregor, I have ceased to be amazed by you. These last few days you have been more alive than at any time in the past. You and your brother are like five-year-olds waiting for Christmas to arrive. Whatever is behind this whole thing I have no idea. Maybe I don't want to know. But one thing is for sure, tonight will be history in the making.'

'No. You're wrong there. This will *not* make history. This may *change* history in the long run but it will go largely unrecorded. This stopover will be remembered as the night that Air Force One made an emergency stop on North Uist for security reasons. We will assist in searching the plane for a bomb that never was. Then I will get in a corner with Jackson and tell him a short bedtime story. You *can*, incidentally, run the story about the bomb and the panic it caused.'

Gus bowed in mock gratitude.

'Then three hours later they will all climb aboard and set a course for Frankfurt to meet with the German Chancellor for urgent discussions on a number of silly subjects that will get the minimum of media coverage, and eventually the whole episode will fade into obscurity.'

He was shaking his head greatly amused. Gus turned to him.

'And you still can't share it with me? I can think of any number of reasons why the leaders of two countries would want to keep their meeting low key, but rarely would it involve the First Minister of a small nation like Scotland and the President of the most powerful country on earth.'

Gregor was pointing out to sea as the great plane switched on its landing lights and made its approach.

'Be that as it may, but tonight, this young David here is going to kick seven bells out of that Goliath we call the President of the United States.'


Gregor, Gus and Hamish entered through the tiny doorway followed by the two special agents who immediately carried out a swift reconnaissance of the premises. Having finished their inspection, much to the amusement of the locals, the first agent returned to the limo to report.

'The venue *is* secured, Mr President but I should warn you, the place is a public house and it's full of peasants. Some of them appear to be much the worse for wear with drink. I would recommend that we call off the rendezvous and find somewhere close at hand that meets our security requirements.'

Nathan Jackson was peering past him towards the small windows of the place, his curiosity aroused, the quaintness of the scene drawing him in.

'It seems peaceful enough,' he muttered. Something about the place seemed vaguely familiar. At that moment Hamish arrived to escort them into the bar.

'Come away in, sirs. The air at this time of year is bad for the health and we won't be taking any chances with yours.'

He led him into the tiny bar, closely followed by Elmer Franklin and Paul Burke. Tom Sherman stood behind them marvelling at the interior, the smell of the place and the time worn fittings. Above the bar, the clock that last chimed for victory in nineteen eighteen was silent.

The shock and the silence that had greeted the arrival of Nathan Jackson were soon ended. The clinking of glasses and the rattle of ice ruining good whisky broke the stillness as Gregor handed round the drams to his guests. Turning to the patrons, he raised his glass.

'Mr President, the people of North Uist bid you welcome. This is indeed an honour. We trust that we can make you comfortable during your short stay. Cheers.'

Turning to Elmer Franklin, he raised his glass reminding him of his last visit to Edinburgh when fair quantities of the twilight wine of Scotland had been drunk over the three day visit. Elmer shook his head at the memory.

In the corner, old Matt struck up with a fiddle tune and within minutes the bar had returned to its chattering self, the drink flowing with only the briefest of inquisitive glances being cast in the direction of the new guests.

Paul Burke stood against the door beside the President's man, the wave of intense nostalgia that he had felt on entering the bar staying with him as he searched the room for Fiona. Hamish approached him from the side, and came directly to the point.

'So tell me young man; are your intentions towards my daughter in any way honourable?'

He chuckled as Paul Burke, straight faced, began to stammer some reply or other.

'Never mind for now, Mr Burke, but I will be keeping my eye on the pair o' ye.'

He squeezed his shoulder affectionately

'She'll be here in fifteen minutes,' he said as he rejoined the party.

Behind the bar Lachie MacDonald called out to him,

'Hey, Paul. Will it be a drop o' the usual?' before collapsing in laughter and being told off by Hamish.

'Behave yourself man. Have ye no shame? The man's working as you should be. Set up another round, laddie, and quickly.'

Nathan Jackson was beginning to settle; a feeling of well-being beginning to lure away the layers of anxiety that had plagued him over the course of the past four months. His mood lightening, he was finding the company of Gregor and Hamish McLeod much to his liking. The atmosphere in the tiny pub, the classless nature of the customers and the camaraderie that he noticed everywhere touching chords within him that echoed sounds and feelings from his boyhood in Texas, the cowboys strumming guitars in the evenings, the sound of a distant harmonica being played and the smell of horses and new mown hay downwind in the early dawn.

He caught sight of himself in the mirror across the bar and was momentarily shocked by his appearance. The lines were now deeply etched around his eyes, his once black hair was now a tousled indeterminate grey. He was killing himself for sure. This business was too much for one man to shoulder. Another glass of the Arran was pushed into his hand and he drank deeply. Across the room the special agent became apprehensive and wondered if he should intervene.

Around him everyone was talking, the soft accents so pleasing and musical. What was that air he was hearing? He turned towards the fiddler, striking out from the small crowd, drawn towards the music. As the notes rang out, he felt a strong rush of emotion course through his being, as childhood memories of family and friends returned to haunt him.

> Ye banks and braes o' bonie Doon,
> How can ye bloom sae fresh and fair?
> How can ye chant, ye little birds,
> And I sae weary fu' o' care!

Beside him, the song started, softly at first then building

slowly as the words came tumbling back to him. Soon he was being joined by others until with a skirl the song ended. Hamish was standing by his side.

'Nathan, I've heard many a singer try that song, but none of them sung it half so sweetly as you just did. Man, that was wonderful.'

Franklin and Sherman were applauding enthusiastically. Jackson looked around him at the smiling, kindly faces around the bar and held up his empty glass.

'Is this a party, or is this a party?' he demanded. 'My turn to buy.' Gregor put an arm around his shoulder.

'Mr President. You are in Scotland now, a land where we know how to treat our guests.' He handed him another glass. Gus gave him a warning look which Gregor acknowledged.

'Don't get him drunk. You need him sober.'

Across the room, the agent noted the exchanges, moved his weight to spread the load more evenly, but did nothing.

'Mr. President, Nathan. Call me Gregor. I always find "First Minister" a bit of a handful.' They were laughing now.

'Can I suggest that we adjourn to the dining room and conduct our little bit of business? After which, I have a feeling there may be a few more songs locked away in there that could well do with an airing.'

They walked through the bar, Nathan brushing off the agents who were determined to stick with him. The President turned to them.

'Keep an eye on that fiddler. Got it? Make sure that he is still here when I get back.'

And with that they were gone, each carrying their glass through to the tiny dining room that hadn't seen excitement like it since Lachie shagged the big Australian barmaid one hot night on top of the big table under the dirty oil lamp with the smoking wick.

The party over, at two o'clock in the morning, Tom Sherman walked quickly down the narrow corridor, past the kitchen and stores and opened the creaking door leading to the rear of the pub. Standing in the dark beside the barrels and empty beer crates, Gregor threw his arms out in greeting.

'Tom, my old friend; we finally did it. He signed up to the draft. I have it here. Fiona will return to Washington tomorrow and she and Sally will conclude a formal agreement. It's in the bag.'

'That's wonderful news, Gregor. I am sure he will keep his word. He needs to bury this thing for all time. I wish I had the time to tell you everything that has gone on.'

He laughed quietly.

'You wouldn't believe half the stories. It's been great.'

'Tom, we couldn't have achieved any of this without your help. You know that. You've risked everything. But man! It was worth it.'

'Gregor; we need to get going. The pilot's been agitating for the last hour or so. We need to leave. Elmer and his man are waiting out front. Jackson is already on board, sound asleep. You must come over to see us. An old man needs friends when he gets to this stage of his life. I'll say goodbye to Hamish on the way out. Take care Gregor; until the next time.'

And he left.

Gregor waited for a moment, then walked around to the front of the inn to wave goodbye to the limo. Hamish and Fiona stood by his side, each with their own thoughts as the car sped away into the night.

They wandered back into the bar, now darkened and deserted, and sat around the fire. Hamish went behind the bar and served them with drinks. Gregor was triumphant, his mood jubilant.

'Would you believe it, in less than five minutes he was only too eager to sign! He'd already concluded that he had no choice. I didn't need to rub it in. We understood each other's point of view immediately. He's a country boy at heart. Scottish ancestry, so he claims. Presbyterian upbringing and church choir as well. The business was all done and dusted then put to one side. We spent more time discussing how we could ensure a steady supply of The Arran be delivered to the White House than anything else. I think he genuinely liked me.

'We struggled a bit with our insistence on pulling the oil companies out of the Arctic Circle, but in the end he reluctantly went along with it. In exchange we will give him concessions over the new fuel. They will set up their own manufacturing plants and produce to agreed quotas. Oh, and I have also agreed that we will assist them in delivering a joint statement that leaves no room for doubt over our findings on the Moon. We'll have to move quickly on that one.'

Hamish lifted his glass, the firelight dancing in the golden liquid.

'It seems a toast is in order, or should I say a couple of toasts? Gregor, to Scotland! And, before I forget, to my future son-in-law Mr Paul Burke.'

Gregor was astonished. Fiona began laughing.

'Is it true? Really? That's wonderful news. My dear Fiona, I wish you all the best. Now if that doesn't qualify us for another round, nothing will. Get Lachie out of bed. Send for old Matt. This place needs livening up. To hell with the time. We want a party. Hamish, if you please.'

# 32

The great conference hall was filled with delegates, visitors and distinguished guests as Gregor, Hamish and Fiona led the way on to the stage to a thunderous round of applause. Behind them, Murdo, Colin and Sandy appeared, waving to the crowd as it rose to give them a standing ovation. For minutes the din continued until Gregor moved to the podium to address the gathering.

Around the room, people were crowding the exits and blocking the aisles. Outside, on the Castle esplanade, the crowds watched on large screens, their cheers reaching through the heavy masonry and adding to the general level of noise in the hall.

'Your Excellencies, distinguished guests, ladies and gentlemen, I bid you welcome.'

A further prolonged burst of applause rang out as Gregor held his arms aloft for silence.

'I know you will all join with me in expressing our heart-felt thanks to our brave crew and share with me the relief and delight we feel in having them back with us safe and well. These past few days have been harrowing for all concerned. I need not remind you all of the tense few hours when they were out of touch, unable to confirm their safety and uncertain if they retained the capability to make the return journey.

'Until, that is, when the transmissions were restored. In those brief few seconds on 22$^{nd}$ and 23$^{rd}$ of October we all knew for sure that they had landed safely on the Moon and had everything under control. I can tell you that nobody was more relieved than I on that occasion. And now you need no reminder from me that we can all take great pride in a worthwhile achievement.

' Before I call on Murdo Sinclair to address us, I would ask you to once again express your thanks to them and everyone concerned with the success of the voyage by joining me in a vote of thanks.'

The room echoed to a huge roar of appreciation that lasted even longer than the first as Murdo changed places with Gregor.

'I thank you all for your kind welcome. Since arriving back yesterday we have been overcome by the warmth of the greetings you have showered upon us. As Gregor has said we did have one or two moments of concern when our communications failed and our relays from the surface to the *Caliban* were severely disrupted. We failed, as you know, to capture the moment when we set foot on the Moon and we regret that we were unable to bring you live pictures of our journeys over the surface. I can only tell you that the experience for all of us has been fantastic. We would not have missed the opportunity for anything. To be able to walk again in the footsteps of Neil Armstrong and the early American astronauts was a great honour.

'We owe a great deal to these early pioneers and to our Russian friends who willingly shared their expertise on re-entry technology with us. I would ask you now to join with me in thanking all those concerned with the success of the project and in particular Fiona, Hamish and Gregor McLeod who had the dream and who steered it so lovingly down the long road to reality.'

As the applause rang out, Gus Simpson sat in the press gallery and watched the proceedings unfold as speaker after speaker added their praises. Somewhere along the way, over the last four months, he had the feeling of having missed the point of it all. Aware that he had been party to something momentous, he couldn't rid himself of the feeling of having been short changed. He had already formed the impression that all the good cheer and bonhomie at the Covenanters was somehow covering up the truth; that something remained unspoken which could explain the pantomime of backslapping and enforced laughter that had somehow failed to ring true on Wednesday night. Only once did he get an inkling as Nathan Jackson had emerged from the dining room with Gregor ... As the pair had passed close by him, he saw the firm handshake and heard the President say,

'Right, Gregor. That's it. And you swear that the first shipment will be delivered in time for the christening?'

And Gregor's reply, his eyes never leaving the face of the American President,

'Trust me, Nathan. I will guarantee it, may my life depend on it.'

On this, the day following the return of the *Caliban*, Rab walked into the "Bletherin' Skite" and chose a stool at the end of the bar. Nursing a pint, which he paid for, he politely ignored the other end of the room where a smiling Charlie Smith was holding court with a group of the regulars. In front of him, the headlines proclaimed the news that the *Caliban* had confirmed the Apollo landings in the sixties and seventies. Charlie Smith sauntered down the bar, closely watched by the regulars.

'Good morning professor, and it is a good morning I trust. I suppose you will huv read the headlines? No need for us tae tell you the news I suppose. But nae doubt you will huv another wee explanation why all the papers are sayin' the same thing.'

Raising his voice now, his face peering into Rab's who was studiously ignoring him.

'Seems they're a' sayin' the same thing. The bloody Yanks were there a' the time. But no doubt the papers are a' wrong. Is that no' whit you said, Mr. Nicol? Huv they got it wrang again dae ye think?'

The crowd around the bar were sniggering now, but still too timid to risk Rab's anger. Ignoring the jibes, Rab waited until Charlie Smith tired of the game and was called away to pull beer. Rab was seething. This was wrong. It was a bloody conspiracy for sure. That bastard Gregor McLeod and that tosser Nathan Jackson. Between them they had carved up the truth.

'Don't suppose anybody's seen a picture yet?' The pub stilled.

'I suppose if there wis a picture now, that would be different. Seein' is believin' is it no'? They say, you know, that one picture is worth a thousand words. Well ah've jist counted the words in this article while youse yins huv been talkin' and for six hundred and forty two words I canny see even one decent picture. Plenty o' smilin' faces mark you, but nae pictures that tell ye anything. So where does this leave us?'

Rab was talking straight at the mirror in front of him. The others remained silent listening but not watching. Charlie Smith had shut up for the moment.

'So ah says tae masel, where are the pictures? The one o' our gallant lads standin' next tae the American descent module. Fur dae ye no' think that if they had found it, they wid want tae huv their photies taken against it? No I don't suppose so. That kind o' thing is only fur tourists. No' that ye get too many tourists oan the Moon. But there we are. Lots and lots o' words, but nae pictures. Makes ye think. Eh?'

Out of the corner of his eye, Rab watched as the argument, carried on in whispers, raged between them.

'And anither thing. Not only is oor gallant Gregor McLeod toastin' his fat bum on North Uist at precisely the same moment that Nathan Jackson has tae divert  tae avoid bein' blown oot the bloody skies, but almost immediately efter, what dae we hear? Aye. Jist what dae we hear?' Turning now to face the doubters, edging closer along the bar, they flinching and retreating as he slowly moved towards them,

'No? Well ah'll bloody well tell ye. The bloody Yanks huv agreed tae sign up tae the Kyoto Protocol.

' "Whit's that?" Ah hear yees askin'. And well might ye ask, ya shower o' ignorant bastards. Whit it means is that the Yanks wull now take responsibility for reeking the place oot wi' carbon dioxide.

' "Whit's that, Rab?" Ah here ye say again. It's pollution pure an' simple. The shite you and I huv tae breathe every bloody waking minute. That's whit it is.

'But now, because o' the wee handshake between that pair o' bastards we can now look forward to breathin' in good clean air again. But, Ah'm asking yees all. At what bloody price? Aye. At what bloody price?

'Oh, ah see. So yees don't know. Well ah'll huv tae tell ye. At the price o' bloody honesty and integrity. That's the price they've paid. They huv surrendered their freedom. They huv embraced injustice. They huv buried the truth. But those two bastards *will* pay the price. One day. You mark my words. Rab Nicol has spoken.'

Charlie Smith laid a fresh Guinness in front of Rab and retreated quickly down the bar.

'And we all know where ye can stick that, don't we Charlie?'

# Epilogue

Gregor sat at his desk listening to the early CNN evening news summary prior to leaving the office.

'Today, it was announced from the North American Space Agency's headquarters in Houston that Monday's launch of the Columbia spacecraft has resulted in American astronauts once again returning to the Moon. Early images received today clearly show the men standing in front of the descent module left over from the Apollo Eleven mission. In the foreground, the footprints of the Scottish crew are evident, made during their visit in October last year.

'The ex-Director of Operations, Mr Tom Sherman, who resigned last month owing to ill health, sent hearty congratulations to the crew and their support staff at Mission Control.

'This new initiative by the United States heralds a new era in space exploration and it has been announced by the White House that President Nathan Jackson has pledged his party's support to setting a team on the planet Mars by the end of the decade.

'Scotland's First Minister sent his congratulations to President Jackson in a memo early today as the news came in of the American landing. We here at CNN wish the crew a safe return journey in four days time.'

Gregor lifted the telephone and dialled a number. The phone rang several times before he heard the voice of Nathan Jackson.

'Mr President. It's Gregor McLeod speaking. May I offer you my sincere congratulations for your magnificent effort? We are all delighted over here and we wish you and your agency our best wishes for your future plans to land on Mars in the coming decade, and of course, every success in the coming elections.'

'Why, thank you Gregor. You are most kind. We are all very relieved to have made it to the Moon and to be back in the field of space exploration. With luck, we may survive to carry through our ambitious plans in the hope of furthering our knowledge of the universe. But all of that is perhaps a long way off. To return to the present for a moment. I thank you for your latest gift addressed to me. It will be treasured as I'm sure you intended it to be. God speed, Gregor.'

The line closed, Gregor reached into his cabinet and pulled out an envelope. He extracted a photograph which he laid in front of him, a wry smile on his face.

Clearly shown in every detail were the descent module, the American flag and the general disruption to the site caused by the Apollo Eleven landing. From the shadow cast by the *Moonraker* at the bottom of the picture a single line of footprints with saltires cut into the soles was seen going to and returning from the site. And gleaming in the harsh light a bottle of The Arran Founders Reserve suitably inscribed *To Nathan Jackson, with kind regards from Gregor McLeod* sat proudly in the dust in the shadow of the American descent module.

Lightning Source UK Ltd.
Milton Keynes UK
UKHW011347080322
399750UK00001B/28